Social
DISTANCE

June Yi

This is a work of fiction. All characters, organizations, and events portrayed in this novel are either products of the author's imagination, or are used fictitiously.

Cover illustrations by Man Hi Park

Cover & Interior design by June Yi

for my family
you are enough

ONE

THEA WOKE TO the natural alarm of the sun shining on her face and the cooing of morning doves by her window. Her daily panic about losing her job, a steady bass beat in the back of her mind, made her want to burrow deeper into her cool sheets. She glanced at her phone. No new emails from her editor at the newspaper. Safe from compromising her morals for another day! She swung her legs off the edge of the bed and stretched.

It was difficult to write a weekly restaurant review column when the county was in lockdown and no one could dine in restaurants. Not that she was eager to sit and breathe the same air as other people at this point in time. Imagining it made her skin prickle with goosebumps.

After a quick shower, Thea pulled her sand-colored linen robe over pajama bottoms and padded to the kitchen. The tub of yogurt in the fridge was almost empty, so she threw in a handful of chopped almonds, fresh blueberries, and a drizzle of honey. She brought her breakfast to the kitchen table and sat down with her phone.

As she scrolled through news headlines, the one notification she'd been dreading appeared at the top of her phone: an email from Ray, her editor at the paper, with the subject line, "Budget for May." It was the end of April, so it made sense he wanted to talk about which columns to schedule for next month. She'd prepared a list of restaurants vetted and ready to go, but it was harder to plan with the unpredictability of the pandemic and decisions from the county health department.

Thea tapped the email. There were only two words in the body: *Call me.*

She scarfed down the last few bites of yogurt and hovered her finger over Ray's number. She put the phone face down on the table. There was no way she was taking this phone call without caffeine.

Thea shuffled around little bags in her tea cabinet until she found something both caffeinated and calming, a charcoal roasted shui xian. She laid out her tea accoutrements on the kitchen counter next to the hot water. The hot water dispenser, a housewarming present from her best friend Olivia when she moved into this house four years ago, was still going strong, even through daily uses.

Tendrils of steam rose from the tea leaves when she filled the gaiwan and the comforting roasted scent of tea wafted up to her. The deep breath of steam she inhaled had her feeling more alive already. She poured off the first brew, the watery rinse, into a small watering can to cool down for her house plants later. She learned from a tea expert that the first brew rinsed dust from the tea leaves. Her plants' dense green foliage thanked her for the tea-infused watering.

Thea decanted the second brew of tea, a dark amber liquid, into her stained and chipped teacup. She inhaled the aroma, remembering sitting on a low stool in front of an elaborate wood table in the tasting room of the tea plantation. What she wouldn't give to be back in Taiwan right now. She made a reminder to call her parents to check in this week.

The bittersweet caramel flavor of the tea swirled around her mouth as her finger hovered over her phone. She took another fortifying sip before dialing Ray's number.

"About time. I was gonna to call you," Ray barked after picking up on the first ring. He didn't smoke, but Thea always pictured him chewing on one end of a cigar when he talked on the phone.

"Good morning," Thea said smoothly. "You want to talk budget for next month?"

"Right, what do you have lined up? You need to do one of the Green Shoots restaurants next month." Ray read off a handful of places owned by a well-known restaurant investment group. Thea swirled the tea around her cup.

The prestigious group's restaurants were large, loud places decorated with poured concrete and glass. The spaces all overflowed with diners before the start of the pandemic. Each restaurant concentrated on cuisine from a distinct part of the world, presented as high acid, high fat, highly Instragrammable dishes. And of course, paired with accessible wines by the glass.

"I can...but I wrote about their Italian place right before the lockdown, remember?"

"They've all pivoted, and it would be good for you to cover what they're offering for takeout," Ray insisted. "We got some press release about their new family-style takeout meals. I want you to check them out."

"But they only do delivery through GrubMates," Thea said. "I've been avoiding those apps after that article I linked you to. Did you read it?"

Silence.

If she had been sitting across from his desk, she would have cracked a joke to ease the tension. Instead, she took another sip of tea, now luke-warm, and waited for a response.

Finally, Ray sighed the bone-weary sigh of a disappointed manager. "We all have to work harder to look good for the new boss and what he cares about is the numbers. Do you want to keep your job?"

"Yes! Of course I do." The previous year, a commercial real estate tycoon bought the parent company that owned the paper. Even though he'd promised that things would stay the same, things were already changing.

"Then you write about those restaurants I told you to. You're lucky that you've got talent and you know your food, but certain restaurants perform better than others with our subscribers," Ray said. Ever since the acquisition, all the higher ups obsessed over page views, subscription numbers, and the vague idea of content innovation.

Thea let him drone on about the importance of looking good for the owner. He ended with, "Subscribers pay the bills. Capiche?"

Who even said that anymore? Thea imagined Ray with a Vito Corleone mustache and had to clamp her lips together to keep from giggling. She took a deep breath to compose herself. "I'll see what I can do."

The food delivery apps were convenient, but she'd read enough articles about them exploiting their drivers and eating up profit from a restaurant's already slim margins to be skeptical. All the spin PR companies put on how great the gig economy was doing didn't help. She'd avoided using them so far, but didn't know how much longer she could hold out. Especially with Ray breathing down her neck like this.

She tried a different angle. "There are restaurants that don't use the apps. Smaller ones that no one is writing about. We can be the first to discover a hidden neighborhood gem or—"

"What gets eyeballs are big buzzy places. That's why we gave you such a high max on your expense card. Use it!" Ray said. "If we just cover the dinky restaurants, we're going to lose readership to the Other paper."

That's what Ray called the other local LA paper. Thea thought of that paper as an alternative paper, not a competitor. Their reader demographics weren't exactly overlapping. She'd written pieces for them before and knew the food and small business editor there. They preferred a different style and voice than her paper's.

"What do the small restaurants use for delivery? I can get Jeff to cover it from the business angle," Ray asked.

"Well..." Thea hedged, "That's kind of the problem, too. A lot of them don't offer delivery because of staffing issues or they just can't afford it."

Ray grumbled something on the line, but Thea ignored it. She jotted down a quick note to herself on a post-it she kept on the table for random ideas. She could do a series interviewing smaller restaurants and how they're coping with the lockdowns.

"Maybe I can use an intern to pick up my food? I can train them on our style guide when they're not doing pickups," Thea offered.

Ray's hearty laughter rang in her ears. "Good one. This summer's interns were yanked up faster than donuts in the break room. You're too late. Terry from Education requested one, and you know how Sports always gets two."

People on the sports beat were Ray's mortal enemies. She tried to stay out of it, but there was a rumor that the Sports editors were always trying to take a bigger piece of the pie when the budget for the coming year was forecasted.

"I gotta call into the editors' meeting. Be glad you're not in this one. Look over the list I sent you and pick at least two restaurants to cover. I don't want to have to remind you again next month."

Thea was pretty sure he just threatened to fire her. She swallowed the bitter taste of fear in her mouth and tried to project a confidence that said she had her shit together. "Got it. I'll email you the rest of the list for next month after I slot in those restaurants."

"Good girl." Ray had a knack for always hanging up first.

Thea felt relieved that this was only a phone call and not video chat, because she could stick out her tongue at Ray. She hung up and exhaled a shaky breath. The good news was that she still had health insurance. The bad news was that she'd have to compromise her morals to keep it.

The previous Food editor, who had originally hired Thea for the paper, had moved to a fancy new online-only publication. It was a shock to learn two months into her dream job that the renowned editor she'd been looking forward to working for was leaving.

Marie had graciously offered Thea a position at the new site after she settled in, but because they were still finding their sea legs, they weren't providing health insurance for any of their reporters. Thea agreed to freelance for them, but stayed at the LA Times for job security. Ray, who was the Business editor, ended up inheriting the handful of staff from the Food section.

She rolled her shoulders back and forth to loosen them. They were always up to her ears after a meeting with Ray. He was a decent editor and knew the ins and outs of what their readers wanted. He just didn't have any passion for food, and he thrived in the culture of the previous generation of newspaper editors.

Her job reporting on restaurants at the Times was crucial for two big reasons: a steady albeit modest paycheck and health insurance. Not having health insurance in the middle of a global health crisis was a worry that woke her up in a cold sweat. What if she got Covid? Not the just-a-cold type of Covid, but a serious case? A hospital stay could bankrupt her without insurance. She couldn't ask her family for help either; her parents were in Taiwan and her brother had his own problems in Chicago.

Thea rose to brew another cup of tea and mulled over her dilemma while the leaves steeped. She hadn't felt safe leaving the house since the lockdown started. Like everyone else privileged enough to do so, she used the ubiquitous online retailer for the delivery of all her groceries and household supplies, even though she hated it. There was no way to fully escape their grasp.

Logistically, she wasn't even sure how she *could* pick up her own takeout and still have time to write — thanks LA traffic! She planned each day at least a week in advance, and the unpredictable traffic patterns were hard to schedule around. If she drove, she'd also need to expense for mileage. Thinking about using the paper's out-dated expense tracking software gave her a headache.

Thea checked her bullet journal for today. Ray would get his writeup about the buzzy restaurant soon, but at least today she could still order food from a mom and pop and not sell her soul.

TWO

Bzzzzt! THEA'S PHONE buzzed with a text from an unknown number: Estimated delivery time 20 minutes.

She dismissed the notification. She had about twenty minutes to clean the mess off her kitchen table and get her equipment ready. She picked up the dirty plates and empty bowls from the table and placed them in the sink. Then she wiped down the table.

The light coming from the kitchen window had softened as the afternoon wore on. If she timed it right, she wouldn't need to use the external light for the photographs. She moved her camera stand and camera to the optimum angle and took a few test shots with two clean, empty bowls.

Her gaze flicked to the clock. Seven minutes to go.

After taking out clean silverware and placing them on the kitchen table, she washed her hands with soap and water. Then she put on a clean mask, this one with an abstract floral pattern on it, and went to the front door. She peeked out of the living room window; no one had pulled up yet. Perfect.

Thea took her laminated sign with the velcro in the back, opened the front door, and stuck the sign below the doorbell. Then she pulled out an empty envelope from the drawer of the little table by the door and put some cash into it. She placed the envelope on her porch and moved her aloe vera on top of it so that only its corner was visible. Then she retreated into the house to wait.

As she sat on her couch, her phone buzzed again.

There was a text message from Olivia: *What're you up to?*

Instead of texting back, Thea pressed the phone icon.

Oliva picked up on the third ring. "You scared me!"

"Sorry, didn't feel like texting."

"No worries. What's up? Feeling better?" Olivia sounded out of breath, like she had just got done running up a flight of stairs.

A week ago, Thea admitted to Olivia that she felt worn down. Not sick, but not great. At first, she thought it was because she wasn't exercising enough, but she'd been spinning with Olivia since the pandemic started. Olivia asked when was the last time she left her house. Other than the ten minutes it took her each week to pull her car out of the driveway and roll her trashcan out onto the street, Thea couldn't remember.

"Besides that. Taking out the trash doesn't count." Olivia said.

Thea pictured her friend's eyes rolling. She thought back to the previous day, the day before that.

"Okay, the fact that you're thinking so hard about it is not good," Olivia interrupted her thoughts. "You gotta get out! Go for a walk —"

"I do go out! I sit on the porch and work every day. And I water my plants."

"How about a walk around the park? Or a hike?"

Thea sighed, "The hikes here want you to reserve a spot beforehand. Seems like a whole lotta trouble."

"What else are you doing all day?" Olivia sounded exasperated.

"I'm pretty busy! I spin with you. Then I have a bunch of stuff I have to read. Write, prep for the food show, then more reading. You know, same old, same old."

"Listen, I gotta go in a bit, but promise me you'll leave your house this week. For a walk. For at least thirty minutes, okay? I think the sun and fresh air'll be good for you. Okay?"

"Alright, fine."

"Promise me!"

"Okay, okay, I promise I'll go outside of my house."

Despite that promise last week, Thea still had gone nowhere. She wanted to complain to Olivia about the call this morning with Ray, but she refrained. Olivia was having her own work issues that were more dire. She didn't need to hear about the minor annoyances of her dream gig gone somewhat less dreamy.

"I'm feeling okay," she said instead. She felt guilty lying to her friend, but she didn't have the energy to get into it right then.

"Did you go outside like you promised?" Olivia asked.

"Um..."

"Well?"

"Sorry, sorry. I got caught up with this article and you know how these days just bleed into each other and —"

"Hey, I'm worried about you, girl. It's not good to be cooped up inside like you are. Do you need me to come down?"

"No, no, I'm fine, promise!" Thea tried to sound convincing. "You don't need to drive six hours for me. I'll really make time for the walk, like I said. It just slipped my mind."

"It shouldn't be this hard to go outside."

The slam of a car door saved Thea from discussing the topic further. "Oops, gotta go. My food's here. I'll call you after?"

"Alright, enjoy your dinner."

Thea hung up and looked out the window. Sometimes people had trouble with finding the latch on her gate. She needed to trim that bougainvillea back one of these days.

The delivery guy found the latch after a couple of tries and let himself into her front yard. His long legs ate up the path to her porch as he moved with an athletic grace. He stepped over all three of her porch steps in one stride and lifted a hand. He paused when he saw the sign she placed on by the doorbell. His eyes were a warm brown that looked golden the way the light bounced off of it.

As if pulled by an invisible string, Thea stood without thinking. She was so drawn to those eyes that she moved toward the front door before stopping herself. He must have felt her gaze on him because he looked toward the window and their eyes met through the parted curtains. She froze, hoping he hadn't seen her staring. Her cheeks heated.

🍃 🍃 🍃

632...634...636...640?

Gabe slowed the scooter to a stop. *Where was 638?* He checked his mirror to make sure the way was clear before backing up. He drove past 632, then started driving forward more carefully. 634... 636... There! No wonder he had missed it. There was a tiny plot of land between house number 636 and 640. The numbers painted on the mailbox were barely visible behind an overgrown bush with bright magenta flowers.

Gabe swung his leg over the seat and removed his helmet, welcoming the cool breeze in his hair. He made sure his mask fit snugly and opened the seat bag of the scooter. He was skeptical when his buddy Veer told him to take the restaurant's scooter, but now he was a believer. The scooter made it easy to squeeze through tight spots, and he didn't have to worry about finding parking on the street large enough for his truck. Like Veer had promised, storage was not a problem with the scooter — the black plastic seat bag was a magical bag of holding.

Gabe pulled out the three paper bags for this delivery, each marked 638 in fat marker. The bags were heavy and one of them made a sloshing sound in its container. Hopefully, nothing spilled in transit. He would hate to waste any of the food that the family here ordered.

Cradling the bags in his arms, he pulled open the low wooden gate of the fence separating the front yard from the sidewalk. It almost didn't open because of the huge bush growing over it. What might have been lawn was sparse and yellow, but otherwise the house looked cozy and welcoming, draped with overgrown greenery. There were several very healthy looking potted plants sitting on the porch, their leaves trailing down the porch balustrade. Some vine-looking plant crept and curled around the top of the porch swing.

There was tape over the doorbell. Someone had taped a brightly colored sign below it.

Doorbell is Broken :(

Please place items on the porch.
Envelope under green pot has tip in cash or I can
can Venmo you if you scan this code.
Thank you!

He gently placed the bags in front of the door. As he bent down, he noticed the aloe vera plant in a terracotta pot painted green. As promised, there was a white envelope sticking out from underneath. He pulled it out and tucked it in his back pocket.

Gabe was about to turn and head back down to the scooter, but the hairs on the back of his neck prickled. A movement caught the corner of his eye and he looked up at the source. He was being watched through one of the large windows at the front of the house. He barely made out a person standing there. Because of the gauzy curtain, he had trouble telling if the person was even looking at him. He gave a tentative wave.

They moved closer to the window and into a shaft of light filtering through the leaves of the immense oak tree by the sidewalk. There was a bright flash as the sunlight glinted off a pair of glasses, but as his eyes adjusted, he looked straight into the loveliest pair of eyes he'd ever seen: dark brown, almost black, framed by thick lashes. With her hair piled in a messy knot and glasses, the woman gave off a sexy librarian vibe. Her eyebrows were raised in surprise as she returned his wave.

"Thanks for the tip!" He shouted, hoping they could hear him through the mask and the window.

She must have heard because she nodded, eyes crinkling in a smile. Then she gave him a thumbs up.

As Gabe walked to his scooter, he checked his phone, where he noted down the address of his next delivery. He glanced at the name of this delivery: Georgia.

With one hand, he closed the lid of the seat bag and latched it secure. With the other, he checked the traffic on his phone. The back of his neck was still tingling, even as he put his helmet back on. He looked toward the house, but the windows were in shadow.

🍃 🍃 🍃

Thea wasn't exactly spying on him, but she needed to wait until the delivery guy left before she opened the door to grab the bags. She watched as he sat on the bike, looking at his phone. He had on a helmet now, but she could see the ends of his light brown hair curling around the nape of his neck. She wasn't the only one who had gone too long without a haircut.

Riding a motor scooter was so far down on Thea's list of sexy things men did, it caught her unaware. She couldn't stop looking at the man in front of her house. He sprawled on the seat, relaxed as a jungle cat. Her eyes made their way up and down his form. A propped foot on the scooter made the denim of his jeans snug, emphasizing the muscle of his thigh.

When the scooter hummed to life and the man drove off, Thea opened her front door. She brought in the three bags and took down the sign for the broken doorbell, dropping it back on the table by the door. She brought the bags into the kitchen, where she placed them on the counter. She carefully removed the contents from the bags, folded the bags up into flat compact rectangles and placed them in the recycling bin by the back door.

Thea took a couple of anti-bacterial wipes from their plastic tub on the counter and wiped down the outside of each container. The CDC hadn't said that surfaces were a source of contracting Covid, but they hadn't ruled it out either. Better safe than sorry. She blamed the pandemic for turning her into a germaphobe.

Satisfied that she wiped down as much as she could, Thea washed her hands with soap while humming "Happy Birthday." The nose-tingling alcoholic smell of the wipes thankfully evaporated by the time she was done.

She scooped the food into colorful bowls and plates that she set out on the table. She rearranged the positioning of the bowls, took a few shots with her camera, then moved things around again. The afternoon light was losing its golden hue, so she needed to get these pictures done fast. A dozen more shots later, she was content that she had enough for editing later.

The camera equipment got shoved off to the side of the table, so they wouldn't be in her way when she walked past. Thea poured herself a glass of chilled wine from the open bottle in the fridge and sat down at the table. Her food-stained notebook was already open to a blank page, and she had a fresh pencil ready.

As she tasted each dish on its own, Thea took notes. She had been looking forward to this particular restaurant because it was known for its curry of the day. It was a small mom and pop place that was barely hanging on during the pandemic, but luckily, loyal customers never stopped talking up the curry. When she dipped a piece of torn naan into the golden stew and sniffed it, her mouth watered.

It was impressive that the food was still hot even after being transported from the restaurant and poured into a different container. Not to mention how long it took her to take pictures of everything. She popped the naan into her mouth and chewed, savoring the warming spices and the richness of the bite. She chased that with a bit of pickled mango and sighed contently. Perfection.

Eating takeout was a privilege in the pandemic, and she liked to do what she could to support independent restaurants. She still missed dining in. Part of it was the atmosphere of each restaurant, whether it was a stand in the middle of an asphalt parking lot, a few stalls in a small market, or even a white linen and bread service type place. The other part was watching other people enjoy the food.

Her favorite thing to do whenever she visited a new place was look at what was on the tables of other customers. It often gave her a good idea of what was popular. Then, she would ask the servers what the restaurant's specialty was. What was popular was not always what the restaurant was known for. She'd written about that paradox for publications. It was interesting to figure out the reason.

At one family-run restaurant, everyone loved ordering food from the Hawaiian-influenced side of the menu. The katsu and macaroni salad from that place was decent, but after talking to the woman who ran the restaurant, Thea learned about the extraordinary fried chicken, off the Indonesian side of the menu.

People rarely ordered it because it usually took longer than they were willing to wait. The cook insisted on the chicken being fried to order. Instead of the typical heavily battered fried chicken made popular by KFC, this fried chicken was lightly battered. The batter formed a thin, lacy, impossibly crispy shell. To top it all off, the restaurant included a house-made sauce that was full of aromatic notes from lemongrass, galangal, and a punch of chili pepper.

The raita that came with her curry tonight was a cooling salve on her tongue. Not that the curry was even that spicy, but the heat level built up with each bite. The dance between the strong spices in the curry and the mellow creaminess of the raita had Thea going back for more, even after she was full.

She stopped before she overdid the eating. It was one of the hardest parts of her job, but she'd gotten plenty of practice. Besides, there was still dessert to get to. She knew that the famous curry was what she wanted to highlight in her review, but she also wanted to try the kheer that she'd heard so much about.

Speaking of kheer, where was it? She would have remembered if she spooned the sweet rice pudding out into one of her bowls. Maybe she had left the container on the counter? She went to the kitchen counter and searched. It wasn't there. It couldn't be in any of the paper bags either, since those were already empty and neatly folded up.

She peered out of the front door. No one was out there. She walked onto her porch, scanning the surrounding space. Maybe she missed a bag behind one of the plants. She looked down the steps to see if anything dropped.

Crap.

She desperately wanted that dessert, not only to write about, but that cool, sweet, creamy rice was exactly what she was in the mood for after that fiery curry. She took out her phone and pulled up the menu posted online. Yep, it was on today's menu and she remembered the person on the phone repeating her order back to her. She hated when things didn't go according to plan, even minor things like this.

She wondered if she should call in another order. Was it weird to order only a single serving of dessert?

As she mulled this over, she checked the porch again. Nothing. She even walked down the steps, thinking maybe the delivery guy dropped it on the path.

The crunch of gravel beneath tires snapped her head up. Speak of the devil.

Thea jumped up the three steps to her porch and ran into the house, slamming the door shut. She'd forgotten to wear her mask when she went out to check, not expecting to run into anyone in her front yard. She went to her living room window and watched as the man looked confusedly at the front door before continuing up the path to the porch. He stopped and waved at her through the window.

She waved back, arching her eyebrows at him in what she hoped was a questioning expression.

"I missed this one," he said as he held up a small paper bag.

Her kheer! Thea clapped her hands. He saved her evening.

"It fell out of the other bag and I didn't notice it."

The man's deep voice carried well, even through his mask and the glass of the window. Olivia was right. She really needed to get laid. She was sweating this guy based on his voice alone. Poor delivery guy. Poor, hot, bedroom-voiced, nice thighs, dreamy eyes, delivery guy.

"Thank you!" Thea said loudly through the closed window, hoping he could hear her.

"Should I leave it here?" He pointed to the spot in front of her door where he had left his other bags.

"Yes, thanks!" she said before mentally face-palming. She had already thanked him once.

"Okay, have a good night. Sorry." The man said before setting down the bag. She was definitely *not* looking at his butt as he made his way down.

Gabe walked back to the scooter. It had been an excellent decision to deliver that little bag. He wouldn't have glimpsed the woman without her mask if he hadn't gone back. Without the distraction of the colorful fabric covering half her face, her expressive brown eyes drew him in. Her rose petal lips captured his attention, causing him to stare longer than he thought was polite, but he couldn't look away.

When she had clapped about the missing container like he'd just performed a magic trick, he couldn't help but let a chuckle escape. The utter look of joy on her face made the trip back worth it. Her shy smile after she stopped clapping was so endearing that he felt warm all over.

He jiggled the keys to the scooter in his cupped hand as he walked.

"Hey, wait!"

His head whipped back to see her standing on her porch, once again masked. The familiarity of her voice surprised him. It was deeper than he expected, with a husky scratch to it that immediately made him wonder what she sounded like behind closed doors. Her skirt glided about her legs in the breeze, hinting at the tantalizing curve of her thighs. In contrast to her full, flowy skirt, her tight fitted top left nothing to his imagination, and yet his imagination still took off to unmentionable places.

The woman took a few steps off the porch and stopped a suitable distance away. "I really appreciate that you came all the way back to deliver this."

"If it's what I think it is, it's worth it." His voice sounded funny, and he wanted to clear it, but he also didn't want to scare her away with a cough in public.

She tucked a lock of hair that had blown free from her bun back behind her ear. She looked down at her clasped hands in front of her.

Gabe resisted the urge to step closer to her. She looked as if she was about to say something, but stopped herself. He waited a few breaths, not wanting to say goodbye yet.

"Sorry you had to come all the way back. Can I give you a bigger tip?" She finally asked.

"Nope," Gabe said, shaking his head. "I should've looked more carefully when I brought out the first delivery."

"I'm sure this happens a lot, right?"

"Not really." Gabe could feel his smile behind his mask, but was pretty sure she couldn't tell. He was sometimes short with people, but he wasn't trying to be rude to her.

"You're the first person I've talked to in, like, a month at least," she blurted out. "Well, in person I mean. Like face to face. Or mask to mask."

Gabe huffed out a laugh. "I know what you mean. I've been talking to my roommate's dog."

"Does he talk back?"

"She's not the chatty type."

"That must be ruff," she said, raising her eyebrows.

Gabe groaned. "Oh wow, that was... I'm not gonna even acknowledge such a bad joke."

Slender shoulders lifted in the briefest of shrugs. "I thought it was pretty good."

Gabe made a face and shook his head.

"Alright, I'll let you go then. I'm sure you have other deliveries to make." She gave a small wave and turned around.

"I don't." He didn't have other deliveries to make. While his body was tired and wanted nothing better to do than go home and sit on the couch, he still didn't want this conversation to end.

"Hmm?" She half-turned as she was about to walk up her porch.

"I don't have other deliveries to make."

"Oh, that's good." Another awkward silence followed while the two of them stared at each other. Gabe didn't think he was this out of practice with small talk, but being alone for the past few weeks got to him.

He realized he hadn't introduced himself. "I'm Gabe, by the way."

"Nice to meet you, Gabe."

"Nice to meet you, too. Georgia, right?"

She looked startled as she glanced up at him. He pulled out his phone and gave it a shake. "You gave your name when you made the order."

"Oh, were you the guy on the phone? You sounded different."

"Wasn't me."

The woman walked back to her front door. She turned one last time and gave him a wave. "See you around, Gabe."

"Bone appétit!"

Her infectious laughter followed him back to the scooter. He didn't feel so tired anymore.

THREE

GABE PULLED ONTO the on-ramp and waited for his turn to merge into traffic. While the little scooter was fun to ride, he was happy to be driving his truck. It had more pickup. On this short on-ramp into speeding cars, good acceleration meant the difference between a good day or not.

Gabe couldn't stop thinking about Georgia, wondering if he should have asked her out. He hadn't asked a woman out on a date for a long time. He felt out of practice. Did people even ask each other out in person anymore?

He still had her number from the delivery. Rustiness aside, even he knew it was creepy to text her out of the blue. He couldn't get her elated look out of his mind. He couldn't remember the last time he had seen such joy from someone about such a small thing. The way her eyes turned into crescent moons when she smiled pulled at the corners of his mouth.

Gabe turned on the radio after he merged onto the freeway. There was an ad for some sort of non-profit organization that covered public policy. No matter how many times he'd heard the ad, he still didn't know what that organization did.

When the radio show came back, the voice through his speakers made him swerve. The nasally honk of a Prius tooted in the other lane. He held his hand up in apology and turned the volume up.

The woman speaking was a weekly guest on the show. He loved her low, melodious voice and the husky laugh that accompanied it. He was embarrassed to admit that he would probably obey every command that woman made. She was a regular guest on Splendid Eats and talked about restaurants. *What was her name?* He was certain it wasn't Georgia.

The car ahead of him screeched to a halt. Gabe stomped down on the brakes. His gaze flicked up to his rear-view mirror in dread, bracing for a collision, but the car behind him was paying more attention and came to a stop. The cars in front changed lanes. There was a folded up mattress in the middle of his lane.

When the obstacle shrunk to a speck in his rear-view mirror, he let out a tense breath. *Why were people always losing mattresses on freeways?*

His thoughts wandered back to Georgia. He had plenty of doubts about asking her out. First, he wasn't even sure if he wanted to start dating again, especially not in the pandemic. Second, his ex, had told him he wasn't exactly boyfriend material, and it was true. Gabe missed very little about dating. He hated awkward first dates in restaurants where he had to come up with stuff to say to fill the silence and high-pressure second dates where he had to read signals of what the expectations were. He had plenty of hookups during his non-dating life. Those were easy and like scratching an itch. Plus, they didn't come with the baggage and expectations that a girlfriend would have.

His friends thought Christina, his ex, had broken him, but it wasn't true. They both knew their relationship was on its last legs by the end. The last straw was him finding out she'd been cheating. The fight that broke out wasn't because of the actual cheating, but because of his non-reaction.

Luckily, his job had taken him out of town for two weeks right after that fight. He hadn't needed to deal with the fallout at all. When he came back, she'd removed all her stuff from his place and left her key with his roommate, Adrian. He hadn't realized how tiring it was to always be tiptoeing around a girlfriend who constantly needed reassurance. Even on local jobs, it was draining to return after 15 hours on set only to have to reassure her he hadn't been sleeping with a coworker.

Sure, he was no angel in that relationship either: never calling at a reasonable hour, disappearing for weeks at a time with little to no notice. He didn't blame Christina anymore for being jealous. It was true; he *was* around tons of gorgeous people, but actors were paid to look good, so of course they were pretty. There was no avoiding them when you worked in the industry.

Gabe thought he was too jaded for crushes, but this heady feeling blossomed tonight. He tried to convince himself it was only boredom and isolation taking its tow. His studio furloughed him and Adrian had moved out, so he didn't have a lot of people to talk to. It was exciting to say even a few clumsy sentences to Georgia. He should just leave it at that.

When Gabe got home, Tails gave an excited bark and met him at the door. The fluffy orange mutt of dubious pedigree was Adrian's dog, but he'd offered to watch her while his ex-roommate got things settled at his mom's house. The dog's devotion to licks and cuddles was especially nice on days when all he wanted to do was flop on the couch and read one of those true crime books that Adrian stocked up on. There wasn't anything the cheerful smile of a dog licking his face couldn't fix.

He toed off his shoes and walked to the bathroom to wash his hands. He pulled on a pair of sweatpants and a clean shirt. Tails sat in the doorway of his room, looking at him.

Coming home to a fluffy companion was enough. He needed nothing more than that.

FOUR

THEA SCOOPED UP the last of the kheer and licked the spoon clean. The cute delivery guy was right; it was worth it. She would have said it was the best part of her meal, but the rest of the meal was also phenomenal.

She made a few scribbles in her notebook and then shut the cover. She didn't like to write right after eating, since she didn't want the satisfaction of a full stomach to cloud her judgment about the food. Plus, it always took her a day or two of mulling over what to write before she could put any words toward a review. But she did like to make sure she had detailed notes about how the food made her feel.

Chucking the plastic takeout containers into the sink, she walked to her living room and took out her phone. 8:43 — it was still early enough to call Olivia back.

"Hi, hi!" Olivia picked up on the second ring. Judging from her background on the screen, Olivia was in her kitchen.

"Hi. Are you still eating?"

"Just finished, you?"

"Me too."

"What did you have?"

"Oh my god, that Indian place I was telling you about.. Their curry is incredible. I get the hype now!" Thea listed all the different spices she could taste in the dish, speculated on the ones she couldn't pinpoint, and went on for several minutes about her meal.

Olivia laughed when she finished. "I can't wait to read your review. Although... I feel like I just got the Spark Notes version. I just had two slices of cheese pizza."

"Oh no! I didn't mean to make you feel bad." Thea said. Olivia was having a hard time in the pandemic because of her soul-sucking corporate job. Her fun hobby job, art with kids, had been cancelled. It wasn't exactly safe to be teaching watercolor in person in the middle of a pandemic.

"No! I love when you describe food. I can almost taste it."

Thea grinned guiltily. She sometimes went on and on about a perfectly seared piece of fish, or a juicy poached chicken. She couldn't help talking about meat with her vegetarian best friend, but Olivia was used to it.

"Oh my *god*, I gotta tell you something ridiculous," Thea said.

"What?"

"I got a really, *really* hot delivery driver."

"Whaaaaat?" Olivia shrieked and covered her mouth. "Like how hot? Was he wearing a mask? How could you even tell?"

"Well," Thea blushed as she thought about the man. "He had really nice wavy hair. Like nice and soft. And you know how guys with nice arms always have those t-shirts that show off their arms? The sleeves are super tiny? It was like that. I think he tall and seemed fit. Oh, and his voice was smooth like butter, but not in a creepy way like that guy on Marketplace."

Olivia wiggled her eyebrows lasciviously. "Girl, wipe that drool off your chin!"

Thea covered her mouth and shook her head. "I know, it's terrible. And I think he's packing."

"Packing an Amazon order or what?"

"Like *packin'* packing!"

Olivia arched an eyebrow. "Did you get his number? Maybe he can pack his eggplant in—"

"What?! Of course not!"

"Why not?"

"Uh, hello?! We're in the middle of a pandemic. I'm not gonna ask some stranger for his number, no matter how good looking he is." Thea rolled her eyes.

"Girl, when have you ever turned down a hot bod?"

"Oh my god, never say 'hot bod' again. I'm gonna vomit." Thea laughed as she cringed.

"What if you got his number and invited him to do something outside? You could go on a walk with him! Kill two birds with one stone."

"What two birds is this?"

"The getting you outside, and getting you some *inside,* birds," Olivia nodded sagely.

"Gross! How did asking some guy to go on a walk with me turn into us banging?"

Olivia gave a look through the camera that was all too easy for Thea to interpret. "I know you. You only talk to dudes to get into their pants, break their hearts, and disappear before they can ask for a second date."

Thea opened her mouth to refute it, but shut it. She pressed her lips into a thin line. "I won't disagree with that, but I don't break their hearts. They know what they signed up for. Whether they believe me is their own problem. Besides, this is all a hypothetical about a total stranger I'll never see again."

"Who knows, LA's a small town. Maybe you'll bump into Popeye again."

"Oh my god, his arms weren't *that* big. They were just nice, okay?" Thea laughed, shaking her head.

Olivia sat up straighter, a gleam in her eye. "What if you order food from that place again? He could deliver it and then you could—"

Thea held a hand up to cut her friend off. "Okay, I'm not gonna engineer this porno. If I was really that desperate, I could probably just text him at the delivery number."

"Yeah, sext him!" Olivia squealed.

"With what? Hey, remember me? You delivered some food the other day. Wanna deliver something good into my pants?" Thea couldn't even say it with a straight face. "That's wild. Anyway, I don't have time for dudes right now. I'm way behind on my book."

"Oh yeah, how's that going, anyway?" Olivia asked.

"Slow, but I think I'm picking up steam," Thea admitted. She'd thought at the start of the pandemic that being in lockdown would give her the time she needed to gain momentum with her manuscript. But between working on the proposal and finally getting it accepted, she lost that momentum. It didn't help that she kept distracting herself by pitching ideas to magazines.

"Well, if you need a break, you could always watch that movie you promised me," Olivia said.

"Crap, forgot about that."

"I didn't."

"I think the dishwasher's acting up again, gotta go!" Thea hung up. To make up for chickening out from the scary movie, she worked on the outline of several features with looming deadlines.

The universe was conspiring to keep her from finishing the outline of her manuscript. First, all of her pitches to the various places she wrote for had been accepted, something that never happened. Then an attractive guy literally lands on her doorstep. But she would not let a hot guy with lame jokes distract her from her work. Definitely not.

FIVE

A WEEK LATER, Thea did what she'd promised Olivia she'd do and made plans to go outside, bright and early on a Tuesday morning. It had been months since she'd left the vicinity of her neighborhood.

Thea flipped to her schedule in her bullet journal. The words "GO OUTSIDE" stared back at her in the space for today. Planning her weeks on paper was a habit she'd picked up from her early days freelancing. It gave structure to her life. Sex was great and all, but it was nothing compared to checking off a tiny square in her To Do list.

Ray's call still lurked in the back of her brain like a black hole. She didn't want to think about it and spiral into depressing thoughts about her moral dilemma. She'd need to sign up for one of those apps this week. For now, she pushed that thought back into its compartment for later. She wouldn't commit to writing that task down in her journal just yet.

Thea looked out her window to check on the weather. Clear blue skies beckoned to her. She should drive somewhere, but where?

After spending an hour goggling the hell out of the potential risks of a public park, she was an expert in exhalation aerodynamics in an outdoor setting. Depending on the breeze, humidity, temperature, and timing, the chances of her walking through a cloud of floating corona viruses was low. She braced herself to venture outside, armed with her new knowledge and a backup mask.

*   *   *

Nerves thrummed under Thea's skin as she slipped a second mask over her first and stepped out of her car. She picked LA Historic Park because, according to pictures posted online, it had wide open paths and enough room to maneuver around people if it got crowded. Judging by the empty spots in the lot, it wasn't likely to be busy at this time of day.

The weather was warm enough. She could finally wear her shorts again. A slight chill was in the air, but under the sun, it was pleasant. Spring in LA always filled her with a sense of renewal and optimism. Relief flooded her as she walked up to the entrance of the park and saw a metal sign reminding people to wear masks. As she peeked beyond the gate, she saw that almost everyone inside the park had their masks on.

She waited until a couple in running outfits jogged through the entrance. After being sure that she wouldn't be walking into a cloud of their exhaled air, she entered the park.

Walking a few minutes in the afternoon sun made her glad that she remembered to bring her straw hat. Olivia always made fun of her about it because the brim was so wide, but her mom, the dermatologist, had instilled in her that protecting her skin from UV rays was a matter of life and death. She should have worn a long sleeve shirt and pants for full coverage, but the sun and breeze felt too good on her skin. Her *titas* would have clucked their tongues at her.

Although the parking lot was mostly empty, the park was not. Some women were playing frisbee in a socially distanced circle. Couples scattered throughout the short green lawn, reclining on picnic blankets and beach chairs. A family perched at the top of one hill with a kite haphazardly climbing the sky.

Olivia was right: she needed this. The sun's warm rays were already burning away the tension in her shoulders. The fresh air, or at least what she could get of it through her double masking, smelled like the promise of a better year to come.

Thea was so busy watching gusts of wind send the kite higher that she didn't notice the dog wandering near her until its cold, wet snout touched the back of her hand. She yelped in surprise and brought her hand up, looking down at the creature. The orange, vulpine bundle of fur sat, tongue lolling out in greeting.

She laughed at the way the dog looked at her with its goofy grin. She extended a tentative hand, and it immediately butted its fluffy head against her palm. Even this dog was enjoying the wonderful weather and fresh air. After a few pats and scratches, it ran back to its owner. The man, wearing linen shorts and a striped T-shirt, was bent over picking up a floppy cloth frisbee. When he stood up and said something to the dog, his voice sounded familiar. *Could it be?*

The guy must have felt her eyes on him, because his gaze immediately found hers. Hot food delivery guy!

"Georgia?" he asked, coming closer.

"Oh, hey?" She was surprised that he recognized her with her masks, sunglasses, and hat on.

"Gabe. I delivered—"

"—I remember. Last week, right? Fancy meeting you here," she said, then cringed at how hokey it sounded coming out of her mouth. She'd forgotten she made the food order with one of her aliases.

"What are you doing here?"

"Just getting fresh air. Apparently, being cooped up in your house for weeks is not great for your mental health," Thea said wryly.

"Yeah, that's why me and Tails are here."

Upon hearing her name, the dog trotted over from where it was sniffing at a tuft of grass and sat in front of Thea, tongue still hanging out. Tails gave her that soulful doggy stare dogs did. Thea laughed and gave the friendly dog a few more scratches behind her ear. It gave her some time to check out Gabe from under the brim of her hat without being obvious.

His shorts revealed nicely shaped, bronze calves. He either did a lot of running or a lot of hikes.

"Weird," he commented. "She's usually skittish with strangers."

"I had some beef jerky on the way here. Maybe your dog's smelling that?"

"Bingo. She's actually my housemate's dog, but I'm watching her while he's outta town."

"That's nice of you."

"She's a good dog. It's no biggie. *And* she's a great cuddler."

The image of him cuddled up with the dog on the couch gave her a warm tingle. What were the chances that she would bump into him again? Thea could practically hear Olivia screaming about how this was a sign from the universe, or Neptune rising, or whatever cosmology her friend was currently into.

"It was nice running into you. I'm gonna go walk the loop around here," Thea said, turning away. Tails trotted happily after her as if on a leash.

Gabe made a clicking sound with his mouth to the dog, but the stubborn animal ignored him.

"Go on. I'm going the other way." Thea looked down at the dog, who looked up at her expectantly with round pleading eyes. She gave the dog a soft push on the bottom, but the she didn't budge.

Gabe chuckled, a rich sound that wrapped around her like a warm scarf. "You said the magic word. You're stuck with her now."

"Walk?" Thea asked, and the dog barked in response.

"Tails, come here." Gabe walked to the dog and clipped a leash onto her collar. The dog let out a dejected whine.

"Do you wanna come with me?" Thea asked before she could stop herself. The path was wide enough for them to be at least six feet apart. It was only a casual walk. It would be fine. That's what she told herself to quiet the quick thumping of her heart.

"Are you talking to me or the dog?" Gabe tilted his head, his eyes crinkling in a smile.

"Both."

"Sure." Gabe handed the dog the frisbee. Tails happily took it in her mouth and started trotting down the path.

Thea couldn't help but notice the way the muscles of his forearm flexed and moved as he adjusted the leash. It was getting hot under her masks.

Dog leashed, they started on the path at a leisurely pace. Thea was relieved that Gabe seemed aware about the distance she attempted to keep from him and didn't walk too close to her, letting her go first where the path narrowed. That Tails liked to walk between them also helped.

Initially, she worried she had lost the people-skills to make small talk, but she found Gabe so easy to talk to that she didn't need to force anything. Her natural curiosity about people, a handy skill to have as a writer, guided their conversation.

He wasn't the most talkative, but he wasn't standoffish, either. He had a quiet, deliberate way of speaking that she could listen to all day. She liked that he seemed to think before saying anything. It was a delightful change from the usual guys she talked to, the ones who couldn't shut up about their podcasts.

As they walked, Gabe told her about all the random things Tails found on walks. She especially liked the way his voice sounded when he recounted the time Tails brought a terrified possum into the house. She wondered what he looked like under that mask when he laughed like that.

During a lull in conversation, Thea asked, "So why are you free on a Tuesday morning?"

"I'm pretty free these days."

"These days?"

"I was furloughed after the first lockdown and we haven't gone back yet."

"Oh no, I'm sorry! That must be stressful."

"Yeah, it sucked, but we all knew it was coming. At least they paid us for the first few weeks. I'm in 'The Industry' as they say." Gabe made air-quotes with his hands as he said the last part.

Thea studied what she could of his face, trying to see if she recognized him from anything. He certainly had the build for a leading man in a movie, but more of a Ryan Gosling body than a John Cena's. It was tricky for her to get the full picture of his face behind the mask.

Gabe noticed her studying him. "Oh, I'm not an actor. I'm a scenic carpenter." At her puzzled look, he clarified, "I build sets."

"Ooooh!" Thea exclaimed. "You must be really good with your hands." She hadn't meant for the last part to come out sounding so flirtatious. She snuck a glance at him, hoping her dark sunglasses didn't make her interest look too obvious.

Gabe's eyes widened at the innuendo. He laughed and scratched the back of his neck. The movement brought Thea's attention to his biceps, and she tried not to gawk too openly at them. He probably did a lot of physical work with wood, hammers, and other heavy things. Those arms were for working, not for her to lust over. "I'm decent. I enjoy working on things where I can see the progress. It's satisfying building something that you can actually touch, you know?"

"You sound like you really like it."

Gabe shrugged. "It's a job and I get to work with my hands. There're plenty of crappy parts about it, like the insane hours and having to take stuff apart that you just built, but it pays the bills. Or it did."

Thea made commiserating noises. She knew something about taking on less exciting jobs to make rent.

"But since I've been free, I started on some projects I put off at home,"

Gabe added with enthusiasm. "I like those much more."

"And you do food delivery too?" Thea asked.

"No. I was covering for my buddy. He does the delivery for his parents' restaurant, but he's recovering from Covid so..."

"Oh, that makes sense." A kernel of an idea was forming in Thea's head.

"Yeah, they're not that tech savvy, so they didn't sign up for Grub-Mates or whatever. They've always been nice to me and they needed someone to cover deliveries last week."

"That was nice of you to help."

"People are tipping well these days *and* they're always giving me free food. Well, you know, since you ordered there, but their food is really great."

Thea nodded enthusiastically. "Yeah, it is. I couldn't believe how much flavor there was in that goat curry."

"Unbelievable, right?" Gabe looked at her and arched an eyebrow. He echoed her question back to her. "So why are you free on this Tuesday morning?"

"I'm a freelancer, sorta, so I make my own hours."

"Freelancer doing?"

"I'm a writer," Thea said after a pause. She wasn't sure how detailed she should get into it. Not that being a food writer was a dirty secret, but she also enjoyed having a certain anonymity about it. It was one reason she used so many aliases when interacting with restaurants.

"Like a TV writer or —"

"No, more like a journalist. I write about food and culture through the lens of the immigrant community here in LA." She didn't mean to lapse into her public voice, the one she used whenever she had to speak to people in a professional setting, but it just happened.

"Wait," Gabe paused mid-stride.

Thea had to back up because she was already a few steps in front of him.

"Are you the one who wrote about that family that runs all the Vietnamese restaurants with the punny names?"

"That's me." She was surprised he'd remembered that. It had been five years since that article came out.

"That was a good one. I loved how you interviewed the older and younger people in the family. It's funny how both generations have totally different ideas about how restaurants should be run. So you're pretty into food, right?"

She felt a little uncomfortable admitting it. She was into food, but she also knew that sometimes she could be too into food. Her ex claimed she had an unhealthy obsession with food, but she couldn't help constantly thinking about it even when she wasn't eating.

Gabe must have sensed her hesitation, because he looked concerned. "Did I say something wrong?"

"No," Thea shook her head, "It's weird talking about my job, I guess."

"You don't like it? It sounds like a dream job."

Thea laughed. "I love it! Sometimes I pinch myself to see if it's all a dream. I get to go to restaurants, well, before all of this, and eat great food. Then I get to write about it. Two of my favorite things."

Gabe started walking again, and Thea let him lead. "So, what's weird about it?"

"I'm not used to talking about it so much with someone I just met. It's not a secret or anything, but I try to keep it on the DL."

"What do you mean? Aren't you a food celebrity? Hold on," Gabe said, recognition dawning in his eyes. "I knew your voice sounded familiar! You're on that food show on the radio, right? Splendid Eats?"

Splendid Eats was a NPR show she had a guest segment on. Thea typically picked a restaurant to talk about and recommended dishes from there. She had to pivot during the pandemic to talking about which restaurants had food that best survived delivery.

"Oh yeah. Do you listen to it?" Thea asked. She never felt comfortable with public recognition like this.

"It's the only reason I tune in to that station. I like your soothing radio voice," Gabe said. The intensity in his eyes made her warmer than the sun directly overhead. He continued, "Great for crappy commutes, but all the food talk on the show makes me hungry."

"I guess that's better than saying I have a face for radio."

A laugh burst out of Gabe. "You don't have a face for radio."

Thea looked askance at him. Casual flirtatious compliments, she could deal with, but what Gabe said made her feel all warm and gooey inside. She found it funny that he was so complimentary about her voice when his own was making her stomach flutter. It was rich and deep, like the dark chocolate gelato from that famous place in the foothills. She mentally shook herself. Now was not the time to think about how sexy his voice was.

"Trust me, you have a very nice face." The confidence with how Gabe said that made her pause. A flirty quip balanced on the tip of her tongue. She knew exactly how to play this game, but as her eyes caught on his mask, she remembered the situation and reality came crashing back. She clamped her mouth shut.

"Sorry, I'm fan-boying here. I made it awkward, right?"

"It's okay. I'm just kinda weird in public about it." Thea clenched her hands. "I do a lot of stuff undercover. Not with a trench-coat and a funny mustache or anything."

He nodded in understanding.

"So... promise me you won't blow my cover, okay?" Thea asked, half joking.

"Okay."

Her hand twitched with the urge to smooth her finger down the little crease forming between his dark eyebrows. "My name's not actually Georgia. It's an alias I give to restaurants. So people working there won't suspect I'm writing about them. And I try to keep my face off of social media—"

"Ah, that's why! I *thought* your name was something different from the show."

"My name's Thea. But don't tell anyone that Georgia is one of my aliases."

Gabe's eyebrows raised as his eyes grew wider. "Okay, you told me one of your secrets, so I have to tell you one of mine."

Thea fought her body to keep from leaning in closer to him. She asked in a mock-whisper, "What is it?"

Gabe looked left, then right. There was no one around him, so he needn't have worried. "My real name is Gabriel."

It confused her at first. Only when she looked at him and saw the twinkle in his eyes did she know he was teasing her. She rolled her eyes. "Okay, hilarious. Do you prefer Gabriel?"

"No, only my mom calls me that." He stuck out his hand as if to shake hers, but curled it into a fist at the last minute. "Well, nice to meet you for real this time, Thea."

Thea reached over and tapped his fist with her own. The way Gabe said her name sent a pleasant shiver down her spine. "So, do you like going to restaurants too?"

"Nah. Not really my thing."

"Really? But you read about them and you listen to a food show about them?" Thea asked, surprised.

Gabe shrugged. "I just like good writing and I like hearing you talk about food."

They reached a small hill on their stroll and walked up to the wooden ramp leading to a platform on top of it. Only one other person was up there, standing by the handrail with their dog. Thea and Gabe stopped at the opposite end of the platform to take in the view while Tails tried to get the other dog's attention by wagging her tail enthusiastically.

Thea was about to ask why he didn't like going to restaurants when she turned toward him and all thoughts in her head disappeared in a puff like a magic trick. Gabe was leaning on the handrail, looking toward downtown LA. She took her time checking him out, since he was facing away from her. She was envious of his long, thick lashes that curled up from his eyes. It wasn't fair that a man had such gorgeous lashes. Even more unfair was how those dark lashes highlighted his brown eyes.

"Cinnamon!" Thea blurted out. A trick of light made his eyes glow like a leaf in autumn under the sun.

"Excuse me?" He turned to her in confusion.

"Your eyes are like cinnamon." Realizing what she'd said aloud, Thea clamped a hand to her mouth. She was mortified.

Gabe took a step closer to her, those eyes of his trained on hers. Like before, her body had a mind of its own and closed the distance between them until she stood in front of him. She couldn't look away from him or the way his pupils grew, inky pools that swallowed the brown. She felt his eyes like a caress as they swept over her face.

She wondered what the rest of his face looked like. She could tell by the way the fabric hugged in places that he had a strong jawline, but what did his mouth look like? Were his lips soft? Thea shook that unproductive train of thought from her head. She watched the rise and fall of his mask with each breath. *Oh right, mask.* She stepped back, surprised at how close they had drifted.

If Gabe noticed her daydreaming about kissing him, he was polite enough not to say anything. He blinked, and the moment was gone. He tipped his head and nodded toward the path. "Keep going?"

Thea led the way off the platform to the rest of the path. There were a handful of groups gathered under the shade of some trees. Other than everyone wearing masks, it could have been any normal day in the park before the pandemic.

By the time they made a complete loop around the park, the sun was high in the sky. Thea hadn't realized how much time had passed. They had stopped along the way to let Tails sniff at bushes and run around, but she didn't think they had dallied for so long.

Gabe was an excellent conversationalist and asked questions without prying too much. Thea was enjoying learning tidbits about him. Where he grew up: just a few miles in the other direction in Boyle Heights; what his hobbies were: building stuff in his workshop; what he'd wanted to be when he grew up: Inspector Gadget.

He impressed her by how well he knew LA. He told her about what used to be at the location of the park they were standing in. What was even better was that he knew all the side-streets to take when the freeway was packed. That was how she knew he was definitely from LA.

Olivia may have been on to something when she said that going out and getting sun would improve her mood. Or maybe it was spending the morning with someone other than herself for once. Thea hadn't felt this good, more like herself, in a while.

As they made their way back to the entrance of the park, Thea's stomach growled.

Any hope that Gabe hadn't heard or would be a gentleman enough to ignore it disappeared when he asked, "Hungry?"

"Yeah, I guess a few pieces of beef jerky for breakfast weren't enough."

"I'd say we go get something to eat," Gabe nodded at Tails, "but I gotta take this good girl home. She might be pretty hot by now."

"I thought you hated restaurants?" Thea asked.

"I don't *hate* them. I just don't like going to them," he said. "I'd make an exception for you."

His flirtatious tone didn't escape her notice. Part of her wanted to volley back an invitation, but the rational part of her brain shut it down fast. She reached over to pet the dog. Tails seemed to be panting more than she was before.

"I'm glad I ran into you today." Gabe said. Even though it was hard to see his expression with the sun behind him, Thea could hear a hint of a smile in his voice.

"Me too." Thea's stomach growled again. She crossed her arms.

Her empty stomach dislodged the thought that had been percolating in her mind. If she didn't come up with a solution that appeased Ray soon, she would lose her job and, most importantly, her health insurance.

What if there was a way to keep her job without compromising her morals?

If she could pay a person to pick up her food instead of putting money into a venture capitalist's pocket, someone who was also willing to travel longer distances than the delivery area of the restaurants, it would give her more places to write about. Places that would satisfy Ray's need for buzzy restaurants as well as her desire to help smaller restaurants. She could even cover the pop-ups she had been following on social media without people recognizing her face. Gabe said he had plenty of time on his hands. He seemed conscientious about Covid precautions. He had a good understanding of LA geography. He already knew where she lived, so she didn't have to worry about him getting lost on the way to her house.

Before she could stop herself, she blurted out, "I have a proposition for you—" at the same time Gabe asked, "Can I—"

"You first," Gabe said.

"No, you go." Thea wiped her palms off on the back of her shorts. She had a feeling she knew what he was about to ask.

"Can I take you out sometime?"

Well, crap, this is awkward. Thea didn't want to go into all the ways she could say no. Besides the obvious, that they were in the middle of the world's most epic pandemic, she'd sworn off dating years ago. It didn't fit her lifestyle for a host of reasons. She gave him the most simple one. "Sorry, I'm not dating right now."

"Okay," Gabe said. Thea liked how easily he took her answer. He didn't immediately go to some saving-face comment like most guys she turned down did. He looked at her and raised his eyebrows. "Now you go."

"Huh?"

"You were about to say something before I interrupted," he reminded her.

How was she going to ask him now? She was certain he was going to decline after she'd rejected him, but she went for it, anyway. "I order a lot of takeout these days for my job. I don't like how if I use an app, the money doesn't go directly to the person doing the delivery or to the restaurant."

"Go on."

"Maybe I could hire you to pick up food regularly for me? I mean, if you want to. Totally okay if you don't. No hard feelings. I'm paying for delivery anyway, so I can just pay you directly. Cut out the middleman." She couldn't help rambling when she was nervous.

"So you'd phone in the order, and I'd pick it up for you?"

"Right. I'll pay over the phone, and then you can pick it up and deliver it. I'd pay you, of course. Maybe we can settle on a weekly fee since I know about how many orders I'd make in a week normally. I'll text you before I make the order or we can figure out a schedule for these things."

Gabe fiddled with the straps on his mask. "Well, this is less exciting than the proposition I thought you were going to make."

Thea's heart skipped, and she took a slow breath to calm herself. "Sorry."

"Don't be. You let me shoot my shot and I missed," he said. Was he still flirting with her?

"So, will you think about it?"

"No." Before she could say anything, he went on, "I don't need to think about it. I accept."

"Really? We didn't even talk about payment yet."

Gabe waved her off. "Why don't you think about it and come up with a number that seems fair? Lemme know later."

"Okay. What days would you be available for this?"

Gabe took out his phone. She thought it was to look at his calendar so that he could give her his availability. Instead, he looked up at her and asked, "Can I have your number?"

"My number?"

"For this to work, you'd need to reach me, right?" he asked.

"Oh, right," she said, trying to hide her blush by looking down and tucking some stray strands of hair behind her hair. She didn't know why she felt so flustered. They were two adults setting up a business transaction.

After she recited her number to him, he tapped a few more times, and she got a buzz on her phone. She reached into her pocket out of habit.

"That was me. Now you have my number." She must have looked more nervous than she thought, because he asked, "You okay?"

"Mm-hmm," she said, distracting herself by adding his number to her contacts list.

He looked at her in a funny way, then widened his eyes. "Wait, did you think I was asking for your number because—even though—"

Thea held her hand up, palm facing him. "No."

"If you change your mind." Gabe gave her a meaningful look. She felt that look to her core, and she was pretty sure her face was turning a brighter color than it already was. "If we weren't in the middle of Covid—"

"That's still a no," Thea said, shook her head. "I don't have time for guys right now."

"Ouch," Gabe gave a small laugh, "It's ok. I get it. Text me later after you figure out the details. Now I really gotta get Tails home or it ain't gonna be pretty."

Thea felt guilty about dragging the poor dog around the whole park with them, but the pooch seemed happy to tag along before. Or maybe that tight sensation in the middle of her chest was guilt about rejecting Gabe and then asking him to do work for her. If he agreed to her terms, it would work out perfectly. Now she just needed Ray to approve.

SIX

"WELL?"

"Well... what?" Thea asked.

"What happened on your walk?" Olivia said. "I can see it all over your face. Something happen?"

"I'll... tell you... but not... right... now." Thea said, gasping for breath between each word.

"Why not?"

For someone also doing the exact exercise, Olivia had no trouble speaking in complete sentences. At that moment, Thea hated her for it. Her friend wasn't even breaking a sweat. Olivia's jet black hair was pulled into a tight bun, not a hair out of place. Thea's own hair was hopelessly plastered around her sweaty face. They'd been on their exercise bikes for at least ten minutes. Five minutes of those were warmup, but still.

Thea pulled the towel from her stationary bike's handlebar and used it to mop up the sweat from her forehead. She glanced at the tablet leaning on the display screen of her bike and made a face. "I'm dying here!"

"Come on, this isn't even a hard workout," Olivia cheerily said. "Let's do another circuit and then we can take a water break."

Thea forced her legs to keep pedaling. She hummed a tune in her head, pressing each leg down on the beat with the song, trying to ignore the burning in her thighs.

Ten agonizing minutes later, the bike chirped a catchy tune that meant the circuit was done. Thea sat back on the bike's seat and greedily chugged on her water bottle. She looked at the screen to see Olivia doing the same.

"So?" Olivia asked after swallowing. "Spill the deets!"

Thea wiped the sweat from her lip. She unclipped one of her shoes out of the pedal and flexed her foot, stretching out her calf. "You remember that guy I told you about? The delivery guy?"

Olivia squealed and pumped her fists. "OMG. Did you see him on your walk?"

"Um-hmm. He remembered me."

"Of course he did!"

Thea summarized what happened at the park to Olivia, leaving out the details she wanted to keep for herself. Like how Gabe's voice made her feel when he chuckled, that low laugh that sounded like a private joke between the two of them. Or how his shoulders pulled the fabric of his shirt enough that she had taken a double-take, or a triple take when he'd raised his arms for a stretch during their walk. She knew Olivia would tease her relentlessly about it.

Instead, Thea explained the arrangement she had offered Gabe.

"Smart!" Olivia said. "That way you can get your food and eye candy, too."

"Olivia!" Thea said in a shocked voice, "He's not just eye candy."

"Right, right. He's also performing an essential job."

Thea rolled her eyes at her best friend.

"But come on, is he cute? What does he look like?"

Thea paused, picturing him. "He's good looking, I think. Or at least, from what I can see of his face."

Olivia's eyes bugged out. "What?! You still don't know what he looks like?"

"I know what he looks like! The top half of his face looks fine. Like *fo-*

ine fine. But I can't really see what the mask is covering, you know. But he has a great voice. Rich like a dark chocolate pot de crème."

"Only you would compare a dude's voice to chocolate pudding." Olivia laughed.

"Fancy chocolate pudding."

"What if he has some un-ironic, terrible mustache or a like... a patchy beard?" Olivia shuddered. "Remember patchy beard guy?"

Thea made a face. "Oh god, don't remind me. That guy had creeper vibes from the beginning."

For a brief couple of weeks in college, Olivia dated a guy from her Eastern Philosophy course who always had a patchy beard. No matter how long he'd let it grow out, there would be sparse areas on his cheeks that were completely bare. Olivia later found out from the guy that he liked to shave off parts of his beard purposely to make it look patchy. He thought it made him more attractive to Asian women.

"What if it's like a 70s porn 'stache?" Olivia squealed.

"Oh no! Now I'm wondering about it, thanks."

"Okay, so super duper 'stache. What else?"

"He takes good care of his body. You know, not like those dudes always posing at the gym, but fit in a way where he actually uses his muscles for normal stuff. I think maybe because of his job. He works a lot with wood and hammers, I think."

"Nice, nice," Olivia nodded. "What else?"

"He's easy to talk to, and okay, this is weird, but he just seems so... wholesome." Thea searched for the word to describe him. "Like, he's really direct and honest—"

"—so not a fuck boy," Olivia filled in for her.

"Yeah. So... not anyone I usually mess around with," Thea said wryly.

Olivia sighed. "You know you're too good for those fuck boys, right?"

Thea laughed, "Yeah, but I like them! They're fun and they don't stick around."

"Yeah, they are," Olivia agreed. "But don't you miss having something substantial or someone who's not against commitment?"

"But I'm against commitment," Thea said.

Her friend didn't say a word, but gave her The Look. She was used to this prodding by Olivia. If it came from anyone but her friend, Thea would have re-directed the conversation to another topic, but with Olivia, she was comfortable. Olivia had seen her at her worst, especially when she was trying to push her away, and stuck through it with her, and that counted for a lot in Thea's book.

"What's so bad about commitment?" Olivia asked gently.

"I dunno. I just like that honeymoon phase when you first meet a guy and he's still trying to impress you."

"Yeah, that is pretty nice."

"See? If I never get serious with anyone, I can just keep having that honeymoon over and over again with different dudes."

"And that's enough?" Olivia asked.

Thea sighed. "I'm just through with that part of my life where we spend so much time at each other's places, then we move in together, then I have to cater to the dude. I like my life. I don't need a man right now."

"I'm not saying you need anyone. But isn't it nice sometimes to be needed?"

Thea shrugged. "I'm not interested in parenting some man-child."

Thea could tell her friend was exasperated. She and Olivia had pretty different outlooks about dating. Olivia was a serial monogamist, even if the pandemic seemed to have broken her streak.

Olivia's shoulder came up in a slow shrug, a movement Thea knew meant she was done with the subject.

"It's not being weak to be vulnerable sometimes," Olivia said as a parting shot. Thea heard some beeps on the other side of the screen, and then Olivia raised her eyebrows in a challenge. "Ready to go for another lap?"

Thea welcomed the strenuous ride to clear her mind, but this time, it wasn't doing much of any clearing. She couldn't stop over-analyzing how she reacted to Gabe. Not that she didn't think he was hot. Her track record of purposely avoiding relationships didn't give her a lot of practice with evaluating her feelings toward him beyond immediate lust. It was easier to act on physical attraction, wait for the novelty to fizzle out, and then move on.

Thea said between labored huffs, "It doesn't really matter if I like Gabe or not. He's just delivering food to me. And it's not like I'm gonna start anything in the middle of this pandemic."

"To start." Olivia said with a knowing look. "Next thing you know, he's delivering flowers, candy, gourmet doughnuts—"

"I don't even like flowers."

"Answer something for me," Olivia said, her face taking up the whole screen.

Thea mirrored her movement and got closer to her screen so that they were about as eye to eye as they could be. Her thighs were burning, so she wasn't sure how long she could maintain this pose while pedaling. Even this close, she couldn't see a drop of sweat on Olivia's face. "What?"

"If we weren't in a pandemic, would you already be sleeping with him?"

Thea pretended to think it over for a few seconds and then nodded. "Of course! Unless he has really has some sort of tragic facial hair."

"Girl, go get it!"

"Pandemic, remember?"

"You two can have a situationship."

"A what?"

Olivia shook her head in disbelief. "Oh my god, you haven't heard of a situationship? You know, a bennie in your bubble."

Thea cringed. "Ugh, I hate that word. It's so... round. Bubble. I'm the only one in my bubble and what the hell is a bennie?"

"You don't know what a bennie is?" Olivia sounded incredulous.

"I know what a beanie is."

"Friends with benefits. Benefits. Bennie. How are you so old?!" Olivia asked. Thea was twenty-nine, only six months older than Olivia.

Thea shook her head. The bike finally beeped to signal the completion of the lap. She huffed and lazily finished pedaling, her legs feeling like overcooked noodles. "Okay, I get it. I just hadn't heard before."

"Yeah, I can tell. You gotta get out more. Well, not right now, obviously, but figuratively. Seriously, when was the last time you got laid?"

Olivia's question took Thea by surprise. Wasn't it obvious? The entire world was going through a pandemic. Unless you were already living with a romantic partner, how else would you be getting laid? Sure, there were reports of people in those other states thinking this whole thing was a hoax, but in California, people were serious about social distancing precautions.

"I dunno," she said. "It's not like I put a notch on my belt. Probably a month before the shutdown started?"

It was with that guy she met at the hipster natural wine bar that had just opened after the new year. She was there collecting info for work to see if there was anything worth writing about. He was the only other person sitting alone at the bar. She struck up a conversation with him so that she could include more detail in her piece about the customers. Turned out he lived only a few blocks from the place. One thing led to another, and he was perfectly fine despite the man-bun, so she went home with him.

"Well, you're a stronger woman than me," Olivia said. Her voice brought Thea out of her reverie.

"Wait, what? Did you start dating someone? How are *you* getting any action? Aren't you scared of catching the virus? This is not a joke! You can't just—"

"Hold up," Olivia raised a placating palm. "Didn't I mention this already? You know, I *do* have a roommate who's a man, right?"

"Sea Bass?!" Thea asked, incredulous. She hadn't forgotten about Olivia's roommate, but she also hadn't thought of him in that way before. Sure, he was pretty cute, in a clueless sort of way, but she didn't think Olivia saw him that way.

Now it was Olivia's turn to blush and stammer. "Yeah, yeah, I know. But we've both been spending so much time in the apartment these days and it was so boring, so—"

"Oh, my god. No! You didn't mention this to me. I can't believe you've been roasting me about not getting laid and you've been doing the dirty with Microwaved Sea Bass." They called him that because of an ill-fated incident with fish in the microwave.

"Shhh! Don't call him that anymore." Olivia looked past the camera at something. Or someone.

"Wait, is he there right now? Was he *in the room* this whole time?" Luckily she could see earbuds in her friend's ears, so hopefully he hadn't heard their entire conversation.

"No. But yeah, he's not so bad."

"Hey," Thea put on as stern of a look as she could, "I don't want you to put your health at risk for 'not so bad.' You know I'm not judging you. Okay, maybe a little about Sea Bass—"

"Shhh!"

"Sorry. Sebastian. You two are both consenting adults and in a bit of a *situation*, I get it. But I'm not that desperate!"

Olivia snickered, "Alright, only because you're my friend that I'm not offended you said that. But because you said that, let's do one last lap."

By the time Thea hung up on her friend, she was thoroughly drenched. Her legs were the forgotten spaghetti strands stuck to the bottom of the pasta pot. She could always count on Olivia to pull her kicking and screaming past the finish line. It was one reason they had these weekly calls. There was no way Thea would get any exercise otherwise. That and catching up with one of her favorite people in the universe.

Even though she texted Olivia daily, and they called each other like this at least once a week, it still felt like something was missing. How had Olivia left out the fact that she and Sea Bass were sleeping with each other? Thea made a mental note to ask more about what was going on in Olivia's life the next time they talked.

SEVEN

THEA'S WRITING WAS captivating. When Gabe searched for her name, he found her site with links to all the recent pieces she'd published, as well as some award-winning articles from the past.

He read through the first page of them. She had a talent for words. In every piece he'd read, she made the people who prepared the food come alive. He felt like he was in the restaurant kitchen with her as she described the people chopping vegetables, stirring enormous pots of broth, and roasting meat.

As he clicked through links, he noticed something. Or rather, he noticed a lack of something. On one site, where the other journalists had a professional-looking picture next to their names, Thea's was missing. He looked at another site and there was only a generic placeholder where her picture would have been. He clicked over to an image-search of her name and found pages and pages of photography from her. Gabe couldn't help but feel attracted to someone so talented.

There were no pictures anywhere of her, probably because of the anonymity she needed to maintain to do her job. It would be difficult for her to ask questions if everyone knew who she was.

Most of her pieces focused on small, immigrant-owned restaurants that were barely hanging on in an industry where profit margins were slim. He knew it was tough to turn a profit because he used to help in his uncle's huaraches restaurant during the summer. Signing up for a delivery service would've cut into their minuscule profits. The setup required technical expertise that most restaurant owners didn't have. If he could help Thea help these people, of course, he couldn't say no.

After an hour of scrolling, he closed his browser and checked his email. He almost deleted a new one he thought was spam. The subject line kept him from tapping the red button: Can you build me a library?

In the beginning of his furlough, he'd panicked about money and started looking for odd jobs he could do. His studio was only promising two weeks of pay at forty hours a week. When he worked on a show, he averaged eighty hours a week, a lot in overtime pay. Not working anymore was a blow to his bank account. His mortgage had been doable when Adrian was paying him rent, but now that he'd moved out, things were more shaky.

With all his newly freed days, he'd finally finished a Little Free Library he'd been promising to build for Katie, a friend from a show he used to work on. She'd sent him pictures of her bungalow-style house, asking if he could make a miniature version of it. It took a few hours of drawing up the plans, but after he'd cut all the wood he needed, the rest was easy. The result was a clean, minimalist miniature of her house that she could fill with free books for her neighborhood.

She must have given his email to this person because they were commissioning him to build something similar. They even included pictures of their house from different angles.

He fired off some questions in reply to the email, suggesting different wood, sizing, and giving an estimated price. Lumber prices were rising these days, and he didn't want the material cost to shock them.

This wasn't exactly like what he did at work, but Gabe enjoyed it all the same. This new library was distinct enough from the one he built Katie that he needed to draw separate plans. Sure, he could build it around a basic box with a facade that matched the house, but he liked the challenge of building something sturdy enough to hold a dozen books with a bare minimum of screws and fasteners. The structural integrity relied on perfectly cut and fitted joins. There was something magical about a finished work where not a nail could be seen, as if the wood naturally grew into that shape.

He welcomed the new project. It kept his mind off of waiting for Thea's text.

EIGHT

"WHAT DO YOU have?" Ray never minced words when he picked up the phone.

"I sent over the list of restaurants for next month," Thea said.

"Right, let me open this."

Over the phone, Thea could hear Ray's ancient mouse going over an equally ancient mouse pad. How that poor device was still working was a wonder to her.

"Those restaurants I mentioned are on there. Good, good."

"About that..." Thea gave Ray a rundown of what she'd proposed to Gabe. She wasn't sure if the paper had a budget for it, or if it would come out of hers.

Ray's heavy breathing on the other line could either mean he was thinking about it, or he was thinking of a way to talk her out of it. The longer the silence went on, the more nervous she felt.

"We don't have a separate item for it in the expense form, but if you note it on your expenses when you submit, it might work. With a cap." Ray told her the maximum the paper could pay for delivery. It was less than what she'd expected, but if she used her own money to make up the difference, she would be okay with it. She'd need to juggle her personal budget to figure out where this extra money would come from.

"Okay."

"Good girl. I'm glad you put your noggin' to it," Ray said.

"I gotta go finish up this week's review. Bye." Thea swallowed a gag and hung up before she said anything career limiting. She took a deep, cleansing breath. One day, working for a patronizing boss like him would pay off. At least that's what she kept telling herself.

🍃 🍃 🍃

Thea ran her teeth along the wood of her pencil. She looked over the numbers she'd jotted on her notebook for the third time. She'd already checked it with a calculator twice. Paying Gabe partially out of her own money would not be easy, but she wanted to compensate him fairly.

Talking about money was always a touchy subject for her, even though her parents had no qualms about doing it. Every time she called home, she had to answer some version of "are you out of money," or her favorite, "are they really paying you to do this?" For her parents, one engineer and one doctor, having a daughter who didn't go into STEM was a point of strife. Her brother the doctor was already the over-achiever of the family. It wasn't until she published her first book and showed her dad a physical copy with her name on the cover that he stopped asking her if writing was really what she wanted to do.

She scrolled through her contact list and found Gabe's number. She could go over the math repeatedly, but the numbers didn't matter until she floated them by him to see if they were acceptable.

She texted: *Hey, it's Thea. You know, the food girl. Lemme know when's a good time to talk?*

Before she could obsess about the wording of the message, she pressed *send*.

Three dots appeared on the screen, showing that he was typing.

They disappeared.

Then appeared again: *Now's good.*

Thea dropped her phone in surprise when it started buzzing. She'd been in the middle of crafting a long text to Gabe.

She scrambled under the table to fetch it and accepted the incoming call. "Hello?"

"Hello, food girl," Gabe said on the other end. She didn't remember his voice sounding like this — deep and full of promising secrets. He sounded like he was right next to her.

She straightened up but bonked her head on the table. "Ow, hello, sorry. You still there?"

A chuckle on the other line. "You okay?"

"Yeah, just bumped my head."

"Ouch."

"So I did some numbers based on how many times I'd like you to do a pickup in a week and how much I typically pay in delivery fees. Then I factored in gas and your time." She gave him the number for the weekly rate. "What do you think? Is it too low? Please let me know if it's too low and we can adjust it?"

Without missing a beat, Gabe said, "It's fine. I may need to charge extra for gas if you make me drive somewhere super far, like Santa Barbara."

"Really," she squeaked, not expecting it to be so easy. "Yeah, of course I'll pay you extra if it's far. Are you sure this is okay? I feel kinda guilty that I'm putting someone at risk like this."

There was a slight pause on the other line.

"I'm sure. It'll get me out of the house and I like that we're sticking it to those apps you don't like, right?" Gabe asked.

She felt a little self righteous when she explained her reasons to him, but she was flattered that he remembered.

"When should I start?"

"Let's see... it's Wednesday now. Does next week on Monday work? I don't know what your schedule is like. I can start transferring you the money on Monday. What app do you want to use for it? Or I can give you cash?" She rattled off a list of payment apps she had.

"Monday should be good. I can rearrange my schedule to work with the pickups. You'll have exclusive access to me. Maybe I'll brand it Guber Eats."

Thea laughed. "I think you need to work with your marketing department on that name."

"GabeMates?"

"Better."

"Text me the details?"

"Yep, I'll text you Sunday night, so you have enough time to plan."

They hung up.

With her notebook on one side of her and a book on the other, Thea settled onto the well-worn dip on her couch. She toed off her house slippers and curled her legs under her, preparing for a few hours of reading.

Thea turned to her notebook, balanced on a pillow. She ran a finger down the soft, buttery page so that it lay flat. The pile of books beside her on the floor reminded her of the work she still needed to do. She had to catch up on reading before she could make any more progress on the outline of her manuscript. Now that she was dipping into her savings, she definitely needed to get this book out.

NINE

THE FIRST WEEK of deliveries went smoothly. Every other day, Thea texted Gabe the location and approximate time for the pickup. So far, they'd been early dinner pickups. Because most businesses either closed temporarily or allowed people to work from home, rush hour traffic wasn't an issue. Gabe clocked a personal best driving from Culver City to Los Feliz in less than fifteen minutes.

Gabe drove deep into neighborhoods he never would have discovered on his own, picking up food from places that he'd never heard of. Once, the pickup spot was a guy's trunk in the back of a Chinese supermarket parking lot. He didn't know how Thea found these spots, but the bags of food he transported made his truck smell delicious. It tempted him to order the same food for himself.

The amount of food he picked up often surprised him. It was enough food for a family, but he assumed she lived alone because she always opened the door, not someone else. He couldn't help being turned on by a woman who knew what she liked and enjoyed food as much as she did.

His distaste for restaurants didn't affect the work, much to his surprise.

As a kid, they never ate out anywhere fancy, so he never felt comfortable in "nice" restaurants. What made his unease even worse were all the fights he and Christina had at restaurants. He would always try to calm her down or leave, but she had no compunction about hashing it out in public. After breaking up with her, even stepping into a restaurant made his whole body tense, as if everyone was staring at him.

Seeing Thea every time he dropped food off was a nice perk of his new job. She usually came out to greet him over bags of food on the welcome mat. They'd started chatting for a few minutes on the porch, but by the end of the first week, a few minutes turned into twenty, then thirty minutes. He never wanted to leave that lush haven of her porch with its heavenly scents and her mysterious eyes.

By the second week, he'd fallen into the rhythm of reading the text from Thea in the evening, and planning how long it would take to deliver food from the restaurant to her place. Mornings, he walked Tails around the neighborhood or to a nearby park that was empty. After, he'd make himself breakfast, check email for any new commissions, and spend the rest of the day working in his garage.

Between what Thea paid him and his woodworking, he was pleased to find he wasn't eating into as much of his savings as he originally thought. It was a relief to see from his rough calculations that if the commissions were steady, he could at least pay his bills.

Tonight, he found Thea already sitting on the porch swing when he walked up the path with her bags of food. There was a circular tray balanced on her crossed legs. On the tray were golden yellow shapes.

"Oh hey," Thea said, waving at him with juice running down her hand. When he got closer, he realized she was holding a piece of mango.

"Do you want me to leave it here?" Gabe asked, pointing to the bottom step of her porch. He didn't know how close she wanted him to get to her since she didn't have her mask on.

Thea nodded and took a bite of the mango. He tried not to stare as the nectar dribbled down from her mouth before she hastily wiped it with a finger. Her tongue darted to the corner of her lips.

"Thanks. Sorry, I didn't think you'd get here so fast. Traffic was good?"

"Roads were deserted." Gabe forced his eyes from the tantalizing sight of her lips to her eyes. Was she torturing him?

"I packed you some mangos to take home. I just got a delivery of ripe ones from a mango farm in the desert. There's no way I'm gonna finish them all before they go bad."

"Mangos?" He said dumbly. It was extremely difficult to carry on a conversation when the juice of the mango was still trickling down her arm.

"Yeah, in that bag there," Thea said, oblivious to what he was thinking. She pointed to a paper bag he hadn't noticed by the planter at the foot of the steps.

"Oh, sure. Thanks. I love mangos," he said, finally dragging his eyes away from her. He took a deep breath and attempted to reign in his untamed thoughts. He picked up the heavy bag. The fruit's tropical aroma drifted up to him from the opening of the bag.

"These are so custardy and sweet," Thea gushed. "I'm excited to hear what you think."

He made some sort of goodbye, opting for a hasty retreat into his truck before he said what he was actually thinking.

TEN

GABE LIKED TO spend Sunday afternoons with his family whenever he wasn't working. He'd go over to his parents' house, where his sister lived with her kid, and they'd grill, or his mom would have a pot of albondigas on the stove. The pandemic had thrown a wrench into that tradition.

He hadn't seen his family since the beginning of March, but his sister convinced him to visit for his niece's fifth birthday party. It was going to be just them, outdoors, safe. When he parked on the curb and walked through the driveway to their backyard, he was impressed with what she'd set up.

There were two outdoor canopies ten feet from each other. Someone had spray-painted a large orange border on the grass below the canopies. Each canopy had its own rectangular foldout table and some chairs.

"*Tio!*" a tiny voice squealed as soon as he got there.

"Hey, birthday girl," Gabe said, holding his hands up to halt the motion of the little girl running for him, "Hold up there. Where's your mama?"

"Right here," his sister called out as she pushed the backdoor open with her foot. She was holding two large bowls of soup. She set them down on one table before telling the girl, "Don't get too close. Remember what I said?"

"I forgot. I got excited," the little girl pouted.

"How about we do an air dap?" Gabe offered, holding his fist up.

The girl looked at it skeptically. "Nope. Look at the new mask mama made me."

The mask in question had a tie-dyed background and colorful Mickey Mouse heads all over it in an artsy pattern.

"Wow, pretty sweet. Your mama's a talented lady." Gabe looked up at his sister, who set down the bowls at the other table. She had on a matching adult-sized mask. "How's the mask making going, Jess?"

Jess shook her head and rolled her eyes. "It's crazy. The more I make, the faster I sell out. I can't even get the fabric fast enough. I'm gonna have to start ordering in bolts."

"Gabriel! How come you'd didn't tell me you were here?" A voice called out from the house. His mom opened the backdoor and stuck her head out. "How many meatballs do you want? I made them the way you like them."

"Mama, mask!" Jess reminded her.

"Okay, okay, when I come out. How many meatballs, *mijo*?" Gabe's mom asked again.

"Just three, mama." He actually wanted four, but right on cue his mom said, "Only three? I'll give you four."

"Thanks."

"Go sit your ass down over there," Jess pointed to the one table under the other tarp.

"Jessica, language!" Their mom hissed before she disappeared into the kitchen.

"I know, geez." Even though he was older than his sister by two years, she still liked to boss him around. When they were kids, she claimed it was because girls matured faster than boys, but the pattern remained even though they were both adults now.

Loud voices from the house instantly washed him in nostalgia. Growing up in this house, there never seemed to be any quiet. Either he and

Jess were fighting about something, or his dad was yelling at him, or his sister, or all three of them were yelling at each other. It was annoying when he wanted a few minutes of silence, but now he sort of missed it.

His mom came out with a large bowl in one hand and a smaller plate in the other. Gabe stepped away from the table to give her enough room to approach with the food. Even through the mask, his mouth watered from the scent of the broth.

His mom put down the bowl and turned to him, looking at him from head to toe. "*Mijo*, you lost weight. You need to eat more. I put some in a container for you to take home. You want a beer?"

Gabe laughed. "You always say that. I weigh exactly the same."

"You're not eating enough," his mom said and shook her head. "*Papi*, bring out the beer!"

His dad came out with a beer but instead of handing it to him, glared at him and put a sweating bottle of beer on the floor by the last step to the kitchen. He then took a seat by the table under the other canopy, sitting with his back facing Gabe. Gabe got out of his seat and fetched it himself. It would have been awkward if everyone hadn't been used to it by now.

Once everyone was settled, Gabe under one canopy, his family under the other, there was a lull in conversation as everyone dug into the soup. Gabe was grateful that his mom made his favorite soup. She even remembered how much cilantro he liked in it. She'd included a small dish full of chopped cilantro and a few wedges of lime. He dumped most of the cilantro on top of the steaming soup and squeezed in some lime. He stuck his face over the bowl, closed his eyes, and inhaled.

The first spoonful of the broth filled his soul. The savory chicken broth was perfectly light thanks to the tomatoes. Secret herbs and spices gave it a depth that no restaurant could ever replicate. He used his spoon to cut a piece of the large meatball. As he chewed it, he couldn't help the sigh that came out. The meat was tender, rich, and brought back happy memories. He suddenly wished Thea could experience this phenomenal soup, too.

When he opened his eyes, his sister was staring. She laughed. "You look like you've found Jesus."

"I missed this," Gabe said, swallowing another spoonful of hot broth.

Nothing hit the spot like his mom's cooking.

Before he was even halfway done with his bowl, his dad stood up with a stretch. He picked up his empty bowl and utensils and walked into the kitchen without a word.

"Why's *abuelo* so mad at you?" Mila asked Gabe.

The rest of the family was so used to the heavy silence between both men by now that the question took Gabe by surprise. Before he could say anything, his sister piped in, "Grownup stuff, Mila. Don't worry about it."

The girl sulked for half a second, then happily went back to slurping up her soup.

Hours later, after two servings of birthday cake, Gabe hosed off the sticky tables while Jess helped put the folding chairs back into the garage. As he rolled the hose back up, his sister leaned against the cinderblock wall of the driveway and gave him a look.

"What?" Gabe asked, even though he knew what was coming.

Jess rolled her eyes and looked toward the house. The kitchen light was still on. Then she looked back at Gabe pointedly. "How long you gonna keep this up?"

"Ask pops."

"You know he's not gonna say anything, dumbass!" Jess said in a loud whisper. "Just talk to him."

"I have nothing to say to him." Gabe folded his arms in front of his chest and looked down at his little sister from the extra foot of height he had on her.

It didn't intimidate her in the least. She mirrored his pose, crossing her own arms, glaring up at him. "I think he's trying to change. I got him to listen to this podcast about Chicano masculinity."

Gabe gave a humorless laugh. "It's gonna take more than one podcast episode to fix this."

"So *talk* to him."

"Why me? If he wants to talk, he can come to me."

"I swear, you two are the most stubborn, stupid, full of *machismo* men —"

"Not even!" That hit a nerve. He was nothing like his authoritarian dad, who overflowed with outdated masculine pride. Not being macho enough was one of the many ways Gabe disappointed his dad.

"No? Then why don't you two talk?"

Gabe cut Jess off. "I'm gonna go."

"Sure, run away. This conflict avoidance is definitely working out for you." Jess pushed herself up from where she was leaning and shook her head.

"Exactly. Works fine for me," he muttered, ignoring his sister's sarcasm.

He'd forgotten how tiresome it was to maintain this Cold War with his dad. When he'd gotten his first job at the studio, he excitedly took his whole family out for a celebratory dinner, thinking they'd be impressed with him working in 'The Industry.' Instead, his dad flipped out at the restaurant as soon as he saw the embossed menu prices.

It was a tense dinner full of snipes about Gabe wasting his money on dinner, which evolved into a heated discussion about him blowing money on college. His dad thought he was an idiot not to take a cushy office job. For Gabe, all it took was one internship the summer after junior year to learn that he'd rather work with his hands instead of typing a bunch of numbers into spreadsheets at a desk job.

It was hard to explain to all this to his dad, who worked incredibly hard to give his kids a better life. Gabe actually enjoyed working with his hands. They'd been fighting about it ever since. The silent treatment was the newest stage of this same old fight. He preferred this stage, since he could ignore his dad instead of rehashing the same arguments over and over.

"I'm not running away. I'm just done talking about this," Gabe said with what he hoped was enough finality that Jess would drop it.

Jess sighed and took the hint. "What are you doing these days? I thought you said they furloughed you."

"They did."

"You need money?"

"No."

"You sure?"

"Yes! Geez, I have some money saved up, okay? I'm making some money on the side, too." He would have preferred having more money saved up, but it wasn't something he wanted his little sister to worry about. Eventually, he'd need to rent out his extra bedroom now that Adrian had moved out for good, but he wasn't that keen on inviting any strangers to live in his house in the pandemic. He also didn't want to mention the work he was doing for Thea for the last month and a half. His nosy sister would surely have endless questions about it.

Jess's voice brought him out of his thoughts of Thea. "Doing what?"

"Custom woodwork," Gabe said, not sure how to describe the Little Free Libraries he'd been making.

"Lemme see," Jess took out her phone, "Text me a picture."

Gabe scrolled through his phone to find a picture of his latest finished project and sent it to her.

"Holy shit," Jess said, then glanced at the kitchen. Even though they were both adults, they both still flinched when they cursed around the house. Gabe half expected a slipper to come flying out of the window and conk her on the head.

"You built this?"

"Yeah."

"Damn, that's a bougie Little Free Library."

"You know what those are?" He asked in surprise.

His sister sighed in exasperation. "I read books too, dumbass. There's one a few streets down, even."

"Really?" He hadn't noticed before, but then it had been years since he'd walked around his childhood home.

"Yeah, those new Chipsters who moved in put it up. I take Mila there sometimes to trade kids' books."

"Here's another one," Gabe texted her the picture of the first library he built.

"So you custom make each one?"

"Yeah. Takes a while, but it's fun and people actually pay a lot of money for it."

"You include the time you take to make it? And materials? When you charge the final price?"

Gabe made a face. "I know how to do math."

Jess blew out some air. "Damn, bro. These are fantastic. You should set up an Instagram for this. I bet a lotta people want one."

"I dunno 'bout that," Gabe started. "I don't really do that Instagram shit."

"You could put other things on there! Like that changing table you built for Mila when she was a baby. People'll pay for handmade things."

Gabe was skeptical. He didn't want to spend all his time on Instagram, which was what he saw a lot of his coworkers doing on their downtime. It seemed like a lot of busy work when he could be actually building stuff.

"Your work is really good! And you like making it, right?" She knew the answer to that. When he was twelve, he'd built a pretty passable treehouse out of old lumber they'd salvaged from a torn-down house across the street. Sure, the treehouse was only about three feet from the ground, but at least it didn't hurt to fall out of. Much.

He took a sip of his beer and put it down after realizing it had gotten warm and flat. He shrugged. "It's just a hobby."

Jess ignored him and busily tapped on her phone. He left it at that and scrolled through his text messages. He worried that he'd missed one from Thea.

A few minutes later, Jess gave a definitive tap on her phone. "Done!"

Gabe's phone vibrated, and he saw a text from her. He tapped on the link, which opened Instagram on his phone. He'd forgotten that it was even installed. The app opened to pictures of the Little Free Libraries he'd just sent to Jessica, as well as a few of his older projects.

"What did you do?" He hissed at his sister.

"I just made you an account for your projects."

"I told you I didn't want to deal with one! Take it down."

"Calm down." Jessica waved her hand in a dismissive gesture. "You don't have to deal with it. I will. Just send me pictures from now on and I'll manage the account for you."

"What do you mean, manage the account?"

"Send me any pictures you have, even work in progress ones. I'll make 'em nice and post to the account. I'll even write the descriptions and everything. It'll get your name out there."

"Why?"

Jessica made a face as if it was the most obvious answer in the world.

"You like building these, right?"

"Right."

"And you like making money, right?"

"I enjoy being able to pay my bills," Gabe said.

"So why not make a little money on the side with something you like doing? There's a market for these, and probably a market for handmade furniture right now, and you have the talent for it."

She had a point there. He was slowly seeing the benefit of having one place people could visit to see what he'd built. "Okay, we can try it."

"Good!"

"What are you getting out of it?"

"I can't just do this to help my big brother?" Jess asked, tilting her head at him.

"I appreciate you helping, but I know you're busy with work, the mask making, and with Mila."

Jessica laughed, "Dude, just chill! It honestly doesn't take that long to post a few pics. I'll let you know if it gets to be too much, okay?"

"You sure?"

"Sure. Just remember us little people when you get big and famous and have your own HGTV show. Maybe introduce me to your sexy co-host."

Gabe laughed. "Fine, fine. But in the meantime, thanks, Jess. I mean it."

"Okay, don't get weird on me. You're still a dumbass." His sister awkwardly brushed off his sincere thanks.

ELEVEN

THEA STRADDLED HIM as their naked bodies pressed together. She pursed her lips and her mouth was a hair's breadth away from his. Something heavy and fluttering took hold of him. He pressed his lips against hers, so plush and silky. Her skin felt so soft, especially when he dragged his mouth along the side of her neck.

Gabe loved the moan that came out of her as he ran a hand down her shoulder, against the curve of her breasts. She writhed on top of him, whimpering when his thumb circled a peaked nipple. Her response to his touch drove him insane.

He needed to hear more. He needed his name on her lips when she lost control. Gabe reached between them, one hand on her hip, but she stilled. Before he could say anything, she pulled away.

She crept down his body, nipping his shoulder playfully. She pushed him back onto the bed. He tensed as her hair brushed a ticklish spot near his side. Her scorching hands splayed against his stomach. When she licked her lips, he thought back to the way she ate that mango and almost lost it. His entire body pulsed in anticipation.

She must have known what he was thinking, because her gaze leisurely moved up until she looked straight into his eyes. She bent over him. Perfect lips paused above his cock. Those dark eyes sparkled as a wicked smile spread across her face and she took him in her mouth.

"Fuck!" Gabe pumped into his fist, his head against his forearm braced on the wall of the shower. Cold water ran off his body but did nothing to cool the heat coursing under his skin. He washed the come off his hands and tried to slow his rapid breaths. He'd woken up hard and knew that he needed to get this out of his system. Now that he was done, maybe he could stop thinking about Thea in that way.

He toweled off and pulled his phone off the dresser. There was a message waiting for him.

Thea: *Change of plans. Meet me in Glendale for trunk lunch?*

He texted a quick affirmative after she sent him a time and address. He had no idea what 'trunk lunch' was, but it piqued his interest. *What was she up to?*

🍃 🍃 🍃

"Order for Macy? Macy? Your order is ready!" A voice called out through the loudspeaker.

Gabe straightened up from leaning on the hood of his truck and headed to pickup their order from the makeshift window in the front door.

They'd both parked in the quiet alley near the restaurant. Thea perched on her back bumper with her trunk open. She wore a pair of jeans and a breezy black shirt. She often wore black because it was the best color for hiding food stains.

Gabe returned with a stuffed paper bag. He pulled two foil packages and handed her one. Her fingers grazed his as she took it from him. The contact made hairs on her arms stand straight up. She hastily retreated with her food, leaning against her trunk as she fiddled with the package. She sank down onto the bumper, then thought better of it and scooted all the way into her trunk, pulling her legs in to sit crossed-legged.

"Is that why you call it trunk lunch?" He laughed.

She nodded. "It's surprisingly comfortable. When it's not a million degrees out, at least."

Gabe took off his mask and placed it on the hood of his car. Joking with Olivia aside, she was dying to see what was under his mask. When he finally looked up, she was relieved he wasn't a butter-face. Quite the opposite.

Gabe looked freshly shaved, but she could already see a hint of a five o'clock shadow coming in along his jaw. She wanted to run her hands over his skin. She wondered if his cheeks would smell like aftershave. His bottom lip was slightly fuller than his top and had a tiny indentation right in the middle, giving him a pouty look. On any other man, it would have looked childish, but on his otherwise masculine face, it gave him a boyish charm. She couldn't tear her eyes away from that little dip on his lip.

He said something, but she hadn't heard over the whooshing of her racing pulse. She could practically feel the endorphins flooding her body right then. She wanted him.

"Sorry, what was that?" she asked, trying to cover her embarrassment by taking a bite out of her wrap.

"This looks like a burrito." His lips curved into a smile and two dimples bracketed his lips, but that mouth was not meant to be a parenthetical. That mouth should be the subject of many, many sentences. This man had no business looking this damn good.

Thea forced her attention back to the food in her hands. It did look like an open-ended burrito. Instead of a flour tortilla, the outside was a thin piece of flatbread filled with tons of chopped herbs and sprinkled with spices.

"It does, doesn't it? Too bad we can't see them make it inside. It's cool how they stuff the dough and cook the whole thing." Thea took another bite, chewing thoughtfully, grateful for the distraction of food. After she swallowed her mouthful, she sighed. "I can't decide if it's the bread that's good, or the filling, or a combination. Once, I tried to ask them what exactly was in the filling, but they said it's a secret."

Mouth full of the food, Gabe could only nod. He brought the wrap closer to his face, but instead of taking another bite, he turned it one way, then the other, trying to get a better look at the filling from different angles.

Her eyes traveled down his body. He was leaning on the truck in that effortless way men seemed to lean on things. Whenever she tried to lean like that, she always caught a corner or a sharp edge and it was never as relaxing as she wanted it to be.

The shirt he wore was tight enough to give her more than a hint of his body underneath. The cotton fabric draped over the planes of his torso, past his flat stomach, tightened around the curve of his biceps. There was a thin, dark scar along the top of one forearm and she wondered what that was from. What would it feel like to run her hand along that scar? She shivered at the imagined sensation.

"Cold?"

She took a deep breath, willing her hot cheeks to cool down. "No, just a little breeze."

As if the mere mention conjured it, a gust appeared. It picked up the napkin laying on Gabe's hood and blew it to the ground. He stepped on it before it could tumble away. When he bent over to retrieve the fallen napkin, his shirt rode up his back, revealing an expanse of smooth skin. Thea could see the black band of his boxer briefs peeking out from the top of his pants.

Gabe straightened and tucked the napkin into his pocket. "Do I have food on my face or something?" The way he lifted his eyebrow told her he knew exactly why she was staring.

Thea shook her head wordlessly, not trusting the sound of her voice, and took another bite. After she swallowed, she asked, "What's the deal with you and restaurants, anyway?"

Gabe was too busy enjoying the looks Thea shot his way when she thought he wasn't paying attention. Her question took him by surprise, and a feeling of unease spread throughout his body. He tried to think of a way to deflect the question, but Jess's voice saying, "Captain Conflict Avoidance runs away again," made him rethink.

When Thea looked at him like that, an open expression with curious eyes on him, he could see why she made such an excellent journalist. He felt compelled to talk to her, even though he couldn't find the words. "My family almost never went to restaurants when we were kids. Definitely not fancy ones. I didn't know it then, but money was tight," he started. "But both my parents are good cooks, so it never felt like we were missing out."

Thea nodded. Her understanding expression made him feel less self-conscious.

Gabe continued, "Now when I have to go, it feels weird, ya know?"

"How so?"

"Sitting down and being served by strangers is kinda weird, isn't it? I guess you're probably used to it since you write about restaurants." He shrugged.

"Hm, yeah, I guess if you really think about it, it is a strange concept."

He didn't want to mention the big fight he had with his dad the last time they'd dined out as a family. Or the time Christina called him a cold asshole with no real feelings. The hairs on the back of his neck stood up as he remembered the prickling sensation of all eyes in the dining room on their table.

"Anyway, it's not a big deal." He shook himself free of the unpleasant memory. He didn't want to think of all the reasons why he was a terrible boyfriend when he was with Thea.

"Are you angry that I dragged you here? I figured since we got stuff to-go—"

"No! I'm glad you invited me." Gabe said. "The food's great. I haven't had anything like this before."

"Incredible, right? Who knew that bread with herbs could be so delicious?" Thea's dark brown eyes were bright with excitement, but he couldn't stop his own eyes from snagging on her lips. The soft curves of her cupid's bow looked like the top of a heart, and he couldn't stop thinking about kissing her right there.

The way her lips pursed together while chewing was short circuiting his brain. He was having a hell of a time not thinking about his shower this morning.

"—and I'm pretty sure there's sorrel in there."

He missed most of what she'd been saying because he was concentrating so hard on keeping his body under control. Too embarrassed by his lack of focus, he only said, "Um-hmm."

Thea's long legs unfolded under her body as she climbed out of the trunk of her car. She dusted crumbs off her lap and licked the corner of her mouth. That brief flash of pink mesmerized him. A wave of wanting spread through his entire body. It had been a long time since he was with a woman.

Thea looked up at him and frowned. She dabbed her napkin to her mouth. "Do I have something in my teeth?" She asked.

Gabe shook his head. His throat was parched. He swallowed, but it hardly helped. He took a sip from his water bottle. That was better.

"That was amazing," he said after finishing the last of his wrap.

"Right?! Whatever magical spell they use on these herbs and spices is incredible."

Gabe loved how excited she was about the flavors. He was never one to watch those *mukbangs* of people recording themselves eat, but he could watch her eat just about anything. Gabe gathered their trash while Thea wiped down the hood of his truck with a paper towel she'd fished out of the back of her car. When he returned, he stood in front of her, thumbs hooked into the pocket of his pants.

"Thanks for inviting me," he said.

"No problem. I'm glad you came. It's nice to have company for lunch," she fiddled with the rubber band tying her hair back from her face. She faced him, but he got the impression that she was avoiding actually looking at him.

"Can I walk you to your door?" he asked, sweeping his arm toward the car door.

Her eyes crinkled. "Of course."

She slammed her trunk closed and walked to the door. She pulled it open and slid into the driver's seat.

Gabe shut the door for her and rested his palms on the top of her car, leaning down so they were face to face, separated by a pane of glass. In the shadow he cast over her, her eyes were black. He was under their spell. She'd pulled her mask down when she got into the car. His eyes drifted down to her mouth, lips parted. He couldn't remember the last time he wanted something so badly. His whole body felt the lure of hers.

"This was fun." He'd wanted to say more, but Thea jumped. Her phone buzzed next to her in the passenger seat. An incoming call. She glanced at it, then turned back to him. "Sorry, gotta go. Talk to you later?"

He stepped back from her car to give her room to pull out. He watched as she pulled into the street and heard the murmur of her voice as she picked up the call. She turned to look at him, surprised that he was still watching.

TWELVE

IN NORMAL TIMES, Thursday nights were notoriously bad for anyone trying to get from one side of LA to the other. But because of lockdowns and people working from home, the freeways were unusually empty, even during rush hour. That's what Gabe was expecting, which was why this inexplicable gridlock was so infuriating.

Gabe thumbed a quick text to Thea while keeping one eye on the road, letting her know he was going to be late. Normally, it took twenty minutes to drive from Little Ethiopia to Thea's neighborhood. He already regretted his decision to take the freeway back instead of the local streets, but it had sounded like a good idea at the time. Now, it would be impossible to make it to the exit lane because that was what most of the cars to the right of him were also trying to do. The aroma of warm spices filled his car and his stomach growled in response.

He craned his head, trying to see over the top of the car in front of him. There didn't seem to be any tow truck lights or sirens nearby, which meant whatever was causing the gridlock was probably further away. When he looked at the map on his phone, the thick red line snaking from his current location to his destination taunted him. This was going to take a while.

An hour later, Gabe pulled up to Thea's sage-green house, nerves tied together in a tense knot in his gut. He rarely minded driving. He could always put on music or zone out to the radio. But sitting for an hour in stop and go traffic when it should have only taken twenty minutes ruined his mood.

He lifted the food from the box he had fastened with a seatbelt in the passenger seat. The bags were no longer warm to the touch, which irked him. He bumped the door closed with his hip and heard a satisfying slam. He walked up the path to Thea's front door. She'd left the porch light on for him.

Before he could put the bags down to knock with his free hand, the door swung open. He stepped back in surprise, holding the bags of food up as a shield.

"Oops, didn't mean to scare you," Thea said, taking a step back. She wore a neon yellow, oversized tank top over a pair of black bicycle shorts. There was a sheen of sweat on her forehead.

"You didn't. Just caught me by surprise. Were you waiting long?"

Thea held up the water bottle she had in one hand. "I was walking by to grab this from the living room and heard your truck pull up."

"Sorry this took so long. Crappy traffic." He rolled his shoulders back a few times to ease the crick in his neck.

"Turn around," Thea said.

Gabe gave her a questioning look.

"I'll fix your neck for you," she said. Then added, "If you want. I'll have to touch you if you don't mind."

Oh. He did not mind. He turned, setting the bags by the floor next to them. The creak of the porch was loud as Thea stepped behind him. He held his breath, anticipating her touch.

Thea's hand felt like a branding iron on his shoulder. She gripped the tense muscle where his neck met his shoulder firmly with one hand and placed her other hand at the top of his head. He forced himself not to jump at the contact, or to imagine her fingers running through his hair. With a gentle touch, she guided his head so that it tipped in the other direction and gave his trapezius a couple of strong squeezes. She did the same on the opposite shoulder, pushing firmly, leaning his head the other way until he felt the pop and release of something in his neck.

She placed both palms on his shoulders, on opposite sides of his neck, and gave him another squeeze, strong fingers digging into the muscle there. Her touch was magic, and the cramp in his neck melted away. A warmth radiated from where her hands rested through to his toes.

His breath had slowed to match her deep breathing, loud through her mask. Was she as affected by the proximity as he was? He reached up, about to place his hands over hers, when she gave him a quick pat on the shoulder and stepped back.

"Better?" she asked.

He searched her face. It was hard to read now that she'd stepped back into the shadow cast by the porch's eave. He rolled his head around tentatively. "Thanks," he said, his voice low. "Much better."

"Sorry for making you sit through so much traffic," she said again.

"The food's cold by now."

Thea shrugged. "Luckily, it reheats pretty well." She looked pensive for a moment.

Gabe took this as his cue to leave and started down the porch steps. Before he got to the bottom step, she called out, "Gabe, wait."

He turned back to her.

"I feel terrible you have to hit the road again," she said, picking at an invisible spot on the door frame. "I always order a lot of food. Maybe too much."

Gabe chuckled. "I'm not judging you."

"Anyway, if it's not weird, do you want to join me for dinner?"

"Right now?" He was one part excited to be asked to stay for dinner, but one part wary about the offer. From everything she'd said since they'd met, she wasn't into him the way he was into her. But he also couldn't ignore the way she looked at him when she thought he wasn't looking, and he couldn't ignore the way his body sang when she touched him. Sure, it had been a while since he'd flirted, but he didn't think his game was that rusty.

"Yeah, outdoors should be safe because of the airflow or whatever, right? If you're okay with it, one of us can sit here," she pointed to one end of the porch, "and the other there. That's a safe distance to eat at, right?"

Gabe raised an eyebrow. He might as well ask for clarification. "Are you asking me out to dinner? Or as a friend?"

She shook her head immediately. "As a friend. Just you know — I ordered a lot of food. I feel bad about making you go back to your car after all that traffic empty handed."

"Technically, you're paying me to do this," he reminded her.

"You know what I mean!" she said, exasperated. "Okay, whatever. Forget I asked!"

He laughed, "I would love to join you for dinner on this not-date."

Thea took the bags into her kitchen and promised to be right out. She returned carrying a large square, which turned out to be a folded card table. She unfolded it and placed it right in the middle of the porch in front of the door. "I figured I could put the food here and we can take turns serving ourselves and then —"

"—back to our corners?" Gabe finished for her.

"Exactly." Her eyes met his, and he had to look away as his heart beat faster at the way her eyes crinkled with a smile.

Thea ducked back into the house and came out with two empty trays. She handed one to him and put the other on the porch swing. "Sorry, I have nothing good we can use as tables, but I figure we can balance our plates and stuff on the trays?"

"Sure, that works." Gabe took his tray and set it on the banister. He held up his hands to her. "Can I wash my hands? I can use a hose if you don't want me to go into the house."

"Oh!" Thea said, walking past him down the porch steps. She went to the side of the house and pointed at something he couldn't see. "There's a utility sink in the back you can use. There should be soap there."

Gabe followed her directions and indeed there was a farm-style sink installed by the back of the house. There was a table next to it topped with terracotta pots of various sizes and a few cuttings. It must be where she repotted her plants. He pumped a few squirts of soap into his palms and scrubbed his hands under the cold water.

When he made it back to the porch, Thea was gone, but he could hear a faint beeping and clanging from the house. She returned with her tray, now heaping with four plates of food. She placed the plates on the card table, then went back in to fetch more. Gabe knew the bags contained a lot of food, but hadn't realized just how much food was in her usual takeout order until he saw the bowls and plates arranged on the table. The poor card table was not made for such a heavy load and shook precariously when she placed the bowl down.

"Can I help with anything?" he asked.

She waved him off before returning to the house. She shouted from the kitchen, "I just have some utensils to bring out. I got it."

She returned with serving spoons and napkins balanced on top of empty plates. Her other hand held two empty glasses. A bottle was wedged under her arm. Gabe stepped forward to carefully take the glasses from her hands. His fingers brushed hers for the briefest moment. Her touch sent a jolt of current down to his toes. The way she snatched her hand back in surprise told him she'd felt it, too.

"Sorry." His voice sounded strange and rough. He moved to take the bottle from under her arm.

"It's okay," she said, avoiding his eyes. She let him take the bottle and placed the empty plates down on the table. "I think that's everything. Not sure what you wanted to drink, so I brought out this beer. Let's split it?"

"Thanks."

They stood on opposite sides of the table now, looking across the food at each other. Thea stepped back a few feet after placing spoons in each dish with food in it. She gestured to the array of food. "Please help yourself."

"I'm not sure how to eat any of this," Gabe admitted. Plate after plate of stews in many colors and textures stared back at him. In what looked like a bread basket were rolls of something gray and spongy looking. "Maybe you should go first?"

"Sure," Thea said as Gabe stepped back to give her space. She took an empty plate and put the gray sponge over it, unrolling and draping it across the entire plate. Then she ladled a bit of everything into separate piles on the sponge, which turned out to be a special type of bread. She explained as she went along, naming each dish. "It's Ethiopian, so the injera, the bread, goes on the bottom. Then you can take a spoonful of everything and see what you like. I usually use another piece for the dipping."

"Oh, kinda like naan for Indian food?"

"Exactly like that."

Gabe followed her lead and made a plate for himself. He popped the top of the beer off and poured it into both glasses. He balanced the tray on his lap after he sat down.

"Is that ok? Not too short?" Thea asked.

"It's fine."

"You're lucky you're so tall," she said. She brought her tray to the porch swing, sitting gingerly so that it wouldn't swing too hard. She raised her glass of beer to him.

He mirrored the gesture and almost put the cup to his mouth before realizing he still had his mask on. He laughed sheepishly and pulled it off, folding it neatly and tucking it into his back pocket.

Thea took a gulp of beer and sighed contentedly. When she back at Gabe, he paused with the glass barely touching his lips. Even though the sky had darkened to night, the porch light gave off a gentle glow that put her in soft focus. Her lips were a dark rosy color, full, and more striking than he remembered. He wanted to trace his fingertips around the perfect line of her lips.

Those lips formed a circle as she frowned at him. "What's wrong? You don't like the beer?" She asked.

Gabe brought the glass back down, then shook his head to clear his thoughts. He brought the glass to his mouth and took a sip. "Beer's fine."

"Oh, you looked weird for a second," she said, eyes flicking up to meet his through her thick lashes.

Gabe could still feel those eyes on him when he studied the food in his lap. He was glad of his coloring and hoped it was hiding the flush creeping up his cheeks. It was embarrassing to be blushing like an idiot, especially when she looked at him like that. The cold stinging bubbles of the beer helped ground his thoughts as he sipped.

Returning to the food at hand, Thea ripped a piece of spongy bread from her plate and used it to scoop something dark green before putting it into her mouth. She closed her eyes as she chewed and let out a soft moan, those sensual lips curving into a small smile.

Gabe had never heard anything more erotic. The look of complete satisfaction on her face made him jealous of the food. He followed her lead and tore off a piece of his bread and scooped it into something saucy. He placed it in his mouth and chewed, taken aback at the texture of the bread. At first, he wasn't sure if he liked the tartness, but the more he chewed, the more the flavors melded together.

"This is great!" he exclaimed, scooping up what looked like stewed cabbage and carrots.

"Isn't it? I miss having this at the restaurant, but we're lucky that it reheats well."

Next, Gabe scooped up something reddish brown with the injera and popped it into his mouth. His eyes immediately watered, and he clamped his lips together, trying to hold in a cough. That only made it worse as the heat on his tongue grew more painful. A fit of coughing erupted from him as he turned away.

"You okay?" Thea asked in alarm.

Gabe took a swig of beer, hoping the cool liquid could save his mouth. "Spicy," he croaked.

"Is it?" Thea swiped some from her plate and chewed thoughtfully. "Hm, it's a little spicy, I guess. Maybe you ate a pepper or something."

"Maybe," he said in a scratchy voice. He was going to avoid that pile on his plate for now. "I can't really eat spicy food."

"What?!"

"I know, I know, whoever heard of a Mexican who can't eat spicy, right?" It was embarrassing, but no matter how much he tried to up his spice tolerance, he still couldn't handle it. His entire family saw it as a personal shortcoming.

"Wait, what about Indian food? Didn't you say you liked eating the curry from—"

"I do. But they also give me three cups of mango lassi to survive it." Gabe could feel the tips of his ears turning red.

"Ah." Thea gave him a sympathetic look.

"Do you see me as less of a man?" He teased to cover up his embarrassment.

Her cheeks colored. Finally, she said with laughter in her voice, "No. You're plenty manly."

After they were done eating, Thea leaned back on the swing and patted her stomach. "Oof, I think I overdid it."

"I know the feeling," Gabe said, wiping his mouth on a napkin. He'd already cleared his second helping.

"My stomach tapped out a while ago, but my mouth kept on going."

"At least it looked like you got some exercise before this," he said, nodding at her outfit. "All I did was sit in a car."

"Hey, that was an important job. Without you, we wouldn't be here stuffed with delicious Ethiopian food." Thea closed her eyes. She stretched her arms up and behind her, her mouth settled in a satiated grin.

Gabe's pulse hammered. His eyes lingered on her long legs flexed under the table as she held her full body stretch. The arch of her back pushed her breasts up, their curves extremely visible through her sports bra. She relaxed and exhaled, her arms coming back down. Her eyes opened sleepily as she blinked at him through her lashes.

"What?" Thea asked, cocking her head in his direction.

He cleared his throat, not trusting his voice right that second. He took a sip of the now warm beer. "Nothing. You just look so happy."

A laugh bubbled from her mouth, seductively husky. The sound sent a shudder of pleasure through his body, and he was grateful for the tray, hiding how readily a certain part of his anatomy reacted to her.

Oblivious to his plight, she said, "There's something to be said about finding pleasure in the simple things in life."

"I know, right? Good food, or a nice hike, is enough to turn my mood around." He tried to focus on the most boring hike.

"Do you go on a lot of hikes?" Thea licked something orange off her finger as she asked, and he almost dropped his tray.

"When I have downtime between projects at work, I try to. Especially if we go on location somewhere else. I like scoping out the area for trails."

"That sounds fun. What are some of your favorites here? I only know of Eaton Canyon and Runyon, which everyone and their mom go to."

Gabe nodded. "Yeah, they're too crowded for me. There are a few lesser known ones up the two, or further east. I can send you pins to my favorite ones."

"Thanks. I'd like to do more hikes. Especially if they're not crowded. It should be easy enough to avoid people on the trail, right?"

"For sure."

Thea stood, carefully placing her tray next to her. She bent over to stack her cup and dish more securely onto the tray and he averted his eyes, trying to be a gentleman and not look at the way the top of her sports bra dipped down when she was in that position. She walked over to his side of the porch and held her hand out for the tray.

He held onto his tray with his life. "I got it," he said more gruffly than he intended. "I can bring it in for you."

She eyed him over her mask. "I can take it in."

"Your hands are full. Lemme just finish the last of my beer." He scrambled for any excuse to keep the tray in his lap.

She gave him a curious look, then shrugged and turned toward the door. "Just leave it on the table when you're done."

When her back was thankfully turned on him, he readjusted his shorts and hastily put the tray where she indicated. He turned to look at the night sky peeking through the canopy of the trees. *Think about basketball. Think about basketball.*

"I can grab these," she said when she returned, interrupting his thoughts. She took his tray back into the house.

Thankfully, his body was under control again.

"I hope I didn't keep you too late?" Thea said.

He turned to face her. The little card table couldn't have been more than three feet wide, but it felt like an ocean between them.

"I don't mind. The food was worth it. And the company."

Thea looked up at him with her dark eyes. He wanted to dive into their depths and never come out. Even with the pesky table between them, Gabe could tell she was at the perfect height for him to barely lean down to kiss. Both her hands pressed on the table, her head tipped toward him.

Her eyes promised irresistible temptations. "I enjoyed your company, too." She blinked and then stepped back from the table.

THIRTEEN

GABE DROVE HOME in a daze, buzzed, but not from the half bottle of beer. He remembered thanking Thea for dinner, wishing he had kissed her, saying goodnight, getting into his car, and the next thing he knew, he was in his driveway.

That alluring shine in her eyes when they stood over that damned table was all he could think about. He wasn't sure he could have resisted without that obstacle between them. Not when she looked at him like that.

Gabe was so distracted by thoughts of Thea that he hadn't noticed that his front door was unlocked. He let himself in and stopped at the threshold. A noise came from the utility room behind the kitchen. He grabbed the closest thing within reach, an umbrella hanging by the door, and held it in his hands like a baseball bat. *Where was Tails?*

He toed off his shoes quietly. Stepping softly to not make a sound, he crept toward the noise. It sounded like someone was opening and closing the cabinets back there. Were they looking for valuables? The only thing in those cabinets were half-empty cleaning supplies, and a broken waffle iron well past its warranty.

He shouted when he got to the kitchen, "Show yourself!"

A figure walked into the doorway just as Gabe was about to swing the umbrella.

"Whoa, whoa!" The man jumped back, bumped into a cabinet, then stumbled forwards. Both his hands raised in a protective gesture.

"Adrian?" Gabe recognized the voice. His roommate had on a royal blue mask and a matching blue baseball cap with a Dodger's logo on it.

"Yeah, of course. Who else?" Adrian eyed the umbrella still in his hand. "Where you flying to, Mary Poppins?"

Gabe leaned the umbrella against the counter. "You gave me a heart attack! Where's your car?"

"It's on the curb. You okay, man?" Adrian peered at him over the mask. "Didn't you see my text?"

Gabe pulled out his phone and noticed the missed texts. "Sorry, didn't check my phone."

"All good. I'm just packing up Tails's stuff. I'm gonna take her to my mom's."

"You sure? I don't mind watching her for you." Gabe enjoyed having the dog around.

"Thanks, man, but I think my mom misses having a dog at home." Adrian jerked a thumb in the kitchen's direction. "You know where her extra food went? I thought I put it in that cabinet above the washer."

Gabe helped his roommate locate all the dog supplies. "Your mom doing okay?" he asked, setting a duffle bag full of chew toys down in front of the door.

"She's okay. It's good I'm staying with her. Keeps her out of trouble. You know she'd be all out on the sidewalk gossiping with all those other old ladies without masks. You know how she is."

"Yeah."

"You? Where'd you just come from? You still helping Veer's fam? I heard he got Covid."

"Not exactly." Gabe filled Adrian in on his and Thea's arrangement.

Adrian gave him a look. "Is it worth it?"

Thinking back to their dinner, Gabe replied, "It's not really about the money, although it's nice that it at least covers gas."

"She hot?"

Gabe rolled his eyes. "Is that all you think about?"

"That's not all *you* think about?"

Gabe couldn't help laughing at that, but he wasn't about to admit how much he thought about Thea. He already knew he was going to have trouble going to sleep tonight without driving himself crazy, thinking about how Thea's bike shorts hugged the curve of her thighs.

"Man, you got it bad!" Adrian clapped a hand on his shoulder and gave him a hard shake. "I can see it in your face."

"Shut up. You can't even see my face."

Adrian turned serious. "You know what I mean. Watch out, okay? Shit's crazy out there."

"True."

"Just don't get into the same mess you did with Christina. I don't wanna bail you out again," Adrian warned. He probably meant it as a joke, but Gabe didn't take it as one.

His breakup with his ex was not even in the neighborhood of amicable. He still felt guilty that Adrian had to deal with the aftermath of it, since Gabe was coincidentally out of town right after. It probably wasn't the best way to end a relationship, but it was easier for him to walk away.

After that breakup, Gabe decided to take a break from girlfriends. Christina had been right on that at least: he couldn't emotionally provide whatever it was that women wanted out of him. He hated their strained phone calls whenever he was out of town. Even on shows that kept him in LA, the hours took over prime date-night hours. Those 14-hour days building new things and fixing old things were fun, but they were also exhausting. Some days, he only made it as far as the living room couch before falling asleep.

That must be why he was so fixated on Thea. He didn't have the crazy hours of his job to take up his time, so he had a lot more time to think about her — to text her clips he found online that he thought she'd laugh at; to read her weekly restaurant reviews; to listen to her voice on that radio show. She said straight to his face she wasn't interested in dating at all, so she was safe and he knew she wasn't gonna get all attached to him.

It was perfect.

"Whatever," he shrugged when he noticed Adrian still staring at him. "It's not like she's interested."

"Uh-huh."

"Anyway, she turned me down. Very clearly."

"Hah! So you *did* ask her out. I knew it!"

"I'm done talking about this with you. Don't you have somewhere to go? I think I hear Tails barking." Gabe made motions to shoo Adrian out of the house.

"Yeah, yeah." Adrian grabbed his box of stuff and headed for the door. He nodded to Gabe. "Take care, man."

"You too. Tell your mom I said hi."

"Will do."

Gabe locked the door after seeing Adrian's car pull away from the curb. He was now completely alone in his house. It was a novel feeling.

FOURTEEN

AFTER LOADING HER dishwasher, Thea flopped onto the couch. She felt exhausted, but happy. She'd written another feature for the paper this afternoon after a spectacularly cranky email from Ray about her output. Nothing like the shadow of looming unemployment to get the creative juices going. She even squeezed in a quick ride after a productive sprint of writing.

The good mood from the ride carried over when Gabe showed up, which was why she invited him to stay for dinner. They had a surprising number of things to talk about and her brain wasn't totally mush afterward. She found out Gabe also grew up in southern California. East LA to be exact, but not as east as where Thea grew up, the Inland Empire. They both were embarrassingly fond of the Fast and the Furious movie franchise, having both watched each one opening day in theaters. Gabe had one upped her and gone to visit all the filming locations in LA.

Gabe's laid back manner drowned out the noisy hum of anxieties about the pandemic that played in the space between her ears. His presence took her out of her head. During dinner, she almost forgot about the big red number she saw in her budget this morning. When she'd opened her spreadsheet to log her expenses, it stunned her to see how quickly her savings account had shrunk. She must have miscalculated something the last time she checked. At her current rate, she'd barely scrape by till the end of the year.

If she could bang out her manuscript faster, she could send the draft to her editor and get that ball rolling. Then her agent could at least negotiate an advance and she'd get a cash infusion into her bank account that would slow down the bleeding.

She *should* use the rest of the night to finish writing that new article about the popular Korean barbecue restaurant's pivot to making a daily dosirak — a Korean lunchbox. She'd promised Ray it would be ready by Monday. Thea opened her laptop, intending to write. Instead, she sat there with her hands resting on the keyboard, her mind still lingering on dinner.

She decided the problem was Gabe. He was too damn hot, *and* he was a decent dude who listened, a dangerous combination. Her stomach had felt all fluttery during dinner. It would be better if he had an obvious red flag, like he listened to the Joe Rogan podcast.

Tonight, she couldn't stop looking at his five o'clock shadow. The dark stubble gave him a mysterious look that made her want to get closer. She wanted to touch his face with her palm. Would it feel like sandpaper?

Thea slapped her cheeks to detour her mind from this dangerous train of thought. She needed to concentrate on ending this article, not on how it would feel to rub her cheek against Gabe's. She was certain what she felt around Gabe was only physical attraction. Because she couldn't actually act on it, she was obsessing over it like forbidden fruit. It *had* been a while since she'd slept with anyone. It was all just her libido demanding some attention. The way her heart raced was not entirely about Gabe at all— definitely not about the rumble in his voice or the way his laugh sent shivers down her spine, or the way his muscles moved under her palm when she helped him with the kink in his neck. And it was definitely not about his thick hair and how she wanted to dig her fingers into those soft waves while his head was between her legs. Not at all.

A chime from her laptop startled her from her steamy imagination.

"Baby!" her dad shouted from into the screen. "Can you hear me?"

A call from her parents was better than a bucket of icy water over her head. She was thankful her dad wasn't telepathic. Even though she missed the comforting cadence of her dad's Filipino accent, Thea thumbed the volume lower to save her eardrums. "I can hear you fine. You don't have to yell."

"Lemme get Mama," Thea's dad turned away from the screen and shouted for her mom.

Thea's mom came appeared in the frame, a smile on her face, "Thea! Did you eat? You look too skinny. Are you sick? Maybe not eating enough." The last sentence was an aside to her dad.

Thea rolled her eyes good-naturedly. "I'm fine."

Every call with her parents started the same way. When she was younger, it annoyed her that they never failed to comment on her appearance as soon as they saw her, but now she tempered the annoyance by reminding herself that these complaints were their love language.

"Honey, you need to cook better for yourself," her mom said. It was ironic because when she was a kid, her feminist mom told her that as long as she studied hard enough, she could get a lucrative job, and be rich enough that she could hire a private chef to cook all her meals. Thea wasn't holding out for that to happen, but she did get to expense most of her meals, so her mom was sort of right.

Thea was grateful both her parents were wizards in the kitchen, but whenever she tried to join them, they got annoyed by her lack of speed and shooed her out. Even when she tried to be unobtrusive and took notes at the kitchen table, they claimed she interrupted their flow and kicked her out. Getting them to write any type of family recipe usually ended with, "Just taste it! If it's not salty enough, add more salt. If not sweet enough, add more sugar."

By now, Thea had given up on cooking any of her family's specialties. It helped that because of her work, there were always plenty of leftovers in her fridge — enough that she couldn't remember the last time she cooked a meal. When she wasn't eating takeout or leftovers, she made do with simple dishes with her limited skills: yogurt, toast, and scrambled eggs. When she craved comfort food, she made porridge in her rice cooker and ate it with a rainbow of pickled and preserved vegetables always in her fridge.

"You want me to send you some serum?" Her mom asked, peering into the camera as if she could see Thea's pores through the grainy video. She was a dermatology professor before she met Thea's dad on a student exchange trip in the Philippines. They'd hit it off right away and her dad followed her mom back to Taiwan. He found a job at the same university she was teaching at. They had a whirlwind romance, got married, had Thea's brother, then five years later, Thea. She often wondered where her parents' life would have gone if they hadn't had to stop and raise the two of them.

"How are you guys?" Thea asked, cutting off any other awkward questions.

"Same thing. No change."

"Are things safe in Taipei? I read some news articles, but it's hard to tell." Thea switched to her rusty Mandarin that she only used with her parents and some unlucky restaurant waitstaff. She had a heavy American accent, but at least she could practice with her mom.

"Yes, yes, all very safe. Low numbers, but we never leave the house. Everything is delivered. All food, even meat. Wow, so expensive!" her dad replied. His Mandarin was decent despite having learned it later in life. He had a gift for languages which Thea unfortunately did not inherit.

"Okay, let me know if you guys want me to order anything from here to ship back over there. I don't know what's available there."

"No need," her dad dismissed. "We get everything already."

Her mom asked, "did you cancel your flight yet?"

"Oh shoot, not yet." It had slipped her mind amid the lockdown chaos. She usually flew back to Taiwan once a year for a month. It was partly vacation and partly work. Thea was collecting, bit by bit, enough knowledge about Taiwanese tea to write a beginner's guide to *gong fu* tea. This type of tea brewing was on the other end of the spectrum from the ubiquitous boba shops in LA. She wanted to write a newbie friendly book about the bounty of loose-leaf teas from Taiwan. She even talked Olivia into illustrating it for her. It was yet another one of her works in progress.

"Make sure you get a refund," her mom said. "If they don't give one to you, get a lot of credit back. With no expiration date!"

"I know. I know." She wasn't sure how easy it was going to be to get her tickets fully refunded.

"Maybe you don't need to cancel," her dad said in a thoughtful voice.

"Baba!" her mom said in a harsh tone. "Not safe to get on plane these days."

"Three months away. Maybe things will be better," her dad shrugged, ever the optimist.

Thea laughed in disbelief. "I don't know how much news about the US you get over there, but I don't think we'll be done with Covid in three months here. It's kind of chaos right now. You're lucky you're somewhere with a government that knows how to deal with it."

"Honey," her mom worried. "You want us to send you anything? Money?"

"No! Stop asking that." She hated that her parents thought she needed money. It made her feel like they didn't respect her work at all. Sure, her precarious juggling act with her finances stressed her out, but it wasn't something she wanted her parents to worry about. Especially since they'd only recently stopped asking if she could make enough to earn a living.

"I'll call the airline tomorrow morning," Thea changed the subject, jotting the reminder down in the notebook on her nightstand. The refund would come in handy. "At least to see what their cancellation policy is. Who knows, maybe they've already cancelled the flight. But then, I didn't get an email about it, so maybe not."

"Maybe international flights from US will be closed by then," her mom warned. "Better call soon."

"I will."

"Okay, bye then." Thea's dad was usually the one hanging up first. He hated long phone calls.

"Alright, stay safe, you two," Thea said.

"You too. Eat more, too skinny. Use sunscreen!" her mother squeezed in before the call ended.

FIFTEEN

THEA CAME OUT of the hot, stuffy closet in her bedroom. She used it as her recording studio for an hour each week to call into the radio show. The good thing about her closet was that it had excellent acoustics. The bad thing was that the excellent acoustics were from the clothes that also insulated the tiny space. It was fine when she first started doing it at the beginning of the pandemic, when March in LA was a beautiful 73°F. It was unbearable now that it was June and twenty degrees warmer. Her armpits were dripping with anxiety sweat. Despite being a regular guest and having notes prepped before each session, she still got the jitters as soon as she called in. It wasn't even a live taping.

The two hosts of Splendid Eats lived on opposite sides of the country, but their friendly banter made it sound like they recorded in the same studio. The woman who hosted had a gift for putting guests at ease with a word or two. She was the reason Thea agreed to the show. That and her small, professional crush on the man who hosted. Sometimes, Thea had to pinch herself when she realized she was getting paid actual money to talk about food with fellow food enthusiasts each week. It didn't pay all of her bills, but she'd come a long way from barely being able to cover the cost of her meal with what certain publications paid her.

She walked by her nightstand, where she'd tossed her silenced phone before entering the closet. When she tapped it, there were a quite a few emails from Ray about the draft she'd submitted in the morning. She wished he would condense his thoughts into one email instead of the usual flurry of one-sentence emails.

There was also a text from Gabe. She tried to ignore the little stutter her heart did when she saw it. She diligently sent her reply to Ray's email, less snarky than she wanted to be because she needed to stay on his good side, thumbs flying across the screen. When that was dealt with, she opened Gabe's text.

Gabe: *Wanna go for a hike today? Asking for a friend ;)*

Thea: *Sorry, just saw this. When?*

Gabe: *5:45pm?*

Thea: *That's oddly specific. Where?*

Gabe sent over a pin that opened up the Maps app on her phone. It was a twenty-minute drive from her. *Wasn't this a residential neighborhood?* She was expecting a trailhead in the foothills or something, not this.

Thea: *You sure this is the right place?*

Gabe: *Best kept secret. See you there @ 5:45?*

Thea: *For a friend-hike, right?*

Gabe: *Right*

Thea checked the time. If she could finish the edits Ray wanted, that still left her enough time to write a first draft of the short piece for the food magazine. She had her notes, not exactly an outline, but it would be enough to get started. Even though she'd been planning on writing all day and into the night, she could condense it by taking out the hours she built in for staring out the window, waiting for inspiration to strike. The reward of a hike with Gabe was inspirational enough to light a fire under her butt.

Thea sent the thumbs up emoji and put her phone down. She sniffed tentatively under her armpit. *Phew*, she definitely needed to jump in the shower, but that would have to wait until she was done with work. She didn't want to show up for the hike, already smelling like sweat.

🍃 🍃 🍃

Thea pulled out a year-old issue of the literary magazine she was aspirationally subscribed to as she sat on the empty bench to wait for Gabe. She wrote a couple times a year for the magazine. What they paid her barely covered the cost of subscription, so she felt guilty about throwing unread issues away. She brought this one along, thinking she could get to the trailhead early and spend the extra time reading without distractions like laundry or dishes.

The cool breeze flowed through her rolled down windows, blowing away the warmth radiating from the asphalt in the parking lot. She caught a quick movement out of the corner of her eye and turned to it. A lizard came out from a low shrub. It climbed onto a boulder next to her car and did some lizard-like push-ups as it decided whether she was a threat.

Her mind was only half paying attention to the words on the page in front of her. Away from home distractions and the impending deadline of her manuscript, her mind was free to linger on thoughts of Gabe.

She hadn't meant to agree to go on this hike. Before she could reason her way out of it, her fingers flew over her phone and she agreed. She *did* want to hike more, and this was an excuse to go out safely. Her thing with Gabe was still in limbo. If only she'd slept with him in the beginning, it would have been easier to think of him as just some guy to mess around with. Thanks to the pandemic, they'd somehow skipped that stage and now... were they friends? A hike was definitely something two platonic friends did.

As if thinking about him conjured his presence, she caught sight of Gabe making his way from the open chain-link gate to the parking lot she was in. She shut her magazine, placing it on the seat next to her.

"Were you waiting long?" Gabe stopped in front of her open window.

"No. I got here early so I could catch up on some reading."

"What're you reading?"

"This overly detailed article about how the Fed figures out when to increase interest rates," Thea laughed lightly. "I was mostly staring off into space because I don't understand any of it."

"This is a great place for reading. It's usually quiet here."

"I never knew there was a hiking trail here. I thought there were only houses here."

"The city set aside these hills for recreation. I think it used to be some sorta utility site for water or whatever before."

"How do you know all of this?"

Gabe shrugged. "I ran into a guy who used to work for the city here years ago."

"Do you live nearby? I saw you walk in through the gate," Thea asked.

"No, I'm in Burbank. I parked on the street because I didn't know if there was gonna be a spot in this lot."

Thea looked around. Other than hers, there were only a handful of cars. "Seems pretty empty."

"Yeah, it's hard to tell. Sometimes it's deserted, other times it's packed, especially around this time."

"What's so special about this time?"

"On a clear day, you get a great view of downtown LA on one side, and rolling hills on the other." Gabe pulled a baseball cap from his back pocket and put it on. "Did you bring a hat?"

Thea fished hers out of her backpack and straightened it out. It wasn't the most stylish, but the straw hat was floppy enough to stuff in a backpack without suffering and popped back into shape easily. She put it on, tucking some stray hairs back under the brim.

"Cute." The corners of his eyes crinkled.

"Thanks." It was a harmless compliment, but she couldn't help the warmth that spread in her chest.

They started on one of two dirt paths leading up a hill that Gabe claimed had the best view. Even though it was after five, the combination of temperature and sunlight made the trail sweltering. It wasn't as bad as when the asphalt radiated heat upwards, but she could still feel the warmth of the day's rays coming off the trail. Thea was glad she wore shorts.

Some parts of the trail were wide enough that they could easily walk side by side with enough distance between them. From the latest articles she read online, being outside and masked cut the chance of transmission down by a lot. Something about droplets being carried away by the wind. She was thankful for the slight breeze bringing much needed cooling to her heated skin.

Gabe walked ahead of her when the trail narrowed through overgrown bushes. She got a superb view of his backside as they trudged up the incline. The muscles on his calves flexed as he trekked up the path, and Thea enjoyed the view. The fabric of his shorts made a swishing sound with each step he took. She resisted the urge to reach out and poke his butt to see if it was as firm as it looked.

Gabe stopped halfway and turned his head to face her. She immediately glanced up, hoping she hadn't voiced her thoughts. He must not have noticed because he brought his index finger to his mask in a "shhh" sign. He'd stepped left off the path and walked quietly around a boulder to the right, pointing to the boulder as he walked past it.

Thea followed his lead and tiptoed around it, giving it a wide berth. When she made her way to the other side of the boulder, she saw what he was pointing at. In a hole in the dirt, close to the back side of the boulder, was a furry head poking out. She stopped to look at it and the head rose from the hole a few inches. It was some sort of gopher-like rodent.

When the animal realized the two humans were closer than expected, it darted back into the hole.

"Aw, so cute!" Thea exclaimed.

"I see their tunnels all over the place, but I've never actually seen one here before."

Thea moved in closer to look, but was so intent on peering into the shadow of the hole in the ground that she missed the one right in front of her. Her toe caught in the hole and her body pitched forward, her arms flailing uselessly in front of her to catch hold of something.

Two powerful hands clamped on to her shoulders and stopped her mid-fall. Gabe's hands felt solid on her shoulders, and she could feel the heat of them through the thin fabric of her shirt.

"I got you," he said, pulling her back to standing.

"Thanks," she said, trying to catch her breath. That was a close one. She could have totally eaten it in front of him.

To her disappointment, he let go and took a step back. She felt the imprint of where his hands had been.

"Let's keep going. We're almost at the top," he said gruffly, leading the way.

When they finally reached the top of the hill, it was still plenty hot, even though the sky was darkening. The residual heat of the day wafted up toward them from the trail. Thea took off her hat to fan the sweat from her forehead and looked out toward the horizon.

"I've never seen downtown so clearly!" she said.

"Nice, right? Wait a few minutes. It gets better." Gabe took a gulp from his water bottle. Despite contributing to the heat, the setting sun enhanced the view of downtown. Usually, there was a layer of smog around it, but with fewer people driving cars these days, the smog had mostly dissipated. The major streets that led downtown looked empty, with a few errant cars.

As the sun kissed the horizon, the sky turned into an incredible blue and orange watercolor. Fluorescent pink light bathed the handful of fluffy clouds in the sky. Against this colorful backdrop, the skyscrapers with their lit up windows in downtown LA looked like something from an 80s science fiction movie.

"Wow..." Thea said softly as she watched the sky changing from blue to dark purple. She wished she had something more profound to say, considering she was a professional writer. But sometimes, the obvious words were the best. "Beautiful."

She slid her gaze from the skyline to Gabe. He was turned so that she could only see his profile. His mask dangled from the same hand that held his water bottle. Thea admired the curl of his long lashes and the strong, slightly upturned slope of a nose. This man was way too hot for his own good. His swallowing brought her attention to his throat, and she traced his jawline with her eyes, liking the way his Adam's apple bobbed up and down.

Gabe screwed the lid back onto his water bottle before turning to face her. Thea's eyes darted back to the horizon. She felt the weight of his gaze on her and fiddled with the strap on her backpack.

"Beautiful," he echoed, not moving his eyes off of her. Then, as if realizing he'd said that out loud, he cleared his throat and looked away.

Thea pulled her phone out to distract herself from what she'd heard. There was no way she could capture the magical blending of violet and orange on the horizon, but she wanted to get close. She snapped a few pictures of the dark skyline of downtown in the background.

"Can I get you in a picture?" she asked him.

He nodded and faced her. The lighting was bad because of the brilliant colors of the sky behind him, but she snapped a few shots, anyway. Of course, this guy was photogenic as hell, too.

"What about you? I can take a picture for you," Gabe offered.

"That's okay," she said immediately, turning away from him. She didn't want to get into her whole picture thing. "Should we head down?"

Gabe was silent for a beat too long, and she worried he would want a selfie together. To her relief, he swallowed whatever he was about to say. "Sure, it'll be dark soon."

"You're a good photographer," Gabe said as they made their way down the path.

Thea was surprised. "You've seen my pictures?"

"I've seen the ones online that go with your reviews. I hope it's not weird?"

"Not weird." She was flattered that he read her pieces.

"I noticed there aren't any pictures of you online," he said. Okay, so he wasn't going to drop it after all. "I think that's why before I met you, I thought that Thea Reyes, the writer, was much older."

"Oh." Unease stroked a frosty finger down her back. She told a lie of omission. "It's easier for me to do my job if people don't know what I look like."

"Makes sense. Also impressive as hell to be so anonymous on the internet. With your picture, at least."

"Heh."

Going down the hill was easier than going up, other than in a few spots where the path was steep enough to require extra concentration so that she didn't slip on any loose rocks. The few people they passed were pretty good about wearing their masks. Even when they weren't, they were at least standing far enough off the trail so that others could pass without getting too close.

It made Thea nervous to even be that close to strangers not wearing masks. Gabe must have picked up on that anxiety because he moved so that he was between her and the other person. She wasn't sure if she liked that alternative either, because she also didn't want *him* to get Covid.

They made it back to the beginning of the trail. At the bottom of the hill, everything was bathed in shadow. An unmasked man tied his shoelace near where the trail opened up into the parking lot. Thea gave him a wide berth, but as she passed him, he stood up and looked at her. She recognized his expression, and a pit of dread opened up at the bottom of her stomach.

"Take your China virus back to your own country," the guy snarled at her.

She glanced around. No one else had heard. Gabe was behind a turn at the start of the trail. He'd fallen back after stepping to the side to let a family pass on the narrow part of the trail. The man glared at her, a sneer on his ruddy face.

"Yeah, I'm talking to you, Chinese bitch!" the man said. He walked closer to her and Thea immediately stepped back.

Sweat slicked her palms. Her heart hammered against her ribs. She'd read about the uptick in anti-Asian crimes, but she didn't think she'd come across it in the progressive bubble of LA. She opened her mouth to say something, but nothing came out. The man was wrong on so many points. She wasn't even from China.

Gabe's footsteps crunched on the gravel beside her. One look from Thea to the stranger, and he stepped between them.

He turned to her. "Are you okay?"

Thea nodded and tipped her head to her car, hoping Gabe would follow. They needed to extricate themselves from the situation.

"Yeah, run away. Back to your own country, ching chong! Take your bat virus with you!" Spittle flew out of the man's mouth.

Before she could react, Gabe spun and walked toward the guy, slow, stalking steps. His arms were loose by his sides, but Thea could see his hands curling into fists.

"What. Did. You. Just. Say?" Gabe asked. Even muffled by his mask, his voice had a dangerous, icy edge to it. Unlike anything she'd heard coming out of his mouth before.

The racist asshole must have realized what was about to happen because, as he looked up at Gabe's towering form, the sneer left his face and his mouth dropped open.

"I asked you a question," Gabe said again in a deathly calm tone. The racist was backing away now. He looked behind him, as if Gabe could be talking to anyone but him.

"Whatever, man." With that, the coward spun around and hurried away, running up the trail. When he was almost hidden by a turn in the path, he shouted, "Chop-suey, lover!"

Gabe lunged to run after him, but Thea grabbed him, clamping her hand over the muscle of his forearm. He felt so hot, as if the anger could bubble out of him like lava. She loosened her grip, hand sliding lower to hold on to his wrist. Gabe looked down at where her fingers circled him and then back at her, his eyes going soft when they met hers.

"It's ok." She didn't like how tiny her voice sounded even to her ears.

Most of the rage had left his eyes, but his voice still held an edge to it. "It's *not* okay to say those things to you. To anyone."

"I know. Forget it," she said. "Racist assholes like him don't deserve the attention."

Gabe glanced down at where they were still touching. She'd slid her grip from his wrist and he'd opened his fist to interlace his fingers with hers. She couldn't remember how that happened.

His thumb swept over the sensitive spot between her thumb and index finger and her breath caught in her throat. Her heart was still pounding.

He gave her hand a squeeze and let go. Thea tucked that hand into her back pocket, wishing she could save that feeling for later. His face was tender when she looked up at him.

"You okay?" he asked.

"Yeah," she lied, trying to steady the tremble in her voice. Seeing his concern for her made her simultaneously want to lean into him and pull away. Lean into him because she wanted comfort, and pull away to prove she didn't need it. Before she could stop herself, she asked, "Can I have a hug?"

Surprise flashed on Gabe's face for half a second, and then it was gone. He held out his arms, and she stepped into the circle of them. He wrapped his arms around her, clasping her firmly to him.

Gabe's shirt was incredibly soft where she bunched it in her fist, a stark contrast to the hardness of his body underneath. Thea pressed her forehead to his shoulder and took a shaky breath. The reassuring heat and weight of his arms on her were soothing. He was a fantastic hugger; not too soft, but just firm enough. He smelled faintly like mint, warm cotton, and something familiar. She wanted to bury her nose in that scent.

Thea stiffened. If she could smell him, then she was too close. There was definitely not six feet of space between them. He noticed the change because he dropped his arms from her. Thea stepped back, pulling at the elastic band of her mask to tighten it.

"Sorry, I just needed..." She was angry at her moment of weakness.

"It's okay." His voice was coarse. He looked at her with so much worry in his eyes that she had to look away.

"I'm just glad that guy wasn't violent." Thea put more distance between them. She'd left her mace at home, not thinking she would need it in broad daylight. She should start carrying it with her again now that she was venturing out of the house.

"Let's key his car." Gabe said, his tone facetious. From the hard gleam in his eyes, Thea could tell he was serious.

"I don't think I saw which car he came out of. But whatever, not worth it." She pulled her phone out of her backpack and checked the time. They'd been here longer than she'd thought.

"What time is it?" Gabe asked.

"Almost seven."

"This trail's gonna close soon. They kick people off of it after sundown."

"We made good time," Thea said. She tried for lightness. "Thanks for inviting me. This is such a hidden gem. I never would have known about it."

"I'm always happy to go hiking if you wanna do it again. Too bad that asshole ruined it," Gabe said. "I'll walk you to your car."

Thea waved away the offer. "Oh, you don't have to. I'm just over there." She pointed to where her car was parked.

"After what just happened, it would make me feel better."

It would make her feel better, too, but she didn't want to admit that. Instead, she said, "No, seriously, my car's right there. How about you stand here and watch me get into it?"

"Fine," he grumbled. His pouty look tugged at something in her.

Thea approached her car, conscious of Gabe's eyes on her with every step. When she unlocked her door, she looked over her shoulder and gave him a last wave. He returned it with a smile. Seeing that dimple in his smile flooded her with a surge of emotion that washed the bad vibes away.

She didn't want to think too hard about what that meant.

SIXTEEN

GABE CLUTCHED MULTIPLE paper bags to his side as he pulled open Thea's front gate. He tripped on a length of hose as he stepped over a mound of dirt on the path to Thea's porch. That wasn't there a few nights ago.

Thea's front yard was in disarray. Instead of the two small patchy squares of lawn on either side of the path leading to her porch, there were huge piles of dirt on top of what looked like a pile of flattened cardboard boxes. A stack of lumber sitting on a large blue tarp occupied one side of the yard. A handful of large bags of more dirt occupied the other side.

Gabe walked up to the porch and knocked on the door. He set the food down and turned to look at what happened to the yard. It looked like Thea was planning on doing major renovations.

"Hey, thanks." Thea said when she opened the door. She was in a pair of worn and faded overalls over a white shirt with the sleeves cut off. She brushed dirt off the knees of her overalls. Even her light blue cotton mask had smudges of dirt.

"You changing it up in front?"

She stepped out of her doorway, over the bags of food, and stood on her porch with hands on her hips, looking from one pile of dirt to the other. A small sigh escaped from her mouth. "Yeah, I'm gonna build two big garden boxes. One here," she pointed to the left of the path, "And one over there. Those are the only places that get a decent amount of sun here."

Gabe looked up at the large tree on the strip in front of the sidewalk and the shadow it cast. It was only six, but shade already covered the front half of the yard thanks to that tree.

"What're you gonna plant?" he asked.

"It might be too late to start big tomatoes. My neighbor offered me her extra squash seedlings. So maybe some cherry tomatoes and zucchini? Fill the rest of the space in with herbs. It'll be nice to have some fresh vegetables to dip in my yogurt in the morning."

Gabe stepped over a partially dug hole.

"Ugh, this mess. I've been working on it all day, but as you can see, there's still a lot to do."

"Where'd all this dirt come from?" Gabe looked, but didn't see any holes large enough to explain where the mounds of dirt came from.

Thea shook her head. "I got it delivered, but I messed up the delivery times. They were supposed to come *after* everything's built. It's fine though. I can finish building the boxes tomorrow and then I can move the soil in."

"You want help?" Gabe offered.

Thea looked up at him in surprise. "You wanna help me build these?"

"Sure."

"And you know how to build garden boxes?" She asked in a skeptical tone.

Gabe smirked. "I do build things like this for my day job, you know."

Thea slapped her forehead. It left an adorable smudge of dirt over her brow. "Oh right! Sorry, I forgot. Of course, you know how to build a simple rectangle."

"There's more to it than just a rectangle. You'll want the walls to bear a certain amount of weight," Gabe said. "Wet soil is heavier than you'd think."

"Right, I think I saw that in one of the YouTube videos." Thea said,

"But I kinda blew my budget, buying the materials for this. Lumber prices are insane right now! I guess a lot of people like me doing these little projects. I don't think I can pay you for the help."

Gabe folded his arms in front of his chest. "I didn't mean as a job. As a favor to a friend."

"I don't know... I feel like I'm taking advantage of you."

He wouldn't mind her taking advantage of him in other ways, but he wasn't meat-headed enough to tell her that. Instead, he proposed an alternative. "How about a trade? I'll help you build this and then you can help me with one of my projects?"

Thea snickered. "I don't know if you'll want my carpentry help after you see how I build these."

"I was thinking of your photography skills," Gabe said. "I could use your help getting pictures of some of the stuff I built. My sister's been complaining about the lighting or whatever in the pics. Maybe you can give me some tips?"

"Hm... okay, that's fair."

"Deal. I'll meet you here tomorrow morning? I think the weather's supposed to be pretty good."

Thea nodded enthusiastically. "Thanks. This'll force me to be outside more. I've been mostly sitting on my ass on the porch, so having something active to do will keep me from slowly going out of my mind."

Gabe's mouth twitched. He almost blurted out that he had no complaints about her ass, but kept it to himself. He liked how animated she was by this project.

"Well, I'm sure you'll regret it, but thank you for offering your expertise," Thea said.

She was wrong. He already knew he would not regret seeing her tomorrow morning.

Gabe rapped on the door with his knuckles and stepped back. When it opened, he clenched his jaw to avoid looking like the cartoon wolf going "awooooogah" with a lascivious tongue hanging out. He'd seen plenty of people wearing all shades and types of coveralls at work, but no one wore them like Thea did.

Thea's coveralls looked well loved, with splotches and smears of paint all over. Its dark green color had faded at her elbows and knees. The zipper stopped about halfway up so that the top gaped open. Even though she had some sort of sports-bra under, the tantalizing band of skin right above her lowered zipper was especially hard not to stare at.

"Good morning," Thea said, bringing his attention back to her face.

Keep it cool, he reminded himself. Hopefully, the blood pounding in his ears wasn't loud enough for her to hear. He cleared his throat and tried for normal. "Morning."

"Oh, you brought your tools?" Thea asked, noticing the large tool bag he had placed by his feet.

"Yeah. I didn't know what tools you had." *Tools, yes, let's concentrate on the tools.* He held up the pink cardboard box tucked under his other arm. "I also brought donuts."

"Thanks! You can set them down over there." Thea pointed to the low table by the porch swing. "I have the perfect thing for it."

When she turned to head into the kitchen, he couldn't help noticing how well the material hugged her curves. Who knew that someone could look so good in a painter's outfit?

Thea came out with a carafe in one hand and an empty cup in another. She placed it on one of the small tables and gestured at it. "I thought you'd want some coffee before we get started. If you like it cold, I can put ice in it."

"Thanks, hot's perfect."

Thea went back into the house to fetch her own mug before coming out again. In the meantime, Gabe put the donut box down and grabbed a chocolate glazed donut for himself.

He held it in his hand and moved to the other side of the porch. He gestured with his coffee mug to the railing of the porch. "Can I put my cup here? On the balustrade?"

"Yeah, that's fine. Is that the fancy name for the railing?" Thea teased as she opened the box and took out a maple bar. "Mmm, these are my favorite."

Gabe took a bite of his donut. He washed it down with a gulp of coffee. "Wow, this coffee is fantastic."

"Thanks." Thea bit into her own donut and sighed, closing her eyes. "I haven't had one of these for a while."

Gabe wasn't sure when he bought the donuts if they were too low brow for someone who probably went to a lot of fancy restaurants with French sounding desserts, but seeing the euphoric smile on Thea's face wiped those doubts away. The pure joy on her face made him feel like he was a donut, fresh out of the oven with gooey, warm jelly inside.

After her third donut, a plain cruller, Thea forced herself to stop.

"Okay enough," she said. "If I eat one more donut, I'm gonna turn into one."

"Same here," Gabe said. He took one last swig of the coffee and stood, pulling his mask back on and flicking the crumbs off his pants. "What should we start first?"

Thea pulled two folded sheets of paper out from her back pocket and unfolded them carefully, smoothing out the creases. "I drew some diagrams of how the pieces should fit together. Here, I made you a copy."

Gabe walked over to her side of the porch to study his copy. He turned the paper one way, then the other. He gave her a puzzled look. "Which way is up?"

Thea rotated the paper for him and pointed to the diagram. "I'm not great at drawing, but it's supposed to be like this. See, here's the shorter side of the rectangle, and then there's the long side."

"Just to be sure, the wood that you bought for the sides is actually straight, right?" He teased.

"Of course!" Thea waved her hand in a dismissive gesture. "I couldn't find a ruler, okay? Anyway, I think it'll make sense once we lay out the pieces."

Gabe walked to the pile of wood and looked at it, picking one piece up to inspect, and then another. She couldn't keep her eyes away from the muscles in his arms, bunching and moving under his bronze skin. She knew the thick pieces he was holding were heavy, having moved them to that spot herself the day before.

"I think before we get to the wood, we should shovel some of this soil out of the way so that we can plop the box around it," Thea said. "Then we can flatten out the soil and add more from the shoveled pile if we need to. What do you think?"

"Yep, you're the boss. One of us can shovel and the other can get started on the frame. Which one do you wanna do?"

Thea mulled over it for a bit, chewing on her bottom lip. She had been planning on doing both tasks herself, but now that Gabe was here, there was no sense in not putting his expertise to use. "I'll do the grunt work, and you can do the frame. It'll probably turn out better that way."

"Suits me. But lemme know if you need a break from shoveling."

"I'm gonna go grab my gloves."

Thea returned with her own tool bag, work gloves, and the electric drill she charged overnight in the garage. She held it up for Gabe. "Hope it'll have enough juice for the whole thing. If not, I can plug it in."

He accepted the drill from her, weighing its heft in his hand. "Wow, I like a woman who has an eye for power tools."

Thea covered her blush up with a retort. "Calm down, Bubba, it's just a drill."

They set off to their tasks in amiable silence, except for the occasional whirring of the drill. Thea liked the rhythm of moving a shovelful of dirt one after the other. She snuck a glance at Gabe on the other side of the yard. He had laid out his tools on the patchy grass by the wood and already started placing parts next to each other in the loose shape of a rectangular garden bed. Once in a while, he referred to the diagram she made. She was glad that it wasn't completely useless.

As he bent over the planks and took the pencil from his ear, he marked off spots with the help of a measuring tape. He had arms women fantasized about. She imagined putting her fingertip on that raised scar on the back of his arm and tracing it up his skin, up his biceps, up those broad shoulders, up his neck, feeling the prickly stubble on his face under that mask.

Gabe stilled and his eyes flicked up to her, curious. "You wanna switch?"

Thea shook her head and blanked out her mind, hoping her face wasn't mirroring her steamy thoughts. "No. I think I need to grab my hat. I'll be right back. Can I bring you some water or something? I think I have cold soda in the fridge."

Gabe wiped the sweat on his forehead off with the back of his hand and accepted her offer. She returned with her straw hat and a cold can of soda.

"Hope you like lime seltzer. It's all I have left."

"Perfect." He cracked open the can with a satisfying hiss.

Thea watched his Adam's apple as he gulped down the cold liquid. She took a long drink from her own water bottle. She was glad she had refilled it with ice cold water.

Gabe set the can aside and went back to his work, methodically measuring things out and marking more spots with a stubby pencil he tucked behind his ear when he wasn't using it. She was grateful that he volunteered to help, even if him being here was a distraction. Maybe working next to his well-toned body would be the exposure therapy she needed to stop lusting after him.

After he got two sides of the rectangle firmly attached, Gabe tested its weight by lifting one corner.

"Can you give me a hand with this part?" he asked. "I think we should move this over there in pieces or else it'll be too heavy to move if it's completely built. We can move it around that pile and then I can screw the sides together in place once we know it's in the right spot."

Thea dropped her shovel and clapped the dirt off her gloves. She walked to where he was standing, careful to step over a pile of screws by the drill. They each grabbed one leg of one L-shaped component of the garden bed and maneuvered it into place. Once Thea confirmed the correct location, Gabe moved the other pieces in place and assembled it.

"Should I do the same thing on that side?" Thea asked, pointing to the pile of soil on the other side. She was done with her current pile.

"How about we switch? I don't wanna take all the fun."

"Deal." Thea dug around in her own toolbag for what she would need to assemble the second box. It wasn't as extensive as Gabe's, but had all the basic things she needed, like a hammer, level, and tape measure.

She followed Gabe's lead and set the various pieces of wood roughly where they were supposed to be, glad that she had ordered the right amount of each piece. She went over each section with a measuring tape and marked where she needed to attach the pieces.

"Yaaaaahrgh!"

Thea's head snapped up to see Gabe flailing around, the cold coffee in his cup sloshing all over. She rushed over to him. "What happened?!"

A loud buzz whizzed past her ears. When she searched for the source of the familiar sound, she found a shiny green iridescent beetle flying off into the trumpet vines at the side of the yard.

"Eeeesh, that scared me," Gabe said, clutching his cup to his chest. "It was right by my ear."

"Oh no! Your shirt!"

Gabe looked down at the front of his shirt, right at the big splash of brown. "Crap. Well, at least the coffee wasn't hot. Oh! I have an extra shirt in the car."

"Here, I can stain stick it for you," Thea offered. "It'll be harder to get off if it dries."

"Thanks." Gabe pulled off his shirt. He did it the way all men seemed to, with a hand on the back of the shirt and pulling it off his shoulders over his head. Was it something they learned in the boys' locker room?

He held his shirt out to her. Her eyes roved his body, from the V-shaped muscles arrowing down into the waist of his jeans, to the dark trail of hair dipping below, up every defined pack of his abs, up his chest, up his neck, partially obstructed by his mask, up his lips, which quirked into a smile, and up to his heated amber eyes, staring hungrily at her.

Thea willed herself to look away, but the hold of his gaze trapped her. It must've been a trick of the light hitting him that made them look glowing and gold. When she finally looked elsewhere, her eyes landed on his abs. They were powerless to the temptation of his naked torso.

"If you keep staring at me like that, we're not gonna finish the bed," Gabe growled.

"You mean the box. The garden box," Thea said, shocked at how husky her voice sounded even to her. She tore her eyes away and grabbed the shirt from him. It was still warm from his body. What he said was an invitation, a challenge. She was very tempted.

Something tickled her forehead, and she reached for it, a stray lock of hair. She tucked it behind her ear, touching the elastic strap of her mask. Oh, right, her mask. The pandemic. She took a few steps back, finally realizing how dangerous it was for her to be so close to him, not only because he had his mask down. Her cheeks were so hot they were steaming up her sunglasses. She stuttered out something. "Lemme just... just go inside and um... your shirt."

There, that sounded normal, right? She escaped from his amused expression back into her house before he could say anything.

♦ ♦ ♦

Gabe stealthily studied Thea in between shovelfuls of dirt. Okay, maybe not stealthily, but he figured less obviously than Thea had been staring at him. He couldn't help showing off and flexing his abs more than was necessary when he helped her lift the walls of the garden bed.

He could have slipped on the extra shirt he grabbed from his truck, but the sporadic breeze on his skin felt good. But not as good as her gaze on him, which felt more exciting than he wanted to admit.

The last time he'd been with a woman was months before the pandemic. He'd forgotten how it felt to be under an appreciative look like that. Thea's dark eyes traveling up his body stirred his blood faster than anything he'd encountered before. If she had asked, he would have happily thrown the shovel down and whisked her into her bedroom — screw the pandemic. Or into her living room. Or even on her porch. No one was around. The thought made him hard. Even the painful constraint of his zipper wasn't enough to discourage him.

Thwack! Thwack!

The loud hammering brought him out of his reverie, and he shifted surreptitiously so that it was not so obvious what sweet torture he was under right then.

Thea straightened up and stepped back a few feet, surveying her handiwork. He was skeptical about her diagram, but the finished product looked better than he expected. Probably because the sides were actually straight, exactly as she'd promised. She began shoveling the rest of the soil into the now completed bed, but stopped after a few minutes.

Gabe tried to concentrate on his own work, but the unmistakable sound of a zipper caught his attention. Thea's brow glistened with sweat.

She'd unzipped the front of her coveralls down to her waist and slipped her arms free of them, tying the top of the outfit around her. She removed her hat and wiped the sweat from her forehead with the back of her arm. He couldn't take his eyes off of her, glad that she hadn't noticed. He was irrationally jealous of the arms of her coveralls and how they hugged the curve of her waist.

The sun was now directly overhead, heat burning off any sign of clouds. He noticed his empty can of soda and how hot it was.

"I gotta grab my water bottle from the truck."

Thea looked up briefly and nodded, not breaking her rhythm of shoveling. When he returned, she was still shoveling dirt into the bed and flattening the mounds so that the soil was level. He was glad he had taken an icy swig of water back at the truck because it gave him a better rein on himself when he returned. Enough self-control to finish his part of the work.

Fifteen minutes later, they were officially done. Thea moved to the other side of the yard, putting away some tools and extra screws. She smiled as he approached her, eyes twinkling. The work and sun had made her cheeks flushed, giving her a gorgeous glow.

"It looks great!" she said.

"Yeah, we make a good team."

A bead of sweat trickled from the spot between her jaw and ear, past the hollow of her collarbone, disappearing into the valley between her breasts. He should not be thinking about placing the tip of his tongue on that trail and following it down into her bra.

"What? Dirt?" Thea rubbed her neck self-consciously with the back of her gloved hand.

Gabe didn't know how long he'd been staring.

She pulled off the glove and rubbed her cheek. A loose lock of hair escaped her hat and stuck to her face.

He resisted the urge to reach over and tuck it back behind her ear. He shook his head and tried to ignore those treacherous thoughts. Words spilled out of his mouth. "You look incredible in that outfit."

She affected pose, one elbow bent, hand on a cocked hip, and said in an amused tone, "Oh, this ol' thing?"

Did she realize what she was doing to him? It took every ounce of his self-control not to place his hands around her waist, the exposed skin beckoning to him so sweetly, and pull her to him.

"I'm not kidding," he said quietly enough that Thea had to lean in to hear him more clearly. "You look amazing."

Thea dropped her arms to her side. A brighter flush spread from the top of her nose across her cheeks. He thought she was going to step closer to him, but she stopped herself, much to his disappointment. Instead, she placed a hand on the side of the newly built garden bed and perched on it.

"Hey," Gabe said, crossing one arm over his chest to scratch at an itch on his shoulder. He should have kept that thought to himself. "Sorry. That was out of line."

Thea gave an almost imperceptible shake of her head and blinked a few times. "It's okay."

Gabe exhaled and closed his eyes in relief. "I made it awkward."

"It's fine. You don't look too bad yourself," she mumbled.

His eyes snapped open, meeting her eyes. He could feel a crackling in the air between them, like before a bolt of lightning ripped through the sky. He was lost in those hypnotic eyes of hers. To keep from doing something stupid, he forced himself to look away and concentrated on her mask instead. It was safe and neutral. The fabric pulled tight against her mouth, moving as she breathed. He desperately wished he was that mask, touching her lips.

Thea chuckled, the husky sound inciting thoughts he was trying to keep out of his head. She moved her hands up and down, gesturing from his head to his shoes. "I mean, look at you!"

Gabe looked down at what she was gesturing about, but only saw what he normally saw. He arched an eyebrow. "I'm looking."

"Your body!" She sputtered, as if it were obvious. "It's like you stepped out of some shiny swimsuit ad."

"Thanks?"

"And your face!" She shook her head.

"My face?"

"You're hot. Like ridiculously hot." Thea covered her mouth with her hands, a hysterical laugh bubbling out of her. "You probably have women lining up for you."

Despite the compliments, a heavy feeling kept him grounded. "Not exactly," Gabe said carefully.

"Yeah, okay, with a thirst trap body like yours?" Thea said incredulously while her eyes meandered up and down his skin.

"Um, thanks?" He liked her attention a lot, but he couldn't help blushing at the compliment. Maybe he should have put his shirt back on sooner, but he hadn't wanted to get it all sweaty. He moved to grab it so he could put it back on, but stopped himself. To do so now would make this situation more awkward. "But I don't."

"Don't what?"

"Don't have women lining up for me," he said. "I'm not 'boyfriend material.'" He even made the air quotes. It wasn't exactly true, but it wasn't far from the truth, either. He had no problems attracting women. It was all the stuff that came after that initial spark of attraction that never worked out in his favor.

Thea shrugged. "Well, I'm not girlfriend material, so that's fine."

Gabe's brows furrowed at that comment. "What do you mean?" In his absolutely objective opinion, she was perfect.

Thea held up her hand with a finger pointing up. "I don't cook."

Gabe shrugged. "That's okay, I do."

A second finger, "I don't clean."

"I don't expect you to."

A third finger, "I write all the time. Like all the time. And it always comes first."

"I like your writing."

A fourth finger, "I love alone time."

"Me too."

Her fifth finger, "I hog the bed."

"I have a big bed." He couldn't help the grin splitting his face.

Thea's eyes widened. She'd drifted closer, caught up in his words. This was a dangerous game they were playing, and he wasn't sure he knew all the rules yet.

"Yoohoo!" A voice shouted from across the street.

"My nosy neighbor," Thea said quietly, so that only he could hear. She moved past him and even from a safe social distance away, he could feel a bubble of warmth.

"Hey Kathy," Thea said from behind her fence. She waved toward the blue painted porch of another Craftsman across the street.

The bush by Thea's side of the sidewalk was partially obscuring his view, so Gabe moved a few feet to the side to look at who she was talking to. There was a woman wearing head-to-toe, pastel tie-dyed athleisure. Even the visor crowning her high ponytail was tie-dyed. He did a double-take; he wasn't used to seeing a woman in her fifties wearing this type of outfit.

"Well, hello there," the woman said, waving to him as he peeked from around the bush. Her glossy, candy-pink colored lips pursed together into an *O*.

He could guess what she was thinking by the way she unapologetically looked him up and down. Now he wished he put his shirt back on.

"This is my friend Gabe," Thea introduced. "Gabe, this is Kathy."

"Hey."

"Why don't you come up here and I can shake your hand," Kathy drawled in a tone that made it clear she wanted to do more than that.

"Sorry, we're in the middle of something." Thea saved him from saying anything.

"I'm sure you were." The woman looked between Thea and him and raised her eyebrow.

"We're making some changes to the front yard," Thea said blandly. She sounded like she knew exactly how to deal with this neighbor.

"Hm, that's nice, dear. That sad grass needed to go away. Well, gotta get my steps in. Good byeeeee." Kathy wiggled her fingers as a goodbye and speed walked away.

Thea shook her head and turned around. When she saw him still looking at her, she rolled her eyes.

"Sorry, just the local busy-body," she said under her breath. "The good thing is she's always home and knows everything going on in the neighborhood. So if a package goes missing, she probably saw who took it. The bad thing is she's always home and knows everything."

Gabe laughed at the truth of that. He had one on his block, too. The old man loved to sit on a lawn chair close to the sidewalk all afternoon. Gabe helped Thea clean up the last piles of dirt and collect the tools strewn all over the yard.

"When are you gonna get plants to put in here?" Gabe gestured to the two newly built garden beds. "You need me to go pick'em up?"

"No, but thanks for offering. I ordered plants from this little nursery in San Gabriel that delivers. I can probably transplant some of those herbs," she gestured in the porch's direction, "into the beds now that there's somewhere for them to go. They're sorta outgrowing their pots, anyway."

"Sounds good."

"Some people have their sourdough pandemic pet, but I just have my plant pets," Thea shrugged.

After putting away his tools in his tool bag, Gabe grabbed his extra shirt from where it hung. He pulled it over his head and smoothed out some stray dirt that had gotten onto one shoulder.

"Thanks so much for helping me do all this," Thea said, moving both hands to gesture at her front yard. "I thought it would take us all day, but now I have the entire afternoon free!"

"My pleasure." It was the truth. He enjoyed the serene silence that settled between them as they worked in parallel. He hadn't felt pressured to fill it with small talk.

"I owe you one for this. Lemme know when you wanna do the pictures."

"It was fun."

Thea wrinkled the top of her nose cutely. "I don't believe that. I still feel bad making you do something that you probably do at your day job."

Gabe laughed. "If only my day job was as chill. It's more like building three things while also tearing apart two other things to reuse the material for the next thing. On a moving train. Seriously, I'm happy to help you out."

SEVENTEEN

"SORRY I'M LATE!" Thea said as she power-walked into the parking lot. "I parked super far away."

"I just parked. You're good." Gabe leaned against the back bumper of his truck, waiting for her.

"I should've warned you about the parking situation before."

The parking lot was a tiny, cramped thing. Thea had enough close calls with her car in there to know to avoid parking in it. Unfortunately, she couldn't find a spot on the same block and ended up walking two blocks to the restaurant. A laundromat flanked the L-shaped strip mall on one side, and on the other side was a space with a "For Lease" sign pasted on the window. In the crook of the L was a tiny Filipino market that also served prepared food.

"Want me to go in and get our food?" He wasn't sure if this was another trunk lunch.

"No, I called just after I parked and they said they can bring the stuff out to us when they're ready."

The two of them made it to the entrance of the tiny market. Thea peered into the storefront window and waved. A few seconds later, the door opened, and a man came out bearing two plastic bags.

"Wow, that was fast," Thea remarked.

"I didn't want to keep you waiting," the young man said in a relaxed Californian drawl as he handed one bag to her. "One pancit, and one rice, right?"

"Right."

"I filled it with good stuff. It's gonna be bomb," the guy said. He looked at Gabe and gave him the guy nod.

Thea could smell the food even through the plastic containers and her mask. "Mmm, it smells so good."

"And here, we just made these, so be careful. Hot hot!" The man handed her a second, lighter bag.

"What is it?"

"A new flavor of turon. Try it out and tell me what you think, okay?" He waggled his eyebrows at her excitedly.

The bag smelled amazing. "Let me pay you for this."

The guy waved it off. "On the house, Cuz. Lemme know what you think."

"Really?"

"Really! It's nothing. A thank you gift for being a reg."

Thea said, "I appreciate it. If they're anything like the other turon, they're gonna be fantastic."

Gabe and Thea walked the three blocks from the strip mall to a tiny park on the corner of a residential block. Mature camphor trees grew around the perimeter of the park. A dozen picnic benches sat under the canopy of leaves. Thea put one takeout container on a picnic table, and the other on the table next to it. The tables were close enough that they wouldn't need to shout to hear each other.

"I've never had Filipino food before." Gabe sat in front of the food, facing Thea.

Thea took off her mask, folded it, and looped its straps over her left arm so that it hung at her elbow. She forgot all about her nervousness earlier now that she was sitting in front of food. She beamed at him. "You're in for a treat."

"Did you get the same thing?" Gabe pointed to the open takeout container in front of him, that was divided into three sections. The largest section contained some sort of noodles on one side, and then rice on the other.

"Yep, I just asked them to give us some scoops of what they thought would be tasty for lunch," Thea said. She flipped the lid off of her container and bent over it, examining the contents.

"What is all this?" Gabe asked her.

"There's pancit, which are the noodles," Thea started pointed to each section. "I forgot what this one is called, but it's like a squash stew, then there's sisig, this pork belly dish. You can eat all of those with rice. Oh, and dinuguan."

Thea peered at Gabe to gauge his reaction. He studied the dark brown stew. "What's dino-guam?"

"Dinuguan," Thea corrected. "Okay, don't be scared by the color. It's a pork stew, but they make the broth with pork blood."

"Heh, I'm not scared by a little blood." Gabe inspected the stew. He picked up a plastic spoon and scooped up some liquid and pieces of pork. He gave it another once over before putting it into his mouth.

Thea watched, holding her breath, as he chewed the food with a thoughtful expression on his face. He looked at her with wide, rounded eyes.

"Wow!" Gabe said with wonder in his voice. "This is good."

Thea clapped her hands gleefully. "Yay, I'm glad you like it! The color scares some people off, but it's one of my favorites and they make a great version of it here."

Gabe scooped the rice onto his spoon this time before dipping it into the stew. Thea approved. The savory, tangy stew tasted even better with fluffy rice.

"The flavor is so unexpected," Gabe said after swallowing a couple more mouthfuls.

"Right?! That sour taste is so addictive and keeps the stew from being too rich." Thea said between two mouthfuls.

"Whoa, this pork belly thing. What did you call it?"

"Sisig."

123

"The sisig is so crispy still. I like that it's sour too. Almost like a pork salad." Gabe said.

"Yeah, a lot of Filipino dishes have that punch of acid."

"So, are you related to that guy? I heard him calling you cousin." Gabe asked.

"Not that I know of. I just go there a lot, so they treat me like family. Mark is always super nice. Actually, one of my *titas* told me about this place, so maybe we are related way up the family tree..."

"Are you Filipino? I know your last name is Reyes, but you don't look..." Gabe trailed off.

Thea knew what he was saying. She sometimes got annoyed with those puzzled looks from strangers as they tried to match her features into something they could categorize. To her surprise, Gabe's question didn't put her off. Maybe because he didn't look at her like she was some optical illusion that just needed to be viewed at a certain angle.

"Yeah, Reyes is from my dad's side. He's Filipino. My mom's Taiwanese. So I'm a mutt," she said in that self-deprecating way.

Gabe gave her a sympathetic look. "Yeah, me too."

"You're Filipino?" Thea asked skeptically. One thing about being Filipino was that she was usually pretty good at recognizing other Filipinos.

He shook his head and swallowed a bite of food. "No, I'm a mutt too. My mom's Mexican but my dad's Peruvian."

For the rest of lunch, they talked about their childhood. Gabe had a lot in common with her, being from two cultures but living in LA. She liked that Gabe understood the exact frustration she had with not being Taiwanese or Filipino enough at home, but being *too* other outside of the home. They swapped ridiculous anecdotes of aunties who lived for family gossip.

"That's one thing I really miss since this whole thing started," Gabe said wistfully. "We used to do these huge family parties with all my *tías* and *tíos* and their families. Like my parents would start cooking the day before and people would start coming around lunch and eat and hang out till two in the morning. It was one of my favorite things as a kid because I got to stay way past my bedtime."

Thea understood. She hadn't seen any of her relatives since the pandemic. Even though they were only about 60 miles away in Riverside, they might as well be in a different country. She hadn't put into words this particular ache in her heart until Gabe had mentioned it.

An hour later, Thea sighed and closed the clamshell top of her container. She was utterly, blissfully, stuffed. Her mouth wanted another bite of the crispy turon and its sweet, aromatic filling, but her stomach sent her loud signals to stop. Or maybe it felt unsettled because of nerves. She still hadn't brought up the real reason she asked Gabe to come out to lunch with her. She wanted to give herself room to chicken out, but now that lunch was over, it was now or never.

"You okay?" he asked in the weighted silence. He finished his second turon and was now wiping his mouth with the flimsy paper napkin.

"Yeah." She looked around. They were alone at the park, other than a family playing with a toddler near the sandbox on the other side of the grass. They were well out of anyone else's earshot. "Can I ask a personal question?"

"Do I have to answer it?" A dimple appeared in his cheek.

"Not if you don't want to," she said in a rush. "Are you in close contact with anyone? Like your roommate, or are you dating someone now? I know you weren't before but—"

Gabe frowned. "No. No one. Last I talked to Adrian, he was planning to be in San Diego for a while. No roommate."

"Okay, that's good. Just wanted to make sure." Thea chewed on her bottom lip, hesitant to go on. "I'm not seeing anyone either. In case you're wondering."

"You told me you didn't date." He cocked his head, eyes wide in mock surprise. "Wait, is this a date?"

"No!" Thea cried out, unintentionally loud. The parents with the toddler glanced over at them. Thea ignored them until they looked away, then muttered. "No, of course not."

Gabe clutched a hand to his chest. "Damn, let a guy down gently next time, will ya?"

Thea pressed her palms on both cheeks and blew out a breath. *Why this was so hard to ask?* She knew exactly how to quirk an eyebrow and smile at a guy to land him in bed for the night. This question should have been easy. Gabe would either say yes or no, and it would be fine either way. She might die of embarrassment if he said no, because then she would have misread all the signs, but at least she'd know.

"Thea, what are you asking?" Gabe folded his arms in front of his chest.

The gesture highlighted his toned arms. She wanted so badly to run her hands along those firm curves. The desire gave her the courage to say the next words. "It's totally okay if you say no. No hard feelings or anything. We can just pretend I never asked and we can go back to being friends. I really will just put it out of my mind, so please just be honest."

"Honest about what?"

"Do you want to just be like hookup buddies during the pandemic? You don't have to answer now. I mean, if it's not obvious already, I think you're super hot... okay, it's very obvious, sorry. You seem responsible about Covid precautions. We're both on the same page there, right? What if we both get tested and if neither of us has it? Then we can, you know... be friends who—"

"—fuck?" Gabe leaned forward, his eyes boring into hers.

She couldn't stop blabbing now. Might as well get it all out, "Yes, and be adults about it. But in a bubble, well not a literal bubble, but we'd both have to not sleep with other people, which I'm definitely not doing right now. We can keep it casual. Nothing serious. Only if you want to, of course." Thea clamped her mouth shut. Her words came out at a machine gun pace.

There was a long pause.

Her breathing was thunderous to her ears, her mouth shut tightly so that more verbal diarrhea didn't come spewing out. She pressed the back of her hands to her cheeks to cool them down. The knocking of a woodpecker above them was annoyingly loud. She stared at the blob of dried gum peeking out from the underside of her table so she wouldn't have to look at Gabe. She prepared herself for the agony of rejection she was sure was coming at the end of this awkward silence. Her face burned with humiliation.

"Journalist spontaneously combusts in public park. You won't believe what caused it!" That's what the clickbait article about her disappearance would read.

This was not what Gabe was expecting. At all. Not even in his wildest dreams — well, yes, in his wildest dreams. An infinite universe of thoughts and scenarios raced through his head, but they all started with "Yes!" He didn't know how many seconds or minutes had passed since Thea had finished talking. He knew he was supposed to say something in reply, but the only thing his stupid brain could produce was "Oh."

Thea looked at him through the fan of her lashes and chewed on the corner of her bottom lip. He had the urge to lick that exact corner.

"You don't need to decide right away. Take some time to think about it, maybe?"

Gabe couldn't believe the doubt in her voice. He must have been better at hiding his interest in her than he thought. It was obvious to him how his body responded whenever she got near. Even now, his breath came in shallow puffs.

"Yes," he said hoarsely.

"Really?"

Was that a squeak that came out of her?

"I'll make an appointment when I get home." This was such a surreal conversation.

"Oh," Thea said. Relief tinged her words. "I did some googling earlier. I'll text you the info on the mobile clinic. They're the fastest with results, from what I've read."

A grin spread across his face. Thea was cute when she was excited.

Her gaze met his. The heat in her eyes made his pulse jump. She licked her lips and pressed them together, like she was stifling a smile. He tamped down the impulse to leap over his table, tip her head back and crush her mouth to his. Instead, he took a calming, deep breath. *Soon*.

EIGHTEEN

THEA RE-READ the sentence. Then she removed it, then rewrote it, then re-read it again. This was her sixth rewrite of the paragraph and she couldn't get it quite right. Her mind kept conjuring up highly distracting scenes featuring her, Gabe, and different pieces of furniture. She time-boxed herself for another ten minutes of heads-down writing time. After a quick stretch of her arms above her head, she placed her hand on the keyboard and started typing away.

When her ten minutes were up, she was slightly more satisfied with the ending of the review. She would let it sit there for the rest of the day and re-read it in the morning. It would give her a newer perspective on her words before she sent it to her editor. Now that her work was done, she turned on the Wi-Fi on her laptop.

A familiar chime notified her of new emails. What she was waiting for had arrived: an email from the Covid test clinic. The test results took longer than expected, but at least it was negative. She hadn't seen anyone other than Gabe in the past week, so it was no surprise that she was cleared.

She took a screenshot and texted it to Gabe. Then, because she didn't know what else to write, she also texted, *how about you?*

She looked at the screen for a few seconds to see if he would respond. Nothing. Maybe he was busy. Or maybe he was having second thoughts about this whole thing. She stood to go put her phone on its charger in her bedroom. It had become a habit of hers whenever she needed to concentrate on writing for a few hours. But she couldn't stop her mind from wandering back to Gabe. Anticipation and dread swirled in the pit of her stomach, threatening to bubble over like a too-full glass of soda. What if he changed his mind? What if he didn't? What if the sex was bad? What if she thought the sex was good, but he thought it was bad?

Thea huffed out a breath, trying to blow those thoughts out with her exhale. She walked out onto the porch with her laptop and placed it on the swing before raising her arms in a big, full-body stretch. It was early, so the chill still clung to the air. A neighbor jogged by and waved at her. She couldn't recognize him thanks to the neck gaiter concealing half his face, but she returned the wave.

She placed her laptop on top of the small plant stand at the perfect height for working on the porch swing, opened up the screen, and began typing notes for the upcoming podcast.

A couple of hours later, she'd finished cross-referencing her notes with as much fact checking as she could. She leaned against the kitchen sink while she gulped down a glass of water. Emerging from the fugue state she usually got in when writing always made her immensely thirsty. She vaguely remembered shoveling a handful of granola and yogurt into her mouth about halfway. She tried to check the time on her phone but it was missing. *Oh right, the nightstand.*

A couple of messages popped up from Gabe. She took a fortifying breath and unlocked her phone. He'd reacted to her text with a clapping emoji. Then, *still waiting on mine,* and a fingers-crossed emoji. Time-stamped an hour after that, a screenshot.

His PCR was negative.

His next message, which was sent half an hour ago, said, *Can I see you later? Call me.*

She hit the phone icon on her screen after taking a few deep breaths.

She could do this. It didn't have to be a big deal. Just two consenting adults making plans for the night.

"Hey," Gabe picked up on the second ring. Goosebumps rose on her arms from how intimate he sounded in her ear.

"I got your message," she said, trying for nonchalance.

"Good. What do you think? Still up for this?"

"Are you?" she cringed, hoping not to sound too eager.

There was a pause. Thea died several deaths in those agonizing seconds.

"If you're having second thoughts about this, it's okay," Gabe said.

"I'm not. I want this." *I want you.* Thea hoped she sounded more confident than she actually felt. She tried to shut down her scary pandemic thoughts. She could do this. They were both Covid-free, responsible adults. It was fine.

Gabe chuckled on the other end. Was he laughing at her? Then, with his voice pitched low, he said, "You have no idea how much I'm looking forward to this."

Thea felt every syllable, like a touch on her skin. She barely stopped herself from melting in a puddle on her kitchen's tiled floor. She was glad they were not FaceTiming because she was sure her face was bright red. She never was much of a blusher thanks to her darker complexion, something her *titas* kept trying to give her creams for, but it was like she couldn't control her body's reaction to Gabe. She said, "Me too" but it came out in an absurdly high-pitched voice.

Thea cleared her throat and tried again. "I'm looking forward to this, too."

"What time do you wanna meet?"

"How about nine?"

"How about earlier? I want plenty of time with you." Gabe's voice was a smokey promise.

Thea's insides were liquid. "Eight?"

"Your place? Mine?"

She chewed on the tip of her thumbnail. She never had men over. Her home was only for her. That and she didn't want to deal with the dance around getting them to leave afterward. "I can drive to yours."

He texted her his address.

"Got it. Should I... uh," she didn't know why she felt so nervous about this. She'd done this plenty of times. "Pick up something on the way? I mean... Do you have protection?"

"Don't worry about it. I'm prepared. I can't wait to see you tonight." His voice sent a shiver of pleasure shooting straight down her spine.

Thea made a sound of approval and hung up. She needed to jump into the cold shower before she spontaneously combusted.

NINETEEN

THEA STUDIED HER reflection in the driver-side window of her car. She tucked some stray hairs back into her usual bun. She'd put on a simple shift dress, basically a long t-shirt that stopped above her knees. They weren't going out anywhere, so she didn't feel the need to get super dressed up. What did one even wear for a pandemic hookup? Might as well call a spade a spade and dress for ease of undressing. Her reflection had the wide-eyed, eager look of someone about to be rocked.

She locked the car and walked up the path to the front door of Gabe's house. She checked the address twice before getting out of the car to ensure she was in the right place. She stood in front of a modest single-family home. The front yard, enclosed by a waist-high chain-link fence, exploded with wildflowers. Even in the weak light from the front porch, Thea could see different colored blooms clustered against the fence.

Closer to the porch of the house, there was some sort of green ground cover that felt soft under her sandals. On one side of the path to the front door were three Adirondack chairs clustered together, facing a round metal Saturn-shaped thing on four thin legs. Upon closer inspection,

Thea saw it was a small fire pit with its cover on.

After donning her mask and adjusting it to make sure it was on correctly, Thea walked up the steps to the porch and rang the doorbell. Through the door, she heard a resonating *ding-dong*. A few seconds later, the unmistakable sound of creaking of the wood floors told her someone was coming to the door. She took a deep breath and let it out through pursed lips, trying to calm her nerves.

Gabe opened the door, a small smile pulling at the corners of his lips. He wore a pair of jeans and a slightly fitted white t-shirt that hugged his arms. "I wasn't sure if you were really coming."

"How'd you know it was me?" Thea asked.

He cocked his head. "I don't get a lot of visitors at this time. I saw you through the speakeasy."

"The what?"

Gabe pointed to the tiny grate and door set at eye-level in his front door. "This peephole thing."

"That thing has a name? A speakeasy?" she tried out the word in her mouth. "I've just been calling those things the hidey-hole, but I know that doesn't make any sense because you're not actually hiding anything in it."

She laughed nervously to cut off her river of words. Now that she was standing at his front door, only a few feet away from him, she buzzed with energy. She'd never been so close to him without his mask before. At this distance, she could see the stubble on his jaw and each individual lash curling up from his eyes. She felt jittery at the proximity.

Gabe stepped aside to let her in. She toed off her shoes at the door, using her feet to push the shoes out of the doorway so he could close the door.

"Do you mind if I wash my hands?" She held up her hands and wiggled her fingers when he finished locking the door.

"Not at all. You can put your mask here." He pointed to an empty hook by the door.

Thea pulled off her mask and hung it on the hook. She followed him through the house to the bathroom off the hallway. She shut the door and turned on the faucet.

The bathroom was tidy and clean, which was both a surprise and a relief. Going into a man's bathroom sometimes revealed horrors she'd rather not think about before sleeping with him. Seeing this bathroom counter with no clutter, no stains and no towels on the floor made her feel conflicted. Who was this perfect man who actually had a clean bathroom? Maybe it would have been better if his bathroom had been in the same state as some other bathrooms she'd seen.

There had been that one guy with incredibly soft hair and a hard, gym rat's body. His bedroom was sparse, with only a platform bed and some milk crates as a nightstand, if she was being generous. There wasn't enough furniture in his bedroom to qualify as messy. But when she stepped into his bathroom and saw the pile of dirty clothes on one corner of the floor, the mildew in the shower, and the open tube of toothpaste on the sink, she wanted to escape out the window. She would have if the apartment hadn't been on the second floor.

Thea splashed some water on her face after seeing the flushed look of her cheeks and patted them dry with the hand towel. Her eyes gleamed with excitement. She was finally going to get some.

Thea wandered out of the bathroom and made her way to the living room. A vibrant red rug stood in the center with a couch on one side, a few armchairs on the other, all turned toward a modest flatscreen and bookshelf on the other wall. His home was inviting.

Gabe was fiddling with something by the bookshelf. When she got closer, she saw him pulling a match out of a box. He lit a candle and brought it to the mantle.

The candle cast an orange glow over the room. She couldn't read any of the spines of the books because the shelf was in shadow, but she could see from the creases in their spines that they were well-loved.

The flip-flopping feeling in her stomach surprised her. It wasn't like she was some inexperienced virgin. Far from it. She was proud of how direct she was in bed and the men usually enjoyed it as much as she did. She laced her fingers in front of her and squeezed them to quell the caffeinated butterflies.

"Nervous?" his face was serious, searching hers.

"It's just so weird being in someone else's house. Without a mask even." She peered up at him through her lashes.

"I know what you mean. We can go slow. Whatever you're comfortable with, okay? Do you want a tour of the house?"

Thea shook her head. Despite what she was here for, a tour of his house seemed too intimate, and she didn't want to know him like that. "No, thanks." She ran her fingers through her hair, brushing strays back from her face.

He didn't seem offended by that. "Come here." He held a hand out to her.

The urgency in his voice excited her. She placed her hand on his outstretched one. His strong fingers closed in on hers and tugged lightly, pulling her toward him.

She stepped close to him so that their toes were almost touching. This close, she had to tilt her head up to look into his eyes. His eyes reflected a dark orange from the flickering candlelight. That was surely why they felt like they were burning a hole through her. She felt flushed under his gaze. A brief panic rolled through her. *Was this Covid?*

He smelled faintly of soap and clean laundry on top of something else she couldn't quite put her finger on. She inhaled more deeply, noticing the slight dampness at the tips of his hair. He must have taken a shower before she got there. She wanted to lean in and get a better whiff of him, but didn't want to be a weirdo.

Gently, as though she might flee, he brought his hand up to cup her face, his thumb whispering over the corner of her mouth and smoothing over her cheeks. His touch held an undercurrent of electricity, leaving her skin humming everywhere it contacted.

Thea exhaled a breath she didn't realize she had been holding. She placed one hand, palm out, onto his chest and felt his muscles flexing in reaction to her touch. She unconsciously licked her bottom lip, and his gaze caught on her mouth.

When he brought his eyes up to hers again, they burned brighter, feverish, the blacks of his pupils swallowing the brown. He leaned down until his mouth was mere inches from her lips. Her heart hammered against her ribcage. She couldn't tell if she was impatient for the kiss, or petrified from the proximity to another person.

"Can I kiss you?" he whispered, his breath feathering across her lips and smelling of mint.

She would die if he didn't. She tipped her head up and brought her hand to the back of his neck, fingers in the soft curls of hair brushing his nape. She pulled him down toward her, closing the distance between their mouths. His lips were silky, an enjoyable contrast to the scratchy stubble on his jaw. She traced the hand that was on his chest higher, up his shoulders, up his neck, rubbing her palm against the fine sandpaper feeling of his jaw. Finally, she was touching him.

"Sorry," he said in a voice that dipped low. "I was planning to shave, but ran out of time. I can go shave now if it bothers you?"

"I like it," she purred, rubbing the side of her thumb along his jaw. A muscle twitched.

Gabe turned his head so he could plant a kiss on her open palm. His hands moved to her waist, pulling her closer before claiming her mouth again. Her legs felt wobbly, like they were about to melt into the rug, but it was okay. She pressed tightly against him, her breasts against his chest, her arms around his shoulders, his thigh between her legs. She should feel claustrophobic being so close to someone else when proximity to another person was so dangerous right now, but she wanted more. She wanted to climb on top of him.

Gabe deepened the kiss, opening his mouth to run his tongue along her bottom lip. She parted hers, tongue tentatively touching his at first, before he groaned and stroked it with his own.

Thea felt his hands sliding down past her waist. He cupped her ass, squeezing gently as he pulled her closer against him. She didn't need to wonder if he was enjoying this as much as she was, because she could feel how much he liked this through the thick denim of his jeans. She was practically pulsing between her legs.

She ran her hands down his broad shoulders to his arms, squeezing the satisfying feel of his biceps. Finally. She wanted to take her time exploring his body now that he was finally hers for the taking. When she softly pressed a spot on his arm, a muscle twitched and his whole body tensed.

"Ticklish," he said between kisses.

Gabe's lips trailed from her mouth. She would have protested if he hadn't been making a delicious path of kisses along her jaw to her ear. She could feel his breaths coming in little pants against her. He nipped her earlobe, and she made a yelping sound which turned into a moan when his tongue flicked out to lick it. His mouth then went down the side of her neck and she was pretty sure he could feel the rapid beating of her heart there.

Gabe breathed in her skin. "You smell so good."

She exhaled as his mouth moved lower. He licked the spot right at the base of her neck, above her collarbone, and she took a deep, shuddering breath at how sensitive she was there. She squeezed her thighs together, clamping his thigh between hers. She ran her fingers through his hair, a soft, tumbled mess now, but she didn't think he minded.

"You're so soft here," he whispered against her skin, pressing his lips to that tender spot.

"Gabe." His name came out more like a gasp than a word.

He pulled his head back and looked down at her. His hair was a sexy bedhead, his face flushed, and his eyes dilated, the huge black pupils eating up the color in them. He arched an eyebrow, as if in challenge. "Do you want me to stop?"

Thea was certain she would spontaneously combust if he stopped. She pressed her lips against the side of his throat, felt his pulse hammering under her tongue. This pandemic was showing her what a precious thing it was to be alive. She murmured, "show me your room."

His eyes never left her face, but his gaze darkened. "Are you sure? If we go in there, I don't think I'll be able to stop myself."

She flexed her hips, pressing against the hardness between them. "Don't stop."

"God, Thea," he breathed her name like a prayer and squeezed her hips. Without warning, his hands moved below her ass to the back of her thighs and he pulled her up so that her legs wrapped around him.

The angle pushed his hard-on right into where she wanted him. Thea moaned into his mouth as he kissed her thoroughly. She loved how he couldn't seem to stop touching her all over with his hands.

With her legs wrapped around him, Gabe stumbled out of the living room. They paused in the hallway, where he pressed her against the wall so that he could wrap his hands around her waist and kiss that spot at her throat that she liked. His lips moved lower, following the neckline of her dress, and she arched into him, needing to feel his mouth on her skin.

His hands moved higher, skimming her rib cage to the swell of her breasts. His thumbs rubbed the sensitive skin through her shirt, then he paused and pulled his head back so he could look at her.

"No bra?" he asked.

Thea shook her head, and he closed his eyes, leaning his forehead against hers. "You're killing me."

She loved that she affected him like that. She straightened her legs, sliding down the length of his body as her feet touched the floor again. She leaned back against the wall and moved her hands up Gabe's front, skirting over abs which twitched after her fleeting touch. He was very ticklish there.

She placed one hand on his shoulder and moved the other to his nape to pull him closer to her mouth. Even with her height, she hadn't realized how much taller he was until they stood toe to toe like this.

Gabe's hand was a branding iron on her hip, absently squeezing as his mouth moved over hers. His other hand skimmed the hem of her dress, pushing the fabric up so that he could palm the skin of her thigh.

It had been a while since she'd done this with anyone, but Thea couldn't remember ever feeling like this. She was burning, a fire roaring so loud inside of her. And they were still mostly clothed. Olivia was right: she needed a pandemic fuck buddy.

Abruptly, Gabe pulled back.

"Wha—"

He grabbed her hand in his and stepped away, pulling her with him. "Come on, if we're gonna do this, let's do it properly."

He led her through the open door to his bedroom. She stepped forward, looking at his bed in anticipation. He'd made it neatly, white sheets tucked in and all the wrinkles smoothed out. She pictured Gabe in here earlier dressing his bed, and the image was so endearing she couldn't stop the smile on her face. The click of the door being shut brought her back to what was about to happen.

She looked over her shoulder at Gabe, leaning against the closed door, arms crossed over his chest. Her eyes traveled down to the noticeable bulge in his pants. He was very happy to see her.

"You sure about this?" he asked again, his voice roughened by lust.

Thea couldn't tear her eyes away from the sharp shadows cast by the light of his lamp. For once, she was at a loss for words. She couldn't believe how much she wanted this. Him. She nodded enthusiastically.

Gabe moved faster than she'd expected. One second, he was by the door, the next, he was pressed against her back, arms wrapped around her waist as he nuzzled the back of her neck. She could smell the minty hint of soap or aftershave on him.

"Can you let down your hair?" he asked, his lips whispering against her skin.

She reached up and Gabe leaned away to avoid catching an elbow.

"Sorry," she said, pulling at the hair tie holding up her bun. Her hair slipped free and tumbled down her shoulders.

With a gentle hand, Gabe swept her hair across her shoulders and placed a kiss on the exposed skin, and then buried his nose in her hair, inhaling.

"Beautiful," he growled softly.

Thea turned around in his arms, pulling away enough to create distance between them so she could slip her hands down to the hem of his shirt. She stopped with her fingers dipped under it and looked up at him through her lashes. His eyes fixed on her mouth. She could feel his chest moving with each breath, could see the pulse in his neck. She arched an eyebrow in question and he answered by covering her lips with his. She smoothed her palms against the dips of his abs and felt them twitch under her fingers. His whole body had tensed up and he let out a laugh.

"Sorry," he said as he pulled his mouth away from hers. "That tickles."

"Hmm," she said, bunching the hem of his shirt in her hands and pulling it up.

Gabe helped her by lifting his arms so that she could pull the shirt over his head. It gave her a teaser of the curves and dips in the muscles of his shoulders. She tossed the garment behind her onto the bed. Then she turned around and took a good look at him. She was giddy with anticipation.

She hadn't wanted to stare the other day when he'd tortured her with his shirtless body. It had taken all her power to keep from touching him in her front yard. Tonight, she didn't need to hold back. They were in his room for one reason only and there was no harm in appreciating what was in front of her. The lamp cast shadows over his skin, adding more definition to the muscles of his abs, to those two lines of his hips pointing down to what interested her the most.

Not wanting to tickle him, she placed her hands firmly on his skin. She liked the way his body flexed under her hand, straining to get closer. She pulled Gabe's head down to meet hers, already missing his lips on hers. This time she was the one who tasted him, licking into his mouth, swallowing his moan as she trailed a hand down his chest, rubbing against his nipple. She marveled at the novelty of touching him and figuring out what made his pulse quicken.

"Take off your dress?" His voice came out hoarse, less of a question and more of a demand.

Thea leaned back and started tugging up her dress. Gabe helped her pull it over her head and threw it behind her to join his shirt. The air behind her felt cool now that she was practically naked, save for her panties, but she could feel the heat from Gabe's body radiating out. She looked up to catch him staring at her breasts and quirked a smile.

"Come here," he said roughly and slipped an arm around her, palm pressed against her back. His skin felt so hot on hers. Her naked skin rubbing against his sent jolts of pleasure coursing through her.

Gabe put his other hand against her jaw and tilted her face up so her lips met his. He traced his other hand against her side, squeezing her hip gently as he pulled her more firmly against him. He exhaled, his breath tickling against the side of her face.

They were barely getting started, but Thea's skin was already hypersensitive, as if a low level electric current surged through her body, primed for more.

Gabe nudged her forward with his body until the back of her legs hit the edge of his bed. She liked where this was going. She hooked one arm around the back of his neck and her lips curled up in a coy smile as she leaned back, letting gravity and her body weight do all the work.

They tumbled into the bed, Thea on her back and Gabe landing beside her, careful not to crush her. He propped his head up on one hand as he looked down at her. His eyes roamed down her body and she could practically feel his gaze like a touch. Naked desire lit his face.

"I'm up here," she said in a faux-sultry voice.

Gabe's eyes flicked up to meet hers, and he gave an impish grin. Looking her in the eye, he leaned over as if to kiss her mouth, but continued lower until his lips met her nipple.

Thea's body arched at the contact. His tongue was hot and firm against her. Her skin was already sensitive and feeling his tongue on her made her gasp.

Gabe looked up. "Okay?"

"No."

He stilled.

"More," she pleaded, grinding against him.

His hand palmed her other breast. His hands were infuriatingly gentle, making her want to press harder against him.

She hadn't realized that she had been gripping his shoulder with one hand until he moved lower and she let go, seeing her nails make crescents against his skin. He kissed between her breasts and the dip at the center of her rib cage. She liked the way the stubble on his cheeks scraped against her skin.

Gabe moved his hand lower, dragging it down to her waist, curved around her hip, met the top of her panties, and dipped lower, pushing the soaked fabric aside.

"Christ, you're so wet," he whispered as he kissed right above her belly button.

Thea spread her legs wider, and he needed no further encouragement as he pulled her panties to one side so he could stroke her with his fingers.

A soft sigh escaped from her mouth at the contact. It had been a long time since someone had touched her like that. She missed it. But it wasn't enough.

Gabe stopped and before she could even voice a protest, he'd hooked his fingers on either side of her panties and slid them off in one smooth motion. Damn, he was good.

Instead of returning to where she was desperate for his touch, he held the heel of her foot in one hand and slid the other one up her calf. The roughness of his hands felt heavenly against the smooth skin of her calf. He bent and placed a kiss on the side of her knee, and she let it fall open. Her legs were jelly.

Thea looked down with half-closed eyes and watched as he kissed a trail from her knee up to the inside of her thigh. By the heated expression on his face and the way he looked up at her, he knew precisely what he was doing to her. When he finally made it to the apex of her thighs, she shook with the need to feel him there.

Gabe had both hands on the inside of each thigh now. His palms were searing an imprint of his hands on her. His thumbs idly rubbed against her, just outside of where she wanted him to touch. A whimper escaped her mouth.

"I've been thinking about how you taste for a long time," he said in that deep, smoky voice. He pressed his hands against her, spreading her legs more, his eyes darting down to look at her.

Thea shifted up the bed, wanting to rub her thighs together. Anything to ease the ache there, but Gabe's hands were firm, holding her legs wide open.

"Please," she said, placing her hand over his.

As though she said the magic word, Gabe slid his hands around her hips to pull her toward him. She was surprised at how easily he did that, but the sensation of his mouth blew all other thoughts away as he bent down and kissed her. Her mind emptied as she arched into him.

Thea could no longer control the sounds coming out of her mouth. Gabe's clever tongue found exactly where she liked to be licked. He worked a gentle but unrelenting rhythm against her. When she thought she could take no more, he slipped a finger inside, making her clench at the sensation.

At some point, Thea had placed her hand on the top of his head. Her fingers clutched in the soft waves of his hair. Her other hand, thrown over her head, scrabbling at the pillow above her. She could feel the pressure building in waves inside of her, roiling with each flick of Gabe's tongue, each thrust of his finger.

When the waves crashed off the cliff, her entire body arched and would have been off the bed if Gabe had not clamped a firm hand over her hip, holding her down and against his mouth. When she finally came back to herself, she realized she was moving mindlessly against him still, chasing the shudders of pleasure.

He had calmed his pace to slow, tender licks and kisses against her soaked skin.

"That was..." Thea fought to catch her breath. "Wow."

She finally let go of the mangled pillowcase. She propped herself up, leaning on one elbow, and looked down at Gabe. His eyes were dark. He licked his lips. She'd seen hunger before, but never like this. She placed her other hand on his shoulder and pulled him up. He crept up her body, trailing wet kisses over her until he was face to face with her. She tasted herself on his lips and tongue.

Thea sat up and leaned into him, running her hands up and down his shoulders, his forearms, his thighs where his hands rested. She trailed her hands to the noticeable bulge straining against his jeans.

Gabe hissed in a breath as she gave an exploratory squeeze. She liked the sounds from his mouth and rubbed down the front of his jeans with her palm before stroking up again. Feeling him through the denim as she stroked her hand up had her quickening her breath. She wanted him.

As she moved her hand to ease him out of his jeans, Gabe gripped her wrist to stop her, his eyes clenched together. Between gritted teeth, he said, "Wait."

"Did I hurt you?" Thea asked.

"No," he huffed out what could have been an awkward laugh. When he opened his eyes and looked at her again, they were dark pools. "I don't want to embarrass myself by coming in my pants."

Thea ran her hands back up his arms, to his shoulders, to the muscles on his back. She pulled him toward her until her mouth met his stomach. She placed a kiss on the hard ridges of his abdomen and trailed a line of kisses from the muscle that started above his hip and arrowed down to where he strained against the fabric.

She smiled mischievously at him and popped the button of his fly open. "I can help you with that."

Gabe held his breath as Thea flicked open the top of his pants. He was heavy and aching exactly where her hands were venturing. Her clever fingers gripped the tab of his zipper. He felt every single tooth of the zipper being released. This was finally happening after so many nights of dreaming about her. He licked the heady taste of her still on his lips, and he knew it wasn't a dream.

Thea's hands were quick and insistent as she pulled off his pants, bunching his boxers. He shifted back in the bed to help her pull the pesky articles of clothing off all the way and returned to kneeling in front of her, his hands clenched at his sides.

The way her eyes widened as they traveled over his body, especially the hunger in her eyes as her gaze settled lower, sent a shiver through him. He closed his eyes and forced himself to take slow, deep breaths despite the incessant pulsing between his legs demanding attention.

His eyes flew open when he felt Thea's hands on him. She circled his length with her fingers and gave an experimental stroke down.

"Fuck." The word escaped before he could stop himself. He thrust against her hand. When she tipped her head toward him, he all but leaned into her.

Thea's lips were soft, her mouth hot and inviting. When she rubbed the tip of her tongue against the underside of his cock, he almost lost it. He'd lain awake countless nights imagining this moment, but having her mouth on him for real was so much better than anything he imagined.

He placed his hands on her shoulder and pushed her away gently even though his body begged for more.

She cast a heavy-lidded glance at him, a question on her lips.

His voiced sounded strained when he said, "We can finish that another time, but I just really, really, need to fuck you right now."

Thea's cheeks flushed at the filthy words coming out of his mouth, but her eyes shone. She leaned back onto her elbows, her heavenly lips quirked in a smile.

Gabe crept toward her, liking the way her body moved toward him as his mattress dipped with their combined weights. He kissed her mouth hungrily as his fingers moved through the wet curls between her legs. An answering throb pulsed between his legs, eager to be inside her.

Reluctantly, he pulled away to reach past her into the nightstand. There was a crinkling sound as he pulled out the condom. He tore open the package with his teeth and sat back to roll the condom onto his straining flesh. Thea's thick-lashed eyes landed on what was between his hands. Her tongue darted out and licked her bottom lip.

Gabe surged forward, nestling between her legs and propping his weight on his elbows above her. Thea wrapped her legs around his waist tightly, bringing her hips off the bed and rubbing against him. He gasped at the sensation as the blood rushed through his body, pooling where they would be joined. She was slick and ready.

A breathy moan came out of her mouth before he claimed her mouth with his. He moved his hips, sliding against her damp skin, and felt a groan deep in his throat. He did it again, loving the way her thighs clamped around him.

Thea broke their kiss and moved her lips to his ears. "Fuck me," she whispered right before she bit down hard on his earlobe.

It broke any thread of control he had left. Gabe pulled back so that only the tip pressed against her and surged forward. At first, he wasn't sure if the low, guttural moan had come out of his mouth or hers. It didn't matter because the sensation of being inside of her flooded him, taking up every corner of his mind. He wanted to pump hard and fast into her, but he didn't want this to be over so soon. He stilled, giving her time to adjust around him.

After half a beat, Thea rocked her hips against him in a motion that told him she was ready. He placed a steadying hand on her hip to still her as he pulled all the way out. He kissed her protest away and slid back in, inch by inch. From the way her hands were clutching at him, nails digging into his skin, and the sigh that escaped her lips, he was fairly certain she liked it.

He'd pictured this in multiple configurations every night, but nothing his mind conjured up prepared him for the way her legs squeezed tightly around his waist, urging him closer, or the soft gasps escaping her mouth as he thrust into her. Definitely not the way her lips seared across his skin, or the exquisite pricks of pain when she dug her nails into his shoulder.

Thea's rhythm changed, her breath coming in staccato pants. She was close. Despite holding off as long as he could, he was almost there himself. The telltale ache in his balls was all the warning he needed. He reached between their bodies, pressing his thumb against the spot his tongue had caressed earlier, right above where the two of them were joined.

He was rewarded by a sweet moan as Thea flexed her hips so that she ground against his hand. He gave her what she needed, moving in time with his quickening thrusts. When he thought he wouldn't be able to hold back much longer, Thea pressed against him, her mouth on the sensitive spot where his neck met his shoulder, biting hard as a strained whimper escaped her, clenching around him.

Her orgasm pulled his forward and he finally let go of what shred of control he still had. He placed both arms on either side of her head, above her shoulders, anchoring her to the bed as he pumped into her with each shuddering wave that overtook his body.

When he at last emptied himself, he managed not to crush Thea by collapsing beside her. He put an arm around her waist and pulled her toward him as he rolled onto his back. The blood pounding in his ears was so loud that he almost didn't hear her satisfied sigh as she stretched out over him.

Thea draped her leg over his. A fierce, possessive feeling blanketed him.

He ran his hand along the outside of her thigh, absently rubbing it up and down as he caught his breath. Her hand splayed over his chest and he was sure she could feel how fast his heart hammered. "Was that okay?" he asked. His voice sounded raw.

Thea moved her head to look up at him through those thick lashes of hers and it took him a few seconds to realize the shaking of her body was her stifling a laugh. She turned her head into his shoulder.

"Yes," she mumbled against his skin. "More than okay, if you couldn't tell."

He relaxed. He'd worried he'd been too rough. When she turned her head again, her face was flushed, her skin dewy with sweat. His chest tightened at how beautiful she was in this moment. He curled his arm, hugging her tight and placed a kiss on her forehead.

"More than okay for me too," he said against her hair. He had broken apart and come back together again. He kept that part to himself.

Thea pulled back and peered at him, as if she could read what he was thinking by looking at his face. He was glad she couldn't. He couldn't give away this blooming feeling resonating in his chest. Whatever she saw on his face must have been okay, because she gave a satisfied smile before leaning forward and planting a soft kiss on his mouth.

Before he could take it further, she pulled away. "Can I use your bathroom?"

Gabe pointed to the half-open door. "Clean towels on the shelf behind the door. Take your time. I'm gonna use the other bathroom."

He watched as Thea stood up, stark naked, gave a cat-like full-body stretch, and walked to the bathroom. Seeing her so comfortable in her own skin like that was so hot, he couldn't wait for round two or three.

Thea shut the door behind her. The bathroom by Gabe's bedroom had that delectable, minty smell with a hint of something familiar she still couldn't pinpoint. She washed her hands and dried them off on the fluffy white hand towel hanging by the sink. It was silly to be impressed by a grown man having a hand towel. She thought about how many times she'd been in a guy's apartment and had to use whatever was hanging on the towel rack — often a bath towel. Sometimes there were no towels hanging at all.

In the mirror she saw a woman who had recently gotten rocked, messy hair and all. She combed her fingers through her hair so it looked less wild. She was glad she opted out of lipstick because it would have been a smear by now.

After taking another sniff of the clean towels, to verify that they actually did smell as good up close as from afar (they did), she took one last look in the mirror.

Gabe had just stepped through the bedroom door and shut it behind him. As soon as he spotted her, he froze in his tracks with a goofy grin on his face. She couldn't quite put her finger on why his expression was so endearing.

She sauntered over to his bed, liking the way his eyes followed her. They'd made a mess of the neatly made sheets he prepared earlier. Her dress was a wrinkled, flattened heap next to his shirt. She lifted the black dress up to her nose and gave it a sniff. It smelled like sweat and sex.

Gabe moved forward, about to pull the dress out of her hands. "I can throw it in the washer for you. It'll be clean and dry in the morning."

Thea startled, dropping the dress in surprise. "Oh," her eyebrows knit into a frown, "I wasn't planning on staying."

"You weren't?" he asked, his mouth forming a pout. "You can, you know."

"I haven't slept over at a man's place for years." Thea pursed her lips.

She slept better in her own bed, by herself. And it would be less awkward in the morning, even though it was plenty awkward in this moment.

Gabe looked surprised. Something flickered in his eyes, then disappeared. "Oh."

"Yeah, I should probably go." She held her hand out for the dress in his hand.

He handed it to her, wincing at how wrinkled it was. There was a particularly incriminating wet spot right on the shoulder. "Do you want to borrow something to wear home? I have some clean shirts that might fit you."

Thea glanced at the clock on his wall. It was late. No one should be around for her walk of shame. "Sure, if you don't mind."

Gabe opened his closet. Clothes hung neatly on hangers. They even seemed to be color coded, with dark colors on one side, light colors on the other.

"Wow," Thea said. "This is quite the organized closet. Are you like a serial killer or something?"

He flashed her a grin. "Makes it easy to find stuff."

He pulled out a plain black t-shirt. In his hand, it looked like her wrinkled black dress, minus the wrinkles. She took it from him and slipped it over her head, giving it a surreptitious sniff. It smelled like detergent, but also like him. The shirt was well worn, so the fabric was soft and clung to her curves. It was long enough to cover all the important bits, which was good enough for her.

"Thanks, this is perfect," she said, stopping him from pulling out anything else.

Gabe had a pair of athletic shorts in his hand that looked way too big for her. "Oh good, because I don't think these are gonna fit you, even if you do the drawstring all the way up."

Thea laughed and waved it away. "I'm just gonna head straight home, so I think this is okay, right? You can't see my ass, right?"

Gabe looked her up and down, lingering on her legs. He drew his eyes up to meet hers. She felt cherished in the intensity of his gaze. His voice was low when he said, "No, you're fine."

She walked over to him and placed her hands on his shoulder, leaning into him for a kiss. She'd planned on a quick peck on the mouth, but Gabe wrapped an arm around her waist and held her tightly to him as he gave her a smoldering, longer kiss. When she pulled away, her pulse pounding in her ears, she knew she needed to leave or the temptation to spend the night would be too much, even for her.

After gathering up the rest of her things, Thea headed to the front door. She pulled it open and took a deep breath in the cool night. The crisp air helped clear her head from the effects of Gabe's kiss. She turned around to say her goodbye but was struck dumb by sight in front of her. Gabe was gripping the top of the doorframe above his head with both hands. It was a casual pose, but his arms and naked chest distracted her from her thoughts. He'd changed into navy blue cotton pajama bottoms that hung low on his hips. The porch light cast shadows over him that highlighted the dips and crevices she had run her hands all over that evening. The taut skin on his abs made her ravenous for more even after she'd been thoroughly satiated.

"Goodnight," she croaked.

A grin spread over his face, making that dimple on his cheek appear. He held onto the doorframe as he leaned in toward her, the movement making the flex of his muscles even more delicious. "This was fun. I'd love to do it again."

As he dipped his head to hers, Thea had a moment of panic, thinking that she wouldn't have enough willpower to leave after one of those searing kisses of his. To her relief, he gave her a quick, chaste peck on her cheek.

To cover her reaction, she called over her shoulder as she left his steps, "Sure. Just don't fall in love with me, okay?"

The sound of his laughter made her float to her car. He said after her, "Text me when you get back so I know you made it home safely?"

Thea gave him a thumbs up. Once she was seated behind the wheel, she looked over at his porch, where he was still standing. She gave a wave. Gabe waved back before closing the door and turning off the porch light. She let go of the breath she'd been holding.

She drove the entire way home, replaying the night. She thought that once she slaked her thirst, her head would be clear, and she'd be able to view this from a better perspective. Just two consenting adults taking care of their physical needs. Nothing more. Her body still hummed with pleasure, but doubts started creeping in. Was she making a big mistake? Would she be able to stop this when the time came?

TWENTY

THE UNUSUAL VOLUME and frequency of the birds chirping outside her window let Thea know she had slept in later than normal. Typically, she woke at eight, when only a few birds were chirping. Now there was a full cacophony of birdsong. She glanced at the clock beside her bed, blurry without her glasses: 10:23.

Thea sat up and stretched her arms above her head, relishing the way her back cracked. She was still wearing Gabe's shirt from last night. She pulled the neck of the shirt to her nose and inhaled. Yup, still smelled good. Minty and that faint, warm smell of his skin. The scent reminded her of being outside on a hot summer day in LA. That extra note in the fragrance was more familiar now. She breathed it in... wood! It smelled like being surrounded by trees.

Her blood coursed through her when she thought about what had happened last night. She almost regretted not staying the night. Almost, but not quite. She hated morning afters. The harsh sunlight usually brought a jarring dose of reality to one-night stands.

At night, it was easier to ignore all the messy and personal things that told her more about the guys she slept with: bikes on living room walls, questionable books on shelves, food on kitchen counters, unwashed clothes piled in the corner. Mornings were when those things didn't seem as minor anymore. She preferred waking up in her own bed, in her own room, with her carefully curated clutter.

That was what was so jarring about seeing Gabe's house. It wasn't empty and minimalist, which she usually found creepy and off-putting. What she saw of his place felt neat and cozy without being cluttered. Maybe he cleaned before she got there. She couldn't help feeling flattered that he was trying to impress her.

An email was waiting for her when she opened her laptop. It was her agent asking about an update on her manuscript. Thea guiltily closed the browser tab and opened up her word processor. She would work the next two hours on it before rewarding herself with lunch, reheated leftovers, then do another two hours before replying to the email. By then, she could have a genuinely substantial update for her agent.

A few hours later, Thea stood up from the table and stretched. She checked the word count in her word processor. Not bad. She got more done than she expected. It was always like that for her. Sometimes, it would take hours to type only 200 words. Other times, the words flowed out of her like water from a faucet. Although she was tempted to return to what she'd already written and re-read it, she forced herself to step away from the computer. She needed to shut off the editing part of her mind if she was going to get this manuscript done on time. She couldn't get caught up in the re-write cycle this time.

Thea shut her laptop so she wouldn't be seduced into an endless cycle of re-reading and editing. Instead, she checked off the item in her bullet journal. She flipped to the section where she kept a rough outline of her manuscript and made more notes.

A message from Gabe was waiting for her when she went to her bedroom. She slid open the notification and peeked at the text with some trepidation. She hated morning after texts as much as she hated morning afters.

Gabe: *Last night was A+++! Would do again!!*

A laugh bubbled out. She knew this wouldn't have worked if he was one of those guys who took things too seriously. She wondered how she should reply. She needed to keep it light and funny, like what he wrote. Definitely not something thirsty, even though that's exactly where she was right now. She couldn't help it. She'd been lusting after Gabe since she'd met him, even if she didn't want to admit it to herself at the time. She had hoped experiencing the real thing would give her mind and body some respite, but instead, she only wanted more.

Thea checked her calendar on her phone. She'd already scheduled a delivery of a special dinner from a local chef on Instagram tonight. She needed to write about it for next week's restaurant review column, so she needed the night to herself to set up for photos and write notes.

Thea: *Tomorrow night?*

She'd started typing out more, explaining why tonight didn't work, but deleted it. She didn't owe anyone, definitely not her pandemic friend with benefits, an explanation.

Gabe: *Can't wait. Your place or mine?*

Thea: *Yours @ 9?*

She hadn't had a man over at her place for... she stopped to think. Never. She loved living alone. No need to negotiate about different levels of cleanliness, or who loaded the dishwasher wrong. Olivia asked her from time to time if she ever got lonely, but she liked being able to do whatever she wanted whenever she wanted.

It also supported her idea of how a writer's home should be: books strewn all over the place, multiple stacks of paper in each room, lots of pens whose caps were lost to the ages. Could it be neater? Sure, but the mess worked for her.

A writer's life wasn't without its stresses thanks to money, or lack of, and an unpredictable schedule, but she was lucky to have saved enough of a buffer from her last non-writing job to not have to check every morning if she had enough money to pay rent. For now, at least.

Gabe: *<thumbs up>*

The night before, she had needlessly worried that he would think it was weird she didn't want him over at her place. She was the one who suggested this arrangement in the first place, and it wasn't like he didn't already know where she lived. But he seemed to take it in stride. Another check in his favor — not that she was keeping count or anything.

Thea returned the phone to her bedroom. She would still see Gabe tonight because he was delivering her food. She resolved to try her hardest to play it cool. She wasn't going to let the incredible night before distract her from her working relationship with him.

When she returned to her office, she was right on time to dial into the weekly editorial meeting. She wasn't sure why Ray bothered to turn the video on, because he was hard to see in shadow against dusty Venetian blinds. It made him look like he was in one of those interviews with someone in the witness protection program. At least the awful lighting made it impossible for her to see his disapproving glare.

After the other reporters gave their status reports on pieces they were working on, it was Thea's turn. She was relieved to be done with the two features Ray strongly recommended she write during the last meeting. Next on her list was a longer article following the career of an LA sushi chef as she navigated male-dominated kitchens before opening up her own very successful restaurant.

"Put that one on the back burner," Ray interrupted her. "I have something else coming up for you."

"You do?"

"Next Sunday's issue is gonna be about the George Floyd protests, so you need to write a review of a Black-owned restaurant."

"Oh!" For once, Ray's suggestion was good. "What about that vegan comfort food place in Crenshaw?" She didn't remind him that he'd told her it was too niche to write about the first time she mentioned it.

"Too weird."

Thea schooled her features into a neutral face. She flipped through her mental Rolodex of restaurants to something that Ray would approve of. "What about—"

"Do one of those spicy fried chicken places."

"Nashville hot chicken? Okay, I can think of a few places."

"Good girl. Get me a draft on Wednesday."

Luckily, she was too busy jotting down ideas for the round-up to roll her eyes at Ray.

TWENTY-ONE

GABE TAPPED HIS steering wheel in rhythm with the music coming out of his radio. He'd hit a bit of traffic on the way back from Santa Monica, so he hoped the food wouldn't suffer from the long drive. He was always on edge at the start of new relationships. It wasn't a sensation he enjoyed, which was partly why he'd stopped dating after his last real girlfriend. Thea had assured him that this was only casual sex and not a real relationship, but he still felt nervous when he pulled up to her house. She sounded normal when they'd texted earlier that day, so he decided to act normal too, not like a messy tangle of nerves.

Thea opened her front door at the banging of the wooden gate shutting behind him.

"Hello. Traffic?" She asked, taking the bags off his hands.

"Yeah. Always at that one spot on the 10."

When he came back from washing his hands, he found Thea crouched on the porch with a cream-colored tablecloth spread out on the floor. On it were various dishes and bowls filled with food. He stood on the first step of the porch, watching her work.

"Don't stand there." She waved at him absently as she arranged and then rearranged the plates. "You're casting a shadow on my shot. Come up and stand here."

"Sorry," he said, moving to where she instructed. This demanding version of her sent a thrill through his body.

He watched as she stood, looking down at the collection of food on the floor. He enjoyed watching her do her work with such confidence. Satisfied, she went back into the house and returned with a stepladder in one hand and a heavy duty camera in the other.

Thea placed the stepladder next to the tablecloth, making sure not to bump the fabric or cause any wrinkles. She then climbed up to the top of the ladder and leaned precariously over it with her camera pointed down at the food.

Not wanting to startle her off-balance, he kept silent as the shutter of her camera clicked away. After a few more positional adjustments of the ladder and twenty shots later, Thea folded it up, leaning it against the railing of the porch, and put the lens cap back on her camera.

"I always wondered how they did those overhead shots," Gabe said. On set, they had camera cranes and all sorts of hardware, but he didn't expect someone to lug the same type of setup out to restaurants.

Thea looked up at him in surprise, then blinked it away. "You were so quiet I forgot you were here. I think *real* food photographers have a stand setup for flat lays. I just use the ladder and put stuff on the floor."

"Clever."

"Yeah, it works if I want the backdrop to be a tablecloth, since viewers can't tell it's on the floor that way. But it's harder if I want to take a flat lay of an undressed table. My dining table's too high to get the right angle, and the light's just better out on the porch for these types of shots," Thea explained as she collapsed the photo reflector into a hand-sized disc.

"Can I help clean up?" Gabe asked, gesturing to the stuff still on the ground.

Thea looked down at the food for a second, then walked through her front door.

Not getting an answer, Gabe didn't know whether to follow her.

They'd had plenty of dinners on her porch by now, but she'd never explicitly invited him into her house, so he'd never stepped past the threshold. He figured it was one of those mysterious rules she had, like never staying over at his house.

Thea emerged, carrying the folding table they usually used on the porch. She handed it to him and he unfolded it on the free side of the porch. She grabbed two plates of food and walked through the front door.

"I'm just gonna nuke these for a few minutes," she shouted through the open window.

"Hope you like upscale Jewish mom food," Thea said as they finally sat down at their places across the square table from each other.

"Is this what this place serves?" Gabe asked. "I looked at the menu before, when they first opened, but it all looked like—"

"White people comfort food?" Thea supplied.

Gabe laughed. "Exactly."

He served her some variation of mac and cheese before spooning a portion onto his plate. Instead of the usual elbow-shaped macaroni, the pasta was shaped like screws. The lightness of the dish surprised him.

"What's this?" He asked, pointing to one dish that Thea hadn't warmed up. She'd said warming it might make it soggy. It was battered and deep fried, but he couldn't quite make out what was beneath the batter.

"Tempura mushrooms, I think." Thea speared one onto her fork and stuffed it into her mouth. "Yep, mushrooms. Oh nice, they're still crunchy too. Try one."

She stabbed another one and held her fork out to him.

He recoiled. "I'm not really into mushrooms."

"What?!" Thea exclaimed, her eyes widening and her lips forming a perfect O. "Who doesn't like mushrooms?"

"Lots of people! I just don't like how they're slimy and squeaky," Gabe said, shuddering.

Thea's brows drew together in a frown. She offered him the bite at the end of the fork again. "This one isn't slimy or squeaky, I promise. Just try a bite."

People had tried to get him to like them before, so he was skeptical. She looked so eager. He wanted to please her. Gabe opened his mouth. Looking at Thea's mouth, the tip of her tongue peeking out as she put the fork in his mouth was almost too much. It wasn't like she was even using her fingers. A pang of lust shot straight down his spine. He was so distracted by it he hadn't realized he was actually eating a mushroom and enjoying it until he had swallowed.

Thea looked at him expectantly.

"It's good." Gabe was shocked. He picked up another mushroom and popped it into his mouth. The light and crunchy batter helped the texture of the mushroom immensely, but the actual mushroom part was savory, nutty, and she was right! Not squeaky at all.

"Okay, now try it with this sauce." Thea's eyes sparkled. Her excitement was contagious.

As they enjoyed the rest of the food together, Gabe felt more and more at ease. He was silly to have been so nervous about seeing her today. Their easy banter continued like usual. Nothing had changed. He only had to convince himself of that.

TWENTY-TWO

GABE SHUT ALL the windows in his house, even the large one above the kitchen sink that he always left open for a cross breeze. It was late July, that time of year where Southern California was on fire again. Not the whole state, but bits and pieces of it. The sky was a burnt sienna wash of color, where the sun touched the horizon. Entire cities were coated in a fine layer of ash.

He turned on the air purifier, something he'd gotten when Adrian was still living there. His roommate's asthma, which worsened whenever there was a fire nearby, improved since they'd gotten the compact square unit. The air in his house smelled less smoky after only ten minutes. Either that or he was getting used to the campfire smell.

An uncomfortable energy pulsated under his skin. At first, he wasn't sure what was wrong, but as he sat with the unpleasant feeling, he realized what it was. He was nervous about Thea coming over. As that realization dawned on him, he shook his head at how silly it was. She'd been to his house before, decidedly doing more intimate things than having takeout with him. They'd been sleeping together for weeks.

Gabe unpacked several containers from the counter, moving the food onto real dishes. He put the menudo in a pot on the stove to simmer. Another thing the had in common: they both hated when soup wasn't served piping hot.

He'd finished putting out plates and utensils when the doorbell rang. *I should give Thea a spare key.* She was regularly coming over once a week, and this would make it more convenient.

"Thanks for doing all this." Thea followed him into the dining room carrying a 4-pack of beer, condensation clinging to the cans.

"I figured with the fires and everything." Gabe took the beer from her and put two in the fridge. While it would have been cool to eat outside with the sky glowing an ominous red, it was out of the question because of how much ash was falling. He'd invited her over to his house for takeout for a change. That and she still hadn't ever invited him *into* her house.

"Can I help with anything?" Thea asked.

Gabe looked around her. She put her purse on one end of his couch when she came in and other than beer, she had nothing else on her.

"I didn't bring my camera," Thea explained. "Already took notes and pictures for this place. I was just really craving their menudo."

"I'm almost done reheating stuff, so why don't you sit down and make yourself at home?"

When he returned, carrying two bowls of soup and a ceramic tortilla crock balanced on his arm, Thea rushed to help him. She took the bowl from him and set it down at one of the place settings. He set down the crock and ducked back into the kitchen to grab the rest of the food.

"This table's so cool," Thea said, running her hands along the grain of the wood. "I've never seen one like it before."

"Thanks, I built it." Gabe said with pride in his voice.

It was one of the first things he built for this house. The tabletop was a solid piece of wood with a subtle grain around a dark knot. He'd designed the legs to be as unobtrusive as possible, disappearing under the tabletop so that unless you looked under the table, it looked like the surface floated. He hated sitting at tables where he was constantly bumping his shin into the legs. It took a few tries, but he'd figured out the perfect placement of them to provide structural support so that nothing could tip the table over, but also so that there would be no bruised shins.

"Whoa," Thea said, running her hands along the edge of the table and looking under it. His eyes caught on the way her fingers lingered on the grain of the wood. "Beautiful craftsmanship."

Gabe colored at the compliment. She had a way of making him feel like what he did was actually meaningful. "Let's eat?"

They sat near one corner of the table. Thea opened both cans of beer and poured the foamy beverage into glasses he'd brought out. One of them had a logo of a show he'd worked on. Thea looked at them curiously.

"Just some swag they were giving out at the end of filming," he said.

Thea sipped at the soup, and a contented moan came out of her mouth. His eyes darted to her mouth, feeling the sudden urge to kiss her. Her eyes were closed and the corners of her lips turned up. She opened her eyes and met his hungry gaze. Her cheeks colored.

"Sorry," she said, "I was just really, really, looking forward to this."

Not trusting his voice, Gabe passed the tortilla warmer to her.

"Aw, this is so cute," she said, taking the heavy flat cylinder. He had borrowed the ceramic crock with matching brown glazed lid from his parents and conveniently forgot to bring it back. They accumulated quite a few through the years, so they hadn't missed it.

Thea took a warm tortilla and tore a piece off, eating it directly. "Their tortillas are so fluffy and full of flavor. Oh man, I need to get one of these things. It's still hot!"

Gabe tore off a piece of his tortilla and dipped it into the hot soup, grabbing a piece of lamb. When he popped it into his mouth, he couldn't believe the tender texture of the meat. The broth for the menudo was bright with lime and herbs and had a deep undercurrent of something he couldn't quite name.

"Whoa," he said.

"I know, right?" Thea said, with awe in her voice. "Not too spicy?"

He shook his head. It was on the cusp of being too spicy for him, but it was worth it for the amazing flavor of the broth.

Gabe tapped out a little after Thea did. They worked together to pack leftovers away into containers. Cleanup mostly done, they stood in his kitchen. Gabe took a sip of his second beer. They were in such a domestic scene that he couldn't help imagining this happening every night. His heart swelled at the thought.

Thea had her back to him as she looked around his kitchen. Her hair was up, but tendrils escaped from their bun and brushed her nape. He was very aware of how much he wanted to put his mouth there.

"You have so many... kitchen things." She sounded impressed. She pointed to the dining room. "You even have dining room furniture! *Real* dining room furniture."

Gabe finished drying the pot he had reheated the menudo in and wiped his hands on a dish towel. He crossed his arms and leaned on the counter, amused at her tone.

"I *am* an adult. Why wouldn't I?" He liked the way her cheeks flushed that irresistible shade of pink when he looked at her like that.

"I know. Maybe I've just been meeting the wrong men. Most of them don't—" Thea yelped as he reached for her hand and pulled her to him.

"I don't want to hear about other men," he grumbled as he wrapped his hands around her waist and buried his nose in her hair. Even though he knew she'd been with other men before, he only wanted to think of her being with him from now on.

Her body melted against his as she rested her hands on his shoulders. Her hair smelled smokey from the fires, but still had that herbal scent that he was starting to crave. Lips skimmed up the side of his neck and his body responded immediately. He needed to feel her bare skin against his. He wanted to have this every day.

"I'll make you forget about them," he promised her as he slipped a hand under her jaw, angling her face and crushing her lips with his.

TWENTY-THREE

JULY MELTED INTO August and the days passed in much the same pattern. Thea spent her days writing or recording the weekly radio show, stopping only to eat leftovers, or order food. If she ordered from a place for work, she took notes and photographed while she ate. Then, if she wasn't at Gabe's, she returned to writing. She thrived in the comfort of a consistent schedule. Her weekly check-ins with Ray were still a pain because of how much she had to hold her tongue, but he seemed to be preoccupied with something else and mostly left her alone to work off her list of restaurants.

Every morning, during her strictly allotted Go Into A Rabbit Hole Time, Thea checked the Covid dashboards she'd bookmarked. If she had told her past self that part of her morning routine would be checking a poop graph for community virus numbers, her past self would have thought she'd gone off the deep end. That downhill slope of the line also corresponded to her level of anxiety.

That evening, Thea was outside pulling the weeds out of her garden bed, when she heard Gabe's truck pull up. She figured they'd have dinner on her porch like any other night he delivered her food.

She waved the clump of weeds and soil at Gabe as he walked up the path to her. "Hey, can you put those on the porch? I'm almost done here."

Thea willed herself not to, but her eyes still drifted over to him as he bent over the porch steps to settle the bags. She thought the novelty of his body would have worn off by now, but her response was now stronger, like her own body was fine tuned to crave being near him. She returned to her weeding when he turned around.

He stopped at where she was still plucking out some unknown seedlings, probably weeds. "Can we talk—"

"Uh sure, what's up?" She felt uneasy about how serious he looked. She wiped her hands off on the bandana tucked into the back pocket of her overalls.

"I got a call from work. They're planning on finishing out this season. They want us all to come in next Tuesday."

"Oh." This was a blow she hadn't expected. Intellectually, she knew that there was an end date to what they'd been doing, but she'd tied it to the pandemic, which had no actual end date in sight.

Gabe was still talking. "—so I'm gonna be out of town for three or four weeks. Depends on how smoothly things go."

"Okay," Thea responded automatically.

"Are you gonna be okay without me?" Gabe asked.

Thea was taken aback. Of course, she would be okay. She'd been okay without him for 29 years of her life, so for him to assume that she wouldn't be okay now was ridiculous. "Yeah, I'll be fine." It sounded convincing enough to her.

"What are you gonna do about the food thing?"

"I'll just do it myself." She knew she was being defensive, but she couldn't stop the words tumbling out of her mouth. "I was planning on doing the pickups eventually, anyway. It'll be easier for me to do the interviews for my book face to face."

"Are you sure?" Gabe's concern should have been poignant, but she was busy feeling peeved that he didn't think she was capable of doing it.

"Yes, don't worry! Let me go wash off and we can set up dinner." She used the excuse to escape and collect her thoughts.

In the bathroom, Thea splashed water onto her face and rubbed the dirt off of her fingers. The cold water gave her some clarity. She was irritated that she'd grown used to Gabe being around. It wasn't like he was going to be around forever. She'd forgotten the boundaries she'd set up in the beginning. This was good. It was a reminder that he was only temporary. He'd go back to his job, and she would go back to hers. They would be adult about it.

After Thea returned to her porch, she went through the motions of setting up the card table, unrolling the yellow hibiscus oilcloth she'd been planning to use for the photos. At the last minute, she changed her mind about moving the food from the takeout containers into the ceramic bowls and dishes she'd planned on using. Instead, she arranged them neatly in their takeout containers. She wanted to remind her readers that yes, there was still a pandemic going on and yes, takeout could still be delicious.

She put the camera equipment away. When she returned, she saw that Gabe pulled over the folding chairs and set their usual places across the small table from each other. The sun was low, the light that peeked through the canopy of the trees bathing the porch in a dreamy golden hue.

Thea sat down and looked up at Gabe, who seemed to study her. All the distance she tried to put between them vanished when he looked at her like that. Her heart swelled in a way she didn't want to think about.

"You okay?" He asked.

"Yeah, just thinking about logistics." It wasn't technically a lie.

"Sorry about springing it on you like that."

"It's okay." She served him some food out of a cooling tub of stew to avoid looking at him.

"Are *we* okay?" He dipped his head so he could meet her eyes.

She concentrated on the slash of his brows. "Yeah, we're fine."

"You sure?"

"Yes! Eat." She plopped the scoop of rice harder than she'd intended onto his plate.

Heavy silence and stilted attempts at conversation filled the rest of the dinner. Thea tried to take mental notes of the food, but her appetite was gone and her heart wasn't in it. She looked down at her plate, where she'd been pushing the rest of her meal around and around. She finally put down her fork and gave up.

Gabe started helping her pack up the rest of the food. They cleaned up the table, moving past each other with a familiar rhythm. When she put everything away in her kitchen, Thea returned to where Gabe leaned on the handrail of the porch steps.

Thea stopped in front of him, a step up so she could be eye to eye with him. "I guess we won't be seeing much of each other?" She fiddled with a twisted section of the vine creeping along the post.

Gabe folded his arms, a frown drawing his eyebrows together. "Is that what's bothering you?"

"I dunno." She didn't like beating around the bush and she owed it to both of them to be mature about it. "I didn't know if you wanted to continue this after," she gestured vaguely in the space between. This close to him, she could smell his woodsy scent and felt the heat of his body. She wanted to press her nose into the side of his throat and save that smell for later.

"Do you?" He raised an eyebrow, daring her to answer.

Thea nodded despite the little voice inside of her saying it would be easier to end this now. "Only if you want to." She wanted to. She bit down on her lip to keep the rest from spilling out.

His gaze darkened as his eyes caught on her mouth.

Thea's body shifted toward him, drawn in by the change in atmosphere.

Gabe's voice was serious. "I don't want this to end."

"Me neither."

Gabe reached for Thea's hand. When his fingers touched hers, she exhaled. He tugged on her, pulling her toward him until there was no space between them. Despite all the many ways they shared each other's bodies, something about standing this close to him in the twilight made her uncharacteristically shy. She didn't want him to know how relieved she was that they could keep doing this.

Gabe brought his hand to the back of her neck, brushing the spot between her jaw and ear, tilting her face up toward him. His breath was a soothing touch on her skin. "We good?"

Thea licked her lips, anticipating what was coming.

Gabe's eyes followed the tiny flick of her tongue. His mouth crushed hers, all warm lips and tender kisses. Being this close to him blasted all of her spiraling doubts away. They were nothing next to the concrete feeling of him right in front of her. She loved the way his mouth lingered on hers, like he couldn't bear to not have his mouth on hers, like they had all the time in the world just for kissing.

Thea placed a hand on his chest, feeling the steady thudding of his heartbeat beneath her palm. Her other hand clutched at his shoulder, pulling him closer. It wasn't enough. She didn't want him to leave. She opened her mouth to nip at his bottom lip. His hand gripped her waist, holding her tight against his body, all tense muscles and hardness.

After too short of a time, Thea placed both hands on his chest, pushing him away. They stood a few inches apart. His breath was rough as his eyes raked over her face.

She knew if she let this go on longer, she would pull him up the steps, into her house. It was tempting. She looked up into his face, pleased that he looked as affected by the kiss as she was.

He must have read some of the hesitation in her eyes because he took a step down, then another. He ran his hands through his hair and took a shaky breath, seemingly more in control of himself than she was of her own reactions.

A banging noise across the street made them both turn toward the sound. It was her neighbor's screen door shutting.

"Ahem." The woman across the street, wearing head to toe mint green, coughed loudly as she let the door go. She looked over at Thea with her eyebrows raised in a disapproving way. She made sure Thea saw her before continuing down her own porch steps to the sidewalk.

"Hi Kathy." Thea gave her a red-faced wave. Her curious neighbor's mouth pulled down into a frown.

Thea wasn't sure what Kathy did all day, other than keep tabs on the neighborhood. She always seemed to pop up at the most inconvenient of times.

Kathy power-walked across the street and stopped on the sidewalk in front of Thea's house. Her gait brought a pronounced bounce to her ample breast. Her mouth was a glossy pink smile. "Hello there. Gabriel, right?"

"Gabe."

"Mmm-hmm, I remember you." Kathy drawled out. Her lips were a flawless pout. Maybe she was a makeup model. She always seemed to have a full face of makeup on. One perfectly plucked eyebrow rose as she continued to look at him. "I've been seeing a lot of you. It's cute of you two to dine *alfresco*. Are you a regular overnight guest?"

"Uh..." Gabe looked over at Thea for help.

"I'm just asking because there are overnight parking restrictions here. I wouldn't want you to get a ticket on that big truck of yours." Kathy continued, unconvincingly.

Thea did not like the way she said *truck*. "Were you on your way somewhere?" She cut in, hoping Kathy would take the hint.

The older woman's eyes darted to hers, not bothering to hide her annoyance. Hint taken. "Yes, I was just going to take my evening walk." Kate stretched her arms over her head and arched her back.

"Please, don't let us keep you," Thea grumbled.

"See you around," she said to Gabe before she walked the other way on the sidewalk, more sway in her hips than Thea thought necessary.

"Well, she was... nice?" Gabe said doubtfully.

"Nice isn't the exact word I'd use," Thea grumbled, spinning to face him.

Gabe took one look at her face and grinned. He hooked his arm around her waist and brought her closer. He kissed the spot between her eyebrows, and like magic, her frown melted away. Better than Botox.

As she was about to lean into him for more, he pulled back and stepped away. "I'd better get going. I gotta do laundry and prep my tools for next week."

"Oh, right." She tried not to sound so disappointed.

"Can I call you tomorrow?" Gabe asked.

Thea loved how arbitrarily old-fashioned this was. They'd been texting each other regularly for months, yet he was asking permission to call.

TWENTY-FOUR

THE NEXT THREE weeks went by in a blur for Thea. She allowed herself to relax after getting over the initial anxiety of picking up her own takeout orders. It wasn't as bad as she expected because she scheduled the orders during off-peak times. She only saw one other person waiting for takeout most of the time, and people kept a respectful distance away.

The first few days without Gabe were a rough adjustment. It wasn't like he was completely out of contact with her. They still texted, but not seeing his face or hearing his voice made her realize how she'd grown used to him. She was now getting used to being by herself most nights again.

Thea chastised herself for letting her guard down. She couldn't slip into domesticity with him. It was lucky that he got called in for work, a reminder that whatever fantasy bubble they were in would not last forever.

By the third day of mindlessly scrolling her social media feeds, Thea shook herself out of her slump and locked her phone in her bedroom. She'd turned in the completed version of this week's restaurant review, so she had a couple of days before she needed to start on a new one. It was the perfect time to switch gears and get more work done on her manuscript.

Thea pulled out her purple notebook she had dedicated to the manuscript and went over her notes from the latest interview. This was the twelfth interview she'd collected for the book. She recognized a pattern. The thing that kept most of these tiny restaurants going through all the upheaval of the pandemic was a strong sense of community. A handful of owners fretted about staying in business, not only because it was their livelihood but also because they worried about some of their regular customers.

There was a Japanese comfort food restaurant east of her that had been around for two decades. The owner, a woman around Thea's age, had taken over the restaurant from her elderly parents only a few years ago. A group of older Japanese men had lunch there every Thursday afternoon. When the county shut down dining-in, the owner pivoted to bento boxes for takeout. She never heard from or saw those men during that period. When Thea interviewed her, she admitted to worrying about them daily. She'd known them since she was a kid scampering around the tables. When restaurants could open their dining rooms again, she wondered if they would return. As if by magic, they appeared the following Thursday after the reopening. They sat in their regular booth, ordered oyakodon and curry with a side of shredded cabbage salad, and ate it as if nothing had happened.

Reading through these interviews caused a wave of longing to wash over Thea. She missed dining in restaurants. When she drove around picking up food, she noticed a bunch of new outdoor spaces popping up. Gabe had mentioned that he was working on a new commission to build outdoor furniture for a friend of a friend. They wanted to expand their cafe to the sidewalk now that the city approved the plans. LA was the perfect place for outdoor dining. The weather was glorious most of the year.

Thea wondered if Gabe would be open to having dinner with her in one of those outdoor spaces when he got back. Did eating outside help with his aversion to restaurants?

TWENTY-FIVE

POSITIVE. THE THING Gabe dreaded had finally happened. He felt a peculiar mixture of panic and relief as he stared at the email from the testing clinic. Panic from all the what-ifs that were about to happen, and relief that the virus he'd been dodging for what seemed like forever had finally caught up to him, so maybe now he could let his guard down.

It wasn't that he looked forward to being sick, but when he received the email from work to head back to the set, catching it became a real possibility. Sure, they all tried to wear masks as much as possible, and people were told not to come into work if they had a sore throat, but not everyone was on their best behavior 100% of the time. The last week of filming was exhausting, and everyone let their guard down. It didn't surprise him to see an exposure notification in his email yesterday. At least he was back at home and could isolate. He'd hate to have had to quarantine for weeks in that dreary motel they were all staying at.

He brought his lukewarm coffee to his living room and plopped down, still digesting the news. He had been looking forward to seeing Thea again. They'd texted back and forth while he was away, but it wasn't the same. He couldn't look into the depth of her eyes over text, couldn't breathe in the heady smell of her skin.

His head was starting to ache. A mounting fear crept into him. She was extremely careful about catching Covid. She wouldn't want to see him while he was recovering, but what about after? He worried that the weeks he'd spent missing her might not have been the same for Thea.

This was the first time he'd dated someone who hadn't tried calling him at least once while he was out of town. It felt strange to wonder if Thea had even missed him at all. She hadn't outright said it in their texts — those all seemed normal, but maybe she only saw him as a friend with a side of benefits. Now that he was damaged goods, would she easily drop him and move on?

He sent her a screenshot of his results. *Might as well rip the bandage off.*

Immediately, his phone lit up with an incoming call. When Thea's face appeared on his phone, his heart beat rapidly. He hadn't felt at home until this very moment, looking at her worried face.

"Oh noooo," Thea groaned, her mouth forming a long oval. "Are you okay?"

"Yeah, just tired." He'd been feeling tired for the past two days but chalked it up to the usual exhaustion caused by weeks of feverish work. He cleared his throat. "I guess my throat's a little scratchy."

"Did everyone on set get sick?"

"Not that I know of. I'm surprised it didn't happen sooner."

"What are you gonna do?"

"Probably just quarantine at home till it's over. Not like there's anything else I can do."

Thea chewed on her lip and Gabe wanted to reach through the screen, cup her jaw, and run his thumb along the corner of her mouth.

"Do you need anything?"

"I'm good for now. What've you been up to?"

Thea filled him in on everything that had happened while he was gone. She'd made incredible progress in her manuscript. The way her eyes sparkled when she described a particular section she wrote made him excited to read the finished product.

Despite his curiosity about her work, he couldn't stifle the yawn that broke through, making his eyes water.

A look of sympathy crossed her face. "Listen to me talking your ear off."

"Don't stop. I like hearing your voice," he said, swallowing another yawn. Covid fatigue was no joke.

"You should get some rest. Drink plenty of fluids!"

"Yeah, maybe I should take a nap," Gabe said, rubbing his forehead with his palm. Was he feeling warm?

"Okay, have a good nap. Keep me posted, okay? If you need anything..." Thea trailed off.

"Thanks Thea."

"Oh, and Gabe?"

"Yeah?"

"Welcome home. I missed you." She immediately ended the call, not giving him a chance to respond.

He sat there, staring at his own image on the phone. He couldn't tell if the growing heat spreading through his body was in response to what Thea had said or if it was another symptom of Covid.

TWENTY-SIX

IF SOMEONE HAD told her she would be hand delivering food to a fuck buddy in the middle of a pandemic, Thea would have laughed in their face. Yet, here she was, five days into Gabe's Covid quarantine, trying to drive gingerly around potholes to avoid having the contents of the take-out containers spill over into her car.

Thea pulled up to Gabe's house in record time. She hoped the food was still warm. He'd sounded so sick when she called in the morning that she immediately thought of bringing him dinner. She felt helpless hearing him suffering like that.

The reversal of roles was not lost on her when she placed the insulated bags of food on Gabe's doorstep. She hopped off his front step and pulled her phone out to text him. Before she could finish typing, her phone rang.

"Hey." Gabe's voice sounded hoarse over the phone. "What are you doing here?"

"Hi, how're you feeling?"

"Can you turn around?"

She turned and saw him behind the front window, phone to his ear.

"Better now." There were dark circles under his eyes and his golden brown skin looked sallow. "What are you doing here?"

"I wanted to drop off some porridge for you. It's what I like eating when I'm sick."

"You should have told me you were coming." He sounded upset.

"Don't worry, I'm double-masking it." She pointed to her mask.

Gabe ran a hand through his messy hair. He looked tired. "Sorry, I didn't mean to snap." He sighed, which ended in a fit of coughing. Her chest tightened, seeing him like that.

"Oh no. That doesn't sound good. Have you talked to a doctor?" She asked, worried.

Gabe took a deep breath, and she was afraid he was about to have a coughing fit again, but he held it in. "It's better than it was yesterday. I just didn't want you to see me this way."

"What way?"

"Sick? It's not very manly to be sick."

"Um, I hope you're kidding," she said. "It's not a weakness to be sick."

He shrugged, the movement seeming to take all the strength out of him. "I know. I feel like shit right now. I think I just need a good night's sleep."

It was strange to have a conversation on the phone with someone she was also standing in front of, but it was the only way she knew to be close to him without risking her health, too.

"Okay, I'll let you go rest. The big container is the porridge," Thea said, pointing to the largest bag.

"Thanks. I'll grab 'em when you leave."

"It's pretty bland on its own, which is nice when you're sick. Then the little containers are toppings you can put in the porridge. Stewed wheat gluten, salted duck eggs, soy-pickled cucumbers..." she rattled off a long list. She wasn't much of a cook, but she knew how to make porridge thanks to her rice cooker and she always kept her pantry stocked with porridge toppings.

Gabe nodded with a glazed over look. He must have been feverish. "I missed seeing you."

"Me too," she replied truthfully. "Hope you have a better night's sleep. Call me if anything changes or you need anything?"

"Thea?"

"Yes?"

Gabe's voice dropped to a low purr. "I'll show you how much I've missed you when I get better."

Thea made an attempt at a response and walked back to the car, flushed and grinning ear to ear.

TWENTY-SEVEN

THEA: *YOU UP?*

Gabe: *Yeah. But still sick, so no booty-call ;)*

Thea: *Ha ha. I wanted to see how you're feeling.*

Gabe: *Mostly better, but lingering cough.*

Thea: *Up for talking on the phone?*

Gabe: *Always*

Thea put in her earbuds and called Gabe. After two hours of banging on the keyboard, the last thing she wanted to do was tap out text messages with her thumbs.

"Hello there," Gabe answered on the first ring. With her earbuds in, his voice, still hoarse, sounded like he was right next to her.

"Sorry, didn't feel like texting." She busied her hands by watering the potted plants valiantly trying to stay alive around her house.

"I don't mind. I love your voice."

She was glad she hadn't FaceTimed him because she would have been embarrassed by how that made her blush.

"Oof, that was a cheesy thing to say," Gabe chuckled. "Let's pretend I didn't say it. So, how was your day?"

"I've been better," Thea admitted. She'd been tempted to say she was fine, but the truth spilled out. It was like she had no filter with him. She told him how screwed she was about her manuscript. "I pitched the proposal back in 2019. The idea was to write a book highlighting immigrants who work in LA restaurants. Like the small places that have a community following. I wanted to interview the people who poured their energy and savings into these places, have accompanying photographs of the kitchens, their regular customers, and just highlight their voices."

"What's wrong with it? The editor wants you to change it?"

"The editor loved it!" Thea said. "But then 2020 happened and some of those places shut down, or moved to doing delivery only. I know it's crappy of me to complain about *my* problems with nothing to write about, but I don't know how I'm gonna finish this manuscript now."

"Not all the places closed down, though," Gabe reminded her.

"Yeah, but they've pivoted to different menus, or they're just struggling to stay open. Even before 2020, some of them were barely hanging on."

"That's all the more reason for you to write about them."

"But what can I write that's not gonna be all Debbie Downer? I can't write about all these places closing down because they can't pay their rent anymore or—"

"—why not? Why can't you write about how they're trying to survive in the pandemic? Aren't those stories worth telling? Wouldn't that make just as good of a book? There's already tension built in." Gabe pointed out.

"Because..." Thea started, but then paused. She'd been mulling over this problem for days, trying to find an alternative to writing about the struggling businesses, but now that Gabe put the question to her, she realized she didn't have a good reason not to.

"Thea? You still there?"

"What? Yeah. Just thinking about what you said. It's crazy, but I never thought of it that way before." She let the idea settle. "Thanks! You just gave me something new to noodle on."

"You're welcome. Are you gonna start working on it now?"

"Nah. I need to let that simmer for a bit. So, what are *you* up to tonight?"

"Lying around being bored, mostly. I still feel kinda out of it, so I don't wanna do any woodworking and cut a finger off. You could say I'm having a pretty wild night."

"Hm," Thea mused. "I've been trying to put off watching this awful movie, but I might as well get it over with."

"What awful movie?"

"It's dumb. Don't judge me. I lost a bet with Olivia ages ago, so now I have to watch A Quiet Place. She's been trying to get me to watch it since it came out in theaters and I kept coming up with things to be busy with. I think she sees through my plan now."

"What was the bet?"

"I don't even remember, now that you mention it. Like I said, it was so long ago. But I really, really don't want to watch it."

"Wait, is that the movie where people can't make noise or something gets them?"

"Yep, that one."

"Why don't you want to watch it? Not a big Sandra Bullock fan?"

"Wait, huh? I think you're thinking of another movie. The Sandra Bullock one is called Bird Box. That's the one where they're blindfolded." Thea corrected him. "This one is Emily Blunt and the dude from The Office."

"You're right. Why don't you want to watch it? You scared?"

"Uh... yes? I live by myself and I don't want to have nightmares." She didn't mind watching horror movies when she shared a dorm room with Olivia in college. They even had weekly movie nights where all they watched were Asian horror movies.

"How're you gonna pay back the bet?"

Thea had been thinking about this for a while. At first, she thought watching it in broad daylight on her porch would make it less scary. She even started it, but something about watching a horror movie on the porch in the middle of a pandemic when there was not a lot of foot-traffic made it even more creepy. She stopped watching after five minutes.

"Okay, don't laugh," Thea warned Gabe. "I wasn't going to watch it on my TV. I was gonna use my computer and put it in a tiny window while I painted my nails or something."

Gabe made a strangled noise that Thea could tell was him trying to stifle a laugh. "Isn't that cheating? You need to at least be paying attention to the movie, don't you?"

"I don't want it to be scary!"

"What if I watch it with you? Would that make it less scary?"

"How would you watch it with me?" The idea intrigued Thea. It would make it more bearable to watch a scary movie with someone else. But she wasn't about to invite him over to Netflix and chill right now.

"Adrian showed me how to do it before. If we both stream it from the same place, there's a way to watch it together so that the timing matches up. And then we can just stay on the phone."

"Hm, if it's easy to set up, that would work. Are you sure you want to watch it with me tonight? Isn't it getting kind of late?" Thea asked.

"I don't have any plans tomorrow morning. You?"

"Alright, as long as you know what you're getting into," Thea said, still skeptical that this would work.

It took less than ten minutes for them to set up their laptops to play the movie in sync. Thea hung up the phone to change into her pajamas and brush her teeth. She had a feeling that she would not want to get out of bed after the movie.

When she got settled in bed, the laptop plugged in and balanced on her blanket, she called Gabe back.

"Hey, wasn't sure if you were gonna chicken out last minute," he joked when he picked up.

"Your voice sounds different." It sounded deeper, richer. Like he was right next to her in bed. Goosebumps pebbled her arms.

"Does it? I put on my headphones. Maybe it's the mic."

"Maybe. Okay, I have to warn you, so you turn down the volume on your phone or something, but I might scream at the scary parts. Sorry in advance."

"Noted." His chuckle made her feel brave enough to start the movie.

It didn't start off too badly. She'd already seen the beginning from her previous failed attempts to watch it. It helped to have Gabe's commentary in her ear. He kept her mind off of the tension building on-screen. Unfortunately, it didn't help the tension she could feel building over the phone. It was incredibly intimate watching a movie with someone late at night, even from different houses.

"Thea?" Gabe's soft voice broke into her thoughts. She hadn't realized she'd stopped paying attention to the movie. Either that or she'd fallen asleep.

"Hmm?"

"Just checking. You were quiet for a long time. I thought you fell asleep."

"No, I'm awake," Thea assured him. She stretched her arms over her head, tilting her head to one side, then the other, to release the crick in her neck.

"That's cute," Gabe said in a gravelly voice.

"What?"

"The little sounds you make when you're stretching."

"How did you know I was stretching?" Thea looked around, as if there were hidden cameras on her bookshelf.

"I can hear your clothes moving around." Gabe's voice was rough.

"Shh, pay attention to the movie," she reminded him in a stage whisper.

"Okay," he whispered back.

Thea couldn't help the smile on her lips. Thanks to Gabe, she was finally paying off her bet to Olivia.

When the credits started rolling, Thea was sad that the movie was over. Even though they hadn't had much of a conversation during the latter half of the movie, it was fun to watch a movie with Gabe. Sure, as the night went on, she could tell he was tired by how hoarse his voice sounded, but if she was being honest to herself, it was kind of hot. No, it was incredibly hot. She was a terrible person, fantasizing about someone who was sick, but she couldn't help imagining him shirtless, lounging against the pillows on his bed.

"—not as bad as I thought," Gabe finished.

"Hmm?" Thea asked. The fuzzy, sleepy feeling made it hard for her to concentrate on his words. She placed her laptop on her nightstand. She slid deeper into bed, stretching her legs so that her feet reached the cool section of the sheets.

"I had low expectations, but it wasn't as bad as I thought," Gabe repeated.

Thea stifled a yawn. "I thought you said you wanted to watch it?"

"I lied. I just wanted to watch a scary movie with you."

Thea could picture his face. One side of his mouth would be pulled in so that the dimple showed. "Was the experience what you had hoped?" Thea asked, wondering why her voice sounded all sultry.

There was no reply on the other end of the line for a bit, but Thea knew the call hadn't dropped because she could still hear Gabe's even breathing.

"Yes," he finally said. "I liked it."

A warm feeling settled over her. It had been a while since such a simple statement from a man made her feel like that. "Me too," she said, right before another yawn burst out of her.

Gabe laughed. "I'm pretty tired too. Let's go to sleep."

"Thanks for watching this with me."

"You're very welcome," he said. "Goodnight, Thea."

"Goodnight Gabe."

Thea hung up and felt a mix of sleepy and giddy. She couldn't help the big grin on her face. She drifted to sleep as soon as she plugged her phone in and her head hit the pillow. She didn't dream of scary monsters at all that night.

TWENTY-EIGHT

"T-Minus six weeks to go," Olivia said gleefully.

Thea clapped her hand. "I can't wait!"

"I know! Did I show you what I made?" Olivia panned her phone to the spot next to her bedroom door, where a long, colorful construction paper chain draped against the top of the doorframe.

"Is that what I think it is?"

"Yep!" Olivia laughed. "Here, I didn't do the one for today yet." She balanced the phone on something and then walked to the door. She ripped a link from the chain.

"Wow, I haven't made those since kindergarten."

"Lemme tell you, this is still as satisfying." Olivia twirled the torn chain in front of the camera and then tossed it in the trash.

"You're really gonna turn in your notice in six weeks?" Thea asked. Olivia had been beyond fed up with her job for more than a year, before the pandemic even started. Thea didn't blame her. She was a designer at a famous internet retailer known for exploiting its employees, and some of the stories she told Thea about work were stranger than fiction.

"Mm-hmm. Got my resignation notice typed up right here."

"How do you feel?"

"Relieved," Olivia admitted. "It's freeing to know that an end's in sight. But I'll be more relieved when I see this next round of vesting hit my bank account."

The convoluted compensation system with cash and stocks was not something Thea had any experience with, but according to her friend, it was all designed to keep people in the dark about how much they were actually making year to year.

"Anyway, enough about that. I just need to keep my head down with this project. Can't rock any boats. What about you? How's it going? Gabe recovered yet?"

"Oh yeah, more than a week ago. Things are okay."

"Just okay?"

Thea sighed. "I dunno. Just conflicted, I guess."

"What happened? I thought things were good?"

"Things *are* good. Like *so* good. I think we're getting too comfortable," Thea admitted. The month and a half she had without seeing Gabe was productive, but also extremely lonely. Thea prided herself on her introvert super powers of enjoying being alone for long stretches of time, but now that Gabe was healthy and she started going over to his house again, she felt like she'd been holding her breath until now. "It's better to break things off before we get too into it, you know. If I wait till the pandemic is over, it might be harder to stop."

"Listen," Olivia got close to the screen and looked serious. "You know I'm all for a wham-bam-thank-you-ma'am, if that's what you want. But do you think you're into him only because of sex or the other thing?"

"Why can't it be because of sex? It's..." Thea struggled to find the words to describe the last few nights with Gabe. Images came to her mind of exactly how good the sex was. She hoped Olivia couldn't see her flaming face in the dim light. "It's really good."

Olivia arched an eyebrow and laughed. "That good, huh? You're speechless. No words from the writer?"

"Pfft. I used up all my ten-dollar words at work. Only one-dollar words for you."

"Well, okay, so the sex is nice and nasty. Great, but are you sure you weren't missing something else while he was away?"

"What else is there?"

"Companionship? Intimacy? Vulnerability?" Olivia yelled as if it were obvious. "Like you don't have to go all in like you did with Peter."

Peter was Thea's ex. She'd moved in with him, fresh out of college, thinking they were soulmates. She felt so adult about it back then, living in a downtown loft with her boyfriend. His requests had been innocuous at first. Could she pick up his dry cleaning because they were closed by the time he came home? Why not fold up his t-shirts too, since she was doing laundry, anyway? Could she wipe down the counters, since she was home all day, anyway? Surely she could take five minutes to do that even if she had writing to do. Peter was often too tired when he came home from a full day's work at the investment firm to do those things himself. Little by little, she felt like she was putting parts of herself on hold in order to be a good girlfriend and roommate. It got so bad that even when Olivia tried to say something, Thea snapped at her and told her to mind her own business.

After their breakup, Thea vowed never to fall into that trap again.

She rolled her eyes at her friend on the screen. "I don't know how you're having sex, but it's intimate when I do it. You're literally letting someone put a part of their body into your own."

Olivia's mouth thinned as she looked serious. "Geez, you really need to work on your dirty talk. You know what I mean. Emotional intimacy."

Thea shook her head. "I'm not looking for that. I don't need that from him. Or from any other guy. That's what friends like you are for."

Even without her saying anything, Thea could tell Olivia did not believe any of it. She did the whole, "say nothing, but look stern" expression that Thea knew was her signature move to get someone else to keep talking. She tried to resist it as long as she could.

Thea sighed, giving up. "I just don't know if I have the energy to deal with more right now."

"That's more honest," Olivia said, nodding. "Go on."

"You sure you don't want me to pay you for therapy?"

Olivia laughed, her grin wide and open. "This is the emotional intimacy you get from me so that you can be a cold-hearted bitch with men, right?"

Thea rolled her eyes at her harsh but loyal friend. Olivia's honesty was one reason why she was such a good friend. Thea missed the sleepovers they used to have, but these weekly calls were better than nothing.

"But seriously, are you feeling okay?"

"Yeah, still recovering from Gabe getting Covid. I was so scared. Now I'm just terrified about this book. I don't know why I even pitched it without thinking it through," Thea admitted, chewing on the inside of her cheek. "I thought the hardest part would be getting the proposal accepted, but they signed me on immediately. Okay, I'm panicking a little. That's why I can't deal with men right now."

"Except for that super good at sex man you have now," Olivia said.

"Yes, except for him. But he's more like a palate cleanser."

"Do the dudes you sleep with know you talk about them like food?" Olivia asked, laughing.

Thea raised an eyebrow. "They haven't complained when I *treat* them like food."

Olivia shook her head. "Girl, you're kinky! But real talk. Gabe knows you're not looking for something serious, and he's okay with it?"

Thea cocked her head. "Why wouldn't he be? I told him this was casual in the beginning. We're just two grownups having fun."

Olivia shrugged. "Okay, as long as you two are on the same page. Honestly, I'm kinda jealous of your ability to compartmentalize like that. It's like you can just switch to a different tab in your brain."

"Oh, my god! I didn't tell you this ridiculous thing I heard at work."

Olivia perked up. "Tell me what?"

"Ray is trying to replace me with a robot."

"Uh, what?"

Thea filled Olivia in on the surreal conversation she had with Ray in the morning. One of the hot shot programmers on the paper's new tech team had some extra time — she whipped up a demo of an article written completely by a computer. Thea wasn't sure of the technical aspects of it, something about AI ingesting all of her previous articles for patterns, but the computer generated article was convincing enough that Ray wanted her to go over it and see if it was publishable.

"Uh, you want me to edit this fake article?" Thea had asked Ray, still not believing whatever alternate timeline she'd woken up to that morning. "I don't usually edit. Isn't that your job?"

"I already gave it a pass," Ray said. "Technically, it's solid. You should read it and see if the contents make sense. You're a better judge about the food stuff than I am."

Thea didn't like where this was going. "Am I helping my replacement? Who's a robot?"

Ray laughed at that, but he didn't sound convincing. "If you can't write better than a computer program, then we got a problem. Just give it a read and tell me what you think. If it's convincing, we could do a whole series with the program. See if our readers can spot the difference. It'll bring in younger subscribers — your generation loves AI, right? We need this type of innovation to keep up with the times."

Thea wasn't ready to speak on behalf of her entire generation on that, especially when she still had a healthy dose of skepticism that AI was going to fix anything.

"Are you fucking kidding me?!" Olivia sounded indignant on her behalf.

"I know, right? I never thought Ray, of all people, would hop on the AI bandwagon. That man still has a flip phone!"

"What did you say to him?"

"What could I? Of course I said I'd look. I need to keep this job!"

Olivia gave a snort. "It's so disrespectful of them! But you have nothing to worry about."

"What?"

"We have, like, fifty teams working on AI generated content here and the stuff the scripts put out is still garbage, believe me."

"I dunno. Ray said it was passable."

"Grammatically correct, yes, but as soon as you read it, you'll see it doesn't make any sense." Olivia's tone was reassuring. She had more exposure to the inner-workings of the tech world, so Thea trusted her take on it over Ray's. "They'd be idiots to replace a talented journalist with some program that outputs gibberish."

Thea let out a breath of relief that she hadn't realized she'd been holding. "Thanks for talking me off this ledge. So I shouldn't start updating my resume?"

"Just write like you normally do and it'll be so obvious the program is shit."

TWENTY-NINE

SEE YOU AT 7 😗

Gabe's cockiness annoyed Thea. That he thought she would automatically agree to a home-cooked dinner at his place was presumptuous, even though he had presumed right. She was dying to know what he was going to cook up, but it was still annoying. He was cheating by using her curiosity about food to lure her to dinner. But since she had been planning to head over to his place that evening anyway, for other activities, it didn't make sense to refuse.

She was still recovering from the drama with her robot replacement from the day before. She read the AI generated article that was supposedly written in her style. On a superficial level, the structure of the paragraphs and sentences read like her style. But as she read more, none of it made any sense. It was a review of a new Spanish tapas spot in Silverlake. Some gems from the article included "a trendy scallop charred service was friendly" and "highlighting a TOTO toilet tasting menu." How those phrases got past Ray was both ridiculous and gratifying. Maybe she could keep her job after all. The article was actually helpful in helping her identify overused patterns in her own writing, so it wasn't all bad.

Thea spent the rest of the day in a low-level, anxiety-driven writing trance. The pressure of proving her worth drove her to bang out this week's restaurant review, then another 4000 words on her manuscript. If she could keep this up for the next month, and if she didn't end up throwing her outline away, she might actually make the new deadline.

She was disappointed in herself for letting her guard down. She'd thought that slowing down and sinking deep into the lull of summer was a radical step in improving her mental health. But how many months had it been? She couldn't even keep track without opening up her planner. The days blended into each other. No wonder she was so far behind. Tomorrow, she would make changes and double down on carving out more time to write. *No more distractions!*

With that promise, Thea took one last look at the reflection in her rearview mirror. The bottle of wine was so slick that she dropped it when she tried to grab it. Luckily, it only fell a few inches back onto her passenger seat, intact. She got a better grip on it and exited her car. She blamed the condensation, but it might also have been her sweaty palms.

The novelty of having Gabe cook for her was both exciting and terrifying. She had never felt so apprehensive about someone cooking for her before. What if she didn't like his cooking? Would she be able to lie to him if he asked her opinion? Was it better to lie or tell the truth in this case?

She paused before knocking on his front door. Friends had told her that she was intimidating to cook for because of what she did for a living, but she always assured them that any level of cooking skill impressed her. She possessed none of that skill herself, so she was very gracious that anyone would want to cook for her. Home-cooked meals were in a completely different category for her than restaurant meals. She still worried. He wouldn't have offered to cook if his cooking was bad, would he?

Before she could reconsider and slink back to her car, the front door flew open. She stepped back in surprise.

"I thought I heard your car," Gabe said, ushering her into his living room. "The door's unlocked. Come in."

"Hi," Thea said, regaining her composure. She held out the bottle of wine. "I brought this for you. I'm not sure if it'll go with what you're cooking, though."

Gabe took the bottle from her and studied the label. He quirked an eyebrow at her and smiled, "A famous food writer once told me a that a bottle of champagne goes well with anything."

At his teasing smile, she felt all of her doubts melting away. This didn't have to be an awkward dinner. They were used to eating together and having effortless conversation. It would be exactly like all the other meals they'd had together.

It was about ten degrees hotter in the kitchen, where she followed him. She sniffed, taking in the delicious scent of cooking onions. She noticed there weren't any pots or pans on the stove. "It smells so good. What're you making?"

Gabe put the wine in the fridge, pulled an apron from its hook and tied it around himself. Thea had seen plenty of men in aprons before. It was a common sight at the restaurants she'd gone to. Especially the sight of tattooed men wearing solid colored canvas aprons over their rolled up chef's whites. None of those men made her drool like *this*, though. The cut of the straps let her appreciate his broad shoulders and muscular arms. He looked like a feast. That dimple on his cheek and the twinkle of mystery in his eyes were irresistible.

He said, "Guess."

Thea sniffed with her nose in the air. "Cooked onions, maybe some garlic or shallots... vinegar... eggs?" She wasn't sure what type of dish would have those ingredients in it. "It also kinda smells like potato chips."

Gabe chuckled, wrapped an arm around her waist and pulled her to him, planting a kiss on her forehead. It was such a casual gesture that it took her off-guard. He leaned against the kitchen counter, pulling her closer so that she stood between his legs.

"You're close," he said, his voice dipping lower as he moved his palms to her waist, slipping a pinky under the hem of her shirt.

"Potato chips topped with caramelized onions and chopped hard-boiled eggs," she guessed.

He pulled back, giving her a skeptical look. "Is that an actual dish?"

"No, but I couldn't think of anything else."

Gabe dipped his head so his mouth touched her temple, then her cheek, then finally her lips. It was a quick kiss, much more chaste than what she wanted. "Guess again."

Thea was having a hard time guessing, with his warm hands on her skin and his thumbs skirting teasingly below her breasts. Forget about guessing. She leaned into him, kissing the rough stubble on his jaw, feeling him swallow. Her lips moved from the line of his jaw down his neck, nipping his skin as her mouth traveled lower.

"Hash browns?" she whispered against his damp skin, licking the salty taste of his sweat.

"Hmm?" Gabe's voice came out as a rumble from low in his throat.

Thea laughed. "Are you cooking hash browns?"

"No." His hands wandered down the hem of her shirt again, bunching it in his fists as he started pulling her shirt up. As he was about to pull it over her shoulders, his phone chimed and shook in his pocket.

"Is that a timer in your pocket, or are you just happy to see me?" Thea asked, laughing before she could finish the lame joke.

Gabe thumbed the alarm silent and gave her such a heated look that she could have sworn the oven was open.

"I am *very* happy to see you." He tugged her shirt back down, much to her dismay. "But I'd better get the stuff out of the oven before it burns the house down. I wanna feed you something edible."

Thea watched him slip on lobster-claw oven mitts and open the oven. A blast of heat came out. Gabe carefully took out a cast iron pan and placed it on the stove. She moved closer, curious about what was in the pan. A golden brown layer of bubbly cheese greeted her, along with the most amazing smell of caramelized onions, potatoes, and egg.

"Spanish tortilla!" she said, unable to hide the excitement in her voice. She clasped her hands under her chin and took a deep breath in. "It smells so amazing. Is that cheese on top of it?"

Gabe nodded, taking off the mitts. "Not traditional at all, but there's nothing a layer of melted cheese can't improve, right?"

"Truth."

"Gotta let this cool down so we don't burn the hell outta our mouths."

Gabe reached for glasses from the cabinet above her.

At that angle, Thea couldn't help noticing the exposed skin when Gabe's shirt rode up. Thanks to his low-slung jeans, she could see that delectable line below his hip bones. She liked to press her thumbs against those twin lines when he was inside of her. At that thought, she brought her fingers to him and he jumped back so quickly he almost dropped the glasses.

"Ticklish?" she asked, an impish grin on her lips.

"No," he said, "You just surprised me."

"Sure you're not ticklish?" Thea asked, wiggling her fingers at him.

The way his shoulders hunched up and his body tensed was adorable. She loved that she'd found his weak spot. He grumbled, "Do you want some wine, or are you going to just keep standing there torturing me?"

"Wine please." Thea batted her eyelashes innocently.

Gabe removed the wine from the fridge and popped the cork with practiced ease. He poured a glass for each of them, topping both off perfectly so the bubbles met the rim. He held up his glass to her. "Thanks for bringing the wine."

"Thank *you* for cooking." She looked at him over the rim of her glass and their eyes locked. She swallowed the cold, bubbly mouthful. There was a lightness in his eyes as he mirrored her and drank his own gulp.

"Can you bring the salad bowl in the fridge to the dining room while I slice some of this up?" Gabe said, finally breaking the eye contact.

Thea brought the salad into the dining room and was about to go back into the kitchen when Gabe called out, "Take a seat. I'll bring the rest out."

He came out with their refilled glasses of wine. Then he went into the kitchen and returned with the tortilla, now on a serving plate, and cut into wedges. He placed the plate in the middle of the table and served her a nice big slice before putting a slice on his own plate.

"Oh, forgot the dressing," he said right before sitting down. He rushed into the kitchen and back out with a small mason jar. He poured the content of the jar into the salad bowl and gave it a hearty couple of tosses with two wooden spoons. "Salad?"

"Yes, please." Thea held out her plate for the pile of greens to go on.

When all the food was finally dished out, Gabe took off his apron and draped it over his chair. He sat down across from her and raised his glass to her. "Cheers."

"Bone appétit," Thea said, clinking her glass with his.

Gabe chuckled. That lame joke had longevity.

Her first bite of the tortilla was hot enough to burn her mouth—perfect. The gooey cheese added a different dimension to the egg and potato dish she didn't know was missing. She fanned the steam coming out of her mouth.

"Careful, it's still hot," Gabe warned her, blowing on the piece on his fork.

"This," Thea said between bites, "is superb!"

"Don't sound so surprised. I'm not on Top Chef but I know how to cook a few things pretty well."

"I'm serious!" Thea said, taking another big, too hot bite. "This is perfect."

Gabe's pleased smile made all her second-guessing of the night vanish. "Thanks. I'm glad you like it."

Thea took a bite of salad. The ice-cold crunch of lettuce with the zesty dressing was the ideal partner to the hot tortilla. She took another bite and closed her eyes, savoring the way the flavors danced with each other. She couldn't help the moan that escaped her mouth.

"Good?" Gabe asked, an eyebrow quirked.

"This salad! Why is it so good? What's in it?"

"It's only lettuce and sliced radish. The trick is to get the vegetables washed and then super dry. Then put it in the fridge to get nice and cold."

"What dressing did you use? It's so zingy and light."

"Olive oil, lemon juice, some chopped shallots, salt and pepper. That's pretty much it." Gabe ticked off the ingredients using his fingers.

"You made your own dressing?!"

He made it sound so easy. "Yeah, it's a pretty generic dressing recipe. I just play with the proportions till it tastes good."

"You should bottle the dressing and sell it!"

Gabe laughed. "Thea, have you *never* made salad dressing before?"

Thea took another crunchy mouthful of salad and shook her head. It hadn't ever occurred to her to make a dressing. She usually had leftover dressing from takeout, and her trusty bottle of Japanese sesame dressing. "I'm not too good in the kitchen."

"What?!" Now it was Gabe's turn to be surprised. "Aren't you a professional food writer?"

"*Writer* being the crucial word. I'm good at *writing* about food. Good at *eating* food. Not good at *making* food."

Gabe chewed thoughtfully on his tortilla, a small frown on his face. "Hard to believe."

She shrugged. "I was never that interested in cooking. It seems so precise and detail oriented. I'm terrible at measuring stuff." She didn't mention how she purposely avoided cooking when she lived with Peter, her ex, because she didn't want to pick up any more domestic responsibilities. She arched an eyebrow at him. "Is that a problem?"

Gabe shook his head. "Why would it be?"

"No reason." She wasn't about to get into it with him about Peter.

"But how do you do your work if you don't know how it's done?" Gabe asked.

"You know that old saying, 'Those who can, do. Those who can't, teach. Those who can't teach, write.'"

"Don't discount your writing. Not everyone can write like you do."

The way he looked at her, with a barest tilt of a smile, made her feel like he actually saw her. All of her. It had been such a long time since she sat across the table from someone at dinner. She was content. This felt normal, even. Like he cooked dinner for her all the time. Like they were a normal couple having a normal dinner together. *Uh oh.*

A cold, tight feeling spread through her. This was why she was behind with her work. This was why a robot was taking over her job. She was too damned comfortable spending time with this man. When the pandemic was over and the two of them returned to their normal post-pandemic lives, there'd be no way they could see each other as often as they did now.

During those long, lonely weeks when he'd been in Arizona, she'd gotten tons of work done. Sure, her head had been in a fog and it was a shaky transition to shift her schedule around picking up her own food.

She had distracted herself from thoughts of him by countless sprints of writing. But as soon as he'd texted that he was back, recovered, and out of quarantine, things had gone back to normal. Or the new normal, where he was a part of her life.

"Want another slice?" Gabe's question jolted her out of her troubling thoughts.

Thea shook her head.

"You got all quiet. Something wrong?"

"No." She felt guilty about lying to him, but she also couldn't put the swirling thoughts in her head into words. She would need to think this through before deciding either way. Thea changed the subject. "I'm getting full, that's all. My mouth wants more, but I should probably stop before I regret it."

"I can pack the rest up for you to take home later. Much later. Dessert?" He sipped his wine, eyes never leaving her face.

The combination of the fizzy wine, the warm temperature of the summer night, and the sultry gleam in his eyes made her feel flushed all over. Her doubts about spending too much time with him suddenly felt very far away. She avoided something as obvious as fanning the heat from her face, barely. "I don't mind staying a little longer after dinner. You made dessert too?"

"Nah. Store-bought chocolate ice-cream and berries in the fridge, okay?"

Thea found some room in her stomach for dessert.

By the time all the ice cream in her bowl disappeared, she was truly full. "Ooof," she said, putting her spoon down.

Gabe's smile turned sensual, hinting at things to come. "Go relax in the living room while I put the food away and clean all this up."

"Oh no, of course not. You did all the cooking, so at least let me help with cleanup."

"I invited you over for dinner. Guests aren't on cleaning duty."

Thea's lips quirked. "I thought you invited me over for other reasons."

The look he gave her made her pulse quicken. A warm, fluttering feeling in her stomach took the words from her mouth. He leaned over, touching the corner of her lips with the pad of his finger. When he pulled his finger away, she saw that he'd wiped off some chocolate ice-cream. "We'll get to those reasons soon," he promised.

THIRTY

GABE LOOKED AT his phone for the hundredth time that afternoon. Still no reply. Going this long without a response from her worried him. Sometimes it took a couple of hours for her to respond, but she always did.

He'd texted her this morning about how much he enjoyed having her over for dinner. She hadn't even replied with an emoji. *Maybe a looming deadline was the reason behind her radio silence?* He didn't want to bug her, so he put his phone back into his pocket and tried to take his mind off of it.

Fortunately, he had a long list of woodworking tasks lined up. After he'd completed the build-out of the parklet in front of the cafe, a commission from a friend of a friend, he received several inquiries from other people who wanted him to build something similar for their outdoor dining spaces.

Then there was the waitlist for his custom-built Adirondacks. He was skeptical when Jess suggested posting them on Instagram, but she had the annoying habit of being right. People wanted a comfortable place to sit in their yard now that they were spending more time at home. Especially hand-crafted lawn chairs made of re-claimed wood. Customers were ordering them left and right. He had to ask Jess to put up a post saying that he was no longer taking orders. That waitlist would take him more than two months to get through, and the wood was getting harder to source.

When he'd made his first chair, it was an exercise to see if he could transform the old wood stashed in the back of the garage into something functional. He found a couple of plans on how to construct the chair online and added a few tweaks to it. The chair got a lot of attention from his family when he brought it home. Jess even snuck him a picture of their dad taking a dad-nap in it when he thought no one was looking.

Gabe finished sanding down the rough edges where the screws holding the chair together dug in. He had an electric sander for the larger pieces, but he liked to do the finishing steps by hand. It made for a smoother finish around where pieces of wood were held together. It felt good to spend the extra time and effort on those details instead of being pressured to finish on time and cut corners like when he worked on set. The time crunch was another thing he didn't miss about his job.

He picked the chair up by both arms and held it in the air, giving it a good shake. Nothing felt loose. Every piece of wood was securely in place. He put it back down on the ground and leaned over it, placing his weight on the arms. No excessive squeaking sounds there.

Finally, he sat down on the chair, plopping down for good measure. It wouldn't be good if the chair collapsed under him, but it would be worse if it collapsed under his customer. His craftsmanship and reputation were at stake here.

Gabe shifted around on the seat, leaning this way and that, hearing the creaks of the wood settling in. Then he got up and re-tightened each set of screws before sitting down again. It was a sturdy chair.

The rectangular inset on top of one arm of the chair caught his eye. This was one of the newest modifications he was offering on these builds: a spot to place a phone so that it didn't get accidentally knocked off when someone bumped the chair. He hadn't known if anyone would want a modern upgrade to a timeless chair, but as soon as he put up a photo of the prototype armrest, someone wrote him about it. The inset itself wasn't difficult to carve out, but took more hand-sanding to get right.

Gabe stood to grab his phone off of his workbench to test with the new chair. He placed it in its designated place and shook the chair a few times, making sure it wasn't easy for the phone to slide out. It was perfect.

The phone buzzed. For a few seconds, the way it bounced around in the rectangular inset mesmerized him. He hadn't intentionally designed it so that it would keep the device from falling off when vibrating, but it was a solid solution.

He finally noticed Thea's name flashing on the screen and accepted the call. "Hey."

Thea's face filled his screen. Her hair was piled on top of her head in a messy bun. It reminded him of the last night they'd spent together. They'd collapsed in a sweaty, satisfied mess on top of his sheets with her resting her head on his shoulder, hair loose. He marveled at how it felt to have all that hair sprawled over his chest. Everything, including dinner, had felt so right. His heart thumping a slow, happy rhythm as he inhaled the soft herbal scent of her shampoo.

"Hi." Thea pushed her glasses up the bridge of her nose. The glare from the phone screen in the reflection of her glasses made it hard to see her eyes.

"I was worried you ghosted me," he joked, about to run his hand over his hair again before he caught himself. Instead, he stretched his arm, bending it at the elbow while bringing his palm against his back.

She pressed her lips together into a thin line. "Sorry," she finally said. "I'm a busy lady."

"Work?"

"Yeah. I accidentally scheduled a bunch of pieces to be done at the same time." She did that thing she did with her lips when she was nervous. He wished they were having this conversation face to face.

"I see."

"Are you mad that I was MIA?"

He wasn't exactly mad, but he didn't feel good that Thea didn't think to at least reply to his texts or tell him she would be busy for the next few days. "No."

"I needed to cut down on distractions so that I could finish."

"I'm a distraction?" He raised an eyebrow.

"Yes."

"Is this an elaborate excuse because you didn't like my cooking?"

"No! Your food was excellent."

"Um-hmm."

"Anyway, I'm glad you're not mad. Sometimes I have to disappear into a cave and write."

She did warn him early on that her writing always came first. He wished she thought enough about him to give him a heads up before she disappeared into her writing cave.

"I turned in all my stuff, so I'm free this weekend." There was a hopeful look in Thea's eyes.

He couldn't help the wary tone of his voice. "Did you want to come over or something?"

"Yeah, if you have time."

"Thea, I always have time for you." He tried not to let his frustration bleed through his reply. He wished that sometimes, she would make time for him.

"Are you sure you're not mad?" She asked.

Gabe didn't like how this felt like a test. He flashed back to all the little tests that Christina had put him through. He failed most of them. Like when he had to work all night on their 6-month anniversary. He didn't even know the 6-month anniversary was a thing. Christina was waiting for him when he finally made it home at two in the morning. Grimy and exhausted, he just wanted to take a quick shower and collapse into bed before having to wake up in a few hours to return to the set. Instead of sleeping, they stayed up fighting until the sun came up.

"Gabe?" Thea sounded worried.

He ran a hand through his hair. "I'm not mad. Just let me know next time, okay? So I don't worry."

Thea looked surprised. "You don't need to worry about me. I can take care of myself."

"I know you can," he started, then clamped his mouth shut. As much as this conversation discouraged him, he didn't want to step over whatever line Thea drew. "Never mind. Forget it."

"So, can I see you this weekend?" Thea's eager look was hard to turn down. He couldn't say no to her even if he'd wanted to.

A humorless laugh came out of his mouth. "Yes, I'll see you this weekend."

While he was happy that he'd passed the test, he wasn't exactly thrilled about how she made him feel like he was only something for her to pass the time with. He hadn't expected to feel so hurt about being used for his body. The truth was, she hadn't led him on. He knew what he was getting into when he agreed to her proposition in the first place. He just didn't think he would feel so deeply about Thea. All the time they'd spent together gave him a pretty good idea of the person she was and he wanted to be with that person, not just occasionally sleep together.

He tried to bury his disappointment about not having an actual relationship with her. Maybe this was for the better. Thinking about Christina brought back all the awful feelings around their dramatic breakup.

"Are we good?" Thea asked, bringing him out of his thoughts.

The vulnerability he saw in her eyes stoked a tender part of him. It was a bittersweet feeling, knowing that she was physically available to him, but kept the other part of herself closed off. He nodded and gave her what he hoped was a convincing look. "We're good."

Thea's bright smile brought him out of his funk. "I'll bring dinner."

There was an email waiting for him from work when he hung up. He almost ignored it, thinking it was another Covid exposure notification. He hadn't been on set for a month.

It wasn't.

It was a new contract for the next season of filming, with an upcoming date he needed to return the contract by. Gabe sank into his armchair and pulled his aging laptop onto his lap to read the contract. He couldn't explain the strange feeling settling over him. At first, he was thrilled because that was a guaranteed paycheck for the next six months. As he read the fine print about the contract, something felt off.

He scrolled back to the first page and re-read it again from start to finish. Nowhere in the contract was there any mention of Covid safety precautions, unlike the last contract he signed. He called his manager, figuring if he had time to send him the contract, he would have time to answer questions.

Dan answered on the first ring. "Is this about the contract?"

"Yup." Gabe voiced his concerns about the lack of precautions.

Dan laughed. "You know everyone on set got it already, right?"

"Yeah, but I read you can still get it again," Gabe countered. "And what about people who didn't get it yet?"

"Look, man. We're gonna be working on top of each other 20 hours a day. There's no avoiding catching it again if it happens."

"So what, they're just giving up completely on masks?"

"You can still wear a mask. No one's stopping you. We're just not going to require it anymore. Personal responsibility or whatever."

"Right."

"So you gonna sign it or not?"

"I'll think about it."

The money was good since the union had renegotiated his rate, but he was having serious doubts about workplace safety.

THIRTY-ONE

THEA DIDN'T KNOW how Gabe could stand the absolute torture of transporting delicious food when he did all those deliveries for her. The mixture of garlic, ginger, and scallion oil made her mouth water. Three more stoplights to go. After the last light, all she needed to do was make a left, then a right, and pull in front of Gabe's house. She could almost taste the savory rice on her tongue.

She parked her car and pulled the bags out of her passenger seat, turning to find Gabe leaning on the open door frame with his arms crossed and a hint of a smile. When would her heart stop tap dancing when she saw him?

"That was quick." He helped her with the bags as she came up the steps. "Didn't you text less than ten minutes ago?"

"Oh," Thea glanced up sheepishly. "I was on my way. From picking up food."

Gabe leaned over and gave her a chaste kiss on her cheek. She liked the spicy, woody smell that lingered when he was near. It was what she imagined sunshine to smell like. The tension left her shoulders as he placed a kiss on her forehead, then her mouth. She was about to run her tongue across his lips, but he pulled back. He gazed down at her and with the orange light of the setting sun streaming through the window onto them, his eyes glowed hungrily.

"Oh! Before I forget." Gabe let her go and strode to the low bookshelf by his door, where he kept his keys and wallet. He opened an old tin and rummaged through it. The thin material of the tin amplified the sound of coins shuffling around each other. "Ah, here it is."

Thea squinted at what he was brandishing like a talisman: a key. Her hand came up before she realized the significance.

Gabe dropped the key into her cupped palm. It felt hot from his hands. The plastic cover over the top was painted to look like a koala.

"What's this for?" she asked, even though dreaded the answer.

"It's a spare key. You can let yourself in if I'm not home."

Thea held the key in her palm like an unpleasant bug she found on her plants. She all but shoved it back at him. "I don't want this."

Gabe's eyebrows drew together. "No? Not like koalas? I tried to get a sea otter, but they didn't have one like that."

Thea shook her head. "No, the key. Why would I come here if you're not home?"

"You don't want it?"

"No."

He plucked the key from her outstretched hand, tucking it into his pocket.

Thea couldn't read his expression. She worried that she'd offended him, but she couldn't keep herself from prodding him. "Are you mad?"

He glanced at her with a puzzled look. "No."

"You sure?"

He let out half a laugh. "Yes, it's fine. Forget about it, okay?"

She nodded and gave him what she hoped was a reassuring smile. "You just surprised me."

"A good surprise?" He looked so hopeful that Thea felt a pang in her chest.

"It's just," she gesturing between them, "I guess we never talked about it."

Something in his eyes shuttered. Gabe held out his hand to her. She placed her hand in his and he gave it an encouraging squeeze. "Relax, it's only a key. Nothing more. Let's get dinner set up and we can talk about it if you want."

The glistening mound of Hainan chicken looked mouth-watering after Thea arranged it on one of Gabe's plates. When she removed the steamed bok choy and posed it on another plate next to the one of chicken, the contrast in colors made for the perfect shot. She poured wine, an effervescent light orange liquid, into mason jars.

She sat down opposite of Gabe once they organized the table to her liking. There was enough light streaking through the window to give everything a rosy, inviting glow.

Gabe leaned over to dig into a morsel of chicken with his chopsticks, but Thea shouted, "Stop!"

He dropped his chopsticks in a clatter on the table.

"Sorry," she said, "Didn't mean to yell. I need to take a picture of the dishes first."

Placing a hand over his heart, Gabe feigned catching his breath. "Geez, you scared me."

Thea pulled out her phone from her back pocket and fiddled with it, but the screen refused to turn on. "Crap. Forgot to charge it."

"Here, use mine." Gabe unlocked his phone and handed it to her. She stood over the table, taking pictures of the food from one angle, then another. Gabe scooted back to give her enough space to move around. He knew she didn't take pictures of food with any people in it.

"Is it okay if I stand on this chair?" she asked.

"Sure."

She stepped onto the chair so that she could get a good top-down shot of the entire table. She took another couple of pictures and then dropped from the chair.

"Okay, sorry for taking so long," she said. "Go ahead and start eating. I'm just gonna send these pics to myself."

Thea opened the photo app on Gabe's phone. She selected the ones she wanted to send to herself. When she scrolled up higher, something earlier in the album caught her eye. Above the pictures of woodworking projects in various states of completion was a picture that made her blood run cold.

✿ ✿ ✿

"Why do you have this?" Thea's tone made the hairs on the back of his neck stand up. Some ancient, reptile brain part of him switched on high alert.

Gabe leaned over the table to look at the screen.

It was a picture of her. In the candid picture, she was looking down at a magazine. Photo Thea sat at the table with her legs crossed, a folded-back magazine in one hand and her chin resting on the other. The light from the window behind her illuminated her like an other-worldly being.

"That's a picture of you," he said cautiously.

"I don't remember you taking it."

"It was from the other day when you brought dinner. Remember? We were waiting for the oven to get hot, and you asked if you could finish this article." He felt like a kid caught with his hand in the cookie jar.

"Why didn't you ask permission?"

"I didn't want you to move before I snapped it."

"You took a picture without my consent!" Thea's voice rose. "Why? Did you jerk off to this picture?!"

"What?! No!"

"Did you send this to anyone?"

"No! Of course not."

"How can I be sure?" Thea rose from her chair, backing away. She picked grabbed her purse from the back of the chair. She mumbled something to herself but Gabe could still hear, "you could be lying."

"Thea, just relax. I'm not." Gabe couldn't help the exasperation in his voice. "You're jumping to conclusions—"

Thea shot him a sharp look, and he could have sworn his balls shriveled. "Don't tell me to relax!"

"I would never lie to you!" Gabe said. It came out more harshly than he'd intended. He had a prickling sense of déjà vu. He stood from the table, moving to close the distance between them. "If you just listen—"

Thea held up a hand that halted him. "Stop."

She strode to his front door, her long legs making quick work of the distance. When she opened the door, she said over her shoulder. "Who knows who you sent those pics to?"

"What the fuck, Thea?!" She didn't know him at all if she'd thought that he'd do that.

The thump of the door shutting was a shock. She didn't even slam it; she closed it like it was the most normal thing in the world to storm out of his house. Gabe wanted to run after her, but his feet were bags of sand. Something deep in his chest was on fire. He was furious at how this whole thing escalated. That accusatory tone of hers humiliated him, especially when he had done nothing wrong.

This was why he avoided relationships. These types of fights, where he didn't even know how they started, made him want to abandon ship. Nothing was worth this sticky, burning feeling creeping up his neck.

Things had been going so well between them. He followed every one of her rules. She'd never freaked out like this before. It was scary. Sure, she was stressed about her manuscript, but even that didn't seem to be the cause of whatever this was.

How long had he been standing in the dining room? He walked to the windows at the front of the house and twitched the curtain aside, expecting to see Thea's car still there. It was gone. *Shit.* He should have gone after her instead of fuming silently in his living room. He hated the thought of her driving home at night while upset. What if something happened to her?

He went back to the dining room table, where his phone was. He swiped his thumb on it and looked at the picture of Thea was still on the screen. Even with the tight, gutted feeling in his chest, she stirred something in him.

One summer, when he was ten, he went to the beach with his family. There was a seagull flying low over the water when a gust hit. Wings spread, the bird soared, higher and higher on that breeze like magic. What he wanted to say to Thea, what he *couldn't* say to her, was that he kept the picture because each time he looked at it, his heart was that bird.

He thumbed over the trash icon and deleted the picture. Then he emptied his trash.

THIRTY-TWO

GABE TAPPED ON Thea's name on his phone. Straight to voicemail. Oh right, out of batteries. Or she could still be driving home. He checked the time. It was only 7:53, even though it felt much later. So much had happened in that short amount of time.

He texted her: *Can we talk? Call me. Please.*

In any other situation, he would have cringed about being so clingy, but his heart was still pounding. He wracked his brain for why she would stomp out like that over a picture. He knew she valued her anonymity, but didn't she know she could trust him?

He went back to the kitchen table, picking at his plate of food. Everything tasted like cold cardboard. He and Thea could have been eating a tasty meal together if he'd only deleted that picture or not taken it in the first place. He didn't exactly feel guilty about having that picture, but hated that it caused this amorphous, terrible feeling pulsing under his skin. It wasn't like her to leave like this.

Gabe checked his phone even though he didn't hear it ding. No replies. He gave up on trying to shovel another spoonful of food into his mouth and cleaned up.

He checked his phone again. No new messages. Thea should've made it home by now.

He sent another message: *Can you at least let me know you made it home okay?*

The phone buzzed before he could return it into his pocket. His heart leapt as he fumbled with it.

I'm home.

That was it. He stared at it for a while longer, wondering if the telltale bubble with the three dots would show up. Nothing.

Should he call again? No, he had already made it clear he wanted to talk. She was the one who didn't want to talk. He rubbed his face with both hands and rested his elbows on his knees. There was an unsettled feeling in his gut. He didn't want what they had to end like this.

A heavy, sinking feeling shot through Thea as soon as she woke up, almost like a morning after. It felt like when she'd drunk and said too much at a party the night before. She played back the scene at Gabe's, scrutinizing every detail of what went wrong. Had she overreacted to the picture? *No.*

She rolled over in bed and grabbed her phone to scroll through her email, then her social media feeds. Then, she searched her name on Google images. Nothing new or out of the ordinary. He hadn't put that picture up on the internet — that she could tell, anyway. That was good. But she couldn't stop reliving the icy feeling of discovering her picture on Gabe's phone last night.

She texted Olivia: *found a pic of me on G's phone that he took without telling me. HELP?*

Immediately, her phone buzzed with an incoming call. She swiped on it and put it to her ear.

"Was it a sex pic?" Olivia asked without so much as a 'hi'.

"No!" Thea said.

"Was it a hidden camera inside the toilet?"

"Ew, no!"

"Well, what kind of pic was it?"

Thea attempted to describe the picture. As she heard herself, it sounded harmless. It was just a regular picture of her reading a magazine. But then she recalled the last time a guy took a picture of her and immediately felt nauseated.

"I don't know," Olivia started, "it doesn't *sound* that bad. I think it's kinda sweet. He probably took it because you looked cute. But I get why you're upset. Did you tell him about your thing with pictures?"

"Not exactly."

"Really?"

"It hasn't really come up," Thea said. "And it's not something I wanna talk about with him."

She was still ashamed about it, but mostly still angry. Yes, definitely still angry about it. Feeling that brief spike of shame made her furious. She shouldn't need to feel guilty about those pictures. No, what she felt bad about was falling for Jake's nice-guy demeanor and letting him convince her to take those pictures in the beginning.

"Thea? You still there?" Olivia asked.

"Yeah, just thinking about what happened with Jake."

"Ugh, don't waste your time," Olivia said. "Look, that guy was a dick. But not all guys are like that, and your new guy doesn't sound like someone who'd do that."

Something warm unfurled in her belly when she thought of Gabe as *her* guy. "I guess not," Thea said. "But why did he have that picture in the first place?"

Olivia made a half snort and half laugh. "Why do dudes do half of the things they do? If I knew, I could have my own podcast about it."

"Please, no."

"Remember that dude in my office who kept cutting his toenails at his desk on Wednesday afternoons?"

"Gross, don't remind me."

"Why don't you ask Gabe for an explanation? I think what he says will tell you one way or the other what to think about this whole thing."

"I kinda... ran out of his house," Thea admitted. "I dunno if I should call him after that or not."

Olivia made a scoffing noise, and Thea could picture her expression.

"Should I call him?"

"Do you want to keep seeing him after this?" Olivia countered.

"I guess it depends on why he took that picture."

Olivia sighed. "So call him, girl! You're not doing any good making up all the answers he could have to that question."

"I dunno. I'm kinda scared."

"Of what?"

"Getting a bad answer. Or... getting a good one," Thea admitted as much to herself as to Olivia.

"Now, why would you be afraid of getting a good answer?"

"I like him. A lot. So if he just had that picture because of something sappy or romantic, it's gonna make me like him more!"

"What's so bad about that?"

Thea sighed dramatically. "I'm just not looking for a relationship right now."

Olivia laughed. "You keep saying that. You're not looking for a relationship right now because you're already in one! What do you call what's going on with Gabe if it's not a relationship?"

"Friends with benefits! What was the word you used for it? A situationship."

Olivia gave her two seconds of silence. "You're pandemic fuck buddies who text every day, have dinner together, watch Netflix together, oh, and have sex together. You just admitted to liking him a lot. It sounds like he likes you a lot. Be honest with me here: what does this sound like?"

Thea grew quiet, the realization coming to her all at once. She'd been avoiding scrutinizing it too closely, but having Olivia spell it out for her made her want to slap herself in the head. As much as she'd been avoiding the label, she and Gabe were in a relationship.

Olivia said, "Just because you don't call it a black kettle doesn't mean it's not a kettle."

"I'm pretty sure that's not how the saying goes." Thea laughed.

"You know what I mean."

"Only because I've known you for so long." Thea stretched out on her bed, taking in a deep breath. "Thanks, Liv. I feel a lot better now."

"That's because you've been spending the past few weeks playing mental dodgeball with relationships when you're already obviously in one. Now that you're not in denial, enjoy it!"

"Oh believe me, I *have* been enjoying it," Thea said, her face already heating at the thought of exactly how much she'd been enjoying it. Not only the sex, which was already better than she'd ever had, but even mundane things like meals together or sending each other stupid dad jokes.

"Just call him already and figure out what's going on with that pic. I gotta run, but I'm glad you called."

"You called *me*."

"I did? Well, you were obviously in some sort of crisis."

"Thanks for talking some sense into me. I'll call him."

"Good luck!"

After a quick shower and her usual morning routine, Thea sat down to a bowl of granola and cherry tomatoes from her garden while she thought about what she would say to Gabe. She didn't want to text. This seemed more like a phone type of conversation. Or maybe FaceTime? She sometimes had trouble getting a gauge of what people were saying if she couldn't see their face.

It also felt weird talking about her thing through a screen. She didn't want to go around in circles re-thinking this all morning, so before she could talk herself out of it, she texted him: *Hi, you up?*

Gabe knocked on Thea's door. There was movement behind the curtains, which could have been the shadows in the room or the wind. All he felt was relief when Thea texted him this morning. After the flash of anger faded the night before, he felt empty. His home was hollow without her.

After an eternity, Thea finally opened the door and, to his surprise, invited him in. This was new. A sick feeling took hold in his gut. Maybe this was her way of telling her they were through.

"Hi." She combed her hand through her hair. There were shadows under her eyes. She stepped back and let him in. "You can put your mask here." She pointed to an empty bamboo basket on the small table by the door.

He followed as Thea led the way into the living room. There were floor to ceiling built-in shelves full of books on the back wall, the spines exploding in an array of colors. Besides the bursting shelves, there were also neat stacks of books in her fireplace.

"You have *a lot* of books," he said appreciatively.

"Oh here, I'll get those. I need to find somewhere to donate them." Thea moved a stack of books off the couch so there was room to sit. She set the stack on the floor by the front door, chattering nervously, "They're too big to fit in the little library box around the corner, so I usually donate them to the actual library."

She gestured to the now cleared couch. "Do you want something to drink? I can make you some coffee. Or iced tea from the fridge? I made some yesterday."

"No, I'm good. Thanks."

Thea sat on one end of the couch, tucking a leg under her. Gabe sat on the other end. He felt oddly formal and at a loss of how to start. His heart was overflowing with emotions but the words wouldn't come to him. Thea was staring at something on the coffee table.

"Are we okay?" He finally asked. Might as well get down to it.

"Kinda nervous," Thea started, glancing up at him.

Gabe scooted closer, wanting to hold her, but she held her hand up to stop him.

"Wait, I have to say this before I lose my nerve." She took a deep breath, as if to gather her courage. "I owe you an explanation about last night."

He waited.

"I wanna ask you about that picture, but I want you to tell me the truth. I'll try not to freak out this time. Why do you have that picture?" When Thea looked up at him, he could see her eyes searching his face, as though if she read the page long enough, an answer would come to her.

He could only be honest, even if it meant revealing more of himself than he'd wanted to. "Every time I miss you, I look at it and it makes me feel closer to you. I know you don't want to see me every single day, but I like seeing you every day, even if it's just a silly picture of you. I really didn't think it was gonna be that big of a deal. I'm sorry."

Thea let out a long breath and blinked several times. Whatever thoughts were swirling behind her eyes cleared. "Really?"

"Really. Don't worry, I deleted it. Here, you can look." Gabe took out his phone, but Thea reached over and put her hand on his, pushing it down.

She shook her head. "No, it's okay."

"Are you sure? I want you to check if it makes you feel better. I don't wanna fight about it."

"It's not the picture that makes me feel bad. Okay, maybe it *is* the picture, but it's not what you think." She'd pulled over the tufted pillow sitting between them and fiddled with its corner. "I don't usually like to talk about this."

"You don't owe me anything. It's okay." His chest physically hurt to see her agitated like this.

Thea took a deep breath. "In college, I dated this guy. I thought we were in love, but I was young and stupid. He went on a guys' trip with his buddies. While he was away, we called each other on the phone before I went to bed every night. One night, he asked me to text him some pictures, because he said he missed me. So I did."

Gabe didn't like where this was going. He suppressed the urge to get off the couch and walk away. Hearing that she had been in love with another man, even if it was in the distant past, filled him with a spiky, unpleasant feeling.

"He said he liked those pictures, but could I take some *other* pictures?" Thea continued, her voice softer now. Her eyes held a faraway look. "At first I told him no, but he somehow guilted me into taking a couple of topless pictures."

Gabe reached over for her hand, removing it from clutching the corner of the pillow.

"He liked those pictures a lot more. He said so many things that made me feel good about my body," Thea whispered. "So I sent him more pictures. He liked those even more. God, I was so stupid!"

"Hey," Gabe said softly, still holding onto her hand. The pit of dread at the bottom of his stomach was growing huge. "You did nothing wrong."

"It gets worse. When I went to pick him up at the airport, he was waiting with one of his friends from the trip. I was gonna give his buddy a ride back, too. This guy kept staring at me with this weird look the whole time. I can still picture him looking at me through the mirror." Thea's complexion looked pale.

"Shit," Gabe breathed, feeling something cold — no, burning, a burning so hot it felt cold, seeping through his body.

"He showed those guys the pictures. He didn't even bother telling me. I found out later when one of them made a comment about it." Thea finally looked up at Gabe, her dark eyes shimmering.

Gabe forced himself to let go of the tight grip on Thea's hands. He'd never felt this amount of anger before. It was hard to keep his breathing even. A freezing icy rage threatened to spill out of his chest. "I'm gonna kill him. Tell me who he is and I'm gonna kill him."

Thea shook her head and gave a bitter smile. "Don't worry, I thrashed him plenty. Verbally. I was at least smart enough not to have my face in those pictures. We had a huge fight about it and I made him delete them. But I dunno if he had them saved somewhere else or what. Obviously, we broke up after that."

"Oh, Thea." Gabe drew her closer to him so that he could put an arm around her. He was an asshole. He'd been busy feeling offended by her accusations when he should have wondered *why* she'd run off like that.

Thea's shoulders sagged, and she leaned into him, tucking herself under his shoulder. He wrapped his other arm around her, wishing he could do something more.

He murmured into her hair. "I'm so sorry my picture brought all this up. I promise I didn't show anyone."

Thea turned her head so she could look into his eyes. If he could pour everything he felt for her into those dark pools, he would have. Something in his eyes must have said it, because she nodded. "I believe you."

Gabe placed his lips on top of her head, inhaling the comforting scent of her. He'd been so close to losing her, he needed to hold her to reassure himself that she was there. She tilted her head up, eyes closed. He placed another soft kiss on her eyebrow, on her temple, on the side of her head. When he kissed her ear, she shivered, then sighed, relaxing into him.

He loved how she responded to his touch. The little sounds she made and the taste of her skin on his lips were a salve to the icy-hot rage he'd felt only seconds earlier.

She believed him. He'd driven over today filled with fear that she was about to put an end to what they had. But she'd not only invited him into her house, but shown him a vulnerable part of herself. It made the incandescent feeling inside his chest swell. He wanted to protect all her soft spots.

He was in deep.

THIRTY-THREE

"MORE," THEA PLEADED in his ear.

Gabe could never tire of that sexy bedroom voice of hers. Thea, her hair loose, riding an unrelenting rhythm on top of him, was incredible. He moved his hands from their firm grip on her waist, circling his thumb across the spot where they were joined, knowing exactly what she needed.

One, two, three thrusts later. Her breath hitched as she ground on top of him, her teeth clamped where his shoulder met his neck. The sweet pain of that bite brought him tumbling over the edge as her squeezing pulled a loud moan out of him.

Thea's body melted on top of his as he smoothed his hands over her back, relishing her soft, slightly damp skin. He planted a kiss on top of her tangle of hair as he caught his breath. He loved the sensation of her sprawled across him and feeling the steady thump of her heart.

Gabe reluctantly let her go as she rolled off of him with a sigh. Before he could say anything, she swung her legs off the edge of the bed and stood, stretching her arms over her head. He felt a surge of passion towards the unfettered way she moved her body.

"Bathroom!" she said as she strode out of his room.

A buzz brought Gabe's attention to his nightstand. Their phones sat next to each other, a sight that made him ache with how much he wanted this to be a nightly occurrence. He'd thought that the misunderstanding with the pictures last week had brought them closer together, but things had gone back to their usual rhythm, with Thea returning to her house after she was through with him. He realized the notification was on Thea's phone, but before he could look away, his eyes skimmed the message from Olivia: *Happy Bday, T!*

The time on the phone said 12:05. There was an unpleasant sensation in his chest. She hadn't ever mentioned her birthday to him. It made him acutely aware of the walls she had set up around certain parts of her life.

Before he could dwell on it any further, the bathroom door swung open and Thea stepped out, padding softly to sit on the edge of his bed as she started pulling her clothes back on.

"It's your birthday tomorrow? Or I guess technically today?" He asked.

Thea stopped in the middle of slipping her dress over her head. "How did you know?"

Gabe nodded to the two phones on his nightstand. "You got a text. Sorry, I didn't mean to, but I thought its was my phone when I looked."

A bare shoulder lifted and lowered. "Yeah, it's my birthday. It's not a big deal."

"Can I make it a big deal? What do you usually do to celebrate?"

Thea finished pulling the dress over her and took a few seconds to smooth out the fabric over her thighs.

"I stay up all night watching horror movies with my friend Olivia," she said as she shrugged. "But I haven't seen her since the pandemic started. She's in the Bay Area."

He could tell that she pretending to be nonchalant about it, but by now he knew her well enough to hear the sadness in her voice. He understood how the pandemic felt especially hard and lonely when you lived by yourself. A plan formed in his head.

* * *

Halloween Horror Nights! Get spooked in the safety of you're car!!

Gabe almost deleted the email as spam thanks to the grammatical error, but something stopped him. It was perfect! Except Thea said that she didn't want them to do any couple-y things like dates. Going to a drive-in *could* be a date. But he'd also gone to them with his platonic friends in high school. Those movie nights amounted to a bunch of guys with nothing to do on a Friday night but hang out, make fun of the movie, eat junk food, and drink cheap beer.

He texted her before he could second guess himself, "Hey, you free to talk?"

His phone buzzed with an incoming FaceTime request. What he saw when he answered it made his heart skip a beat. He had an incredible view of Thea. She had on a maroon sports bra, and the angle of the camera made it very hard for him not to gawk at the delicious curves of her breasts. There was a sheen of sweat on her flushed face and her breathing was heavy.

"Hi," Thea said, looking down at the screen with an apologetic smile. "I'm just finishing up this bike ride."

"I like the view." The bead of sweat trickling down the hollow of her throat transfixed him as it disappeared into her sports bra. He swallowed hard.

"Stop, you." Thea grinned as she rolled her eyes, oblivious to how she affected him. "I don't like to text while I'm riding. Makes me wanna barf. What's up?"

Gabe tried to remember why he'd called her. Oh yes, Halloween Horror Nights. "The drive-in's playing scary movies this month. Can I take you for your birthday? They're playing some older stuff right now."

"Oooh! That sounds so fun." Thea's eyes widened in surprise. Then her face fell. "I can't. I really need to work on my manuscript."

"Not even one night off? For your birthday?" He asked.

Thea chewed on her lip. "It's tempting, but I already have every night this week scheduled."

"Just use your usual booty-call night, except we'll be watching a movie instead." He wagged his eyebrows suggestively. He was not above pouting. "It's a birthday present. You can't say no."

She laughed a hearty belly-laugh. She must have had a good day of writing. "Fine, fine. That's one fewer booty-call for you then."

"I'll try to survive," he said solemnly.

Thea slowed her pedaling. "Wow, a drive-in. I haven't been to the movies since, well, since the before times. I don't know why I didn't think of this sooner. A drive-in is totally Covid safe. What's playing?"

"Don't look it up! I want it to be a surprise."

"Hm... I like this kind of surprise."

Gabe let out a breath of relief. It was silly to feel nervous about asking her on a not-date to the drive-in, especially after they'd been sleeping together. The jitters in his stomach were only now settling down.

"Just checking." Thea narrowed her eyes. It was like she'd read his mind. "This isn't like a date-date, right? I strictly have a no-birthday dates rule. It's just too much pressure."

Gabe could see doubts flit through her eyes. "Not a date. Just two friends who really like scary movies. You're not gonna be too scared afterward, right?"

"I hope not! It's not too bad when I'm watching with someone else. Isn't a drive-in where teenagers go to make out?"

Gabe snickered. "Uh, okay, if you're a teenager from 1960s or whatever, yes."

Thea stopped pedaling and reached off-camera. A sleek black water bottle came into view. Gabe watched her drinking from the bottle, his body growing warmer as he watched the slender line of her throat. Was she going to change her mind?

"Are you asking me to go to the drive-in to make out?" she asked after she swallowed a few gulps of water.

Gabe shook his head slowly, nailing her with a look. "I didn't realize I needed an excuse to make out with you."

Thea's mouth dropped open. When she finally recovered, she said, "You don't. But I'm not gonna go if it's like a date-date."

"It'll be strictly platonic. Don't worry, I'll be have myself."

"Okay, fine, you've convinced me. As long as there's no hanky-panky, I'm game."

"*Are* you a teenager from the 1960s? Y'know, no one says hanky-panky anymore, right?"

THIRTY-FOUR

THE SOFT PINK glow of sunset illuminated Thea's front porch. Vines and leaves tumbling over the balustrade added to the cozy atmosphere. It was no wonder she enjoyed sitting out there so much. A nervous energy thrummed beneath Gabe's skin as he walked from his truck. This was far from his first time at her house. And they were already intimately acquainted. So intimately. But that didn't reign in his anxiety about picking her up for their not-date. He tried to act natural as he knocked on the door.

When Thea answered, he couldn't stop the goofy grin from spreading on his face. Seeing her erased any doubts about the evening. She wore an oversized black hoodie that dwarfed her frame. Under that, she had on simple black leggings and some brightly colored socks.

"What?" she asked in a teasing tone. "You told me to dress comfy, and this is dressing comfy!"

"I know. You're just —" he struggled to find the words to describe the overwhelming sensation spreading through his chest. He shook his head, giving up. "You're just so adorable sometimes."

Thea locked her door and heaved a bulky tote on her shoulder.

"What's in here?" Gabe pulled it away from her. It was heavier than he expected.

"You told me to pack snacks, so I did! And some drinks." She wiggled her eyebrows.

"By snacks, do you mean an entire three-course meal?" he asked, weighing the bag in his hand.

"Hey," she smacked his arm, "I like a variety, okay? If you're gonna make fun of my snacks, then you can watch while I eat them. Every. Single. One."

Gabe put his free arm around her shoulders and gave her a squeeze. "I'm sure these are very good snacks. I would be honored if you shared your snacks with me."

Half an hour later, Gabe pulled his truck behind a line of other cars making a right into a parking lot bordered by tall trees.

"I didn't know there still were drive-ins like this!" Thea said as the car crept forward, getting closer and closer to the entrance, where it looked like someone was checking for tickets.

"Yeah, this place has been around forever. I used to go with my buddies in highschool. Cheaper than going to a regular theater because they charge per car *and* you could bring your own food."

"This is awesome!" Thea looked at him, a big smile on her face.

He wanted to kiss her, but stopped himself in time as he leaned over. Instead, he opened the glove compartment and pulled out his wallet. Out of the corner of his eyes, he saw a hard to read expression on her face. She looked almost disappointed. The quiet in the car while they inched their way forward was thick.

"Hey, you okay? We can leave if you don't think this is safe. I read on the site that the cars have to park one car space away from the next car and that people aren't allowed to get out other than for the bathroom."

"It's not that. This just feels so much like a date. More than I expected."

Gabe tried for a casual tone. "We're just two buddies watching a scary movie."

"Two buddies at a horror movie?" Thea raised an eyebrow.

"Yes. I promise, no hanky-panky and after this, I'll drive you straight home. Okay?"

Thea turned to face him, her eyes roaming his face as if she could read what he was thinking. She nodded firmly. "Okay, deal. No funny business, okay?"

Gabe raised one hand as if taking an oath, "I promise. No funny business. Just two pals watching The Ring."

"The Ring?!" Thea shrieked. "Japanese or American?"

"Japanese, of course."

Thea clapped gleefully, her eyes wide in anticipation.

Darkness cloaked the parking lot of the drive-in. Thea peered at Gabe while he focused on the screen. They had a few awkward moments when their hands brushed each other while reaching into the chip bag, but so far, he'd kept his promise and they were behaving like strictly platonic friends.

A loud noise on the screen startled her out of her thoughts, and she let out an unintentional squeak. She pressed herself back into the passenger seat, as if those few inches of extra distance between her and the screen would protect her.

Gabe looked at her and whispered, "You okay?"

Thea nodded. She pulled her hoodie up over her hair and tugged on its strings. If things got too scary, she could always hide in the hood.

Gabe gathered the half-empty shrimp chip bag, the box of mushroom-shaped chocolate covered cookies, the can of wasabi peanuts, and the unopened bag of beef jerky. He dumped those in the seat well behind them. Then he folded the middle console down so that it was no longer a barrier between them.

"Come here," he said, patting the space to his right.

Thea eagerly slid closer. She'd forgotten how scary this movie was, especially in the dark of night when she couldn't see anything else outside of the car windows. Gabe draped his arm over her shoulder and gave her a reassuring squeeze. She immediately felt better. Still scared, but this time a good kind of scared. She snuggled into the crook of his arm, his shoulder at the perfect height for a headrest. By tilting her head, she could watch the screen and still sneak glances at Gabe. He seemed unperturbed by the movie. She was distracted by the strong column of his neck and the urge to put her mouth there. What was it about dark cars and movies that made people want to make out?

Halfway through the movie, the music turned eerie and slow. The camera creeped along the scene in anticipation... BAM. Even though she knew it was coming, the jump scare started her. Thea jolted back in her seat and flung an arm down to grab anything she could — Gabe's leg.

"Sorry," she said, embarrassed at her reaction. She pulled her hand away, but Gabe reached down and put it back on his thigh. She could feel the heat of him through the denim.

He smoothed his palm over the back of her hand and gave it a gentle pat. "It's fine."

🍃 🍃 🍃

For the rest of the movie, Thea kept her left hand on his leg. When something scary happened, her hand tensed and clutched at him. Gabe reminded himself at least once every five minutes that this was *not* supposed to be a date. He calmed his reaction to her hand on his thigh, even though she was mere inches away from a crucial part of his anatomy. He was definitely not having thoughts about her that a buddy would.

He snuck glances down at her when she wasn't looking. With the faint light shining through the windshield from the movie screen, he could barely make out her features. At this angle, her eyes looked startlingly black. When she gasped, his attention slipped to her full, parted lips. He tried to fight back the memory of how silky her lips were and the little moan she made when he kissed her just right. He harnessed all his self-control to keep from kissing her right then. If he started kissing her in the car, he wouldn't be able to stop and they definitely wouldn't be able to finish the movie.

Thea's eyes slid to meet his. The sounds of the movie were far away like they were coming to him from the other end of a long tunnel. He saw her take a steady inhale, her eyes going soft and her lids lowering. He knew that look. He wanted to lean down and touch his lips to hers.

Gabe moved toward her, inches away from her face. He moved the arm that was around her and dug around in the footwell until he pulled out a candy bar. His lips twitched as he held it out to her. "Chocolate?"

Thea's dreamy expression shuttered. She pursed her lips and took the candy, noisily tearing it open and breaking off a piece. It was a rookie mistake to watch her pop it into her mouth. The tip of her tongue darted out to lick a crumb of chocolate from her finger, and he almost lost it. She slanted her eyes up to him, with a cat-like expression of smugness. She knew exactly what she was doing to him.

He took a shaky breath to gather his wits and gave her what he hoped was a friendly and totally not a "I want to jump your bones" smile. He tore his gaze away from hers and looked back at the movie, mentally cataloging all the tools in his workshop so that he could hold on to the willpower to behave as a strictly platonic friend.

When the credits rolled, Thea let out a long breath. She'd forgotten how immersive it felt to watch a horror movie on the big screen. She stretched as best as she could in the confines of the truck, twisting one way, then the other, to work out the kinks in her back. It was good they were in his truck and not her tiny car. Gabe did the same, rolling his neck a few times and causing some cracks and pops.

He gave her a shy smile. "It happens if I don't move around for a long time."

Thea started collecting the discarded wrappers and crumbs from her side of the car. She busied herself stuffing them into an empty snack bag so that she could avoid the awkward moment that came after the credits rolled and they needed to decide what to do.

She thought she'd packed everything up when Gabe said, "Wait."

He moved toward her, his left arm curving over her body. His head bent close to hers. She felt his warm breath over the fine hairs on her temples. She froze, her breathing hitched, wondering if he was going to kiss her. She wanted him to.

"Forgot this," Gabe whispered into her ear. He straightened away from her and held up an empty wrapper that had been wedged between her seat and the door.

"Thanks." Despite her trying to keep her voice neutral, it came out rougher than expected.

Gabe looked at her, a knowing glint in his eyes. He arched an eyebrow. She wanted him to kiss her right then, but the infuriating man only grinned at her.

"Alright, buckle up. Looks like we have an opening here," he said, pointing to a space after the long queue of cars waiting to get out of the parking lot.

Gabe was a calm and competent driver, holding the wheel loosely with his right hand as his left rested on the rolled down window. Even in the dark, Thea could see the muscle in his forearm move as he maneuvered the truck onto the freeway. She never took herself for an arms girl, but she had to admit there was something alluring about all that bronze skin with its light dusting of hair over it. She forced herself to look out of her own window to keep from doing anything stupid.

It wasn't until they reached the curb in front of her house that Thea realized he had driven her home instead of to his house. She must have drifted off while looking out the window. She wiped the side of her mouth, embarrassed that she had drooled. They hadn't explicitly talked about it, but based on the tension between them, Thea hoped they'd go back to Gabe's house.

By the time she'd gathered her stuff and opened her door, Gabe was already on the other side. Her now empty cooler bag was slung over his shoulder.

"I can get that," she said, moving to pull the strap from him.

"I got it. I'll walk you to your door. As a friend," he said, his lips curling in a teasing smile.

As she fumbled with her keys at the front door, she heard him stop close behind her. She could feel his heat on her back and she fought to keep from leaning back toward him like a plant to sunlight. The key finally unlocked the deadbolt with a satisfying click.

Instead of opening the door, she turned around to face him. He was closer than she expected. She took a step back, leaning on her door. The solid wood on her back gave her a firm foundation so that she could meet his gaze. The lack of light on her porch threw his face in shadow, which emphasized the strong angle of his jaw and the depth of his eyes.

Thea held her breath as he moved toward her, his right hand reaching for her hip. She closed her eyes and tilted her head up, eagerly expecting the warmth of his mouth on hers. She felt his breath on the side of her face, tickling her ear.

"Goodnight," he whispered in his sex voice.

Thea's eyes flicked open in surprise. She must have had some tragic expression on her face because, as Gabe pulled away, she heard him chuckle, rumbling deep in his chest. A click behind her. She realized he had been reaching to open the door. There was a twinkle in his eye when he pulled back.

"Hilarious," she grumbled, narrowing her eyes at him.

"Hey, don't get the wrong idea." He stepped back and raised his hands up in a placating gesture. He gave her a soft punch in the shoulder. "Happy belated birthday, buddy."

"Yeah, yeah." She stepped through the doorway and then turned to face him. "Have a safe drive home."

"I will."

Thea leaned against the door and watched him saunter back to his truck. She would never get tired of watching his backside. When he finally pulled away, she closed her front door and let out a deep breath. She fanned her flushed cheeks. Don't be silly, she chided herself.

THIRTY-FIVE

GABE PUT HIS phone down and hopped into the shower. He mulled over the text from Thea. He couldn't quite place his finger on it, but something was peculiar. He hadn't seen her since the drive-in last week.

She'd asked if he would be around. Once he confirmed it, she just wrote, "I'm coming over."

He hopped in the shower to wash away the dirt and wood dust of the day. He'd gotten sweaty this afternoon doing a delivery, his largest order yet: eight Adirondacks. Thankfully, all with the same specifications. Getting all eight stacked into the back of his truck securely was a real life game of Tetris.

The doorbell rang as he stepped out of the shower. She got there so fast, he wondered if she was already on the way when she texted him. Gabe rubbed the towel through his hair one last time and pulled on a clean pair of shorts.

"Hey," he barely got out as Thea stalked in, right past him.

She walked in like a woman on a mission. *What she was up to?* She spun to face him. Her eyes widened as they drifted down. He hadn't had time to put on a shirt before getting the door. Her gaze was palpable.

"You okay?"

"Yeah," she said breathlessly, right before she crashed into him, her mouth hot and hungry.

Gabe braced himself against the door, returning the kiss. *Oh, was that what she was here for?* His body responded instantly, attuned to hers like he was made for her. She placed her hands on his shoulders, pulling him towards her or her towards him. He wasn't sure which. He slipped an arm around her waist, the other on her nape, fingers buried in her thick hair. He would never get enough of her.

When she finally pulled back, her lips were swollen and flushed. He was about to dip his head down to continue kissing her when she held a finger up.

"What you did at the drive-in," she started, poking him in the chest with her finger as she made her point, "Wasn't very funny."

"No?" His mouth twitched. She looked so serious, it was adorable. After all, she was the one who laid out the rules about how it was *not* a date-date. He was only following her rules. It wasn't his fault if she didn't like how well he followed her rules.

"No! Not at all," she answered softly, her eyes meeting his. He felt her dark gaze searing into him. "You can't tease me like that and..."

Her palm settled over his chest. He'd been craving her all day. Could she feel his pulse jumping at her touch? "And what?"

"And not do anything about it!"

Gabe smoothed his hands down her shoulders to her arms, then up a feather-light touch on the delicate skin of her neck. He lived for the flushed color of her cheeks. He tilted his head and searched her face. His voice deepening, he asked, "what would you like me to do about it now?"

Thea's eyes held a vicious gleam. Her mouth spread into a mischievous smile. Gabe was hypnotized. He realized her hand was still on his chest when she started moving it lower. She trailed it down and he couldn't control the clenching of his abs as she pressed a sensitive spot. She skirted over his belly button, then lower, tickling the line of hair below his stomach, until she hooked her finger on the straining waistband of his shorts. His breathing was loud in the sudden silence of the room.

"Come into the bedroom and I'll show you." Her voice was husky as she tugged on his shorts. She walked backwards toward the direction of his room.

He followed her as if he had a choice, as if his body didn't already belong to her. In his bedroom, Gabe grabbed the wet towel hanging over the door and tossed it toward the bathroom, not wanting to waste any more time.

Thea pushed his door closed with a click. She looked at him with a teasing curve of her lips and he swallowed, suddenly parched. The feverish look in her eyes made his blood rush south.

"I'm glad to see you've started undressing," she said in a sultry voice, her eyebrows raised at his half-dressed body.

"Just... the shower." It was hard to form sentences when she looked at him like that.

"Hmm." She reached down for the hem of her dress, a sleeveless shift that draped her body and ended mid-thigh. In one fluid motion, she pulled it up over her head and threw it over the chair in the corner. It slid down the back of the chair. Neither of them cared.

"Fuck," Gabe mumbled as she stood in her panties before him. He reached for her, but she stepped just out of reach.

"Nuh-uh," she said, wagging a finger at him. "Get on the bed."

Thea was never shy about what she wanted, but this new, commanding version of her thrilled him. His pulse doubled, and he was so hard it ached. He sat on the edge of the bed and looked up at her expectantly. She gave an imperceptible nod and walked toward him. She stood in between his legs, so close, but not touching. Seated on the edge of the bed like that, he was at a convenient height. The sight of her perfect breasts in front of him made him lick his lips. If he leaned forward an inch, he could pull her nipple in into his mouth and make her moan.

He glanced up.

Thea's lips came crashing down on his as one of her hands grasped the back of his neck, fingers curled into his hair. Her other hand cupped the side of his jaw as she kissed him desperately. He placed his hands on her hips, fingers kneading her skin as he lost himself in the feeling of her scorching lips.

When they finally broke apart, she was panting and her eyes shone. "I've been wanting to do that since the end of the movie."

"Get on," he said roughly, not able to hold back any longer. He scooted back on the bed until his back hit the headboard. He scooped an arm around her waist, pulling her toward him, over his legs so that she straddled his lap.

Thea needed no encouragement as he wrapped his arms around her, a steady hand at her back. He nuzzled the side of her breast, sighing at the feeling of her against his cheek. She gasped at the contact, arching into him willingly. His tongue flicked over her nipple, already taut. Thea's hands tangled in his hair again, her nails digging into his scalp.

Gabe kissed the valley between her breasts, inhaling the sweet, intoxicating scent of her skin. If he could bottle up that smell and save it for the day when she wasn't with him, he would. His cock strained against his shorts so painfully that he was glad he hadn't changed into jeans before.

Thea's uneven breath was hot and loud in his ear as she sat down on his lap. The layers of fabric between them were too much to bear. He hooked a finger into the waistband of her panties, pulling them over her hips. He gave her ass a playful slap, loving the way her flesh molded to his hands.

Instead of settling back down on his lap, Thea slid her hands down his shoulders, the pads of her fingers grazing his nipples and sending shivers up his spine. When she started moving down, scooting lower on his legs and pulling his shorts down with her, his breath hitched. He helped her pull his shorts off and settled back down against the headboard.

Thea flipped her hair so that it tumbled in waves down one side. She must have pulled her hair out of that bun sometime between entering his front door and getting to his bedroom, but he couldn't remember when. She slid down his body with that delicious friction between her soft, pliant skin and his. Her warm hands grasped him at the base gently, and he almost came from the expression in her eyes as she looked at him. Before he could warn her to go slow, she'd dipped her head, swirled her tongue around the head of his cock.

An uncontrollable shout escaped from his lips, and he clenched his bedsheets in his fists. Thea's mouth was so hot and wet, and the thing she was doing with her tongue! He closed his eyes and tried to take some deep breaths before the sensation washed over him. His hips flexed uncontrollably, wanting to pump deeper into her mouth.

He called on hidden reserves of willpower he didn't know he possessed to cup the side of her face with his hand and pull her away. As much as he wanted her mouth on him forever, he knew that if he let it go on even a second longer, he would lose that thin thread of control he had on his body.

Thea looked at him with questioning eyes. The way her kiss-swollen lips glistened made her irresistible. He pulled her up, settling her on his lap again, and kissed her, tongue sweeping into her mouth. She made a delicious sound in the back of her throat when he nipped at her lip softly.

Gabe wrapped his arms around her and placed a hand on the base of her neck, tugging her hair gently so that she tipped her head back. It exposed the soft skin on her neck and he kissed a path from her ear to the tender spot where her neck met her shoulder. He dipped the tip of his tongue in that hollow, licking the salty taste of her skin.

Thea made a contented sound while she rubbed against his length. Gabe groaned at how wet she was. He moved a hand to her hip, fingers squeezing as he carefully explored the taste of her skin, wanting to savor every single inch of her with his tongue. He didn't care if it took all night.

"Gabe," Thea moaned when he slid a hand up the side of her breast and he swirled his tongue around her nipple. "Please."

"Please what?" He asked against her skin. He liked the way her nipple pebbled at his breath.

"Fuck me," she pleaded, arching into him.

"Patience." A powerful feeling of possession surged over him. He chuckled against her as he continued to kiss and touch each squirming inch of her. She did not like that one bit because she slid partially off of him. He was about to pull her back, but she reached over to his nightstand and pulled out a condom. She made swift work of opening it and rolling it onto him. He couldn't take his eyes off of her hands gripping his cock. He was still admiring the view when she spoke.

"You evil, evil, man," she murmured as she straddled him, bracing her hands on his shoulder.

He angled himself into her as she sank onto his lap, felt her moan through his entire body. He relished the feeling of being inside her. Thea started moving up and down in a slow rhythm above him. With her eyes closed and her head thrown back, she looked amazing.

Gabe couldn't stop the glowing feeling welling up inside of him, something more intense than the impending orgasm he was trying to fight off. The heat of it flooded his whole being, and he shut his eyes, burying his face in the waves of hair cascading over her shoulder, hoping whatever this emotion was, it wasn't beaming out of his eyes like a beacon.

Gabe jolted awake. A glance at the glowing ticks of his wall clock showed that he'd drifted off for almost an hour. A sigh came from Thea's warm body sprawled over him. He looked at her, melting at the way sleep relaxed her face into something unguarded.

He nudged her shoulder. "Thea," he whispered, not wanting to startle her.

She snuggled into his shoulder.

He gave her shoulder a firmer shake. "Thea."

When she blinked sleepily and rubbed her nose, it was so endearing that he couldn't help hugging her closer to him. He could never tire of the way her body felt draped over his.

"Hmm?" she said, stifling a yawn. "How long was I asleep?"

"An hour? I fell asleep too."

"Oh, sorry." She levered herself up, one hand on his chest. "I should go, it's late."

He placed a hand over her hip. "Stay. It is pretty late. We'll just sleep."

She looked down at him, blinking in thought. Her dark hair tumbled over her face, cloaking it from view. Gabe lifted his hand from her hip to brush it back and tuck it behind her ear.

"It's fine. I'd feel better if you stayed over instead of driving back so late." It didn't escape his notice that she still hadn't spent the night with him. Whenever she left for the night, he couldn't fall asleep until she texted him that she made it home. And now that they'd been spending less time together, he wanted to keep her with him as long as possible.

"Are you sure? What if I have terrible morning breath?" she asked while worrying at her lip.

"What if *I* have terrible morning breath?"

"You don't know if I snore or not."

"Do you snore?"

"I don't think so. Do you?"

"No." He stifled a yawn. She'd worn him out.

"What if I look terrible in the morning?"

A bark of laughter came out of him. "There's no possibility in any universe where you'd look terrible."

"I dunno. I don't want it to be all awkward and weird and in the morning."

"I like it when you're all awkward and weird. It'll be fine, I promise."

Thea's eyes lids lowered and her lips curled up in a bashful smile. Even in the dim light, he could see the blush spreading on her face.

"Well, it *is* pretty late. As long as you don't mind."

Gabe wrapped an arm around her waist and nudged her, so she turned over. He curled his body around hers, pulling her snug against him. He pressed a kiss to her ear as he felt her relax against him. Having her tucked against him so sweetly was the closest he'd ever felt to her. He drifted off to the thud, thud, thud of her heartbeat pressed against his chest, fervently wishing this could be forever.

THIRTY-SIX

THEA WOKE UP to the unfamiliar absence of birds squawking. She opened her eyes. It was dimmer in Gabe's room in the morning than it typically was in her room.

She was shocked that she enjoyed the novel sensation of waking up with Gabe's heavy arm wrapped around her. She was the small spoon, curled up on her side, her back fitting comfortably against the cocoon of his body. She lay still for a moment, waiting for that sinking sensation she associated with morning-afters. It wasn't exactly a hangover, but more of a sense of dread about having to face the guy in the morning. That feeling didn't come. Not even a little bit.

Thea shifted, pressing herself against his firm length nestled behind her. A sharp intake of breath behind her, and then his arm moved, a strong hand on her hip. Gabe buried his face into her tangle of hair. He moaned a low rumble that she could feel resonating in his chest behind her.

"Good morning," she said, arching her back in a stretch, intentionally rubbing herself against him.

Another groan escaped from him, which encouraged her to do it again, grinding the curve of her ass into him. She rubbed her thighs together, trying to ease the pressure between her legs, but that only made things worse when she felt how wet she was for him.

Gabe's hand slid from her hip, caressing her thigh and squeezing it gently while he flexed his hips against her. She felt soft kisses against her temple. He swept the hair off her face so that he could plant a kiss on the edge of her ear.

She gasped as his tongue flicked out and licked her ear. His labored breath was hot against it. He bit her lobe and sucked it into his mouth gently and she let out a high sound, clamping her hand over his hand, still clutching her thigh. She shifted her thigh on top of his and guided his hand to her pussy.

Gabe moved infuriatingly slowly, sliding his hand to her inner thigh, rubbing teasing circles against her skin. It wasn't enough. She must have made a sound of protest because he chuckled, the sound like thunder rumbling past her ear. Finally, he gave her what she wanted and placed his palm between her legs, pushing the pesky fabric aside and dipping his finger into her.

"Fuck me, you're soaked," he whispered in a strained voice. She pulled off her panties, tossing them to the floor at the foot of the bed.

Freed from the constraints of her panties, Thea turned to lie on her back, her thighs falling open as his hand trailed up the inner part of her thighs again. She shivered as his hand made its slow journey up. By the time his hands returned to where she was desperate for his touch, she was panting and wound up so tight she was about to beg. If this was her reward for staying the night, she needed to rethink her rules.

Gabe's mouth moved on from her ear and was now over her lips, nibbling and licking her as his hand did its magic. She opened her mouth to him, licking his bottom lip, liking the rough feel of the surrounding stubble. Her tongue met his, and he pressed into her. She could feel him hard and ready against her hip. She'd never hungered for something so desperately in her life.

When he swirled his thumb over her clit, she moaned into his mouth. He thrust two fingers into her agonizingly slow. She clutched at him as he pulled out.

"Please," she pleaded, not recognizing the throaty voice coming from mouth.

"Shh," he said between kisses and thrusts of his fingers, sounding like someone trying to calm a spooked horse. "You'll get what you want. Eventually."

Thea realized her right hand clung to the tangle of sheets next to her and placed it against Gabe's taut stomach. She was helpless against the way his abs flexed under her touch. She trailed the hand lower, rubbing against the trail of hair skimming over the band of his boxer briefs. When she reached the unmistakable bulge tenting the front, she gave him a firm squeeze, pleased by the hiss of pleasure from his mouth.

With a sigh, Thea stretched out on her back, limbs liquid and wobbly. She rested her hand on Gabe's head, which was pillowed below her breasts, his breath tickling against her stomach. This felt nice. Like they were the only two people in the world. She rarely allowed herself to enjoy the warm afterglow with men in the past.

Her stomach growled, ruining the moment.

"Sorry."

Gabe raised himself up off of her, leaning on a bent elbow. "I'm a poor host for not offering you breakfast. I'll whip something up. What do you like? Sweet or savory?"

"You're gonna make me breakfast?" Thea squeaked, then cleared her throat. She was thinking of a gracious way to leave. "Are you sure? I don't want to impose or anything."

He gave her a look as if she was out of her mind. "You spent the night at my house for the first time and we just had mind-blowing sex, if I'm being honest. You're *not* imposing. Let me feed you before you run away."

"I wasn't about to run away!"

Gabe rolled his eyes as if he knew better. "Okay, if you say so. Lemme feed you. Then you can escape. Please."

Thea's stomach growled again, which decided it for her.

Gabe was already off the bed and pulling on a pair of clean shorts. He left the bedroom, but then popped back in as if he forgot something. "I'm gonna get started with breakfast. Clean towels behind the door in the bathroom. Use anything else in there. There's a new toothbrush out for you in the holder."

Before he left a second time, he bent over the bed and kissed her so sweetly that she couldn't keep the smile off her face. Thea stretched her arms over her head, taking advantage of the empty bed to also stretch out her legs.

There wasn't only a clean toothbrush still in its packaging, but also a small unopened tube of toothpaste like the ones she got from the dentist. Sure, it was silly to feel squeamish about germs from sharing the same tube of toothpaste, but that he thought of her made her heart hitch in a way she wasn't ready to process. It distracted her from questioning why he was so prepared for an overnight guest in the first place.

When she emerged from the bedroom, freshly showered and wearing one of his shirts, Gabe was still busy in the kitchen. Thea thanked the gods that he hadn't pulled on a shirt, as she enjoyed watching the powerful lines of his back and shoulders while he wasn't looking.

He must have known she was there though, because without turning, he nodded to the Chemex on the counter. "The coffee should be ready. Not sure if it'll be as good as the one you make, though."

Thea stepped up to the counter and filled the two empty mugs with the steaming hot beverage. She wrapped her hands around one, closed her eyes, and inhaled. "Smells great."

Gabe turned, and an expression of surprise lit his face. He started, lips pressed into a firm line. A muscle in his jaw twitched. "Um…"

Thea looked down at the shirt she put on. It was a faded Ramones shirt. By the soft cloud-like texture, she knew it was an old shirt, not fake-old. "Oh, oops. I just took the first shirt I could find in your closet. I can return it if—"

"No!" he said roughly, running a hand through his hair, still in its adorable bed-head mess. "Keep it. You look great in it."

"Are you sure?"

His gaze moved up and down her body. "My favorite shirt just got better. Here, sit down. Breakfast is ready."

Thea brought the two cups of coffee to the small breakfast bar and sat. Gabe placed a plate in front of her. Then he went to the fridge and pulled out a jar of jam. Thea looked down at her plate, where a perfectly cooked sunny-side up egg stared back at her.

Gabe sat beside her and opened the jam, placing it in the space between them. "Dig in."

Thea spread jam on her bread. "Wow, this toast is like diner toast."

"Is that good or bad?"

"It's good. Impressive! I could never get my bread toasted like this."

"My secret is toasting it in a pan over the stove on low heat," Gabe fake whispered.

Thea noticed the empty place setting in front of him. "What about you? You're not having breakfast?"

"Just coffee for me. I'm not usually that hungry in the morning. I'll have some toast after, maybe."

This was a tidbit she wouldn't have known if she hadn't stayed the night. As she dipped a corner of her toast in the runny yolk, she watched Gabe. He had his cup of coffee in one hand and was looking out the window, a thoughtful expression on his face. She bit down on the bread and chewed. The silence in which they ate their breakfast was easy, like an everyday occurrence.

Her phone buzzed from the table. She flashed it an accusing look for interrupting the peace.

"You can take it," Gabe said, nodding to the phone. "I don't mind."

"Sorry, it might be a work thing." She wiped her hand on her napkin and picked up her phone. There was an email from her editor with the subject line: URGENT!!

Thea swiped open the email with more than a little trepidation. She had a feeling bad news was coming.

"Shit," she said, putting her phone face down and taking an angry bite of toast. She was so upset she couldn't even look at the phone. *Of course, this would happen.*

"What's wrong?"

Thea sighed and shook her head. "Nothing, just stupid work stuff."

"Anything I can help with?"

She pursed her mouth and pushed the remnants of her breakfast away. Her appetite was gone. She took a swallow of coffee. The bitter drink calmed her.

"Jeff, the other food reporter, he covers more event type stuff, tested positive for Covid this morning, so he can't go to the Jonathan Gold thing tonight," Thea explained. The paper did an annual tribute event to the late restaurant critic that also doubled as a charity event. The money they raised went toward fighting food insecurity. They always raised a ton because large companies loved to measure swords by sponsoring more and more tables. During normal times, it was an important event, with restaurants from all over LA preparing little bites to eat. Everyone in food around the country attended, so it was typically treated as a reunion of sorts for people in the industry.

She went every year to pay tribute to her idol turned mentor. Or at least, she did before the pandemic started. She'd used the excuse of not wanting to come into contact with too many people to avoid going this year, but now it seemed like they would force her to attend.

Thea continued, "So now that Jeff can't go, they want me to. Thankfully, I don't have to do a writeup for it, but Ray says I need to take Jeff's place. It'll look bad if his table's empty."

"Can he force you to go?" Gabe asked skeptically.

"He *is* my boss. Technically, it's a work event and I'm already on thin ice with him, so I don't think I can turn it down." Supposedly, the tables were going to be very far from each other. It didn't sound like a very fun event with all the Covid safety precautions, which was why Thea hadn't wanted to go in the first place.

Thea glanced at Gabe and her anger softened. "Hey... it's totally okay for you to say no, but do you wanna be my plus one tonight? You'd be doing me a huge favor. I won't have to sit there alone like a loser. I know you hate restaurants and it's technically *not* a restaurant—"

Gabe chuckled, "Sure, I'd love to go."

"Not like a date," Thea warned him with a raised eyebrow.

"Not a date," Gabe assured her, but with a glimmer in his eye that sent a thrill through her thoroughly satiated body.

THIRTY-SEVEN

THEA FINISHED APPLYING the last layer of lipstick, the sealer, when she heard the slam of her gate. She'd rushed home after discussing logistics with Gabe over breakfast. Luckily, she had checked the old press release for the event. She had totally forgotten that there was a dress code: semi-formal.

"I'm almost done! Meet you in front?" Thea yelled through her bedroom door when she heard her front door open and close. The good thing about living in a small house was that her voice carried well in it.

She fanned her lips with her hand, hoping that the breeze would help dry the sealer. After a few seconds, she tentatively touched her lip. It felt dry. She blotted it with a piece of tissue. Nothing came off! She'd been skeptical about this new lipstick and sealer duo she ordered thanks to a well-placed Instagram ad, but it actually worked. Now she didn't need to worry that the lipstick would rub off inside her mask.

Thea took one more look in the full-length mirror. The person staring back at her looked glamorous. She wore a simple black sleeveless dress with a v-neck cutting across her collarbones. It looked quite demure in the front because all the drama was in its plunging back.

She opted for a more classic look for tonight's makeup. It had been almost a year since she'd put on a full face. Black cat-eye eyeliner, a neutral eye-shadow, and bright red lips. She piled her hair on top of her head in a more complicated style than usual. She wasn't sure she could do it herself even after watching a YouTube tutorial, but with enough bobby pins, it felt secure for the night.

Gabe was standing by the front window, flipping through a book she'd left on the couch. He looked up at her approach. His mouth dropped open as his eyes traveled over her.

"Too much?" She asked, putting a hand on her hip and striking a pose.

"It's beautiful. You're beautiful." He dropped the book onto the couch.

"Thank you. You're not so bad yourself," she teased. Gabe looked more than not bad. He looked like he stepped out of a glossy men's magazine with his cream slacks, royal blue blazer, and white button-up shirt open at the collar. The fluttering in her stomach made her feel like she was crushing on him all over again.

Thea stepped up to him, touching the floral silk pocket square that gave his outfit a burst of color. "I like this." She looked at him through her lashes. Up close, his five o'clock shadow was already coming in, giving him a dangerous devil-may-care look that contrasted with his outfit. Her blood heated as she breathed in that warm man smell of his. *How can a man smell so good?*

Gabe put a hand on her back, stopping in surprise when his palm met her bare skin. He turned her around. He hummed a sound of appreciation and then smoothed his hand up and down her spine. She shivered in pleasure. He moved a hand to her waist, pulling her toward him until she met the solid mass of his body radiating heat through his clothes.

His mouth feathered against her ear when he asked in a hushed voice, "Wanna be fashionably late to the event?"

Her toes curled. She liked where he was going with this, but Ray would blow a gasket. She could already picture the vein in her boss's forehead pulsing at her as he chastised her about the importance of punctuality.

"I want to, but I can't. I'll never hear the end of it if I'm late." She turned in Gabe's arms and leaned up to give him a quick kiss on the lips. "Let's go."

Gabe had lied. Thea wasn't only beautiful. She was a goddess. His eyes were so glued to the curve of her butt as she walked to her car that he tripped on the bottom step of her porch. He recovered before Thea noticed. The open back of her dress exposed a wide expanse of deliciously soft skin, and stopped right before things got really interesting. He never thought much of the logistics of women's clothing, but he marveled at the magic behind this dress.

He slid into the passenger seat of Thea's car. They'd decided that she would drive since she wouldn't be drinking much at an event she was working. The front of the car was neat, but the back was another story. There was a haphazard pile of takeout menus in one of the seat wells in back, and another pile of reusable shopping bags in the other.

"Sorry, it's a little messy in here," Thea said as she slid into the driver's seat.

The movement made her dress fall open at the leg slit, revealing almost her entire thigh. Gabe forced his hands to be still on his lap to prevent himself from reaching over and pulling her to him. He wished he hadn't noticed that slit because now he would have to spend the entire night *not* imagining the convenience of a dress that opened like that.

The intoxicating floral smell of her hair teased him as she leaned over to his side and plopped a pair of black heels with rounded toes by his feet. "Thanks. It's hard to drive with these on."

She must have noticed his stiffness because she asked, "Are you okay? I'm an excellent driver, don't worry."

"I'm fine," he said, his voice sounding funny to him. He cleared his throat.

"Oh! Before I forget." Thea dug around in the tiny purse she'd brought. She pulled out two black objects and handed him one.

He unfolded the packet: a black, disposable mask.

"I wasn't sure what mask you were going to bring, but I figured these new black ones I ordered from Korea would look more formal. Or dressy?" Thea said.

"A more dressy mask? What a world we're living in."

They'd parked in a lot near Grand park and walked the block to the entrance of the event at the south end of the park. The party was in full swing by the time they arrived, a few minutes late. It was rare for this many people to be on time for something in LA, but Gabe chalked it up to everyone's excitement about finally dining out.

One of the handful of greeters led them through widely spaced tables until they got to their own. They were seated at a small round table covered with a white tablecloth. An elegant black place card in the center read: Jeff Lopez.

Gabe gave Thea a questioning look. "They couldn't make you your own place card?"

Thea laughed. "Yeah, I'm officially Jeff's unimportant and unnamed intern for tonight. Ray said he's gonna spread the word about Jeff getting Covid. It's fine. Other than people from the paper, no one knows my face, anyway."

A masked server swung by with two flutes of champagne and instructed them to scan the QR code on the back of the place card to view the "food and wine program" for the event.

"These things used to be run differently. Before." Thea said, looking around at the other tables. There was a tautness in her shoulders and Gabe wasn't sure if it was because she was at a work event or she was nervous about being around so many people. "They used to set up booths for the restaurants and people would line up at them for food.

Then you'd have to fight everyone else to get to one of the standing tables while balancing your wine glass and two or three tiny plates in your hands."

"This seems more civilized."

Most people were keeping to their tables.

"Does it feel weird to you to be outside like this?" Gabe asked.

Thea nodded emphatically. "I'm low key freaking out." She looked at the other tables. "At least they're masked."

A breeze blew by, making the tablecloth flap against his leg. There was a brief speech by someone he didn't know on the stage toward the top of the hill. Because of the natural slant of the park, it was easy to see the panel of speakers sitting on chairs up there. Sponsors were mentioned, restaurants taking part were thanked, and then there was a toast to the memory of Jonathan Gold.

Gabe remembered the first time he'd read a Jonathan Gold review. He was in high school when he came across it. It was in one of the Sunday LA Times issues he'd brought home from his AP English class. He couldn't remember what the actual assignment was, but the memory of randomly flipping through the pages and landing on a picture of a steaming stack of tamales was so clear it could have been yesterday.

Curious about the picture, Gabe read the article accompanying it. It was a review of the tamale restaurant by his *tía's* house in Montebello. Finding such rhapsodic prose about one of his favorite things to eat during the holidays was jarring enough, but he also never expected to see a neighborhood restaurant written up like that. He thought only restaurants with valet parking got reviewed in a major publication like the LA Times. After that, he couldn't resist flipping to the food section whenever he got his hands on the paper and seeing what else the food critic waxed poetic about.

Thea unhooked her mask from one ear and pulled out her phone, checking her lipstick on it. She held out her champagne flute to him and he tapped it gently with his. "Cheers," she said.

The bracing liquid slid down his throat as a server whizzed by and plopped two small plates on the table, gone before Gabe put the glass down. It was the start of at least two dozen small bites landing on their table for the next hour. The speed at which the morsels of food appeared, all varied and delicious, made it slightly harrowing. He had a much better understanding of Thea's job.

The onslaught of tiny bites slowed down to a trickle, then ended with a gravity defying miniature sculpture made of chocolate. Gabe felt like a stuffed pig. Looking at Thea's rosy-cheeked, satiated expression, he could tell that she felt the same.

"Wow, that was intense," he said.

The event planners had done a good job considering the restrictions from the health department, and it seemed like people were happy. He'd gone for another glass of wine, an orange one that Thea recommended. While it wouldn't have been something he would've ordered himself, it had a funky aftertaste, and he was glad he'd listened to her suggestion.

Gabe looked around at the other tables and based on the expressions on everyone's faces, from happy to slightly shell-shocked, he guessed they were also done with their food. The background volume of people talking, whether from the free-flowing alcohol, or the excitement of being at the event, was louder than when they'd first arrived.

A few other people from different departments at the paper wandered by to chat with Thea. He noticed she was careful to keep the table between her colleagues and her. This was the first time Gabe watched Thea put on her work persona. She was still herself, but there was a slightly different tone or cadence when she spoke.

"What?" Thea asked when she turned to him after the last person drifted away. No one else approached. He guessed interns at the paper weren't the most popular people to talk to at the party. "Do I have something on my face?"

"No, I just like listening to your work voice."

Thea laughed. "I have a work voice? What does it sound like?"

"Hard to describe. More formal. I think that's why I didn't recognize your voice from the radio sooner. I always thought that person was way older."

"Um, thanks?"

"I didn't mean it like that. Just more mature, I guess," he said.

"I'm plenty mature! You weren't complaining when—"

"Thea?" A man walked to their table.

"Derrick!" Thea exclaimed, her eyes lighting up.

Derrick stopped in front of Thea, moving in as if to hug her, but Thea put her hand out in one of those awkward pandemic waves. He stepped back. "Sorry, forgot. How've you been?"

"I'm good, considering." Thea made a vague gesture with her hands. She turned to Gabe. "Meet my... friend Gabe." If he hadn't been hyper-attuned to what she was saying, Gabe wouldn't have noticed the slight pause in her introduction.

"Hey, man. I'm Derrick."

Gabe stood and did an equally awkward elbow bump with the man. He rarely considered how guys looked, but this blonde-haired, green eyed, secret Hemsworth brother was hard to miss. He didn't fail to notice how the servers walked by and unabashedly checked the guy out. Some of them even circled their table twice.

"... an honor to have my wines here," Derrick was saying by the time Gabe turned back to the conversation. Of course, this guy was a wine-maker.

Thea laughed, that husky sound hitting him right in his core. "Don't be modest. Your wines are wonderful. I still remember that sparkling rosé I got from you in 2018. I blame you for ruining all other rosés for me."

Gabe looked from Thea to Derrick. She used her normal voice, not her professional writer's voice. The two seemed pretty friendly. He felt a chilling sensation in his chest. He always strove to be a modern man and not a possessive caveman, or so he thought. Was this what real jealousy felt like, or was it the second glass of wine clouding his judgement?

"This year's whites are going to be great," Derrick said. He looked at Thea knowingly. "I know you're gonna like them."

"Wow, I'll have to try some. Are you gonna be in the usual places? Everly's?" Thea rattled off a couple more names, and it took Gabe a few seconds to realize they were the names of wine shops in LA.

He studied the two of them standing across from each other. They made an amazing-looking couple, he thought begrudgingly.

"I'll bring you a case. On the house. A sampler of this year's offerings. I insist, Thea." The way Derrick said Thea's name grated on Gabe. He did not like what the man was insisting on at all.

Thea demurred, saying something about the paper not accepting gifts.

"You don't have to write about any of the wines, I promise." Derrick assured her. "A gift from one friend to the other. How far back do we go? I wasn't even *making* wines when we met."

Thea finally relented.

"I'll personally deliver the case next week. Are you in the same place? The little jungle cottage?" Derrick asked.

That twisting, cold sensation intensified. He was someone who'd been to Thea's house, so they must be close.

Luckily, someone else from across the park called out to Derrick. He apologized for having to mingle and left after a nod to Gabe. Gabe wasn't sure if the eye contact they'd made was a challenge or not, but he wasn't exactly thinking charitable thoughts right then.

Thea turned back to him and tilted her head, surveying his face. Her eyebrows drew together. "Are you okay?"

"Fine," he said, not meaning to sound so gruff. "Friend of yours?"

"Yeah, from way back."

"Like how we're friends?" Gabe asked, hating how it came out. This wasn't like him at all, but it was as though he couldn't stop that awful feeling from tainting his words. Was this how Christina felt whenever he was on work trips, when she thought he was messing around? No wonder it drove her to do strange things.

Thea placed a hand on his forearm and squeezed it. Her touch immediately soothed him. When she looked up at him, her eyes were shining with desire. Her cheeks reddened as she stared at him through lowered lashes. Her voice dropped to a whisper that only he could hear. "No, not like how *we're* friends."

He realized he was being stupid.

"Shit," Thea said under her breath as she looked at something over his shoulder.

Gabe was about to turn, but Thea squeezed his arm.

"Don't look," she said. "My boss is coming this way."

She inhaled deeply, blinked, and while he couldn't pinpoint what had changed in her face, it was like she'd slipped on a mask.

"Hi Ray!" she said in a cheerful, professional voice. She made introductions.

They had a few rounds of small talk, if he could call it that. It was mostly Thea reassuring Ray that various pieces were on track and would be delivered to his inbox on time, and him raving about some sort of AI thing. Gabe wasn't sure if he heard correctly; something about an article generating robot. Then Ray went on for another five minutes with complaints about *his* boss. Thea's boss seemed to think her responsibilities included being a vessel for grievances about his own work. The conversation finally sputtered to a halt and Ray said a hasty goodbye, moving on to another table.

"So that's your boss, huh?" Gabe asked, pressing his mouth into a thin line.

Thea sighed dramatically and took a swig from her glass of mineral water. "Yep, that's Ray. Now you know how I feel."

"He's uh..." he tried to think of something positive to say.

"The life of the party?"

A bark of laughter erupted from him. He loved Thea's ability to accurately describe something with only a few choice words.

Thea blew out a breath, and her shoulders slumped. Gabe looked around. It looked like the party was winding down. Guests were still mingling, or as much mingling as one could do while six feet away from each other, but there was a definite movement toward the exit.

"You want to go soon?" He asked, reading the tenseness of Thea's shoulders.

She looked at him gratefully. "Yes, please."

"Good, me too." He placed a hand around her, not missing the chance to rub his thumb against the skin of her back. She shivered and he could not mistake the promising look she cast up at him. "Let's go home."

THIRTY-EIGHT

THE REST OF the year came and went swiftly like winter in LA. Thea had been so busy with writing and deadlines that she hardly noticed the seasons turning. Her garden bed still held her winter crops. It was already hot on her porch when she stepped out with her tea tray. In a few more weeks, if the temperature continued to climb, she would need to make cold brew. She gingerly placed the tea tray on the low table in front of her swing and sat.

After ten minutes of staring at a dense volume about the tea trade in ancient China, she gave up. Thea zoned out and drank her tea. It was a treat to be drinking dragon well tea from this spring's picking. She had to special order a bag of the elusive tea from a fancy tea vendor. She'd befriended the tea shop owner after writing about her previous shop on the west side of LA. Now, every year, she placed an order with her for a bag of the first-picked leaves of the spring harvest.

The liquid that those special leaves brewed was a light yellowish green color. It had an incredible fragrance that always reminded her of that first sniff of spring: verdant and floral. Thea thoughtfully sipped, loving how the fresh sweetness coated her mouth. *What a treat!* She wondered how the leaves would taste cold brewed. She didn't think she could bear using that much tea at once for an experiment.

Thea made a mental note to brew this tea for Gabe the next time he came over. They'd started alternating whose house they spent time in. Bringing her laptop to his place for a change of scenery worked wonders when she had writer's block.

They'd been seeing each other so often these past six months that she noticed her daily routine had shifted to accommodate him. The changes were so gradual; it hadn't hit her until last week, when she looked through the previous pages of her bullet journal for some notes she remembered jotting down around December. The two weeks looked significantly different when she flipped back and forth from a week in December to the current week.

When she needed to get work done at his house, he left her alone for hours at a time. They worked together in amicable silence in the shady backyard. Other times, she liked to sit at the bar stool on his kitchen counter where she could look out the window and see him working on his latest piece. When it was time for a break, she took pictures of him and his projects in the garage-turned-workshop.

She couldn't believe they'd been in their little pandemic bubble for this long. Every day was a repeat of the day before. It was so hard to keep track of time when it was pleasant and sunny every day. A small part of her worried that while they were floating comfortably along in their pandemic bubble, like any bubble, it would eventually pop. What would happen when the bubble burst and she and Gabe came tumbling out of it, forced into the real world?

THIRTY-NINE

THEA SHUT HER laptop with a satisfying thump. She never thought this moment would come. Finally done with the rough draft! A very imperfect, probably full of trash sentences, but hey, at least it's done, rough draft. The sun cast long shadows that crept through her yard. The sky exploded with royal blue and magenta wisps to help her celebrate.

Even though she wanted to open her screen and re-read the beginning of the manuscript, she stopped herself. The best thing to do was to put it out of her mind for at least a week. After that, when she went back to it, it would be with fresh eyes.

Thea stood from the porch swing and stretched. The spot between her shoulders gave a series of pops and cracks as she rolled her head left and right. A weight had been lifted and she felt free. She dumped her writing stuff onto the cluttered dining room table and walked into the bedroom to check her messages. A couple of texts from Gabe from hours ago, asking what her plans were for the rest of the day. He asked if she wanted to come over and help him paint that afternoon. Well, that opportunity had come and gone.

In the relaxing afterglow of finishing this phase of her book, she felt celebratory. She wrote back: *How about my place? I can order delivery.*

He immediately replied with a thumbs up.

The old Thea would have balked at asking a man over to her place. But with Gabe, it felt different. The mornings where she woke next to him, she felt zero regrets. It was so pleasant that when she woke up alone in her bed this morning, an unfamiliar feeling lodged in her chest. She missed him.

Thea scrolled through her phone for the new roasted chicken pop-up she'd been wanting to try. It was a small operation run by a couple who wanted to showcase the flavors of their respective cuisines through flavorful chicken. As she scrolled, she had a difficult time deciding on whether to order the Jeera chicken with Indian spices and caramelized onion, or Pibil chicken with its garlicky, citrusy punch of chiles. Both sounded so wonderful and she *did* need to try both options to write about it. Strictly for research purposes, she placed an order for both chickens.

🍃 🍃 🍃

When Gabe arrived at Thea's door, mouth-watering scents wafted from the house. He automatically ignored the broken doorbell and knocked. Thea peeked out of the front window. She startled him when she wrenched the door open and threw her arms around his neck. He caught her around her waist and returned her hug.

"Hello to you too," he said into the messy knot of her hair. He pulled back and looked at her. "Did something happen?"

She stepped back, excitement shining in her eyes. "I just finished my first draft. It's finally done!"

"Congratulations!"

A buzzer went off from the kitchen and Thea pulled him through the front door. "Shut the door, would you?" she called out, already on her way into the kitchen. "I gotta check on something."

Gabe put his folded mask in the basket. He took a second to look at both of their masks sitting side by side, and something warm and fuzzy bloomed in his chest.

"What smells so good?" he asked as he stepped into the kitchen. The temperature was several degrees warmer in there, even with all the windows wide open.

"I thought we could have a nice dinner to celebrate," Thea said, glancing from the oven window.

Gabe tried to hide the look of surprise on his face.

"Don't look so shocked! I'm just warming these up in the oven. I didn't actually cook them."

"Can I help with anything?"

Thea pointed to a sink full of greens. "I washed the lettuce from the garden. Can you make one of your special dressings for them?"

Gabe went to work whipping up a dressing with oil, lemon, and fresh chives Thea had grown on the windowsill. The two of them moved around each other in the kitchen as they readied dinner. There were a few accidental bumps and not quite accidental touches.

After he dressed the salad, Gabe helped set the table. He found some candles while looking for wine glasses and lit them. When he returned to the kitchen, Thea pulled an aromatic roasted chicken from the oven, then another.

She fanned herself with the oven mitt and looked at him with a rueful smile. "I forgot how hot this kitchen gets whenever the oven's turned on."

"You got *two* whole chickens?" Gabe asked.

"I couldn't decide which seasoning to choose, so I got both. For research!" With her cheeks flushed pink and a thin sheen of sweat making her face glow, Thea had never looked more stunning.

He must have been staring because she self-consciously wiped a lock of hair from where it was stuck to her forehead. "Sorry, I'm super sweaty. If you're hungry, we can start eating the salad. The chicken just needs to rest for a bit."

Gabe grinned and placed his hands on her hips, pulling her toward him. He tucked the lock of hair behind her ear. "I love it when you're sweaty. And I can think of a couple of things we could do besides eating salad while the chicken rests."

Thea's eyes widened and her smile spread as she stepped closer to him, her bare feet on either side of his. "What things?"

Gabe touched his mouth to hers, licking away the salty sweat from her lips. A satisfied sound emerged from the back of her throat. Her hand rose to the back of his neck, pulling him closer as she sucked in his bottom lip.

A low chuckle came from him and he backed up, leaning against the counter as he pulled her against him. She came willingly, one hand clutching the hem of his shirt, the other one buried in his hair. At this rate, Gabe wasn't sure if the chicken would still be hot by the time they were done. He could spend an eternity being kissed by her like this.

Some time later, the buzzer on the oven went off again, making the two of them jump.

Thea stepped back, her breath coming in little pants that drew Gabe's attention to the quick rise and fall of her breasts. He desperately wanted to lick that sheen of sweat off of the dip of her collarbone. Her lips were red and swollen from his kiss, and her heavy-lidded eyes were hard to resist. He reached for her again, but she took a step away.

"We should —" Thea cleared her throat, "we should probably get started with dinner."

Gabe reluctantly agreed and helped her carry the salad bowl to the dining room. Thea followed behind after grabbing the champagne from the fridge.

At the dining room table, she threw a dishcloth over the top of the bottle and eased the cork open with a loud pop.

Gabe arched his eyebrow at her, and she grinned. "Just in case the cork flies out. I learned the hard way that an exploding cork is hard to control."

"Uh oh, what happened?"

"No one got their eye shot out or anything. The waiter opened a bottle, but the cork exploded up and hit the ceiling, taking a chunk out."

"Good tip."

Thea poured the champagne into the two wineglasses.

Gabe held up his glass before drinking, "A toast."

"To what?"

"To rough drafts," he said.

Thea clinked her glass with his. "To rough drafts and making friends even through a pandemic."

Gabe looked up in surprise. It was true; they were friends, but he must have been doing a great job of hiding his feelings if that was the word she used to describe them. It felt like not enough. Before she could notice anything, he echoed, "to making friends."

The champagne fizzed in his mouth, its tart flavor reminding him of crisp apples. Thea swallowed and closed her eyes. Her mouth widened into a smile. She hadn't looked this light-hearted for a while.

"What?" Thea opened her eyes to find him staring.

"I love how much you enjoy food."

She lowered her lashes as she took another sip from her glass. "Sometimes I feel like I'm in a very good dream."

"Me too."

After Thea took pictures of the massive amount of food on the table, they ate with gusto. It was far too much food for the two of them, but everything smelled so good that he knew they'd at least make a dent in it. There were two large plates of chicken, a bowl of herbed rice, roasted cauliflower, salad, and various small bowls of pickled things to eat with the chicken. Under a warm towel, there were even stretchy, flakey flour tortillas.

"Your salad dressing is amazing as usual!" Thea said, taking another bite. "What's in it?"

"It's probably the fresh lettuce from the garden."

It was shocking how impressed she was by a simple salad dressing. This type of praise from someone who dined at Michelin starred restaurants was a boost to his ego.

"No really, what's in the dressing? There's no way I grew lettuce this good."

Gabe ticked off on his hand. "Olive oil, lemon juice, mustard, salt, pepper, your chives, oh, and sumac."

Thea looked confused. "I have sumac?!"

"Yeah, I found it in your spice cabinet."

"Wow, you know my kitchen better than I do," Thea laughed.

Gabe dug enthusiastically into the chicken. By the satisfied sounds coming from Thea's mouth, he could tell that she was enjoying the meal. He couldn't blame her. The two chickens were differently spiced, but good in their own ways. The Pibil was bright, but a bit too spicy for him. He washed it down with the champagne. The Jeera chicken was so tender and juicy that he didn't mind the slow burn building in his mouth. He'd never had a chicken so flavorful before.

"Sorry, I didn't know they were going to be so spicy." Thea said, noticing him gulping his glass of water.

He was pretty sure his nose was sweating. "I'll manage," he croaked, helping himself to more salad.

"Oh!" Thea ran into the kitchen and returned with a tall mason jar of creamy orange liquid from the fridge. She handed it to him with a flourish.

"What's this?" He asked, unscrewing the lid and giving it a sniff.

"I made you a mango lassi! To help with the spices."

"You made this?" He asked with a tentative sip. It was good!

"I know how to use a blender!" She rolled her eyes.

"Thanks." Gabe couldn't describe the fizzy sensation spreading throughout his body.

In the silence that followed, he looked up to see Thea's hands had paused. One hand was halfway to her mouth with a piece of chicken, while the other was on the knife resting on her plate. She was looking at him with a strange expression on her face.

"Do I have a lassi mustache?" He wiped his mouth with the napkin.

Thea shook her head and gave him a smile he couldn't read. "I'm still not used to having someone eating with me in the dining room."

"Oh."

"It's... nice," she said with awe in her voice. Her eyes met his and he could swear he wasn't the only one feeling this depth of emotion.

That fizzy sensation intensified. Gabe now knew how that champagne bottle felt, with so many things wanting to come out, that he was about to pop.

Thea queued up the next episode of the medical drama they'd been watching on her TV while Gabe finished the dishes. She helped load the dishwasher, but there were plenty of things that either didn't fit, or couldn't go in the dishwasher, so he'd offered to wash them. She hit pause on the remote and walked into the kitchen.

"Can I help dry?" Thea asked, seeing that Gabe was running out of room to stack things.

"Thanks. I don't know where a lot of these things go."

Thea fetched a clean dishtowel from a drawer and started drying some of the larger items from the rack. She liked how easy it was to clean up with him there.

After the dishes were done, they flopped down in the living room. Gabe leaned back on the couch, crossed his ankle over one knee, and threw an arm around her shoulders. Thea pulled her legs up so that her knees rested on Gabe's thigh. She glanced at him, the red glow of the TV reflecting off his face.

Gabe looked back down at her. The corners of his mouth lifted in a smile. One time, Thea watched a chef flip a six-egg omelette in a wok with a flick of his wrist. Her heart felt like that omelette right then. She wondered when she would stop feeling this way whenever he looked at her with that secret smile on his lips. Even in the dim light of the TV, he was so handsome that she sometimes had to look away. It was like looking into the sun.

"Hey," he said softly, interrupting her thoughts. "Thanks again for dinner."

"My pleasure."

"When this is all over, I'd like to take you out to dinner. A nice restaurant, you can pick which. To celebrate."

When this is all over. She knew he meant the pandemic, but it was still jarring to think about what would happen after. When they found a cure for this virus, when the quarantine and the shutdown rules were over, what would happen to them? She was actively avoiding thinking about it. Instead, she thought about how he'd asked her to go to an actual restaurant. Her heart filled with a swooping feeling.

"Thea?" Gabe asked, cocking his head and looking at her. "Where'd you go?"

Thea blinked her eyes and snapped back to the present. "Sorry. Just weird to think about... you know. Whenever this is going to be over."

"It's bound to happen, right?"

"Yeah, but we still don't know what's going to happen after. It's like everything's changed, but at the same time, everything's still frozen in time."

Gabe took her hand, interlacing his fingers with hers. "I know what you mean."

It was wrong to feel grateful for the pandemic, since so many people got sick and passed away. But if it hadn't happened, she would have never met Gabe. A universe where she'd never met him wasn't something she could even picture now. It was scary how easily he'd fit himself into her life without her even noticing it.

"What's wrong?"

She gave a tiny shrug. "I dunno. Just kinda sad, I guess."

"It's a pretty crappy time for everyone right now."

"It's just weird how quickly I got used to all of this. And who knows what it's going to be like when this is over, like you said? Are things gonna go back the way they were? I don't know how I feel about that."

"Are we still talking about the pandemic?" Gabe asked.

Thea's eyes flicked up to meet his. He looked wary, like he wasn't sure if he wanted to step into the deep end of the pool or not. She understood his reluctance. They'd started this whole thing on the assumption that they would keep it casual. They were both past that line now.

"Maybe not," Thea admitted. She watched an unnamed emotion flick through Gabe's eyes. She wished she could tell what he was thinking. He looked like he was steeling himself for something.

"I think things are bound to change between us," Gabe finally said. Before she could say anything, he held his hand up. "Lemme finish. Things are already changing between us. We both know how this started, and I'm not gonna lie and say I wasn't crazy into you from the beginning. But for me, this is more than friends with benefits. I mean, the benefits are great, incredible, some of the best benefits of my life. But this," he gestured between them, "is what I look forward to. I love spending time with you."

Her pulse was a whoosh in her ears. She hadn't been expecting The Talk right now. But Pandora's box was about to be opened and there was no closing it. Or *was* there? She turned her body so that she faced him and leaned in, lowering her lashes. She knew of one way to distract him from where she wasn't ready to go yet.

Gabe opened his mouth, but before he could get another word out,

Thea closed the remaining distance between them and pressed her lips to his, swallowing what he was about to say. He responded enthusiastically, firm hands grasping her shoulders, pulling her over him.

The TV remote clattered off the arm of the couch. Thea settled over him, her thighs straddling his lap, her hands digging into the soft curls at the back of his head. She nipped at his bottom lip before swiping her tongue over it. A sound halfway between a moan and a sigh escaped from his throat. His mouth tasted like champagne. She was comfortable in this familiar territory.

When his hands worked their way under the hem of her dress, pushing it up over her thighs, she knew she had won.

FORTY

GABE CHANNELED HIS nervous energy into sanding down the rough edges on the seat of the bench he was building. Physical work usually let him escape whatever he was on his mind, but today he couldn't help glancing at the old clock leaning crookedly on the pegboard every five minutes. He'd texted Thea earlier that he was working in the back and that she should let herself into the yard. His entire being felt jittery with anticipation. He hoped she would like the surprise.

The high-pitched squeak of the front gate, louder than any doorbell, signaled her arrival. He turned off the sander and set it down. Thea wore a loose tank-top patterned with tiny flowers, tucked into cut-off shorts. The shorts accentuated her mile-long legs. Gabe forced his eyes away from admiring all that skin by looking at her face. Was she taunting him? He felt abashed at being caught ogling.

"Hey," he managed to say.

"Hey yourself. Whatcha working on?" She headed into the workshop, but stopped when she saw all the tools on the floor. Her camera bag bumped against her hip.

He'd made up some excuse about taking pictures of the bench when he asked her over this afternoon.

"Sorry, it's a disaster in here. I'm sanding down this bench for delivery tomorrow." It was another commission from the same coffee shop he built the parklet for. They were expanding their outside area thanks to the increase in customers and needed more seating.

Thea ran a hand along the surface of the bench. "This is gorgeous."

Instead of the usual flat surfaces and sharp corners, the bench had smooth curves and bevels. Not so much that people sitting on the edge would slide off, but enough for the edge to not cut into the back of their legs.

"Can I try sitting on it?" Thea asked.

"Not yet. It's dusty from sanding," Gabe said. "Actually, there *is* something you can try sitting on. Come here."

He stepped over the pile of tools and led her by the hand to the side of his backyard, right under the old magnolia tree bordering his yard and the neighbor's. The Adirondack he built for her sat in the cool shadow of the tree. It had extra wide arm rests to hold not only a cell phone but also a circular hole for holding a drink.

"Sit," he told Thea.

She gingerly sat down and looked up at him, eyes wide in wonder.

"This is so comfy!" She scooted her butt around the chair and placed her arms on the armrest. "And these are at the perfect height."

"I thought of it after you said these chairs aren't comfortable for working in," Gabe said. The armrest was lower so that it was at a better level for Thea to rest her elbows on when she had her laptop. He also made the seat surface beveled to contour around her body. Then he smoothed out the edges of the seat to prevent it from digging into the back of her knees.

Thea took out her phone and put it in the divot designed to hold it. "This is perfect." She looked at the shaded area around the chair and noticed the low table next to the chair. "Oh, and a little matching table? How cute!"

"I'm glad you like it," Gabe said, glowing at her praise. "I made it for you."

"For me?"

Gabe nodded. "It usually stays cool back here because of the tree, so I thought it would be a good spot for you to write. The Wi-Fi's not bad back here."

Thea looked down at the jute rug under her.

"Do you like it?" Gabe felt giddy. He was terrible at keeping secrets.

"You made me a space to write?" She asked again, something off in her tone.

"Come inside. I wanna show you something else," he said, holding his hand out.

She placed her hand in his tentatively, and he pulled her up. He strode through the back door to the kitchen. He pointed to an empty shelf below the kitchen bench.

"Where'd your books go?" She asked, looking up at him in confusion.

"I cleared the shelf for you. You can bring over some of your books and leave them here. That way, you don't have to lug them back and forth. I also emptied a drawer for you in my dresser, in case you wanted to leave pajamas or a change of clothes."

Thea dropped his hand. An icy tendril of dread touched the back of his neck. She looked surprisingly pale. He asked, "What's wrong?"

She took a step back from him, slowly shaking her head. "I didn't ask you to do this."

It was like she threw cold water on him. Gabe wondered if what he said came out wrong. He replayed it in his head. Nothing. He tried again. "Since you're spending so much time here, I thought you'd like some space of your own."

Thea looked at him as if he were speaking in tongues. "I have space of my own. My house."

Gabe ran a frustrated hand through his hair. "I know that, but I'd like you to have a place to put your stuff here. To feel at home here."

"But I don't bring any stuff here."

"But you could if you *wanted* to."

The way Thea looked at him, her face purposely blank, was enough to shut him up. This complete 180 of his emotions made him dizzy. Had he been misreading the whole situation? He liked it when she spent time at his house, whether they were in bed or not. He thought she enjoyed it, too. It wasn't like he was asking her to move in with him.

"I *don't* want to." Thea said, interrupting his thoughts.

"Oh." What more was there to say? She made it abundantly clear. He was only good for fucking, not boyfriend material at all. It was stupid of him to think they could be anything more. She'd told him from the beginning that she only wanted one thing from him.

"I think I'm gonna go," she said, looking everywhere else but at him. She twisted the strap of the camera bag in her hands.

Gabe barely heard her through the roar of blood rushing through his ears. He was burning with embarrassment at how eager he was to show her all of this. In fifth grade, he'd carved a wooden bookmark and given it to his crush on Valentine's day. She accepted it, but then, at recess, he overheard her laughing about it with her friends by the swings. When they left, he went to the swings and found the bookmark dirty and splintered in the sand. The same awful feeling was bubbling in him now.

He swallowed and schooled his features. "Fine."

Thea opened the door and stepped out onto his porch. She turned and when she looked up at him, he couldn't escape her fathomless gaze. He felt like she saw everything. The angry crash of rejection pulsed through his body. He opened his mouth to say something, but was cut off when she placed a hand on his chest.

"I can't do this," Thea said.

The disquieting feeling of humiliation crescendoed. It was such a powerful feeling that it surprised him when he blurted out, "Wait."

Thea stilled.

He didn't want her to leave. It scared him that if they didn't name whatever this was right now, everything would come tumbling down. "Can we go back in and talk about this?"

Thea shook her head, looking down at where they touched. She dropped her hand.

"What did I do wrong?" He kept his voice steady even though he wanted to shout.

Silence.

For once, he didn't turn away from the uncomfortable sensation, no matter how much he wanted to. What he wanted more was to understand what was wrong, but Thea said nothing. The feeling of helplessness frustrated him. He squeezed the back of his neck just to have something to do with his hands. "I see."

"I'm sorry." The way she kept glancing away hurt him.

"For what?" He asked, trying to sound normal. She had stuck to her end of the deal. She'd warned him that all she wanted was a warm body in bed. He was the lovesick idiot who thought he could have more; that they could be more.

"For all this," she shrugged. She looked tired. Defeated. "Leading you on and letting you think that there's more for us. Or that there's a future with this."

Gabe wanted to pull her into his arms and demand she to stop talking. Her words were rusty daggers piercing him. He crossed his arms over his chest to keep from reaching out.

"It's fine," he said, proud that his voice remained calm and detached.

Thea glanced up in surprise. He thought he saw pain flash in her eyes, but she blinked and it was gone. He was concentrating so hard on holding his body still, taking deep breaths in, that he didn't hear her goodbye. His eyes followed her down the steps to the noisy gate.

FORTY-ONE

THE CLINKING OF ice cubes in her glass brought Thea back from staring off into space. She was glad that she had the foresight the night before to make cold brew coffee. As she poured the thick black liquid into her glass and diluted it with ice-cold water, she thanked her past self.

She brought the frosted glass out with her onto the porch, where it was already getting warm. Even though she could still see dew on the weeds in her garden bed, she had maybe an hour left before it became too hot to the garden. She gulped down the coffee, welcoming the cold, fruity taste of it on her tongue. After the restless night she had where Gabe weaved in and out of her dreams, the bitter beverage was precisely what she needed to feel more awake.

Thea found her discarded gardening gloves on the low table on the porch. She grabbed them by the fingers and shook each one out, in case there were critters like spiders hiding inside. Satisfied that nothing was waiting to spring an attack on her fingers, she pulled them onto her hands and walked down the porch steps. The clouds in the sky provided enough cover that she didn't need to pull on her gardening hat. She didn't think she'd enjoy gardening as much as she did, but mornings like these, when thoughts of Gabe pressed in on her, the repetitive physical motion helped her compartmentalize her thoughts.

The ice cubes in her coffee were already melted by the time she returned to her glass. She looked over at the two garden beds in front of her. It was ironic that the first project they built together was now what she used to distract herself from thinking about him.

Her front yard looked completely different now that the basil and tomato plants had filled out. Instead of two sections of admittedly patchy grass, the two bountiful garden beds made her front yard look inviting. Her thoughts drifted to how simple everything had seemed that day they built the boxes. She was wrong about the garden being a good distraction; everything about it made her think of Gabe.

The forlorn way he looked at her yesterday staggered her each time she pictured it. As soon as she'd drifted to sleep, she saw his face, and the guilt jolted her awake.

She was angry about how she'd let her guard down. She'd warned him she wasn't looking for a serious relationship in the beginning. She thought he understood, but now it seemed like he was ready for her to move in with him. After Peter, Thea knew that she never wanted to live with another man ever again. She never wanted to make the compromises she did when she was living with him, with anyone. She was older, smarter, and knew herself better.

This was why she preferred one-night-stands with men. It was easy to avoid heartache when she knew she'd never see them again. She couldn't see how things could ever work in the real world with Gabe, not with what he wanted from her.

The coffee was gone from her glass. She pulled her gloves back on and returned to weeding. If she couldn't yank her heart from her body and stop the pain, yanking undesirable plants from her little garden was the next best thing.

She welcomed the cool spray of the hose as she scrubbed the dirt between her fingers. She watered the garden thoroughly. A heat wave was coming soon, according to her weather app. Thea chuckled to herself because she was now one of those people who actually checked the weather daily.

By the time she had sufficiently watered the two beds deeply enough that she didn't have to worry about a freak heatwave hitting them in the next couple of days, it was time for her exercise. She changed out of her overalls and pulled on her bike shorts.

She called Olivia as she climbed onto her bike.

"Hey," Olivia said when she picked up her FaceTime. Her friend fiddled with whatever held her camera in place. She thankfully stopped because Thea felt nauseated by the moving camera.

"Good morning." Thea took a good slug of cold water to prepare herself for whatever hellish circuit Olivia was about to put her through.

"Were you just outside? Looks like you got a little sun."

Thea looked at herself through the small thumbnail on her screen. She did look flushed, but didn't remember it being that sunny that morning.

"I figure we start off slow and then do a hill climb or two. Sound good?"

Thea pulled a face, but nodded, turning the resistance knob on her bike.

"How are you holding up?" Olivia asked once they'd settled on a nice warmup speed. Thea had filled her in on what happened as soon as she got home last night.

Thea shrugged. "I couldn't sleep. I kept replaying the whole thing in my head all night."

"Yeah?"

"I was so stupid," Thea continued. "I had something good going with Gabe and I thought we could be adult about it, but maybe I led him on."

"Aw, don't say it like that."

"You were right. You tried to warn me, but did I listen? No way."

"I know how to call it," Olivia grinned on the other side of the screen. Her usually radiant smile then lowered into a sympathetic look. "But I'm sorry you're going through this! It's hard breaking up. Trust me, I know."

"Does it count as a breakup if there was nothing really to break up? Ugh! I hate this."

"I think so."

"The dumbest part is the guilt. I didn't want to catch feelings or whatever, but I can't stop thinking about how sad he looked when I left."

"Let's crank it up a few notches."

Thea grunted as she worked harder to push the pedals. Her heart rate increased and sweat collected at her hairline. A few beads dripped down the side of her face. Although her legs were protesting, she enjoyed the growing burn in her thighs. It took her mind away from the emptiness in the pit of her stomach.

"It'll take time to get over him," Olivia said, no change in her voice. Did her friend *ever* get winded?

Thea pouted. "What if I don't *want* to get over him?"

"Is that what you want?"

"I don't know! Maybe I'm just feeling this way because it's something I can't have. Ugh, listen to me. I sound so pathetic," Thea said, wiping sweat off her forehead with the back of her hand.

"Hey," Olivia said, looking serious. Or at least as serious as someone who was bouncing along on a stationary bike could look, "you don't sound pathetic. You sound like a woman who's coming to terms with big feelings that she hasn't had in a long time."

"You think so?"

"Let's say you could rewind. Would you have asked Gabe to start whatever this is with you two if you knew this was where it would lead?"

Thea took a while to think about it. Mostly, she had to concentrate on her thighs, pushing the pedals down and pulling them up. Pedalling at this resistance, which hadn't seemed that bad in the beginning, was getting more and more difficult the longer she kept at it.

Olivia let her concentrate on the pace, urging her along. "Just a few more minutes of this... Almost done."

Thea tucked her chin into her chest, braced herself on the handlebars, and lifted her butt off the seat. The leverage gave her more strength so she could keep pushing the pedals even though her thighs trembled.

"Yeah, that's it," Olivia called in encouragement. "You got it."

"Ugh," Thea gritted out between her teeth. She wasn't sure if she could take any more of this.

"Okay, back to 3," Olivia said at the same time Thea was about to slither off her bike.

She let out a puff of breath as she dialed her resistance knob down. Her legs thanked her, although they couldn't stop trembling. She was still mulling over Olivia's question. She couldn't think of any way it could have gone differently. The unnamed thing between her and Gabe was inevitable. She couldn't control it even if she tried.

"Yes," she said, the realization coming to her with a sudden force. "I would have done exactly the same thing." She wanted Gabe in her life, but she just didn't know how to keep him and still hold on to all the things she wanted to keep in her life.

Olivia nodded, and her mouth spread into a grin. "Nothing like some high-intensity exercise to clear your head, am I right?"

Thea rolled her eyes and shook her head at her exercise obsessed friend, "I'm not saying that crazy circuit you put me through is worth it, but it might have helped."

"Are you gonna call him after?" Olivia asked. "Oh yeah, we're only halfway done, by the way."

"No. I still don't know what I want out of this. Like how is it ever going to work between us?" Thea said.

"That sounds like a conversation you should have with him. Let's keep going, but crank it up to 6." Olivia said as she started pedaling furiously.

"You're killing me!" Thea whined, leaning forward on her bike for some leverage. She was grateful for the insane pace Olivia set for her. Her best friend knew what she needed to detangle her thoughts.

FORTY-TWO

A HUNDRED LITTLE things reminded Gabe of Thea's absence each morning. When he drank his coffee, he thought of the way she took the first sip, closed her eyes, and sighed. When he ate toast, he remembered how she called it diner toast. He lurched into wakefulness when he reached over to her side of the bed and found it empty.

Every lonely morning this week, he had to remind himself that he wasn't in a nightmare. The fight had been real. He couldn't get that trapped, panicked look in her eyes out of his mind. They had actually broken up, but over what? The fact that he wanted more than she could give? He felt the sting of rejection as fresh as it was the first time. The one time he wanted to stick around and work things out in a relationship, and this was what happened.

Now that she'd ghosted him, his home felt like it was missing an entire room. It was weird because it wasn't like she left anything at his house. The whole reason he set aside space for Thea was that he wanted those little reminders of her. Part of it was him selfishly wanting her to spend more time with him, but part of it was also because it felt strange not to have any evidence of her in his house at all. When she left, other than an extra toothbrush and the gaping maw in his chest, it was like she'd never been there at all.

He rolled over to Thea's side of the bed and put his head on the pillow she liked to use, inhaling. To his disappointment, it only smelled like clean laundry. He forgot that he'd washed his sheets the morning before.

Gabe allowed himself a few more minutes moping around in bed. If he didn't get up, he didn't have to start his day without Thea. He rubbed his face and pulled on his running shorts to get some fresh air.

The run around the reservoir the day before, and the day before that didn't help clear his head, but maybe today would be different. Today, he couldn't zone out like he wanted to. It was still early, but the dirt path around the greenish water had speed-walkers he needed to dodge. Running was the only way he could escape the constant ache of missing Thea. No matter how hard he centered himself on his breathing, three breaths in, four breaths out, his heart still beat a steady rhythm: Thea, Thea, Thea, Thea.

After two loops around the reservoir, he slowed to a walk, giving his body the chance to cool down. He immediately regretted that decision because without the sound of his breath bellowing, the only thought he'd been trying to quiet came roaring back: He loved her.

He never told her. He *couldn't* tell her. It was the one thing she was crystal clear about not wanting. He knew it would scare her away. Not that keeping it from her helped anything now.

Gabe couldn't ignore the twinge that shot up his body when he thought about how she was so against having a real relationship. He knew she had bad experiences in the past, but it wasn't fair of her to make him endure the punishment of past injustices from other men.

By the time he stumbled back to his truck, Gabe wasn't sure if the run had helped at all. His radio clicked on when he started the ignition. Thea's voice came through his speakers. *Of course,* an episode of of her food show was on. He thumbed off the radio.

His thoughts were still spiraling around what he could have done differently. He should have taken her proposition at face value and treated their interactions as purely physical. Two adults scratching an itch. But how could he resist falling for her when she was so easy to love? The husky laugh she had when something delighted her. The way she closed her eyes and her lips curved into a small smile when she ate something delicious. Her unending curiosity about all the people who played a part in the food she ate. The way she wrote, making him want to grab a chair and join in at her table. That crease between her brows when she was lost in a book. He was an idiot to think he was strong enough to resist falling in love with her.

FORTY-THREE

THE MAN AT the nursery had warned Thea that the bird's nest fern she wanted to buy craved humidity and wasn't easy to keep alive in LA's harsh desert climate. Two years in Thea's humid, light-filled bathroom and the plant was now an overgrown, verdant monster brushing against the ceiling.

Thea rotated the pot so that it wouldn't favor one side, then finished toweling off her wet hair. She used the towel to wipe the steam from the bathroom mirror. After stepping out of the bathroom, she checked her phone. She was half hoping, half dreading the missed messages. It had been over two weeks (but who's counting?) since she had talked to Gabe. A few nights ago, she let her phone run out of batteries and didn't bother charging it until the next day, so she wouldn't succumb to temptation and text him.

That first week, she had to stop herself from sending him links to funny things she saw online. She'd renamed him in her contacts list as "Not Today!" Now that she eased herself back into her old routine, especially with a few looming deadlines, she barely thought about Gabe.

Like how she wasn't thinking about him right now, nor was she wondering if he was in his workshop building another gorgeous piece of furniture.

No new texts on her phone, but her calendar dinged. Thea thumbed it open and almost dropped it. Staring back at her was a reminder to pack for her Taiwan trip scheduled for tomorrow morning. She checked the date again on the calendar. Hadn't she already cancelled the flight? Did she forget to delete this calendar reminder with the flight details?

She remembered calling the airline to cancel. *Wait a minute.* She called the airline and *asked* about cancellation policies but hadn't actually cancelled.

"Crap." She frantically scrolled through her inbox. Her flight was in less than twenty-four hours. Was the flight even still happening?

Thea plopped down on her dining room table with her laptop. She navigated to the airline's site and checked the flight status, hoping for a cancellation message. No such luck. The flight was still scheduled. She navigated to the CDC's website on travel guidance. Then she looked up the procedure for international flights to Taiwan. She needed to get a negative test, then quarantine for two weeks when she got to Taiwan and test negative again on the last day.

Next, she checked the Covid numbers both in LA and Taiwan. The number of cases in Taipei was shockingly low for a densely populated city. She double-checked it from another source: same thing. Hell, if she could board the plane safely, she'd be safer in Taipei than in Los Angeles. She hadn't been able to compartmentalize and stop thinking about Gabe, so maybe a change of scenery would help her figure out what to do. And she could see her parents.

Her parents! They definitely would not appreciate a call in the middle of the night from their daughter, who had forgotten to cancel her flight. Best to send them an email with the details. She closed her inbox after hitting send when her phone started buzzing with an incoming FaceTime.

"Hi baba," Thea said. "Isn't it the middle of the night where you are?"

Her dad waved that concern away. "I got a good idea in my dream for this project, so I woke up to try it. Not so good an idea, but gave me another idea."

Her dad had that faraway look he often got when he was thinking about something at work.

"Did you read my email?" Thea asked, directing him back to the problem on hand.

"That's why I called," her dad said. "Mama's not going to be happy you're getting on a plane, but we'll both be happy to see you. You want us to pick you up from the airport?"

"No, I have to do the quarantine hotel," Thea said. "After that, I can probably take the train home. Are the subways running?"

Her dad nodded. "But make sure you wear a good mask. You have masks there?"

"Yeah, I just got a whole pack I ordered," Thea said, thankful for the box of what seemed like an excessive amount of disposable masks at the time.

"Be safe on the plane," her dad reminded her, even though she was a grown adult and didn't need the reminder.

"I will. See you soon."

"Love you," her dad said and hung up first, looking like he was ready to get back to his work.

Thea put down the phone and opened her packing list on her laptop. She hadn't updated it in over a year, but most of the items were still valid. She added extra masks to the list and printed it out to prepare for packing. Being stuck in a hotel for two weeks would not be fun, but she could use it to force herself to make progress on some of her unfinished pieces.

She looked up the nearest testing place that could provide rapid results and made an appointment.

FORTY-FOUR

A SAVORY STEWED tomato scent greeted Gabe when he pulled up in front of the familiar house. The nostalgic aroma took his mind off of the palpable absence Thea left in him. He trudged to the back of the house, following the cheerful voices.

"Gabriel! *Ay, mijo!*" His mom clasped her hands when she saw him.

Jess raised her eyebrows. "Dude, you look like shit."

"*Mija,* language!"

"Thanks, Jess."

"Seriously, you sure you recovered? Maybe you have long Covid or something."

Gabe sat heavily on the chair at the end of the table, the plastic creaking under him. He was pretty sure his state wasn't because of any lingering effects of Covid. He'd felt fine until this thing with Thea. Now he was exhausted from nights of tossing and turning and days of agonizing over how things could have gone differently.

His dad emerged from the kitchen hauling a huge, battered pot. When they were kids, Gabe and Jess used to pretend to use the pot as a bathtub.

Gabe moved to help his dad with the heavy pot, but one glare from his dad and he halted.

"I'll get the bowls," he offered, standing to head into the kitchen.

"No, sit," his sister said and rushed inside before he could protest.

Soon, everyone was bent over large steaming bowls of seafood stew. Gabe inhaled his first bowl, then served himself another helping, settling down to devour the second serving. He was silently grateful that this standoff with his dad didn't extend to his cooking.

Gabe glanced over at his dad, who was looking at him over his own bowl of soup. Caught looking, his dad grunted and looked away at the same time Gabe did.

Jess coughed, and he looked over at her. She shot eye lasers at him and then looked pointedly between him and their dad. He ignored her and concentrated on scooping the tender pieces of fish out of the rich broth. It brought him back to childhood when they used to have this regularly on Fridays.

An hour later, Gabe returned from helping clean up the kitchen, surprised to find his dad sitting on the chair he'd built. It was one of his first custom Adirondacks. Not perfect, but still comfortable and solid. When he'd brought it over for his parents months ago, his mom had made appreciative sounds, but his dad took one look at it, shook his head, and walked back into the house. That his dad was now lounging in it was some sort of concession, right?

The tension between them drained him, but it had been going on for so long now, he wasn't sure if there was a way to ease it. He sat down, nursing his own half empty bottle of beer. Both his sister and mom were suspiciously absent, but he could hear Mila's soft chatter through the kitchen window. She was probably holding court with them in there.

The silence between them was so thick that, finally, Gabe gave in and cleared his throat. The beer stilled in his dad's hands, halfway to his mouth. Gabe asked, "How do you like the chair, pops?"

His dad turned to him and, under that scrutinizing gaze, Gabe was a ten-year-old again. His dad opened his mouth. "It's good."

"Really?" Gabe's jaw dropped.

His dad took a sip of beer, continuing to look at him. "Craftsmanship is good, but why do you have to ask?"

"I dunno. I'm just—"

"—you don't have to keep asking. Be a man." His dad said.

Oh geez, here we go, again. Gabe took a deep, calming breath. "Pops, stop."

"Don't tell me to stop!"

"I don't want to fight with you," he said evenly over his dad's raised voice.

"Then don't tell me to stop when I'm telling you—"

"—that I'm a disappointment. I know already, okay? You don't have to keep saying it." Gabe rubbed his face. He regretted trying to talk to his dad. He should have kept the silent treatment going.

"What?" His dad looked confused.

"I know I let you down by not staying at the internship, okay? And not having a fancy office job like you. But that was years ago. You don't have to keep bringing it up."

His dad set the beer bottle down and leaned forward, elbows on his knees. "That's not why I'm disappointed."

"No?" This evening was full of surprises. "When I started working at the studio, you made such a big deal about—"

"—is that a job you like doing?"

"Yes!" Gabe paused, then amended. "It was. I'm not sure now."

"That's what I mean. You're too good for that job."

"Wait, what are you saying?" It was like he stepped out of the kitchen door into Bizarro Land.

"All your hard work making things for pretend. What's the point? It's a waste. You make good pieces that people should keep, not tear apart." His dad thumped his finger on the arm of the chair.

"Wait, you're *not* mad I'm a carpenter?"

"I'm mad you don't go for what you want. You want to work forever for a big Hollywood company making pretend backgrounds and never sleeping?"

"I dunno," Gabe admitted. "I thought I did. I'm good at it and it pays the bills." He didn't want to bring up the latest problem at work around the lack of Covid safety protocols. He still hadn't signed the contract.

"*Mijo*," His dad sighed and put his hands on his knees. "We didn't work this hard just for you to be stuck at a job that just pays the bills. Don't you want the American Dream?"

"But my dream isn't working in a cubicle on mountains of paperwork." He hoped his dad wasn't offended by him calling him out like that.

A flash of anger lit his dad's eyes. "Not what I mean! Do something you *love*."

"I love working with my hands! And it pays decent money. That's why I wanted to take you guys out that time! So I could show you."

An exasperated noise came out of his dad. "You don't need to show off like that. I don't want to eat a $60 piece of meat they didn't even cook."

"I wasn't showing off. I just wanted to take you and Mama somewhere nice!" Gabe stared at his dad. They were finally talking again, but he was worried it would go nowhere.

His dad made a dad-like grunt. "If you want to work there forever and you're okay with it, I'm okay. But are you okay with it?"

"Forever is a long time, pops."

"Your new stuff. The things your sister showed me on her phone. You still doing those?"

"Yes."

"You like doing it?"

"Yes."

"So keep doing it." His dad made it sound so simple.

"Yeah, but I dunno if that'll keep paying the bills," Gabe said, finally putting words to the doubt gnawing at him. "Like after all this is over, maybe people will go back to their normal jobs or whatever and not want any of this."

His dad laughed. "People always need furniture." He cast a stern look at Gabe, a look that Gabe used to wilt under as a kid, but now he forced himself to face it and not look away. Finally, his dad said, "Do what you want. You're a man now. Being scared is okay, but don't let it stop you living your life."

Gabe was taken aback. This was not the way he thought this conversation would go. He was prepared to raise his voice and stomp off, like all the other times he and his dad talked, but something had shifted. He couldn't help how small his voice sounded when he said, "For real?"

His dad stood to stretch, and Gabe automatically got up with him. In his head, his dad was always this person with a disapproving scowl on his face, towering over him. But now, practically standing next to him, Gabe realized he needed to look down to meet his dad's eye.

"Gabriel, you're a man now. I can't tell you what to do anymore."

FORTY-FIVE

IT WAS A mild morning, the type that promised one last hurrah for the summer. Gabe sat in his backyard, in the chair he'd made for Thea, with his second mug of offee and pulled out his phone. He tried to enjoy the coolness of the day before the sun's heat made it unbearable.

He scrolled through his Instagram feed idly. He now understood why so many people were addicted to the app. Endless squares of perfectly restored cottages and storybook homes scrolled past. The algorithm must have lumped his tastes together with people who were renovating their houses during the pandemic. One square caught his eye mid-scroll. It was a picture of a dish in a very familiar setting. The constant ache in his chest deepened. He recognized the color and grain of wood of the table in the background. It was a plank of wood he'd given to Thea for overhead shots. It was thin enough for her to move onto the porch herself, where the natural light was best.

He remembered the exact night they had eaten that dinner. Thea had removed the food from styrofoam containers and artfully plated each dish into an appetizing composition on top of the wood. A colorful spread of baked catfish topped with fragrant herbs, a mango and papaya salad, and pungent seafood stew covered the wood surface.

"You ordered a feast," Gabe teased. "Did you invite anyone else to help eat this?"

Thea shrugged, snapping the lens cap back onto her camera. "I figured you'd be able to help."

"This is enough food for six people."

"I know, but I wanted to try a bunch of stuff. This is the edited down version of the order, trust me."

Gabe lifted the wood, food and all off the floor now that the photoshoot was done, and placed it on the card table Thea brought out for this purpose. He watched, fascinated, as she dipped a flat round translucent disc into a shallow dish of water and placed it on an empty plate. She arranged rice noodles, some of the grilled fish, herbs, and pickled vegetables onto the disc and then started rolling it up. To his surprise, the disc had turned into a pliable sheet after touching water.

"Voila!" Thea exclaimed, holding out the finished roll.

"How did you do that?" Gabe asked, amazed. For someone who claimed she didn't know how to cook, her hands were dextrous around food.

"Practice," she said, wagging her eyebrows. She spooned some brown sauce onto the end and held the roll to his mouth. "Here, try it."

Gabe let her put it in his mouth and bit down. The wrapper was stretchy and chewier than he expected. As he chomped down, a burst of flavor met his tongue. The sauce was sweet, tangy, and had a familiar earthiness he couldn't put his finger on. The filling, chewy, crunchy, and refreshing from the herbs, was incredibly tasty. He swallowed. "This is so good!"

"I know, right?" Thea said, finishing the rest of the half-bitten roll. "Here, I'll make you another one."

"Lemme try."

They laughed at his failed attempt. It was less of a roll and more of a flat, sticky sheet with filling half in, half out. Wrangling the rice noodles, fish, cucumber, and other contents into the delicate wrapper was much harder than it looked.

"No, like this." Thea stepped close to him so that she could place her hands over his. With confident fingers, she guided his movements so that he could pull on the roll with the right amount of tension. Too much, and it tore. Too little, and it made a limp, floppy mess. "You have to wrap it tight."

The floral, green scent that followed her wherever she went distracted him from paying attention. With her body so close to his, he was hungry for something else.

Gabe forced his mind away from dwelling on the memory. It had been weeks since she'd walked out. He tried texting, then calling her, but only reached her voicemail. Ghosted. He tapped on her post from Instagram instead and landed on her latest article.

He read the opening sentences, hearing Thea's voice as though she were next to him: *Like most children of immigrants, my parents never said they loved me, but I never doubted that they did. Their love language was food. I knew they loved me because there was always something to eat at the table...*

At the end of the article, he blinked, startled to feel moisture in his eyes. She had a way with words that conveyed her love of food and how it could be used to talk about other things. Sure, this piece was about the family-owned Vietnamese restaurant that specialized in baked catfish, but it was also about loneliness and isolation, something that especially resonated with him today. Seeing her words on the page like that made him fall in love with her all over again. He went back and re-read the article three more times, each time feeling more and more resolved.

Gabe hadn't been truthful about his feelings either to himself or to Thea. He thought he could shield her from the extent of his feelings because of the way she shied away from anything serious. But what he was really doing was keeping those feelings from her to safeguard himself against the ball-shrinking fear of rejection.

FORTY-SIX

Gabe always enjoyed the spike of dopamine after fastening the last screw into place with his drill. He stepped back to look at the finished product. It was his best work yet, but he wouldn't be satisfied until he saw it in front of the house it was based on. He looked at the picture on his phone, to compare. He'd followed the diagram he sketched out based on that picture, and it turned out better than he expected. Gabe felt wistful now that the project was done. He'd wanted to surprise Thea with a Little Free Library that looked like her house. He'd built it so that there would be ample room for the large cookbooks she wanted to give away.

On his phone was a picture of her porch, where he'd fallen in love with her. The unceasing yearning in his chest intensified. Gabe missed the way she ate her food, savoring each bite like a treasure. He missed the playful way she swung her legs back and forth on the swing while they talked. He missed how easily they could be together with no words between them at all.

Gabe checked his phone multiple times an hour, even without meaning to, hoping to see her name on his screen. It had been so long since her final text to him. He skimmed through the headlines of all the publications she wrote for in case there were any new pieces by her. It wasn't stalking if it was all out in the public. He caught himself looking for her whenever he passed a restaurant, even though he knew LA was an enormous place and the chances of two people running into each other during a pandemic were slimmer than finding a free parking spot in Pasadena.

The memory of Thea's face the last time he saw her was still fresh. That familiar expression in her eyes finally came to him. She had the frantic look of someone wanting to run away. He kicked himself for letting her go so easily.

Gabe's finger hovered over his phone. He was at a loss for what to say. What he wanted to say wasn't something he could fit into the tiny screen. He wasn't even sure what he wanted to say could be contained with only words. He needed to see her, even if it was going to be the nail in the coffin.

His eyes fell to the finished library lying on its back on the garage floor. Delivering it would give him the perfect excuse to go to her house, and then maybe she would be more inclined to give him a chance to talk.

He carefully wrapped the bulky library up with a cloth tarp. It was unwieldy to carry, but he managed to slide it into the bed of his truck. He slid the wooden post next to it along with his toolbox, his shovel, and his posthole digger. He went into the house for a quick shower since he didn't think showing up in a dirty T-shirt smelling like BO would earn him any extra points with Thea.

After a rushed toweling off, Gabe ran his hands through his still-wet hair. It was getting longer, and he needed to cut it soon. He pulled on a clean shirt and the pair of dark jeans he knew she liked. Was it barely a month ago that she'd slid her hand into his back pocket and squeezed his ass? The memory buoyed him and he caught himself with a love-struck grin on his face in his reflection.

Gabe took it as a sign from the universe that there was a parking spot right on her curb. He allowed himself five minutes of doubt in his truck, working up the courage to step out of it. What if she wasn't home? Had she left the house at all? What if she'd been holed up for weeks indoors, working? That couldn't be healthy. Was she getting enough to eat? Was she exercising? What if she refused to even talk to him?

When he'd decided not to renew his contract with the studio and strike out on his own, he wanted to celebrate with her. Her absence was a continual reminder that he needed her in his life.

Shoving down all this uncertainty and holding on to the one thing he was sure about, he slammed the door, louder than usual, hoping she would hear from inside. When he peered into the living room window from the sidewalk, he couldn't see any movement. Okay, so she wasn't in the living room or she would have definitely looked out the curtains.

He tried jiggling the wooden gate to the front yard. He waited a minute. Still no sign of anyone inside.

Gabe walked up the path, eyeing the tall bushy tomato plant and the leggy basil going out of control below it. When he'd last seen them, they'd barely had a couple of blossoms and now they were full-blown plants with light green fruit hanging off of them. A sea of large leafy greens crowded the other planter. Below the leaves, there were two green and yellow squashes.

His boots made heavy thudding sounds on the steps of her porch as he trod up them. He had a bad feeling. There was no twitch of the curtains nor any signs of life from the house. Maybe she was avoiding him.

His heart hammered as he raised his hand to the door. Before he could chicken out, he knocked on the door, firmly, but not too loudly. Thea hated when people pounded on the door like they were going to break it down.

No answer.

He cupped his hands around his eyes to shield against glare and looked into her living room window, through a crack in the curtains. The house was dark inside, but the hallway light was on. He knocked again, holding his breath so that he could hear for any footsteps from the house.

Silence.

Her car was in the driveway, so she couldn't have driven anywhere. She wasn't working in the front yard or he would have noticed. Maybe she was in the back.

He leaned over the side of her porch and looked toward the back of the house. "Thea?" he called out.

The only sound from the backyard was the chirping of the birds and someone else on the block running a leaf blower.

"She's not home." The voice came from somewhere out on the sidewalk.

Gabe followed it, trying to locate the source. There was no one on the sidewalk that he could see, even when he peered around the overgrown bougainvillea.

"Hello?" he called toward the source of the voice.

"She's not here," the voice said again. Closer now, he realized it came from across the street. A familiar woman sat on the porch across the street and another woman stood on her lawn. He hadn't noticed them there when he pulled up. She waved at him.

He left Thea's front yard and closed the gate behind him. He walked up to them. "Do you know where she went?"

It was the neighbor who kept tabs on everything.

"Yeah, she left early this morning," she said.

What was her name? Kathy, or something that started with a K.

She turned to the other woman and said, "That's Thea's boyfriend."

Gabe didn't bother correcting her and instead asked, "Do you know when she'll be back?"

Kathy gave him an odd look. Her mouth opened, then closed again, this time in a thin line. Her eyes narrowed. She looked curiously at the other woman.

The other woman waved at Gabe. "Hi, I'm Grace. I live next door."

"Hi. Do you know when Thea said she'd be back?" He didn't mean to sound rude, but he was starting to worry.

"Hm, I think the 5th of next month." Grace said. "She didn't tell you? She asked me to water her plants till she got back."

Gabe did the math in his head. That was over five weeks from now. "Did she say where she went?"

"The airport," Kathy finally said. "Something about Taiwan."

"What?" Gabe cocked his head, hoping he'd heard incorrectly.

"She really didn't tell you?"

Gabe shook his head. He remembered her mentioning her parents lived in Taiwan and some reference to waiting out the pandemic there, but he'd thought she'd been mostly speculating, not that she was actually going to do it. It had been one of those nights where she couldn't stop worrying about her manuscript deadline and getting enough time to work on it.

"Sounds like you two'll have a lot to talk about when she gets back," the woman said with a pursed expression. The glint in her eye made her look like she was enjoying this exchange very much.

"She left this morning?"

After checking her watch and confirming with Kathy, Grace answered, "Yeah, maybe an hour ago?"

An hour. It would have still been in the middle of morning rush hour. If she'd gotten stuck in traffic on the way there, he wasn't sure how the laws of physics would allow for this, but he could still catch up to her.

🪶 🪶 🪶

Los Angeles International Airport was the only one that had flights to Asia. The airport, famous for its illogical twists and turns, its expensive short-term parking, and stress-angered drivers, was the tenth circle of hell. People had broken up over the stress of driving to LAX. If he could catch Thea before she boarded the flight, he'd gladly take on the burden.

Traffic was thankfully light, and he drove a healthy amount above the posted speed limit, but it still took longer than he'd liked to finally make it to the freeway offramp that led into the airport. The sinking feeling when he'd heard what the neighbor said scared him. He forced himself to take deep breaths to keep his frustration from bubbling over. Him and his stupid, stubborn pride. He should have called earlier. Why did he wait so long to see her?

His knuckles were white as he gripped the steering wheel. There was nothing he could do but guide his car behind the line of other cars heading to the airport and wait. He hoped her flight hadn't taken off yet. His left foot jiggled with impatience. His hands curled into fists to keep from laying on the horn. Intellectually, he knew that honking would not speed everyone up, but maybe some people would move out of the way for him? No, not likely.

Ten minutes, which felt like ten years, passed before he finally parked his car in the first spot he could find. He slammed the door, sprinted out of the parking lot, saw the crossing signal was yellow, and ran out onto the crosswalk. An angry driver yelled something out of the window at him, but he didn't bother returning a finger.

Groups of people clustered around carts of luggage at the curb. It seemed like the pandemic didn't dampen *everyone's* appetite for travel. Masked travelers glaring at him reminded him that his mask was still uselessly dangling around his neck. He pulled it up over his face and continued his quick jog into the terminal.

Seeing the inside of the airport relatively empty was an eerie sight. The world was a very different place than it was a year ago. The fact that even in this time of disaster, he'd found a connection to someone like Thea was something that he'd been taking for granted. He checked the tower of departure screens. The only flight to Taiwan this morning was leaving in less than twenty minutes.

Gabe scanned the overhead signs to see where everything was. A small line of people headed toward a pair of conveyor belts of luggage. The people scanning machine at the front of the line beeped at steady intervals. This had to be it. None of the travelers in the line looked familiar.

He was too late. She'd already gone through the security checkpoint. He tried calling her. Straight to voicemail.

He stood still, staring at the line of people being processed through the gate, hoping for one of them to be her so he could at least wish her a safe flight. Other travelers streamed around him.

If only he had found a parking spot sooner. If only he had bypassed the line of cars and cut in front. If only he'd driven to her house faster. If only he had put his bullheaded pride behind him and called her sooner instead of trying to wait her out in this stupid, stupid game of chicken. Infinite alternate universes spun out of his head. He almost didn't hear his name.

"Gabe?"

FORTY-SEVEN

"Gabe?"

Thea's luggage thumped to the floor. She hurried to right the fallen suitcase. Even through her fogged up glasses, she knew it was him. It was like she conjured him from sheer will. Her heart pounded as thoughts raced. What was he doing here? Was he even here for her? Why would he be here for her after she ghosted him?

He spun to face her, eyes wide with surprise. Time stopped when his gaze met hers. No words came to her. His Adam's apple bobbed up and down in a swallow. It looked like he opened his mouth, but no sound came out.

"Thea," he finally said. It sounded like something was caught in his throat. "I heard them call your flight. I thought I was too late."

Thea gripped the strap of the purse slung over her chest with both hands. It was the only thing she could do to prevent herself from walking closer to him. It felt like they were in their own bubble, the rest of the world rushing by around them.

"I couldn't go," she breathed, not sure if he heard her.

He stepped closer.

"I cancelled my flight."

"What?"

"I cancelled it. I can't go," she repeated.

"Why not?"

Thea had left her house at the crack of dawn, thinking this was the right thing to do. She needed a break from the pandemic, from LA, from thinking about Gabe. Once she got some distance from him, about 7000 miles of distance, then maybe she could figure out how to fit him into her life. Except, as her rideshare crept along in traffic, her anxiety only increased, bit by bit.

At first, she thought it was just the dread of boarding a plane with a bunch of strangers, flying through the sky in a metal box, breathing recycled air for fourteen hours. When she tried to rationalize her fears, she realized that wasn't the primary source of her worry. No, it was the fact that she was leaving unresolved issues behind. She didn't want to run away to Taiwan without figuring out what to do about Gabe. He deserved closure, one way or another. Her parents taught her to be fearless, to go for what she wanted and not let anything stand in her way, yet here she was, slinking back to them because she didn't want to deal with what was in front of her. When had she gotten so timid about doing scary things?

"Thea?" Gabe interrupted her thoughts. "Why aren't you on the plane?"

"I had some unfinished business." She shook her head, trying to clear the cyclone of emotions whirring around it. "What are you doing here?"

"I went to drop something off at your house, but you weren't home."

"I was here," she said, feeling dumb for pointing out the obvious.

"Your neighbor told me you went to the airport. I didn't want you to leave before I could see you."

She wanted to wrap her arms around him, tell him she missed him, that she was sorry about everything, that she still didn't know how this was supposed to go. That she didn't want to hurt him. Instead, she just stood there, shifting her weight from one foot to the other.

A determined look lit Gabe's eyes. He approached her, one step, then the next, as if he was wary of scaring her off. The inside of her mask was sticky on her mouth when she inhaled.

"I love you," he said, the words coming out muffled through his mask. She was certain she'd misheard. "What?"

"I love you." Louder this time. His brown eyes looked into hers and she felt the honest truth of it.

A sharp intake of breath pulled her mask flush against her face. Her eyes watered and all she could hear was the thumping of her heartbeat. She braced herself, waiting for the suffocating feeling to enclose her. It didn't. Instead, a warm, tingling sensation spread through her, pooling in her stomach. She felt like she'd stepped into sunlight after sitting in the shade for too long. All the thoughts flying around her head stilled. One by one, they dropped away until there was nothing but a luminous feeling radiating through her.

"—I didn't tell you before," Gabe was still talking. Thea missed the first part, but forced herself to focus on his words. "I'm sorry. I tried to keep it to myself because I thought it might scare you away. But I was the one who was scared. I don't know what this is between us. Whatever it is, I need you to know I love you. I love you and I'm not scared to tell you that I want you in any way that I can. If I'm too late, if you don't feel the same, it's okay. I just needed to tell you."

Thea let go of her purse strap. She reached a hand out and placed it over his, curled in a fist by his side. His hand automatically opened, turning so that their palms touched each other. He wrapped his fingers around hers. She missed this. His hands were always so warm.

Thea never thought she'd be the type to have an emotional airport scene, but here she was, hand in hand with a man who'd just declared his love for her. Her mind was shockingly blank. She blinked, her eyes stinging.

"I—," she said, then stopped. Where was she going with this? She wasn't prepared for this at all. Her throat constricted. She tried to clear it. "Um..."

Gabe squeezed her hand. She looked away from the tender look he gave her. When she raised her eyes to his again, he said, "Don't worry. I don't expect an answer."

Thea peeked at her wristwatch. Her plane was probably on the runway by now. She thought she'd feel regretful, but all she felt was relief. It was like all the mismatched, jutting out pieces in her finally settled in place.

"Do you... want to reschedule another flight?" He asked, trying to read her face.

She shook her head vigorously.

"Do you want me to take you home?"

Thea nodded. "I'm sorry you came all the way to LAX. I know you hate it."

He let out a laugh and let go of her hand to take her suitcase for her. "I'll pick you up from LAX anytime."

Thea paused mid-step and looked at him, trying to see if he was serious or not. Her throat still felt tight and tears welled up in her eyes. She pushed her glasses up and swiped the tears away with the back of her hand.

Gabe shook his head. "A guy pours his heart out to you and you're unmoved. An offer to pick you up from the airport and you're crying." He twined his fingers around her other hand and pulled her toward the exit.

Thea let him lead, glad that her mask hid the silly grin on her face.

FORTY-EIGHT

GABE TRIED TO still the drumming of his fingers on the steering wheel. He glanced over at Thea after he merged onto the 105. She had said little else to him. The relief of finally telling her his feelings was short-lived. Her silence made him uneasy. He felt like an animal pacing around a too-small cage.

She hadn't gotten on the plane to Taiwan. That counted for something, right? He didn't know what her unfinished business was, but that she had talked to him at all was progress. She didn't seem angry, but he couldn't take his eyes off the road long enough to look at her. It frustrated him because he could usually tell what she was feeling by the tilt of her eyebrows.

The agonizing drive back to her house, still in rush hour traffic, was an exercise in sitting with unpleasant emotions. He imagined all the ways this could go, some of them rainbows and riding off into the sunset, others pouring rain and LA traffic on a Thursday night. His mood ping-ponged from one extreme to the other.

Thea looked over at him and asked, "Are you feeling okay? You look kinda pale."

"Yeah."

Thea placed a palm on his forehead. The gesture sent a shot of affection straight to his gut and he felt dizzy thinking about how close he'd been to losing her.

"You feel fine," she mumbled to herself.

"Just tired. I had some late nights working." He didn't mention that working late into the night until it thoroughly exhausted him was the only way he could fall asleep now.

Thea tucked her hands under her thighs and returned to looking out the window.

🍃 🍃 🍃

Thea barely remembered the drive home. One second, she was in the parking lot, standing in front of Gabe's truck. The next, he was taking the keys out of the ignition.

"Hey, you okay?" Gabe asked, reaching for her.

She leaned into him, his hand cupping her jaw, tilting her head one way, then the next. She missed the feel of his hands on her.

"Did the drive make you carsick?" He asked.

"No." Her voice was froggy. She made no movement to leave his truck, and he made no movement to shoo her out.

"You must be tired—" he started.

"I love you too," she blurted over him.

His gasp was a sharp sound over the silence in the truck.

That was easy. So easy, she repeated it. "I love you."

A plane didn't drop out of the sky on her. She didn't automatically regret it. Nothing had changed, other than the overwhelming sense of rightness in those words. She was a hot-air balloon soaring after the weights came off.

Gabe blinked, and then his face split into a dazzling, incandescent smile that blasted all of her lingering doubts away until only the two of them remained, sitting in the truck, his warm brown eyes searing into hers.

"I don't know what happens next," Thea admitted, clutching her fears like a shield of armor. "I'm still a terrible girlfriend. I still don't want to cook. I still hog the bed. I want my alone time. I don't want to move in with you. I don't want you to move in with me."

"Hey," Gabe shushed her, skimming his thumb over her still moving lips. "I just want to be with you, like this."

"But—"

Gabe shook his head and repeated. "It's okay. I'm so happy when I'm with you. I promise, none of that other stuff matters. We'll be okay."

"What if that's not enough for a real relationship? I might never want to—"

"Thea, you are enough. You're enough for me. I just want to be enough for you." A muscle in Gabe's jaw twitched as his brows furrowed. She thought he would be upset, but his voice was calm.

She looked at him, at his vulnerable, hopefully look. A flowering feeling filled her entire being. "You are."

Gabe's eyes widened. She didn't know why he looked surprised. He'd always been more than she'd ever asked for, more than she'd ever hoped for. That's what made it so scary. There had to be a tradeoff somewhere.

"What if you change your mind?" She chewed on the corner of her lip. She didn't like that all her fears were bubbling out of her mouth, one by one, but she couldn't help it when he looked at her like that. It was like he shone a light right into her, seeing everything.

Gabe looked up from the movement of her mouth. His eyes were clear when they met hers. "Forever. You'll be enough for me forever."

"Forever's a long time," she whispered.

"I don't care," he said, moving closer to her. "I'll love you even longer than that."

Thea's lips parted at the feel of his breath on her cheek. Her pulse pounded like she'd biked up ten hills. She didn't think it was possible for her heart to feel so empty of doubts, but so full of love.

Gabe's voice was rough when his words feathered across her lips. "Any other questions?"

She barely shook her head.

"Can I kiss you, now?" He stared at her mouth.

Thea reached for him, her palm on the rough stubble of his jaw, her thumb touching the dimple at the corner of his mouth. She slid as close to Gabe as she could. When his mouth melted into hers, hot and yearning, the knots of tension between her shoulders loosened. He kissed her like he couldn't get enough of her, fingers digging into the back of her head, snaking through her hair.

When she opened her mouth to his, tentatively touching his lip with the tip of her tongue, a guttural sound came out of him. She wanted more, but he held her shoulders, squeezing firmly as his kisses softened, tapering off with a chaste kiss on the corner of her mouth before pushing her away.

She blinked in confusion. Their breaths were loud and harsh in the car, even over the parrots squawking outside. Her lips felt bruised and swollen in the best way. Gabe's pupils swallowed the brown of his eyes as he pulled away, fighting for control of his breath. He rubbed a hand along his jaw, where her hand had been. He squinted through the front window at something in the distance.

"I love you. I want you. But I don't want Kathy to interrupt us." He said, turning to her.

Thea followed his gaze and couldn't help the snicker that escaped from her. "Say it again," she demanded.

"I love you."

The rightness of those three words caused a warm tingle from the top of her head, pooling in her belly. She slid back to her side of the truck and unlocked the door. Halfway out of the truck, she said over her shoulder, "Are you coming in?"

"Do you want me to?" His voice was rough with desire.

Her mouth curled into a smile. "Yes."

FORTY-NINE

TEARS STREAMED DOWN Thea's face. Her cheeks felt flushed as she tried to keep it together. She couldn't stop. After a few seconds of gasping for air, she could breathe again.

"Oh my god," Olivia croaked, wiping her forehead. "I'm laughing so hard that I'm sweating."

Thea erupted in another fit of laughter. "I'm gonna pee my pants." She set the tablet on the couch and ran to the restroom, still trying to stop the giggles.

"Okay, back." The splash of cold water on her face helped calm her.

"I still can't believe he actually apologized," Olivia said.

Thea was reading excerpts from the AI generated reviews that ran in the paper aloud to Olivia. She hadn't told Ray that she'd cancelled her flight and would be home for the rest of the month. He'd already lined up a trial run of the AI content generator with a made-up byline to cover for her while she was gone. He said her vacation was the perfect time to test it on readers.

When she'd mentioned her concerns over the quality of the generated articles, he dismissed them as her as being too emotional about her work. After hearing that, Thea was happy to let him dig his own grave.

She couldn't have imagined it going better. The taste of the *schaden-freude* was exquisite. The first article that went out incited immediate feedback in the comments section. Readers were *not* happy about this new writer. Some of them even took the issue to Twitter, calling out the paper publicly and complaining about the quality going downhill. After the second review went out the weekend after, things got worse. One celebrity subscriber posted a screenshot of him cancelling his subscription and said that the writing was no better than their kid's Mad Libs.

The outrage was so extreme that there was even a trending hashtag for unsubscribing. Ray pulled the next scheduled article. Thea wasn't sure if it was his own idea, or pressure from their CEO, but in the next issue, instead of a restaurant review, there was a full apology from the paper penned by Ray, taking full responsibility for the catastrophe.

The sweetest part of it was that Ray had blown up Thea's phone, begging her to call him. She was technically still on vacation for one more week and she'd planned to use it to edit the pages her book editor had sent back. The Times needed a new review for the upcoming weekend edition. They had reserved the spot for the big reveal of how the LA Times had some fancy AI that could write exactly like a human. They weren't running that piece anymore.

After a slew of over the top compliments, cajoling, and a written promise of a 10% raise in the next budget year, Thea agreed to help. It was good to feel vindicated.

FIFTY

THREE WEEKS LATER, Gabe was on his way back to LA. The arid drive through the desert from Nevada to California always filled him with awe. The plants that survived the relentless heat of the day and the plunging temperature at night looked otherworldly in the harsh afternoon sun.

He must have zoned out in the latter half of the drive because next thing he knew, he was pulling into his driveway. A familiar car parked in front of him. An eerie sense of déjà vu hit him. He thought about the time he came home to find Christina, his ex, waiting in his house. He shook his head, ridding himself of the memory, and pulled his toolbox out of the back of his truck.

The house was empty, but there was a pitcher full of iced tea on his counter, condensation dripping off the outside. The cool water of the kitchen faucet felt nice on his hands after the long drive home. He'd had an early start this morning, loading his truck with a patio table he'd built, driving to the border of Nevada to deliver it to a customer, and driving back. He thought about jumping in the shower before he saw movement in the backyard, partially blocked by the enormous trunk of the magnolia tree.

"Hey." He stepped out into the backyard. He took a refreshing gulp of iced tea. He could never go back to Arizona Green Tea now that Thea had introduced him to the wonders of cold brewed tea.

Thea looked up from her laptop in surprise, "Hi, didn't hear you come back."

Her smile made him feel like he was home.

"Thanks for making tea," he said, bending over her for a kiss.

"Mmm, it was for me." Thea tilted her head toward him. She had a glazed over expression on her face. One he recognized as her brain still being on her work. Her lips were soft on his. "How'd they like the table? I'm jealous I don't have one like that."

"They said it was better than they pictured. Do you want me to build you one? It'll look good in your backyard."

She made a noncommittal grunt, eyes already returning to the screen.

"I'm gonna hop in the shower," he said, heading back toward the house.

The spray of water, just shy of being too hot, felt amazing on his back. He finished lathering his head. Two weeks out, and it still felt weird to touch his shorn hair.

Gabe had finally tired of how long it was, especially during a heatwave. He took a pair of clippers to it and cut it all off. He wasn't sure if Thea would like it, but when she saw it, she immediately reached for him. As soon as he felt her hands on his shaved head and heard her husky, "I like this," all his doubts disappeared.

The suds sluiced off his chest in rivulets. He didn't care that they might never move in together. If the pandemic had shown him anything, it was that being too rigid about plans for the future was pointless. He was satisfied with what he had with Thea. Each day with her, even if all he saw of her was a text, brought him so much joy, he couldn't imagine how it could get any better.

As the water flowed over his face, he felt a draft of cold air. Hands came around him, palms pressing into his chest. Thea's soft body pressed into him from behind. He turned in her embrace, shielding her playful face from the spray of the shower. Her eyes were dark pools, pulling him under.

"Mind if I join you?" She asked, her voice liquid and sultry.

He wrapped his hands around her waist, pushing her against the shower wall before covering her mouth with his. He was wrong: he could never get enough of her, but it was okay.

What Happens Next

"I don't like waiting for food, so I'll keep this short. I didn't think I was gonna finish this book, especially with everything going on, so it means a lot to me that you're all here at my little book party. Thank you. Now, LET'S EAT SOME BRISKET!"

Hearty applause and a round of cheers ended Thea's speech. She sat and took a swig of beer, a grapefruit gose with a refreshing tang.

"Congratulations," Gabe whispered in her ear before kissing it.

"Ugh, you two, get a room!" Olivia squealed across the table from her. Her friend held out her hands and Thea took them, squeezing her fingers.

She beamed at Olivia, thrilled that she was finally seeing her best friend. It had been almost two years. When Thea mentioned her book launch, her friend had insisted on driving down for the party, even to a BBQ spot that had nothing vegetarian on the menu. Now that everyone had gotten their two rounds of the vaccine and the infection rates were still on a steady decline, she could relax. Her book couldn't have launched at a more convenient time.

"How's everything?" The co-owner of the BBQ joint asked as she plopped a tray of steaming sausages stuffed with cheese on the table. The side patio filled with the enticing aroma of smoked meats.

"Mm-hmm," Thea mumbled, her mouth full of smoky, tender brisket. She swallowed and tried again. "Great, thank you so much for letting us do this here."

Thea's publisher had bought out the restaurant, a barbecue place in Lincoln Heights, for the book launch. She'd interviewed the husband and wife owners for the book. Each chapter featured a story about an independent restaurant in LA and the people behind it as they navigated the struggles of the pandemic. Initially, she wasn't sure if enough people would want to talk to her, but as she went along, she found that everyone she met was open and gracious with sharing their experiences. Their honesty inspired her.

"Looks like your adoring fans are already lining up," Gabe said, pointing to the line forming at the front of the restaurant.

Thea looked through the crowd and tried to calm her nerves. She dreaded public events like this, but her publisher had convinced her, or more like bribed her, with a launch party. Her agent knew she couldn't turn down an opportunity to share delicious food and drinks with her friends.

"You'll be fine." Gabe put his hand on her thigh. The warm weight of it made her stop jiggling her leg. "Think of all the books you'll sell."

He was right. She'd convinced her publisher to split a share of the book sales so that they could donate to No Us Without You. The LA branch helped provide food security to undocumented immigrants, many of them hit especially hard during the pandemic thanks to the unpredictability of restaurant lockdowns and closures.

Thea looked down at her half-finished plate. She'd lost her appetite now that she thought about all the people she was about to meet.

"Go! We'll save you some food," Olivia urged her.

"I promise not to finish the ribs," Nate said. His tone was so dry that Thea had to look twice to make sure he was joking. This was the first time she'd met Olivia's new boyfriend. Her friend was uncharacteristically secretive about him, not telling her she'd met someone new until a month ago. Thea had no idea how Olivia had jumped from Sebastian to Nate.

Nate didn't seem like the type her creative, arty friend would usually go for. His neatly combed, dark hair, and buttoned up short-sleeved shirt made him look out of place next to Olivia with her cotton candy pink bob, red-framed glasses, and ink-stained hands.

Looking between Olivia and Nate, especially at the obvious chemistry between them, she knew her friend was in deep. She needed to get the complete story from Olivia soon, but for now, she used a wet-nap to wipe off her greasy hands and got ready for book signing. She pulled out a package of Sharpies.

Two hours later, she signed her last book of the day. Thea sighed and sank onto the bench in happy exhaustion. She'd been smiling so much that her face hurt.

"I'm proud of you," Gabe handed her a fresh shandy.

"Thanks." She took a sip of the foamy beverage. It tasted like heaven.

Gabe chuckled and tapped his upper lip. "You got a little somethin' here."

Thea tried to wipe the beer foam off her mouth, but she must have missed a spot. Gabe leaned over and swiped his thumb across her upper lip. Her thoughts narrowed to the touch of his warm hand on her jaw. A pleasant shiver ran down her spine. His lids lowered as he stared at her mouth.

"Uh, we're still here, guys," Olivia said, waving a hand in the space between them.

Thea snapped out of it and laughed. She'd been nervous about introducing Gabe to her friends once things began opening up again. Part of it was because she didn't want anything to shatter the magical bubble that surrounded her whenever she was with him. She needn't have worried because as soon as they met him, they all loved him. She couldn't blame them. He had the type of relaxed vibe that put everyone at ease.

Thea met Gabe's gaze, and a surge of fondness overwhelmed her. Nothing in the past six months had changed. She didn't move into his place; he didn't move into hers. The extra drawer he set aside was perfect for stashing her pile of unread magazines. They were happy together. It was enough.

Dear Reader

I hope you enjoyed this book. It would help me immensely if you leave a review or recommend this to a friend. Good reviews of books really help indie authors like me. Here are some handy links:

Goodreads:
  https://www.goodreads.com/book/show/62985471-social-distance

Amazon:
  https://www.amazon.com/dp/B0BJXD9CR9

Follow me on the usual social networks or subscribe to my newsletter if you've enjoyed my work:

Instagram:
  JuneYiBooks

Sincerely,
June Yi
juneyi.com

Acknowledgements

It takes a village to make a book, and I owe a debt to a lot of villagers.

Thank you to Will, for the idea, for the support, for giving me the time, and for knowing the right words I want to use even when I don't. Thank you to Robin, you are the best.

Thank you to Meg Yardley, for early feedback, improvements, and for fielding neurotic-writer-texts and finding humor in the process.

Heartfelt thanks to Vijay Singh, CJ Smith, Tara King, Samantha Zeitlin, and Lisa Lau. You have my sincere gratitude for your patience in reading very rough drafts, and providing invaluable feedback.

Lightning Source UK Ltd.
Milton Keynes UK
UKHW040644051222
413345UK00005B/737

9 798986 949529